Back in His Bed

KIMBERLY LANG
HEIDI RICE
AIMEE CARSON

MILLS & BOON

Published in Great Britain 2015
by Mills & Boon, an imprint of Harlequin (UK) Limited,
Eton House, 18-24 Paradise Road, Richmond, Surrey, TW9 1SR

BACK IN HIS BED © 2015 Harlequin Books S.A.

Boardroom Rivals, Bedroom Fireworks!, Unfinished Business with the Duke and *How to Win the Dating War* were first published in Great Britain by Harlequin (UK) Limited.

Boardroom Rivals, Bedroom Fireworks! © 2010 Kimberly Lang
Unfinished Business with the Duke © 2010 Heidi Rice
How to Win the Dating War © 2011 Aimee Carson

ISBN: 978-0-263-25197-5
eBook ISBN: 978-1-474-00376-6

05-0115

Harlequin (UK) Limited's policy is to use papers that are natural, renewable and recyclable products and made from wood grown in sustainable forests. The logging and manufacturing processes conform to the legal environmental regulations of the country of origin.

Printed and bound in Spain
by CPI, Barcelona

BOARDROOM RIVALS, BEDROOM FIREWORKS!

BY
KIMBERLY LANG

Kimberly Lang hid romance novels behind her text-books in junior high, and even a Master's programme in English couldn't break her obsession with dashing heroes and happily ever after. A ballet dancer turned English teacher, Kimberly married an electrical engineer and turned her life into an ongoing episode of *When Dilbert Met Frasier*. She and her Darling Geek live in beautiful North Alabama, with their one Amazing Child—who, unfortunately, shows an aptitude for sports.

Visit Kimberly at www.booksbykimberly.com for the latest news—and don't forget to say hi while you're there!

This one is for my mom:
If books are like children, then this book was me at
fifteen: headstrong, occasionally wilful, and not afraid
to do its own thing. But, based on your example, I just
kept faith in it, and it turned out to be fabulous and
totally worth it in the end (hopefully also like me!).
I love you, Mom. Thanks for putting up with me.

CHAPTER ONE

"THEY'RE ready, Brenna. I'll call Marco and tell him to have the crews here in the morning."

"It's too soon." Brenna double-checked the number on the refractometer in shock. No one else in Sonoma had grapes ripe this early; that was for sure. "We should have a couple of more weeks, at least."

"You doubt me?" Ted's affront was only partially feigned, and, though they'd been friends and coworkers for years, Brenna rushed to smooth the ruffled feathers of her viticulturist.

"Not at all. No one knows these vines better than you. I'm surprised, that's all."

Placated, Ted popped a grape into his mouth and chewed, a small, blissful smile crossing his face. "Obviously these grapes like our sunny summers and this drought. You just don't want to harvest in the heat."

"True." But that was only part of it. The new tanks had only arrived last week and were stacked haphazardly around the building. The main pump was still being temperamental, and there was so much paperwork left to do...and...and...she *needed* those couple of extra weeks just to finish getting her head together. She wasn't ready to start the crush right now.

Brenna looked at the vines, all heavy with ripe fruit—fruit that wasn't going to hold on while she adjusted to the new situation at a leisurely pace. Amante Verano Cellars was her responsibility now.

Well, mostly.

Ready or not, these grapes were coming in. She knew what to do; she'd been doing it her entire life. But she'd never done it alone. That responsibility weighed heavily on her shoulders.

"I just wish Max were here." The sigh in Ted's voice brought her back to reality with a jerk.

"I know. These vines were Max's ticket to wine-world domination—or at the very least a gold medal." She smiled weakly at Ted as her inspection of the grapes digressed to aimless fiddling. "He really should be here for this. It's not fair." She blinked back the tears threatening to escape again. She couldn't fall apart in front of Ted—or anyone else. Max would expect her to solider on, and everyone at Amante Verano needed to believe she had this under control. "Call Marco. We'll have the first grapes in the tank by tomorrow night."

They walked up the hill together, stopping occasionally to test the sugars and make notes on the grapes on different acres. The other vines were being slightly more predictable in their timelines. Another two weeks—give or take—and they'd be ready. September would be high-gear time.

"Have you talked to Jack yet?" Ted asked the question too quietly, too casually.

Her heart thumped in her chest at the mention of his name. "Not since the funeral, and then only for a minute." And that had been awkward and difficult, not to mention painful on more levels than she cared to admit. She'd exchanged condolences, shaken his hand and left. End of story.

"Does he know?"

"Oh, I'm sure he does. Max's lawyer called me to explain the partnership and what it meant, and I have to assume Jack was the first to know."

"And?" Ted was the first to brave asking the question she knew was on everyone's mind.

"There is no 'and.' I'm sure Jack has his hands full with the hotels, and the lawsuit against the driver that hit Max's car, and everything else, so we've got to be pretty low on the priority list." Max's death had left them all scrambling these last few weeks, just trying to sort out the wide range of Max's businesses and projects. In a way it had helped her grieve as well; she hadn't been able to lose herself in her grief as she'd wanted to, and the pain seemed a little easier to deal with when she could concentrate on keeping Max's beloved winery running smoothly.

Ted didn't look relieved.

"After the crush I'll make an appointment with the lawyers and we'll get it all sorted out." She patted his shoulder fondly. "Go on home. We've got several very busy days ahead of us."

"In other words, I should see my daughter while I can?"

"Yep." The crush would give them all something to

focus on. And when it was over she would have proved to everyone she was more than capable of shouldering the responsibility Max left her.

"Do you want to come to the house for dinner? You know you're always welcome, and Dianne will happily feed you."

It was tempting, very tempting, but she really needed to learn to cope on her own. Dianne had been mothering her way too much in the weeks since Max had died, and she needed to be strong now. She needed to be a grown-up. "Thanks, but no. Give my goddaughter a kiss for me, though, okay?"

"Will do." With a wave, Ted was gone, leaving her standing in the shadow of the main house alone, while his long legs covered the distance to the little house quickly. She could see the lights on upstairs in the apartment over the wine shop, which he shared with Dianne and baby Chloe.

She'd left a light on in the house as well, because she hadn't gotten used to coming home to a silent and dark house yet. She wondered if she ever would. Maybe after the craziness of the crush was over she'd get a puppy. It would keep her company, make the house feel less empty, and give her someone to talk to when she got home at night.

Her footsteps echoed in the hallway as habit directed her toward the office—just *her* office now, since Max was gone—where the winery's paperwork waited for her. As always, the work gave her something to do, a way to fill the long evenings.

Pressing "play" on the stereo filled the room with

music and chased the dreadful silence away. Max's huge desk dominated the space, and she turned her chair away from his empty one as she tried to focus on the invoices and orders that kept her inbox overflowing no matter how much time she spent on them.

But her usual focus wouldn't come. Ted's earlier question had brought everything she was trying so hard to repress right back to the forefront of her mind.

Amante Verano would make it to the top of Jack's to-do list eventually, and she had no idea how she'd handle that once it did. Avoidance—her time-honored and safe way of dealing with anything Jack-related—wasn't going to work this time. She had to make this work, because she couldn't run a business if she couldn't talk to her business partner.

The thought of Jack brought up all kinds of feelings she didn't want to deal with. Their history was just too complicated to pretend it didn't exist. Max had been her mentor, her friend, her surrogate father, and she, Max, and her mom had been a happy—if slightly oddly configured—family. Jack, not solely by his choice, had never been a part of that. Add in their private history, and the whole mess would put any soap opera plot to shame.

But she'd have to meet with Jack eventually. The thought kicked her heartbeat up a notch, and all the cleansing breaths in the world couldn't help calm it. She needed to be an adult about this. She needed to concentrate on the present and not let the past interfere.

Her glib response to Ted was starting to sound pretty good: a meeting on neutral ground, with lawyers doing most of the talking so she wouldn't have to. This was business, not personal, and surely she could swallow all the competing emotions long enough to get through a business meeting.

Many years ago Jack had told her how important it was to keep her personal life from rolling over into her business dealings. "Don't ever let one affect the other," he'd said. It was a major point of pride with him, and it seemed to work well as he expanded Garrett Properties all down the west coast.

Jack would want to keep this strictly business. If she could do that, it would make things a lot easier. For everyone, but most especially for her and her sanity.

Brenna took a deep breath, feeling a little better after her self-therapy session. They could come to a workable situation. One that was business only and ignored all the messiness of the past.

The fact she'd been crazy enough to marry him once wouldn't be a problem at all.

Jack sincerely hoped insanity didn't run in the family. That Max's will was merely an act of early-onset senility caused by too much wine over the years, or even some kind of weird joke on Max's part. There had to be an explanation, and he'd love to have just five minutes with his father to find out what the punch line was supposed to be.

Otherwise, insanity was the only explanation he had for the fact he now owned half of a winery in Sonoma. Him *personally*—not the company.

And the other half belonged to Brenna Walsh.

Brenna should be a footnote in his dating history—a cautionary tale about youthful infatuation and reckless decision-making—not a recurring character in his life.

Bad decisions must go hand-in-hand with anything Brenna-related, because he spent most of the drive out to Sonoma questioning his decision to handle this in person. His attorney, Roger, had offered to take care of it, but for some unknown reason, he felt this was a discussion he and Brenna should have face-to-face. The closer he got to the vineyard and Brenna, though, the more he realized this probably wasn't the best idea he'd ever had. God knew he had enough work on his desk waiting for him, and his trip to New York to negotiate the expansion of Garrett Properties should be his main focus right now, but he'd decided to get this off his plate first.

He rolled his eyes. He should have waited, gotten through more important, more pressing issues first, instead of letting his desire to cut ties with this place override his common sense.

The vines almost covering the sign welcoming him to Amante Verano had matured in the five years since he'd been out here for Brenna's mother's funeral, and grapes hung heavily from the canopy. As he turned on to the property the acres of vines laid out in perfectly aligned rows, the white stucco house at the top of the hill, and the weathered wooden winery building created a picturesque scene straight out of a movie's stock footage file.

Change came slowly to Amante Verano—if it ever

came at all—and it looked much the same as it had when Max had bought the winery twelve years ago.

That had been before Max's hobby had turned into his obsession. Before he'd left San Francisco for good and moved out here full-time to play in his grapes. Before Jack had become the Garrett in charge of Garrett Properties and the responsibility had consumed his entire life.

He drove slowly past the little house—that was Brenna's free and clear now, even if Max *had* converted it into the winery's shop once Brenna and her mother had moved into the main house—and noted the gravel parking lot was empty. Well, it was still early in the day for the tourists on their trips to wine country.

Where to find Brenna? Her lab? The office? He just wanted this over and done with as quickly as possible, so he could get back to civilization and his life. This place hung like an albatross around his neck, and the sooner he could get Brenna's signature on the documents, the better.

He didn't even *like* wine, for God's sake.

As he crested the next low hill he could see a tractor lumbering its way in the direction of the winery, the trailer overflowing with grapes.

He had never learned the intricacies of grape-growing or wine-making, and what little he had picked up he'd tried hard to forget, but even he knew it was early for harvesting. A strange turn of events, but it answered his first question nicely.

Brenna would be somewhere in those damn vines.

He sighed. He could either trudge through the

vineyard looking for her, or he could wait at the house until she was finished for the day.

"Let's just get this over with," he muttered to himself.

Cursing the entire ridiculous situation, Jack took his overnight case and laptop into the house, dropped them in what had used to be his room, and headed down the hill on foot to find his ex-wife.

"Brenna, they need you at the building. The pump's acting up again," Ted called from the end of the row she was working on. "Rick kicked it and nothing happened, so he asked me to get you."

Brenna sighed. The new pump was on backorder, and wouldn't be here until sometime in the next couple of weeks. Which would have been in plenty of time for the crush if Ted's grapes had kept to their usual time-table. "Did he kick it in the right place?"

Ted nodded. "Twice."

Straightening, she slid her clippers into her back pocket and pulled off her gloves, before wiping a hand across her sweaty forehead. "Great. Exactly what I didn't want to do today. Do you have this under control?"

"Of course. I didn't need you out here to begin with," he teased.

They didn't have time for this, and they would only get further behind if she had to take the whole pump apart again. Beads of sweat rolled down her spine, and she grimaced at the feeling. At least she'd be out of the heat sooner than planned. She'd call Dianne and get her to bring a clean shirt along with their lunches.

She pulled her cellphone out of her other pocket, replacing it with her gloves. Dialing Dianne as she walked, she didn't see the man who stepped into her path until she ran face-first into him. The force knocked her hat off her head, and the cellphone hit the dust at her feet.

"Sorry," she said, as strong hands closed around her arms to steady her. In the split second that followed her brain registered the fine cotton shirt—far too nice for any of her guys to be wearing while they worked—the strangely familiar feeling of the man's grasp, and the subtle spicy scent tickling her nostrils.

And then her brain shut down altogether as one thought crystallized: *Jack.*

"It's a bit early to be harvesting, isn't it, Brenna?"

His deep voice rumbled through her, causing her brain to misfire in shock, but the bite of sarcasm brought her world back into focus. Shrugging off his hands in what she hoped was a casual way, she tried to match his tone. "The grapes are ready when the grapes are ready. You should know that."

She made the mistake of meeting his eyes when she spoke, and the smoky blue stare caused her to take a step back. She bent to retrieve her hat, but as she stood, she saw the assessing roaming those eyes made down her body, taking in her sweat-darkened T-shirt, battered jeans, and dusty work boots before settling back on her face.

She just hoped the flush she felt on her cheeks looked like a response to the heat of the sun, not the heat of his stare.

One of his dark eyebrows arched up at her in surprise

as she captured her ponytail under her hat and pulled the brim down to shade her eyes.

"You really need a new hat, Brenna. That one's seen better days."

Damn it, he'd recognized it. Jack had bought her this hat—a silly gift from the early days of their relationship—and if she'd had even the smallest clue he'd show up she'd have left it at the house today. It was her favorite hat—wide brimmed and very comfortable—and she'd absolutely only kept it because it worked so well for her, *not* because it was a gift from him.

She hoped he didn't think otherwise.

Brazening it out regardless, she lifted her chin. "It's perfectly serviceable." Shifting her weight onto her heels, she put her hands in her back pockets and tried to act normally, although she felt anything but normal. Her heart pounded in her chest and her palms felt clammy. *Be an adult.* "What brings you to Amante Verano, Jack?"

Her words seemed to amuse him. "I know the lawyer explained Max's will to you. You had to be expecting me."

"Actually, no. I was expecting another phone call from your *lawyer*—not a personal visit from you." This was the longest conversation they'd had in over five years, and she wasn't handling it well. She knew she sounded defensive and prickly.

"We don't need lawyers for this." He pulled a folded manila envelope from the back pocket of his jeans. "If we could go somewhere quiet—"

Somewhere quiet. Brenna's knees wobbled a little bit

at the rush of memories those two words brought. That summer after graduation, when finding "somewhere quiet" had always led to…

She shook herself, forcing the memories and the tingle they caused back into the past, where they belonged. Concentrating on the envelope in his hand helped; she had a very sick feeling she wasn't going to like what was in there, otherwise Jack wouldn't have wanted to take the conversation elsewhere. Hoping for steadiness in her voice—if not her knees—she met his eyes. "In case you haven't noticed, I'm a little busy at the moment. Surely you remember how this place works?"

"Brenna…" The muscle in Jack's jaw tightened, showing his frustration with her.

That helped. Irritation flowed through her body, displacing the earlier, more disturbing emotions. Jack was *not* going to walk onto her property after all these years and act as if he owned the damn place. Okay, so he owned half of it, and the guilt that she was the reason he never came out here anymore nagged at her a bit, but still… She focused on her irritation.

He wasn't the boss of Amante Verano. Or her. Whatever was so all-fire important enough to pull him away from the excitement of his life in the city could just wait. "I have grapes losing quality while I stand here talking to you, and I need to go fix a stupid pump if I want to get them into the tanks tonight. You'll just have to wait your turn."

Pleased with herself for getting the last word, she brushed past him, intent on getting to the winery and back to work. Jack grabbed her arm, halting her steps and pulling her too close for comfort. His face was only inches from hers—something her body reacted to instantly. And embarrassingly.

Heat, *real* heat, the kind she hadn't felt in years, surged through her. He was so close she could see herself in the pupils of his eyes, smell the spicy scent of his soap. She swallowed hard. "Not now, Jack. I'm—"

"Busy, I know. So am I. Do you think I *wanted* to come out here?" His dark brows pulled together in a sharp vee as he gritted out the words.

He might as well have slapped her. The pain and shock were the same. In a way, she welcomed it. It would help her focus on the present.

Then the heat dropped out of his voice. "I'm selling my half of the winery."

Outrage replaced her shock. *What?* "You can't. Max set up the partnership—"

"Oh, I'm well aware of how this ridiculous partnership is set up. It's barely legal and completely beyond reason. But I've found a buyer, and all you have do is sign off on it."

She hadn't planned on owning Amante Verano right now either—much less sharing it with him—but he didn't have the right to go selling off his part of it. His attitude wasn't exactly helping the situation any either. "There's no way in hell I'm signing anything. I'm sorry if you find the arrangement distasteful. Trust me, it's not exactly a picnic for me either. But we're stuck with each other."

"You won't have to be stuck with me once you sign off on the sale."

The grip on her arm was bordering on painful, and

she smacked his hand away. He stepped back, the muscle in his jaw still working.

She bristled. "To whom? Let me guess: you found someone who fancied the odd break from city life and wanted to come stomp grapes on the weekends?" The look on Jack's face told her all she needed to know. "That figures. My answer is no."

"That's not an option, Brenna. I don't want a winery. Not even half of one."

Bless Max for his forward-thinking and iron-clad partnership clauses. Otherwise she'd be royally screwed about now. "Tough. I'm certainly not turning half of everything Max and I worked for over to someone who doesn't know squat about this business."

"You'd rather deal with me? Isn't that worse?"

How could she explain her reasoning to Jack? It barely made sense to her. And would it make any difference if she did? "I'll take the devil I know any day."

Jack opened his mouth to argue, but her phone rang. A quick glance at the number reminded her of all the things she needed to be doing instead of standing here fighting with Jack. "I'm going to go take a pump apart now, because I have wine to make. This conversation is over."

This time Jack didn't move to stop her—which was a good thing, because with her temper riding so high she would probably take a swing at him if he tried. But it didn't stop him from flinging the last word at her back as she stalked off.

"This is not over, Brenna. Put *that* in your damn tank and ferment it."

* * *

Jack let her stomp away, recognizing the signs of a full-on Brenna fit brewing even after ten years. She had her shoulders thrown back and her head high, but he could tell she was talking to herself by the agitated movements of her hands.

Maybe confronting Brenna like that had been a slight tactical error. He'd let his desire to get this over with override his business sense. Hell, his common sense seemed to have checked out—as it always did with Brenna.

It was the only explanation he had.

He'd had the whole conversation planned—he knew Brenna well enough to know how to approach her—but when she'd slammed into him his body had remembered each and every curve of her and promptly forgotten his earlier plan. Then his hands had curved around her biceps, and the muscles there had flexed in response…and he'd felt the tiny shudder move through her when she'd realized who he was.

He should have known Brenna would react like this to his news. It wasn't as if their history didn't complicate this situation even more than it should have been. When you added in Brenna's temper… What was it Max had said shortly after Brenna and her equally copper-headed mother had moved in? "The only things I've learned to fear are red-headed women and downhill putts." Since Jack didn't play golf—he simply didn't have the time or patience for the game—he'd dismissed both warnings at the time. He'd learned the hard way the truth of at least half of

Max's statement. Pity he'd forgotten it before he came out here.

He should have let his lawyer handle this instead of thinking he and Brenna could do it the easy way. Hell, hadn't he learned long ago that nothing with Brenna was easy?

With a sigh of disgust, he folded the envelope again and put it back in his pocket. Tonight, after Brenna had the day's harvest safely in the tanks, they'd talk again.

She couldn't put him off forever, and the house, while large, wasn't big enough for her to avoid him. Red hair aside, Brenna's anger rarely had lasting power, so that would work in his favor as well.

He still had to go through some files in Max's office, but even with the delay caused by Brenna he should have plenty of time to deal with her, take care of business, and get the hell out of Sonoma tomorrow.

CHAPTER TWO

SHOWER. Dinner. Drink. The thought of those three rewards kept Brenna's legs moving as she dragged herself back to the house, but the black Mercedes parked next to her Jeep was an unwelcome reminder of Jack's presence. Not that she needed one. He'd been circling her thoughts all afternoon, distracting her and keeping her temper on edge. While she'd bemoaned rattling around the house alone recently, Jack wasn't exactly the company she'd been hoping for.

She left her boots in the mudroom and headed straight for the safety of her bedroom. Jack must be holed up in his old room, because the house still echoed like it always did these days. Technically, Jack's room was the guest suite now, but Max had always held out hope that Jack would make use of it again one day.

And now he was. It had only taken Max's death and inheriting half the winery to get him back out here. That familiar guilt settled on her again as the shower washed away the dirt from the vineyard and she scrubbed the grease from the pump from under her fingernails. Max had never said anything to her face, but Brenna knew that deep down he had to blame her, to *resent* her for Jack's absence and the breach in his relationship with his son.

She'd been trying to make that up to Max every day for the last ten years, at the very least by making his winery everything Max had wanted it to be. Even if he'd made it more difficult for her now, by bringing Jack into the mix. Rationally, she knew why Max had split the vineyard between them, but it was still a difficult situation to handle.

The confrontation in the vineyard with Jack still had her cringing. Could she have been more juvenile and defensive? In all of the possible scenarios she'd imagined, Jack accosting her in her vineyard with some crazy idea about selling to a stranger had never crossed her mind. Not to mention how totally unprepared she'd been to actually be that close to him again. It had taken her an hour just to calm down.

She turned off the water and sighed. If this wasn't a disaster, she didn't want to know what was. Amante Verano had always been the one stable pillar in her life, her haven, and now even that foundation was shaking. She needed some time to think. And food.

Her stomach was growling loudly by the time she'd dried off and slid into a clean pair of pajamas, so she left her hair to dry naturally and padded to the kitchen in search of something to eat.

Dianne, bless her, had left a plate in the fridge for her, and in less time than it took for her to pour a glass of wine her dinner was ready. She took her plate to the counter and grabbed the TV remote.

Just as she took the first bite Jack walked in, causing her to choke on Dianne's homemade quiche.

A black sleeveless T-shirt exposed shoulder and arm muscles covered in a sheen of sweat. Gym shorts rode low on his hips, giving her a glimpse of tight abs between the hem of the shirt and the waistband as he reached into the cupboard for a glass and then filled it with water. Powerful thighs. Defined calves.

Mercy.

Oh, she remembered his body all too well—and far too frequently—but to have it displayed for her in reality had her coughing painfully as her mouth went dry and it became hard to chew. A look of concern crossed Jack's face and he reached for her.

She did not need him touching her. Even if it was for the Heimlich maneuver. Waving him away, she swallowed with difficulty.

Jack offered her his water, and she waved that away as well; the thought of sharing his glass just seemed too familiar and intimate. She reached for her own glass, but the normally smooth wine burned her throat on the way down. She coughed one last time and willed herself under control.

It didn't quite work, but at least she wasn't choking now. She forced her eyes back to his face. "I see you found Max's gym."

"I did. Nice set-up you've got in there." Jack's eyebrows went up as he belatedly noted her pajamas, and Brenna felt a flush rise on her neck. *Get real. They're just pajamas. Boring ones at that. Just eat.*

"Max seemed to think we needed one, but I never

have understood why." *Stab, lift, bite, chew, swallow.*
"We tend to get our exercise the old-fashioned way
around here."

Don't stare, for God's sake.

"I remember."

Jack leaned against the other side of the counter,
and she could feel those blue eyes boring into her. She
concentrated on eating, ignoring the impulse to take her
plate to her room. The weight of his stare, though, got
to be too much. "*Must* you watch me eat?"

"You're a bit hostile tonight." Calmly enough to make
her even more jumpy, Jack lifted his glass and drank.

Mirroring his calm, she placed her fork carefully on
her plate. "You expected something different?" She
latched on to the easiest excuse, the one that was much
easier to deal with. "You come storming out here, telling
me you want to sell out—without any discussion at all—
and I'm supposed to be happy about it? Get real, Jack."

A bead of sweat trickled down the side of his face
and he swiped at it, giving her another quick glimpse
of his abs as his shirt rose. A familiar heat settled low
in her belly. "You want reality? Good. We can skip past
all the small talk and get straight down to business."

His tone doused the heat nicely. Brenna straightened
her spine and tried to pretend she was wearing more than
a pair of thin cotton pajamas. "Business. Excellent. As
you saw, we have an early set of grapes coming in—a
hybrid vine Max and Ted have been babying along for
the last couple of years. I'm going to make an excellent,
yet deceptively simple white from them, and it's going
to put Amante Verano on the map." She stood and moved

around the counter, put her plate into the dishwasher. "I'll be sure to let you know when it's ready to taste."

Jack hadn't moved, and getting to the dishwasher had put her in close proximity to him. So close she caught his scent, reigniting that heat again. She tried to breathe shallowly through her mouth as she closed the machine and stood to face him.

"Brenna, don't."

Feigning innocence, she met his eyes. "Don't what? Talk business?"

He crossed his arms across his chest casually, looking completely unruffled—to someone who didn't know him, at least. She, however, knew better, and his next words confirmed it. "I could not care less what you're doing with those grapes—or any of the grapes. I just want you to sign off on the sale."

"In case I was unclear earlier, I'll sign off when hell freezes over. You're not selling half of this place to some stranger."

In that same even tone—the one that meant he was only barely keeping his frustration with her in check— he asked, "Then what *do* you want, Brenna?"

"I want you to go back to San Francisco. Go run your empire and leave Amante Verano—" *and me*, she added silently "—alone." The words came out in a rush, and she took a deep breath to stem the flow. "You can be a silent partner—just let us do our thing, and we'll mail you a check for your share of the profits."

"Profits?" He laughed, a mean humorless sound that stabbed her. "This place is nothing but a money pit. Without Max's bankroll—"

"We had a couple of lean years, yes, but we're about to turn a corner. Do you have any idea how long it takes for a winery to become profitable? *Years*, Jack. We're nearly there, *ahead* of all our predictions."

"I've seen your books, Bren."

Bren. The nickname caught her off-guard, throwing her momentarily. "Then you know what I'm saying is true."

"It doesn't matter. How many times do I have to tell you that I don't want a winery?"

Her frustration was starting to build, and she wished she had the ability to control it like Jack. "It's just a winery, for God's sake, not a brothel."

He snorted. "No, brothels are profitable."

"And so are wineries. You just have to be patient. Not that you'd have any idea what *that* concept is like," she added under her breath.

"Brenna…" Impatience tinged his voice, and the muscle in his jaw was working again.

Enough defense. Time to take offense. "Who's being hostile now?"

"If I'm hostile, it's only because you're being completely unreasonable. Again."

Talk about a time warp. Less than a day and they were already settling back into their fighting stances. Oh, she'd love to throw something at him. "Don't start."

His fingers tightened around his biceps. "I'd love to finish, actually."

She took a step back. "Why are you so hot to sell? This is Max's legacy."

"Max's legacy is Garrett Properties."

There was that sting of the slap again. "So would you be so quick to sell off a piece of that?"

"If the price were right and the situation called for it, yes. It's called business, Brenna." He finally levered himself out of his casual lounging against the counter, and suddenly she felt as if she should keep something between them. This would be easier with a barrier keeping him from looming over her.

"There's the difference, Jack. This is more than just a business for me. It's more than a paycheck and a profit margin. It's my *home*. It's all I've ever wanted and you know that."

"Really, Bren? *This* is what you want?"

The question shook her, but she fought not to let it show. Instead, she crossed her arms, copying his earlier casual stance. "Of course."

Jack looked at her strangely, and she struggled to keep her face impassive. "Since when?"

Another memory slammed into her. *Of course* Jack would have to remember the *one* thing she'd hoped he would forget. "It's been a while, Jack. People change."

That damn eyebrow quirked up again. "Obviously."

Don't let this turn personal. Focus on the business. "I'll buy you out."

Jack looked at her in surprise. "You have that kind of money squirreled away someplace? I'm impressed, Bren."

"Well, no." She paced as she tried to think fast. "I can't do it now, but I will eventually. Maybe a little at a time over the next few years…"

"I'm not shackling myself to this place indefinitely."

That's right. He was just as trapped as she was with this partnership. That knowledge gave her a little spurt of courage and she smiled. "Then we seem to be at a stalemate." Oh, that *had* to bother him, and the narrowing of his eyes told her she was right. She could end the night on a high note. "I'm going to bed. I have to get up early to get the grapes in. Make yourself at home. Or, better yet, go home. We're done here."

He stepped in front of her, blocking her path of retreat. Once again she was too close to his body, and her libido reacted immediately. "No, we're not."

She needed distance to get her body back under control, needed quiet and space to figure out what she was going to do. "Move."

"What? So you can stomp off again? Try to stall some more? Stave off the inevitable?"

She had to tilt her head back, but she met his hard stare. "Inevitable? Selling is inevitable? Hardly."

"If you knew a thing about business, you'd know there's no way this partnership can work as long as we're at odds. You can sell now, or lose everything later."

Cold prickles climbed her spine. "You wouldn't. You'd never intentionally let a business—*any* business—fail. It's not in your DNA."

Jack stepped back, finally giving her the space she needed, and she inhaled in relief. The relief quickly faded, though, as he tossed down the gauntlet. "There's a first time for everything, Brenna."

The sobering knowledge of what he was threatening settled around her. Granted, he couldn't sell without her approval, but he could certainly make it next to impossible for her to do business at all. That scenario had never occurred to her, but something in his eyes told her he could do it. *Would* do it. Easily. Her eyes burned at the thought, and she bit the inside of her mouth to distract herself with physical pain. She would *not* cry in front of him, not now. She couldn't get her voice above a whisper, though, when she asked, "Do you hate me that much?"

His eyes raked over her before he answered. "It's just business."

Oh, no, this crossed a line, no matter what he tried to say.

"Go ahead and stomp off now, Bren, but think about what I've said. We'll talk again tomorrow."

Her knees were trembling, but Brenna tried hard to keep her head up as she left the kitchen. Once in the safety of her bedroom, she closed the door and leaned against it before her legs could give out completely.

She'd never seen Jack like that. Not even after their last fight, when she'd packed her bags while Jack had called a car to bring her back here. When pushed, Jack turned silent and broody, not coldly calculating. And since Jack never made empty threats… Damn it. She'd been fooling herself to think they could move beyond their past and forge any kind of business relationship. She'd had no idea his dislike of her was so strong that he'd rather destroy everything Max had created out here than work with her.

She looked skyward. "Why'd you do this to me, Max?"

No answer came, and she flopped on the bed, wrung out, yet still jumpy from the evening.

Jack's sarcastic rebuttal of the one argument he really shouldn't be able to question had thrown her off her game. Of all the things for Jack to bring up… Hell, she'd practically forgotten; why hadn't he? Oh, the optimism and arrogance of an eighteen-year-old girl in love. She groaned and pulled the pillow over her head. Back then she'd figured Max and her mom would run Amante Verano forever. She, on the other hand, would take her knowledge out into the wide world, educating the masses on wine-making, visiting wineries in France and Italy and bringing new ideas back to their vineyard— in general, just getting the hell out of Sonoma and doing something more. Jack had embraced that idea, encouraged it.

But the wide world hadn't had a place for her, and she'd come home. Then her mom had died…

Amante Verano was where she belonged, it seemed. And she'd accepted that, thrown herself into it, made it her life.

She couldn't let Jack undermine that. Not now. No matter how much Jack hated it.

Or her.

For the second time that day Jack let Brenna stomp away, wondering when he'd lost his lauded ability to finesse a situation. What had possessed him to think he'd be able to handle this negotiation just like any other of the hundreds he'd done? Make the plan, work the plan—common sense and good business tactics had always worked for him before. Except when it came to Brenna. Bren just knew the right buttons to push to cause him to lose his temper—a hard pill to swallow, since he never let his temper loose any other time.

Hell, who was he kidding? Brenna *was* his button. Nothing between them had ever been steady or calm or predictable. It was all drama and tension and theatrics.

Oh, they'd started with a bang. But once the initial glow had faded their relationship had fallen apart with alarming speed. All the dreams and plans and excitement had crumbled under the strain of reality, and "love" just hadn't been enough. Before long they'd just made each other miserable.

Except in bed. The familiar heat spread over his skin. Making love to Brenna was like holding a live fuse too close to the gunpowder: hot, dangerous, explosive.

And ultimately destructive.

But they'd been young then, too young and stupid to realize sex wasn't enough to hold them together until it was too late. No matter how great it was.

If tonight was any indication, his body hadn't forgotten *that* in the intervening years. Her plain, most-likely organic cotton pajamas did a good job of camouflaging what was underneath, but his body had reacted anyway, reigniting that old urge to get her under him as quickly as humanly possible.

But reality hit home pretty quickly once Brenna started in on him. While his hands had still itched to touch her, he'd been reminded exactly why they were in this mess in the first place.

Regardless of their past or their present, he didn't necessarily relish the idea of destroying her dreams for this place. But that didn't mean he wanted to be a part of it, either. Max might have found someone willing to build his little wine-making dynasty, but Jack didn't want to play along. And, Brenna, for all her talk of a partnership, couldn't really want him around either.

Not after everything.

He needed something stronger than water to drink. A look around revealed several bottles of wine but little else, and nothing of interest. Wine on the counters, wine in the cupboards, wine in the largest non-commercial fridge he'd ever seen. Was there a damn beer anywhere on the property?

Max would have Scotch in his desk. He always did. His passion for wine-making couldn't have squelched his love of a good single malt.

Jack had to pass Brenna's bedroom to get to the office. Light escaped around the doorframe, but the room was silent as he paused in front of the door, debating whether he'd made a mistake in letting Brenna walk out in the middle of their discussion.

Discussion? Right. He seemed incapable of having a civilized discussion with Brenna about anything. Between her temper and the emotional attachment she had to this place, the chances of any civil discourse seemed remote.

The Amante Verano business office was large—larger than such a small operation probably needed, but that was just Max's style—and Max's desk dominated the room. A smaller desk he assumed was Brenna's sat at an angle to Max's. He recognized the set-up; he'd learned the family business in much the same fashion—except the view from the offices of

Garrett Properties encompassed San Francisco Bay and the Golden Gate Bridge, not acres of vines.

The second drawer on the left-hand side produced the Scotch he had been looking for. He leaned back in Max's chair as he poured two fingers and contemplated Brenna's desk. His father had initially planned for that desk to be Jack's, from where he would run the winery as well as the hotels. It hadn't mattered that he didn't want to.

Hell, after Max had gotten over the shock of Jack and Brenna's elopement he'd been practically gleeful over the "merger." The divorce had given Jack a valid reason to stay away all these years, but it seemed Max was trying to have the final say after all.

"Sorry, old man. You can't make me run this place."

No matter what Brenna wanted to believe, she wasn't even the main reason he wanted out from under Amante Verano. Max's first business ate up enough of his life as it was, especially since Max had all but turned the hotels over to him completely once this winery had become his focus. The complication of Brenna didn't add any appeal, though.

His body disagreed, growing hard again at the thought of her. Good God, it had been ten years. Shouldn't he be past that by now?

He sipped the Scotch in silence for a few minutes, willing his body to get over it. When he heard a noise to his right, he looked up to see a barefoot Brenna slip quietly into the room.

"I thought you had to get up early in the morning."

Brenna jumped, a small cry escaping her as she

turned around to locate the voice. Her hand fell away from her throat as she found him, and her shoulders dropped. "Damn it, Jack, you scared the life out of me. What are you doing in here?"

He shrugged. "I could ask you the same thing."

"It's *my* office." Brenna's chin lifted in challenge.

Unable to resist prodding her, he raised the glass in salute. "And now it's half mine."

Brenna shook her head. "Whatever." She slid into her chair and turned her back to him as she booted up the computer. "I need to do some work, so if you'll excuse me…?"

She wanted him to retreat so she wouldn't have to? Hardly. "Go ahead. You won't bother me at all." Brenna's hands tightened around the armrests of her chair, and even in the semi-darkness of the room he could see the white knuckles. If he listened carefully, he'd probably be able to hear her grinding her teeth next.

He heard her sigh, then her fingers moved quickly across the keyboard, the clicking sound filling the silence. "The new hotel in Monterrey is selling the Pinot faster than I can get it to them. Max's idea to market our wines in your boutique hotels was a fabulous one."

"That's nice."

"It is." She pushed her hair over her shoulder, causing it to spill over the back of the chair, where the light bounced off it in a coppery glow. "It means you may be seeing those profit checks sooner than you thought."

That was supposed to convince him he wanted to own half a winery? "I don't need the money."

Brenna shrugged. "Good. I'll buy new tanks instead."

So much for polite conversation. "You just bought new tanks."

Brenna spun in her chair, sputtering. "Are you questioning—?"

He shouldn't prod her, but he just couldn't stop himself. "Yeah, I am. You just bought new tanks. Italian ones. Very expensive. I saw the invoice."

Bren straightened her spine, and she seemed to be trying for a lofty, all-business tone. "I'm slowly trying to replace all the old ones that desperately need it, and the best tanks come from Italy. Since the best equipment lets me make the best wines, it's money well spent." She took a deep breath. "Anyway, why are you poking around in my invoices? I thought you didn't care about this place."

"I don't. But since I now own half of it…" he loved the way her eyes narrowed every time he reminded her of that fact "…I have to make sure it's running properly. It's in my DNA, remember?"

"You know nothing about *this* business, so I think the silent partner idea is best."

"I don't do silent. Until I sell my half…" He let the sentence trail off and let her fill in the blanks.

It only took her a second to make the leap, and her hackles went up again. "Are you seriously planning to buck me on every decision I make around here?"

"Of course. Weren't you listening earlier?" Brenna's eyes widened, and he was lucky looks couldn't kill. "But you know it would be really easy to get me away from your books. Sign on the dotted line, Bren, and I'm out of your hair."

Brenna rolled her eyes and turned back to her computer. She started to type, then stopped as she leaned her head against the chair-back. "First you threaten to drive my winery into the ground. Then you threaten to drive me insane. To think Max used to say how good you'd be for this place."

"There's a simple solution, you know."

"It's not simple at all." She moved her chair slightly, turning her profile his way. Her eyes were closed, and her throat worked as she rubbed her hands over her face.

"It's a lot easier than you're making it, Bren. You don't want me in your business, and you know it. Sign off on the sale and I'm gone."

"I've already said no. Come up with a new idea."

Lord, the woman was stubborn. "There are no other ideas."

"You're going to tell me that the great Jack Garrett doesn't have a Plan B?"

He swirled the drink in his glass. "I don't need a Plan B."

Brenna turned to face him again, and her voice turned conciliatory for a change. "Max wanted Amante Verano kept as a small family business. He didn't want outsiders involved."

"And what, exactly, are *you*?"

Brenna pulled back as if she'd been hit, and he regretted the harshness of his words.

"That's unfair, Jack. We were a family, and this is a family business."

"Brenna—"

She held up a hand. "Wait. Just— Just—" She took another deep breath and faced him across the expanse of Max's desk. "I don't want to fight any more. Especially not with you."

"Then don't fight me. Neither of us wants to be in this situation."

She opened her mouth, then closed it and chewed on her bottom lip for a moment while she thought. "You're right, you know. I don't want you around anymore than you want to be here. But…" She took a deep breath. Her voice dropped to a whisper as she turned to meet his eyes. "I *need* you."

The desire that slammed into him with those three simple words nearly caused him to drop his glass. Oh, part of him knew she was still talking about the damn winery, but his body was reacting to that throaty whisper—she'd whispered those words in his ear countless times as she'd wrapped herself around him.

Need. She'd always referred to him as a need. He'd nearly forgotten, but the response of his body proved those six months they'd had weren't as deeply buried as he'd thought. He shifted in his chair, attempting to bring the reaction under control.

Brenna seemed not to notice. "Max was the brains behind the business. I'm sure you know that. And I could learn, but Amante Verano would suffer in the meantime. I know that's why Max put us in this partnership—he always said the Walsh women made great wine, but they needed Garrett men to make it profitable." She folded her hands in her lap, squeezing her fingers together as she talked. "It took me a while to figure out what he meant—beyond the MBA-approved business model, at least. The Garrett name opens a lot of doors."

"You should know that from experience. You were a Garrett for a short while."

She paled a bit at the reminder. "Don't go there, Jack. What I *mean* is that as long as there's a Garrett behind Amante Verano I can do business. Get loans to expand, for example. A small winery is a bank's nightmare—unless there's a Garrett on the books, of course, and then we're golden. I just need you to back me—in name, if not spirit—for a few years. That's all I'm asking."

"You ask a lot."

"Why? How? You don't have to do anything."

He just looked at her.

She nodded. "Except deal with me. And you hate that more than anything else."

He'd never heard Brenna sound so flat, so lifeless. He'd almost prefer her anger to that toneless resignation. "I don't hate you, Bren. But I'm not going to be your partner either."

She cocked her head. "Once bitten?" she challenged.

"I'm not afraid of your bite." In fact, the thought of her teeth on his skin brought back a slew of sensual memories. Unwilling to circle this topic again or battle with his body any longer, he stood. "Decide what you're going to do. I'll leave the sale paperwork in the kitchen."

Brenna's jaw dropped at his words, then she spun her chair back to her computer. He heard her mumble something under her breath as he turned to leave.

He doubted it was a compliment.

CHAPTER THREE

"I SWEAR, Di, it's frustrating. I just want to scream. Or something," she muttered. Brenna positioned her clippers and separated the grape cluster from the vine with a satisfying, overly forceful snip.

"Picturing Jack's neck, are we?" Dianne teased from the other side of the row of vines. Chloe napped peacefully in a carrier strapped to Dianne's chest, her hat with its embroidered Amante Verano logo shielding her fat baby cheeks from the early-morning sun.

"It's cathartic." She snipped two more clusters and added them to the bucket at her feet. "And safer for Jack."

"What are you going to do?" Dianne asked the question casually, but Brenna knew everyone in the vineyard was on edge, waiting to see what would happen next. Jack's plan to sell would affect everyone in some way.

"Honestly? I'm not sure. I'm open to ideas if you have any." She'd been up most of the night, tossing and turning as she tried to figure out her options. There weren't many.

"I wish I did."

"Stubborn. Arrogant. Domineering. Jerk." She punctuated each comment with a snip of the clippers.

"Max could be like that sometimes. He's his father's son; that's for sure."

Brenna laughed. "Oh, I dare you to tell him that. It'll really get his goat."

"I don't think antagonizing Jack further is really the best idea right now, do you?" Dianne was always so calm, so unflappable. So annoyingly right most of the time.

"I was trying to be nice last night. Trying to be reasonable. That didn't work out so well."

"Because you have a history with Jack."

"*Ancient* history," Brenna clarified.

"Still, it complicates things."

No kidding. She'd seen the papers in the kitchen this morning; she'd even glanced through them while she waited for her coffee to brew. Turn over fifty-percent of the vineyard to the highest bidder? She'd been tempted to feed Jack's stack of papers into the shredder and leave a bag of confetti hanging on his doorknob.

For the thousandth time, she wished she had the money to buy Jack's share. But while the banks would be happy to loan her barrels of money as long as Jack was a co-owner, no bank in the world would loan her the money to buy him *out*. It still wasn't an ideal solution—buying Jack out only solved one problem while causing a whole slew of others.

In the small hours of the morning, though, she had realized how much of their current problem was rooted in their heated, reckless past. She needed to recognize it and figure out good ways to move past it. Dianne wasn't the only one realizing that. "That knowledge—however truthful it may be—doesn't make the situation suck any less." It certainly didn't make her feel any better. She was drowning—in anger, frustration, guilt, worry, and a dozen other emotions she couldn't quite name. The painful knot in her stomach was bordering on debilitating.

Dianne nodded understandingly, then looked at her watch. "I hate to harvest and run, but I need to shower so I can get the shop open in time. Plus, I think Chloe is waking up." Dianne cooed at the baby as she stripped off her gloves.

"I appreciate the help. And the company, of course. Getting up at dawn goes above and beyond the call of duty."

"But it's fun—at least for the first couple of hours," she added, as Brenna raised an eyebrow at her in disbelief. "Do you think you'll finish today?"

"Marco brought a full crew, so if not today definitely tomorrow."

"Good. I'll see you at lunch. Tuna salad okay with you?"

"That's great. You're the best."

"I know," Dianne tossed over her shoulder as she left.

Brenna had enjoyed the company—having Di to talk to had been a nice distraction, one that she missed as she fell back into her rhythm and her mind started to wander.

There *had* to be a solution. She just needed to find it. If she'd only known Jack would carry such a grudge...

It wasn't *all* her fault, she thought as she carried the full bucket of grapes to the bin at the end of the row and emptied it. He was just as much to blame for their disastrous relationship and the fallout as she was. The early days had been fantastic—the type of thing romance novels were written about. The boss's handsome son, descending from the city to sweep the winemaker's daughter off her feet. Picnics in the vineyard; stolen kisses behind the barrels of Merlot. Making love under a canopy of Cabernet vines, then feeding the ripe grapes to each other in the afterglow.

It had been everything she'd ever dreamed of. Romantic and passionate and all-encompassing. Jack had made her feel like the center of his universe—beautiful and sexy and interesting. It had been too easy to fall in love.

But, while opposites attracting worked great in movies, the reality hadn't been dreamy at all.

While it had all gone to hell later, she did have fond memories of being eighteen and head-over-heels in love. Jack had been different then, too: more carefree, with a smile that melted her knees even in memory.

The old Jack would be more reasonable and much easier for her to deal with. The old Jack wouldn't want to sell her winery out from under her, or ruin everything she'd worked for simply out of spite. He'd changed so much in the last ten years. He'd become more reserved, harder and colder. Sometimes she wondered if he was really the same man.

She missed the old Jack. The one she fell in love with. The Jack who didn't hate her.

She shook off the reverie and the sinking feeling. She had to deal with *this* Jack. And quickly—for the good of Amante Verano and her own mental health.

"Daydreaming on the job, boss?" Ted grinned at her as he upended his overflowing bucket into the bin. "You seem pretty far away."

"Trust me, I'm here. Just sending up quick prayers that the pump doesn't die again."

"After the way you cursed at it yesterday? It wouldn't dare."

She laughed. "It deserved it. Cantankerous thing." *Much like someone else she knew.* She pulled off her gloves. "Unless you need me here for some reason, I'm going to head back to the winery. Lots of grapes to process, and…"

"You have a cantankerous pump to deal with," he finished for her.

That explanation would do. "Exactly."

But the pump seemed to be working fine. At least that part of her life was moving along on plan. Although it freed her mind to stew over other issues for the next six hours, she didn't discover any new solutions to her problems.

She took her time hosing out the crusher for the last time, then puttered around the lab, stalling for time. Calling it a day would put her back in the house with Jack. For such a big house, it felt very small with Jack in it, and, since she was still having trouble controlling her hormones while he was around, putting herself in close proximity to him didn't sound like a great idea. Plus, there was no way to avoid more discussion of the future of the vineyard, and without any bright new ideas she wasn't in any hurry for another round with Jack over *that*.

But she couldn't hide in her lab forever, and as the

sun went down her irritation grew—both with herself and Jack. She was avoiding her *home*, for goodness's sake. Just because of *him*.

That irritation fueled her up the hill to the house, and as she toed off her boots in the mudroom she felt ready for a fight and actually *hoped* Jack was nearby.

Then she heard Dianne's voice in her head: *"Don't antagonize him."* That deflated her indignant bubble a bit. She'd be nice if it killed her.

But Jack wasn't around. The kitchen was empty, the sale paperwork still sitting on the counter. The living room was just as empty. She glanced down the hallway, but no light or noise came out of the office either.

Jack's car sat in the driveway, so he hadn't gone far. Of course his room and the gym were on the far side of the house, but she didn't have a good excuse to go wandering down that hallway to see where he was. Plus, she didn't want to take the chance of running into him while he was hot and sweaty and half dressed again. Last night had been bad enough.

For the time being she was alone, and for the first time in a long time she didn't mind the quiet. With her stomach still tied in a knot, eating was out of the question, but a glass of wine sounded like a great plan.

She grabbed a glass and a bottle of last year's Chardonnay and retreated behind her bedroom door.

She still had a lot of thinking to do.

The sun was completely behind the hills and he still hadn't heard Brenna come in. She'd been gone early, too, probably around dawn, because the coffee she'd left in the pot had tasted old when he'd made his way into the kitchen this morning.

The early morning was to be expected; he remembered all too well the rush to get the grapes in before it got too hot—for the grapes, not the people. But sunup to sunset? That meant something had gone wrong at the winery with the crush, and Brenna would be in a bad mood when she finally did make it back to the house.

He wasn't going to concern himself with her mood—beyond the fact it would make any conversation even more difficult than last night's had been. The papers were still on the counter, unsigned, but in a different place than he'd left them, telling him she'd at least looked through them at some point.

He'd spent the day in Max's office, alternating between talking to his secretary and going through the winery's books. He didn't want to leave until he had this settled with Brenna, because he fully intended to never darken the doorway again once he left this time, but he couldn't be away from the city indefinitely. At some point he did need to finish the preparations for his meeting in New York next week. Unfortunately, he hadn't been able to come up with many ideas that would both placate Brenna and sever his ties with this place at the same time.

Dianne Hart, whom he only vaguely remembered as one of Brenna's friends from high school, had brought two plates of dinner to the house late in the afternoon, explaining as she did so that she normally fed Brenna during harvest time, and bashfully explained she'd figured he'd need dinner, too.

She'd chatted to him as she moved easily through the kitchen, balancing a wide-eyed baby on one hip, explaining how she'd moved to Amante Verano five years ago, shortly after Brenna's mother died. When Brenna took her mother's place as vintner, she'd hired Dianne's then newlywed husband Ted as viticulturist. Dianne seemed loyal to Brenna to the core, and had only glowing things to say about her, yet she didn't seem to share Brenna's animosity toward him.

Or if she did, she did a better job of hiding it than Bren. He hadn't missed the way her eyes had strayed to the papers on the counter, though. No doubt Dianne was fully up-to-date on the situation, and he vaguely wondered if Brenna had sent Dianne with instructions to help smooth the path.

But before he could question her, to uncover any underlying motives, she'd been gone. Dianne was Brenna's polar opposite in both looks and temperament, but she had that same earth mother wholesomeness. Years ago that had been part of Brenna's allure—so different from the women he'd grown used to at home. He'd learned his lesson well, though. He'd take Gucci over granola any day.

Boredom and an empty house drove him outside to the pool, where he pulled up short. He'd forgotten how Max had recreated his rooftop retreat at Garrett Tower here—only on a larger scale. White flagstones, warm under his feet, formed the pool deck, while large pots of hibiscus, hellebores and yarrow divided the space, providing secluded seating areas and privacy for the hot tub. Eerie. Almost like being at home.

He swam several laps, then hooked his arms over the edge and listened to the quiet sounds of the evening. Even with the sun down the night was still warm—no need to heat the pool here in the summertime. With nothing more than a few vineyards scattered over the surrounding miles, the lack of light pollution made the stars seem brighter, clearer. A few wispy clouds crossed in front of the rising moon, but no high-rise buildings blocked the view.

This was possibly the only thing he didn't dislike about Amante Verano. When Max had bought the vineyard, *this* was what had first brought Jack out here, not some love of the *vino*.

The French doors to Brenna's bedroom opened, and she stepped quietly onto the patio. Her hair was pulled up and secured with a clip, leaving her profile and the long column of her neck exposed. She drank deeply from a large wine glass as she walked, obviously unaware of his presence, the belt to her short robe trailing behind her on the flagstones. Brenna set the glass carefully on a stone table and shrugged out of the robe.

And then he remembered what else had attracted him to Max's vineyard.

Even in the dim light he could see the defined muscles in her slender shoulders, arms and back— muscles developed from hauling endless bins of grapes, not on some piece of equipment in a gym. The dark bikini didn't cover much, allowing him a sight he hadn't seen in years but had never forgotten. Her body was compact, strong. He knew from experience the power in those thighs, the way the firm muscles covered in soft skin would flex under his hands.

The water, warm just a minute ago, now felt cool against his heated skin, and that old flame sparked to life.

Then Brenna stretched, her back arching gracefully as she lifted her arms over her head, drawing his eyes to the generous curve of her breasts and down the flat plane of her stomach.

And the flame seared through him like a flash fire, fanned by the rush of erotic memories tumbling through his heated brain. He flattened his palms on the pool apron and pushed, heaving himself out of the water.

At the noisy rush of water Brenna spun, the force causing the clip to lose its grip and sending the mass of red hair tumbling around her shoulders. "Jeez, Jack, *when* did you take up skulking in the dark as a hobby?"

He was already reaching for her when her words registered, and he grabbed a towel instead, busying his hands by drying himself off and knotting the towel around his waist in an attempt to camouflage the raging erection she'd caused. "Since when is swimming 'skulking in the dark'?"

"Since you started doing it here." Her hands weren't entirely steady as she gathered her hair and secured it back on top of her head. He felt as well as saw Brenna's eyes move over his chest like a caress, tracking downward until her cheeks reddened. When her eyes flew upward to meet his, he recognized the glow there. It had been a while since he'd seen it, and it stoked the fire burning in him.

Brenna shifted uncomfortably as he returned his slow gaze to her body, and she reached for her robe.

"It's not like I haven't seen it before, Bren. No need to be modest."

Her jaw tightened, but the goad didn't bring a retort. Instead, she stared beyond him into the dark vineyards. The silence stretched out for long minutes as they stood there, until Brenna finally cleared her throat. "If you'd— I mean, are you tr— Um, I'll leave you to it."

"Retreat again, Bren?"

Her shoulders pulled back and settled. "No, no retreat. But I came out here to relax, and fighting with you is not on my list of things I'd like to do tonight."

Images of what *he'd* like to do tonight swam in front of his eyes, and he forcefully shut them out. His body's reaction to Brenna might be beyond his mind's control, but he wasn't a kid anymore. He'd learned his lesson the hard way and, while she was very tempting…

Who was he kidding? He wanted her. Badly. "Don't let me stand in the way of your swim."

"Swim? Oh." She smiled weakly. "I wasn't planning on a swim."

He looked pointedly at her swimsuit. "Interesting choice of attire, then."

Brenna rolled her eyes at him as she reached for her wine glass. "I've had a long day," she said as she stepped around the pots of hellebores and sank into the bubbling hot tub with a sigh. She arched an eyebrow at him. "Do you mind?"

He knew he shouldn't, but he took the opening anyway. "Not at all." He'd dropped his towel and taken the seat opposite her in the hot water before Brenna could stop sputtering. "We have a lot to talk about."

Brenna closed her eyes and sank lower, until the water covered her shoulders. "Not tonight, Jack."

She didn't realize the vineyard was the last thing on his mind at the moment. "Why not?"

"Because I really don't want to fight with you again. It's exhausting, and I'm exhausted enough already."

"Who said we had to fight?"

She opened her eyes, giving him a "get real" look. "We haven't had a civilized conversation in years. You think we'll succeed tonight? Under these circumstances?"

Brenna had a point, but the soft, husky voice had him mesmerized. Even her snappy comebacks lacked any real sarcasm or heat. It boded well. He leaned back, mirroring her position, and shrugged. "So far, so good."

She laughed softly. "Well, there's a first time for everything, I guess."

He was actually suffering from *déjà vu* at the moment. Brenna, quiet if not quite relaxed, the steam rising in wisps around her face, her legs stretched out on the bench only inches from his. His body reacted to the memories, wanting to pull her into his lap…

"How are things with the hotels? Max said you were planning on expanding to the east coast?"

Brenna's question snapped him back to the present. "Everything is going well. I'm headed to New York next week to finalize the deal."

A small smile pulled at the corner of her mouth. "Max would be pleased. He always wanted a hotel in Manhattan."

"And all this time I thought he just wanted a winery." He winked at her, enjoying the look of surprise that crossed her face at the gesture.

"Well, he got that. But you know how Max was always thinking ahead to the next thing."

"Garrett men aren't satisfied easily." He met her eyes evenly, and held the stare until her cheeks flushed and she broke away.

Brenna's eyes traveled over his chest and shoulders hungrily, before she snapped them back up to his face and coughed awkwardly. "They're also hard to please sometimes," she retorted, but she did it with a smile on her face so he couldn't take it as an attack.

Brenna closed her eyes again and sank a little deeper into the water. Her legs brushed against his, and she moved them away quickly. They sat there in silence for a few minutes, and he watched the tension slowly begin to ease from her body. When she finally spoke, her voice was calm and casual again. "We got the last of those grapes in today. It was a really nice yield, and they made gorgeous juice."

Small talk seemed oddly easy at the moment. It certainly beat fighting, and his hopes that this night might turn out to be interesting grew. "Only you would call grape juice gorgeous."

She smiled. "Gorgeous juice makes gorgeous wine. And that makes me very happy indeed."

"What else makes you happy, Bren?" The question came out of nowhere, shocking him almost as much as her.

She sighed tiredly. "Are we going to fight now?"

He couldn't stop the small smile her question caused, but Brenna's eyes were still closed and she couldn't see it. "Not unless you start it. It's a simple question."

Her shoulders sagged. "Fine. Let's see." She thought for a long moment, floating her hands on the water's surface and humming. "Good grapes and good wine."

Did she ever think about anything else? "Besides wine, Bren."

Brenna pursed her lips in mock annoyance. "Um… Walks through the vineyard right at sunset—when it's peaceful and cool, but not dark yet."

They'd been on several memorable sunset walks together, but he didn't think Brenna would appreciate the reminder at the moment.

"Brownie fudge ice cream. And… And… Can I say good wine again?"

"That's not very creative."

That caused her eyes to open again. "What can I say? I have simple needs. What about you?"

He had to think. "Board meetings where no one brings me a disaster to fix. Fast cars. Single-malt Scotch."

Brenna shook her head. "That's a strange list."

"Well, we all can't be blissful just hanging out at Amante Verano making good wine." He shrugged.

He'd said it off-hand, but Brenna's chin dropped and her teeth worried her bottom lip. He knew that look, too, so he waited to see what she was working up the courage to say.

"I'm very sorry, Jack."

An apology? He'd expected a volley about the sale of the winery, or even a statement about Max, designed to play on his sense of duty to the vineyard. Not an apology. What was she angling for? "What for, Bren?"

"A lot of things. But mainly for keeping you away from here."

He snorted, and Brenna looked at him in question. "Brenna, if I'd had any desire to come out here, your presence wouldn't have stopped me."

Confusion wrinkled her forehead. "But you used to love it here—you were out here all the time. It was just after…after, you know, the divorce that you quit coming. I know that was because of me, and I am sorry for that."

Interesting. There were many ways he could respond, but something about Brenna's honesty brought out the same in him. "I don't like wine, I don't like grapes, and I certainly don't have any interest in agriculture of any sort. Think about it—how often did I come out here in the two years after Max bought the property?"

"Maybe twice that I know of…"

He leaned forward and held her gaze. "That's because you were in school and I hadn't met you yet. Then I came out with Max for your graduation…"

Brenna's eyes widened and her jaw dropped. "Are you saying you only came out here to see *me* that summer?"

He nodded, enjoying the waves of shock that moved over her face as she re-aligned her thought processes. "And after we were over there was no reason for me to come back."

CHAPTER FOUR

BRENNA struggled to make sense of his words. The chirp of crickets and the bubbles of the tub's jets covered the sound of her rough, shallow breaths as the ramifications of his simple statement hit home. "I always assumed it was me keeping you away."

Jack shrugged a muscular shoulder, drawing her attention back to his body. Thankfully, much of it was submerged, and no longer quite the magnet for her eyes. Jack in nothing but swim trunks brought back too many memories, and her brain simply couldn't balance both important conversation and gawking at Jack's body at the same time. She struggled to focus on what Jack was saying.

"Why? You knew good and well by the time we got divorced that there wasn't much attraction out here for me."

She'd been the attraction before. That explained some things… "But you didn't even come to see Max after the divorce."

"Staying under the same roof with your ex—especially when your former mother-in-law is sleeping with your father—isn't exactly a tourist attraction." A wry smile crossed his face. "No matter how nice the scenery."

Okay, she knew that. She'd even considered moving back into her old house at the time, only Max and her mom had talked her out of it.

Jack's legs were so close to hers under the bubbling water they rubbed against hers as he shifted position. The brief contact sent a zing through her. But she couldn't hold eye contact, because the smoldering look there wreaked havoc on her insides. If she kept her eyes on his forehead it was easier to concentrate, and she'd be able to keep up with this conversation.

"Then Max started spending even more time out here and less in the city," he continued, as if he didn't know how she was having trouble following along, "and the company took over my life. What little free time I had left I wasn't going to spend it out here, regardless."

Suddenly she realized that for the first time since… well, since the beginning of the end, there was no anger underlying Jack's words. While that absence calmed her guilty conscience, and the part of her that was always so on edge whenever she so much as thought of him, she wasn't deaf to the other heat adding weight to his words. *That* heat her body recognized immediately, even though she hadn't heard it in years. To her great embarrassment her breasts began to tingle and a familiar ache settled in her core.

It was gratifying to know that after everything Jack wasn't completely immune to her. That he didn't hate her enough to make his body forget what had brought them together in the first place. Her skin felt flushed, and she hoped the steam and the hot water would take the blame.

. But she couldn't lose focus. This conversation was too important. His concise explanation didn't quite explain as much as his casual demeanor implied. "But Max always…" She stopped herself, unwilling to say the words.

Jack looked at her closely. "You think Max blamed you?"

She nodded. "He had to. He was so disappointed after the divorce."

"Max didn't like having his plans thwarted. He had this whole hotel-slash-winery empire planned, and you managed to accomplish the one thing he couldn't do— made me give a damn about this place. The divorce put him back at zero—at least until he came up with this ridiculous scheme. Max didn't blame you for the divorce, Bren. He saved all the blame for me."

Jack didn't sound bitter, just matter-of-fact. If anything, it made her feel worse about the situation. "Then I'm sorry for that. I'm sorry I caused a rift between you and Max."

"Quit apologizing. You didn't cause anything. You were just a handy excuse."

Just an excuse? No way. "There's got to be more to it than that. Your relationship with Max—"

"Has nothing to do with the current situation." He brushed her words aside with a wave of his hand.

She pulled her legs up to her chest and hugged them. The stress she'd come out here to alleviate was building instead. Hot tub jets were no match for the knots Jack caused, but the stress was much less disturbing than her inappropriate tingling. "Then why? If it's not because of me and it's not because of Max, then *why* do you want to sell so badly?"

She worked up the courage to look at him then, but he didn't look angry. More like resigned and tired of talking about it. "How many times do I have to say it? I don't want to own a winery. I know that's an alien concept for you, because you *do*, but not everyone has a burning desire to make wine. You need to get off the property more. Expand your circle of friends and see there's a whole world out there *not* obsessed with grapes."

There it was. The snide remark. The dismissive tone. She should have known it was coming instead of being lulled by his civility and the intimate atmosphere caused by their surroundings and the conversation. She needed more space, and she pushed herself out of the steaming water. The air felt chilly against her heated skin but did nothing to cool her rising temper. "God, you're such a jerk."

Jack had the nerve to look taken aback. "What now?"

The tingle thankfully disappeared as old resentments bubbled up. This was much easier. "You. Acting so superior and condescending. Little Brenna is so sheltered and naïve, she couldn't possibly know any better."

"You can't deny you've been sheltered out here. You used to admit that readily."

She started to pace in agitation. "Maybe. That

doesn't mean I'm naïve. Just because I never went to college…"

Jack pushed out of the water as well and sat on the edge of the tub. "That was *your* decision. UC Davis would have let you in."

"Only because my last name was Garrett at the time. And why would I spend all that time at school for them to teach me what I already knew about wine-making?"

"You might have enjoyed it. Or you could have gone to a different school and studied something else."

Now a pang of old hurt joined the resentment. "Oh, I'm *so* sorry my lack of formal education was such an embarrassment in front of your snobby city friends."

"Having interests other than grapes makes them snobs?"

"No, looking down on people makes them snobs." She crossed her arms over her chest. "*You* should know from all the practice you've had."

Jack ran his hands through his hair in exasperation. "Why are we having this fight again? We're not married anymore."

And they'd just run through many of the reasons why. *Again.* "Thank goodness for that." She reached for her wine glass and drank deeply.

"If anyone's a snob, Brenna, it's you."

She choked on her wine. "What? Hardly."

Jack stood and walked to within an inch of her. "You're a wine snob. All that 'fruit of the vine, nectar of the gods' garbage. It gets old. And quite boring."

The comment stung, but she stood her ground. "Gee, I'm sheltered, naïve, snobbish *and* boring—and you're an overbearing, condescending jerk with a superiority complex. I don't know how we ever ended up together in the first place."

She regretted the words the moment they left her lips. When would she learn not to wave the red flag in front of the bull just because she was angry?

Jack's eyes lit alarmingly and traced a path down her body, leaving her skin tingling again in their wake. *How* had she forgotten she was practically naked? And that he was, too? Her nipples tightened against the fabric of her bikini, and a slow half-smile crossed Jack's face. "Oh, I think you remember why, Bren," he said quietly. "I know I do."

His husky voice moved through her and every nerve-ending came to life. She was close enough to feel the heat radiating off his body. A rush of desire slammed into her, making her knees wobble and her heart beat faster. Damn him. "D-don't change the subject."

"I'm not. This has always been the subject." He traced a finger over her collarbone and down the top of her arm. Gooseflesh rose up in its wake, and a shiver moved through her. "We've always had this."

"Jack, don't." Her voice sounded breathy and unsteady even to her, but she couldn't pull away from the tease of his touch or the promise in his voice. Her body screamed for more, and all she'd have to do would be to take a tiny step forward…

No. She closed her eyes, blocking the sight of temptation, but her other senses were still under assault and she swayed on her feet. Sex wouldn't solve anything. *It never had*, she reminded herself. They'd been down this path many, many times. Fight bitterly, then have fabulous make-up sex. It never made anything better. In this case it could only make things worse. More complicated.

She *had* to remember that, no matter how much her body begged to differ. No matter how strong the ache was.

No matter how much she wanted him.

She knew what his hands could do to her, remembered the feel of his skin against hers. And from the fire in Jack's eyes she knew he was remembering as well. A tiny shiver of desire rippled through her.

His finger finished its slow path down her arm and now tickled across the sensitive skin of her waist, over her stomach, where butterflies battered her insides.

"Jack, I…I mean *we* shouldn't. Can't." She didn't know exactly what she was trying to say, but weak protest was better than none at all.

Jack's voice rumbled through her. "But we *can*. And you know you want to." The tickling fingers became a warm caress as his palm moved over the dip in her waist to the plane of her lower back.

Be strong. Brenna inhaled, filling her starved lungs with oxygen and the enticing smell that was uniquely Jack. *Now step away.* The signal to her feet to move got lost in transit as Jack's arm began to encircle her.

She was wavering, and she hated herself for it. *What harm could it do?* her body argued.

A lot, her heart responded.

Hundreds of reasons—solid, rational reasons—why this would be a mistake raced through her mind, but that didn't stop her from taking a step closer to him. Jack's fingers tightened on her back, urging her closer still, until she could feel the hairs on his chest tickling faintly across her skin.

Brenna's brain felt foggy, and she lifted her hand to his chest to create a barrier. Jack inhaled sharply at her touch, and the muscle under his skin jumped in response.

Just a taste.

Jack's hand came up to lift her chin, angling it for his kiss, and reality intruded one last time. She'd regret this either way, but which choice would she regret more?

His mouth was almost on hers when she clasped her hand around his wrist. She could feel the heavy beat of his pulse under her fingers, matching the thumping in her chest. Jack's cheek slid across hers as she turned her face away.

"You want me, Bren. I can feel it," Jack whispered.

Oh, he was so right about that. And she could feel how much he wanted her. All she had to do was say yes…

"I'll make this easier for you." Jack kissed her temple, then moved to her ear, his breath sending shivers down her spine. "Give me tonight, and I'll give you the winery."

Jack heard her sharp gasp a second before her hands landed on his chest and pushed him forcefully away from her. Anger hardened her jaw as her fingers flexed, then curled into a fist. Closing her eyes with the effort, she lowered her hand to her side.

When she opened her eyes, the heat blasted him. "Are you *kidding* me?"

Her anger cut through the last of the sensual haze that had snared him and had to have been the source of his offer. The thought of simply giving her the winery *had* crossed his mind briefly, as a quick and easy way out of this unholy mess, but he hadn't entertained it seriously. After all, as Brenna had pointed out, business was built into his DNA, and *giving* one away wasn't exactly approved business practice.

But the offer was out there now, even if he didn't know what had possessed him to make it. "I'm serious, Brenna." He held the stare, watching as Brenna moved from anger, to shock, through disbelief, and finally settled on outrage. He wasn't going to back pedal, not even as he watched the angry flush creep up Brenna's neck as her temper boiled. Even with indignation radiating off her in waves he burned for her. His fingers itched to touch her again, to feel that smooth skin quiver in pleasure and desire. He knew her taste, and the craving was awakened, familiar and frustrating at the same time.

It would give her the excuse she needed to give in to the desire he knew she felt without recriminations in the morning. He'd be able to get Brenna out of his system *and* break their stalemate over the winery at the same time. Win-win all around.

"Oh. My. *God.*" Brenna took another step back, shaking her head in disbelief. As her shoulders tensed, he braced for the full blast of her temper.

But the blow-up didn't come. Her anger seemed to drain away as quickly as it had flared. She moved to the table and perched on the edge, her hands folded against her chin. "I always thought we'd hit every low possible, but this is a new one." Her shoulders slumped as the last of the ire went out of her voice, and she laughed hollowly. "It's a hell of an offer, Jack. Prostituting myself in order to keep my vineyard. It's appropriate, though. I'm screwed no matter what I do."

Put like that, his proposition sounded tawdry, instead of expedient yet pleasurable for them both. "If you want to look at it that way—"

"There's another way?" she scoffed. "If I sign off on the sale I get you out of my life permanently, but I gain God-only-knows-who as a partner, and there's no telling what *that* will do to my business. If I don't sign off on the sale you'll make my life hell in a multitude of interesting ways." Brenna started to pace, her hands moving in agitated circles as she talked. "So I can sleep with you, throwing away what little self-respect I still have, but gaining my business free and clear. In theory, that sounds really great—except I've already told you that I need your name backing me for a while."

She finally faced him, her hands on her hips, her chest heaving under her skimpy bikini top. The anger was back. "Tell me, *exactly* what other way there is to look at it. The way where I'm not screwed, personally *and* professionally?"

Wide-eyed and expectant, she glared at him, waiting for an answer. He didn't have one readily available. He'd backed her into a corner, and she had no graceful means of escape. The professors from his MBA program would be proud—hell, Max would be proud—

of his use of the time-honored strategy of putting his adversary into a position where he definitely had the upper hand in the negotiations.

Except putting Brenna there didn't bring the satisfaction it would in any other situation.

As the silence stretched out Brenna's breathing turned ragged, and he saw the tears gathering in the corners of her eyes. She closed her eyes again and took a deep breath, as if she were trying to pull herself together and hold the tears at bay.

The action stabbed him in the chest, as he'd never seen her tear up before. *Brenna didn't cry.* She exploded, she shouted, she slammed doors, and she even sulked occasionally, but she *didn't cry.*

He'd pushed her too far this time. Considering their past, that was an accomplishment in itself. Their marriage had fallen apart and she'd never shed a single tear. Hell, she'd sat dry-eyed and stoic through her own mother's funeral. But her beloved damn winery brought out the waterworks. Astonishing and insulting, but he still felt like a snake.

Neither of them had a graceful escape route, but he could try to defuse the situation. It wasn't easy—not with his body still wired and ready to finish what he'd started—but he managed a toneless "Forget it, Bren. Chalk the offer up to temporary insanity."

Brenna's eyes flew open, widening in shock as her jaw dropped. She looked as if she'd just been slapped. "What?"

"I said forget it."

"Oh, I don't think so." Brenna's hackles were back

up, but it beat her tears. "You can't toy with me like that and then just walk away. Things have changed, Jack. I won't let you hurt me again."

Where had this come from? "Hurt you?"

"Maybe you can keep things in little boxes, all compartmentalized in your head, but I can't. You can't come out here and turn me inside out and expect me to just take it. You broke my heart once, Jack. I'm finished crying over you."

Her? Heartbroken? Crying? She'd walked out dry-eyed and never looked back. "You left me, Bren. Don't forget that."

Her mouth twisted. "Yes, and you were kind enough to order a ride for me while I packed."

"What, exactly, was I supposed to do? You said you were miserable and that you wanted to go home. I couldn't force you to stay."

"You didn't want me to stay. You were just as miserable as I was."

"Did I ever say that, Bren?"

"You didn't have to." Her voice broke on the last word, and Brenna cleared her throat. "You're right. We should just forget this."

Oh, no, he wasn't going to let Bren retreat. Not after tossing down the gauntlet. "Here's a newsflash for you. *You* left. *You* served me with divorce papers. Don't blame me for your broken heart when you're the one who walked out."

Brenna pulled back as if he'd slapped her. Then her eyes narrowed. "You're saying it was all my fault? Don't even try. It takes two people to make a relationship fail that spectacularly. I loved you, Jack, and it hurt too much that you didn't love me."

Had he heard her correctly? "You think I didn't love you?"

"You *wanted* me." She made it sound distasteful.

"I'm not denying that. But if you want to talk pain and heartache, try your wife telling you she'd rather live at a damn vineyard in Sonoma than with you. We can divvy out blame however you want to for the rest of our problems, but don't try to tell me I didn't love you. Because you'd be wrong."

He was rewarded for his honesty when Brenna's eyes grew wide. She opened her mouth to speak, then closed it again with a snap. "Maybe we were better off when we weren't speaking to each other."

No one could wind him up like Brenna could. This debacle of an evening was proof of that. "I'm inclined to agree with you."

"Then why—?"

"I think we've taken this discussion as far as it can go. No sense circling back and rehashing the past again. When you're ready to sign the sale papers, let me know." Picking up his towel from where he'd dropped it earlier, he draped it over his shoulders and left her standing there, glaring at him.

It certainly wasn't for the first time. Oddly, though, this time he felt as if he deserved it.

Watching Jack walk away was like reliving yet another painful scene from their marriage. Except this time there wouldn't be the fabulous make-up sex later on.

Knees shaking, she made her way carefully to the table and sank into a chair. She heard the door to the house close, and now, safely alone, she let her head drop into her hands. So much had been thrown at her tonight, and she wasn't sure she could process it all.

This was a nightmare—the kind she couldn't wake up from. She'd been so close—too close—to giving in to the sensual pull of Jack that if he hadn't whispered his indecent proposal into her ear at that exact moment she'd probably be happily under him right now.

But to have him offer her… God, it didn't bear thinking about. She didn't know which was worse: the fact Jack thought so little of her now he believed she'd be willing to sell herself for Amante Verano, or the fact she'd seriously considered it for a nanosecond.

And how to explain the pain that had shot through her when he withdrew his offer altogether?

No one could rip her apart with the effortless efficiency of Jack Garrett. She'd thought—make that *hoped*—time and maturity would have made her immune to him. Or that he'd forgotten how.

Tears burned in her eyes. *No*, she told herself angrily as she took deep breaths. She would not cry over him again. She'd long ago grown weary of crying after one of them walked out, and she was finished with that. It had to be the rehashing that had her so close to blubbering again.

She'd loved him so much back then, but over the years she'd decided it had been a one-sided affair. To have him say he'd loved her? To hear that she'd hurt him when she left? That was a one-two punch she hadn't seen coming, and her head was still reeling.

Once upon a time she'd believed her love for Jack could solve anything life threw at them. But the cold reality of their endless cycle of fight-truce-sex-fight had shown her how big the gap between them really was. The inability to bridge that gap had always been her secret failure, the thing she'd never admitted to anyone.

But for a few minutes tonight she'd thought they'd almost built that bridge. She'd briefly felt that old connection—the one they'd had in the very beginning, when they could talk for hours about everything and nothing. That feeling had been buried quickly in the ensuing mess, and she felt a pang of disappointment at the loss.

Brenna sighed and lifted her head. Everything looked exactly the same, seeming to belie the upheaval she'd just gone through. The glowing lights from the pool, the bubbling hot tub, the chirp of the crickets and the smell of the flowers created a serene setting designed to soothe—exactly what she'd come looking for tonight. But it was wasted on her now.

Her insides tumbled over each other and her head ached from the emotional extremes and pressure. Even her wine couldn't calm the storm within her. Grabbing her robe, which she didn't bother putting on, she concentrated on making her shaky legs move her back to the privacy of her bedroom quickly.

Because, damn it, Jack had made her cry. Again.

CHAPTER FIVE

"'EVERY day is a beautiful day at Amante Verano.' Isn't that your motto?" Dianne sing-songed the greeting as she poked her head around the lab door and extended a steaming mug in Brenna's direction.

Brenna accepted the coffee with a grateful smile. After another restless, miserable night, the heady aroma of Di's high-octane brew was a welcome jolt to her sluggish system. "Ever since you printed it on my coffee mug it is."

"Then why do you look like someone kicked that puppy you claim you're going to get?"

She wouldn't be able to avoid this conversation for long. She might as well go ahead and get it over with. "One guess."

"Jack." Dianne pushed a rack of vials and testing supplies to the back of the counter and pulled herself up to sit, her legs swinging gently. "Are you two still fighting? Come on, Brenna, surely there's a better way to sort this out?"

"I wish. Every conversation—no matter how nice I try to be—always deteriorates into a shouting match.

And last night was a nightmare. I thought exes were supposed to get more civil as time progresses. Not us." Brenna shook her head and leaned back in her chair.

"Unfinished business, I think."

Brenna stared into her coffee. "I don't know what you mean."

Dianne snorted. "Try that with someone who didn't witness the whole thing. I watched you fall goofy-stupid in love, elope, and then divorce in less than six months. I also know what that did to you—even if you tried to hide it from everyone else."

Her stomach was hollow enough at the moment. She didn't need Dianne making it worse. "Where's Chloe?" she asked with forced cheerfulness.

"With her father, learning the intricacies of wine-making, testing and probably teething on your new digital refractometer. Now, don't change the subject." She shook her head in disappointment. "It was a weak attempt, anyway. No points for effort."

"I thought it might work there for a minute," Brenna grumbled.

"With someone else, maybe. But you can't fool me. Now, spill. What is going on with you two?"

She certainly wasn't going to go into detail. She still hadn't made sense of it yet herself. "You know the basics. Then, last night, Jack offered to *give* me his half of the winery."

Dianne lit up and she clapped her hands. "That's fantastic! It's not perfect, I know, but it beats…" She trailed off as Brenna shook her head slightly. "Oh, no. There's a 'but,' isn't there? I hate the 'but.'"

"No 'but.' An 'if.'"

Dianne's forehead wrinkled in confusion. "I'm not following you. An 'if'? What kind of 'if'?"

Brenna glanced over to make sure the lab door was firmly closed. "Jack offered to give me his half *if*—" She took a deep breath. "*If* I slept with him."

Her eyes widened. "You're not serious?" Brenna nodded, and Dianne's jaw dropped. "That's—that's—that's…"

"Disgusting? Amoral?" she offered. "Brilliant? Good business sense? I honestly don't know."

"But you didn't." Di looked at her carefully. "*Did* you?"

"No! Do you think I'd be in this bad shape if I was now sole owner?" Brenna leaned back in the chair and took another sip of coffee. "I have to admit, though, it was pretty tempting." And if she'd given in to that temptation she wouldn't have been turned inside out by the rest of their conversation.

"And I can see why. You get everything you want just for a little nookie? That's a helluva return on your investment." Brenna felt her own eyebrows go up at the words, and Dianne cleared her throat. "Not that you would, though. That would be wrong."

"I had no idea you had such a practical Machiavellian streak. In some ways it does seem like a relatively minor thing to do—I mean, it's not like I've never had sex with him before."

"Ah-ha!" Dianne jumped off the counter. "*That's* what was tempting you. Not the vineyard. Oh, no. Sex with Jack again was the temptation."

That much was true. No sense in lying. "Yes. Jack was the temptation. I haven't forgotten what it was like. I remember every single detail." Images danced through her memory, bringing a physical response. *"Vividly."*

"So do I, and I only heard them from you," Di said, fanning herself.

"But I'm not stupid. Physically and financially it sounds like a pretty decent deal, but honestly—and if you repeat this I'll kill you—I'm afraid it would hurt too much. In here." She placed a hand over her chest.

"Afraid you wouldn't be able to respect yourself in the morning?"

"That, too." She'd come to several conclusions in the wee hours of the morning. Including that one.

"Ahh." Dianne bit her lip. She understood. "Jack still has a piece of you. I suspected as much."

"I don't know how or why, but, yeah, it seems he does. You'd think I'd be over him by now. It's been a long time."

"Avoidance doesn't mean you've been dealing."

"I guess not. Now look at me." Brenna balanced her elbows on her knees and let her head rest in her hands. "I'm a mess. And I'm *in* a hell of a mess."

"That explains a lot of the fighting." Dianne returned to her perch on the counter and drummed her nails on it.

"What do you mean by that?"

"Unfinished business, remember? Maybe Jack has some, too."

"Oh, please." Jack didn't sound like someone with unfinished business—unless she counted the winery, of course. "You're insane. And that noise is making *me* insane."

Dianne stopped the drumming and folded her hands in her lap. "Jack doesn't need to bribe or blackmail women to get them to sleep with him. There's got to be a reason he propositioned you."

Her heart skipped a beat. She'd thought about that, too, and decided not to dig too deep lest she find something to make her even worse off than she already was. "I have to admit, though, it's the one thing we were really good at. It was everything else that didn't work."

"Still…even good sex can't be that hard for him to come by. There are lots of women in San Francisco, and he's rich, young, and unbelievably handsome. He doesn't need to hit you up for ex-sex for a little relief."

Pulling her hair out sounded like a grand plan about now. "*Argh*. Can we pick another subject now? Please?"

"Just one more question." Dianne turned serious. "What are you going to do?"

"I don't know. I don't think the offer is open now anyway—not after last night's blowout. I may sound like a broken record, but I just don't *know*."

"You'll figure it out. I know you will." Dianne left her then, squeezing her shoulder in comfort and support as she passed Brenna's chair. Dianne also left the Thermos of coffee for her, but her stomach didn't seem stable enough to take more.

Brenna stared at the walls—old pictures, notes written in her mother's elegant handwriting, label prototypes, newspaper clippings and lists of local growers all competed for space. She would figure it out. She had to. But last night's revelations wouldn't leave her alone.

She'd loved Jack, but he'd also offered an excitement

she'd lacked living out here on the property. When that had gone to hell she'd slunk home, to the one place where she understood who and what she needed to be. She'd thrown herself into Amante Verano—partly because she loved it, but also partly to fill the gap losing Jack had created.

Right or wrong, though, this was her life now. Everything she'd worked for in the last ten years had come to this moment. Jack's presence had just created a wrinkle; the blast from her past shaking her world a little. She needed to come to a workable arrangement with Jack, and once she did everything would go back to normal.

And Jack himself... Well, she needed to get past old hurts and old feelings and remember what they were *now*—not what they had been. All she had to do was ignore that pull he had on her and take back that little piece of her he still seemed to have. Needless to say sleeping with Jack was out of the question. *For any reason*, she told herself.

In the meantime, sitting around moping in frustration wasn't going to change anything—at least she knew *that* much. She also had a to-do list a mile long, and she wouldn't accomplish any of it hiding out in her lab.

Her first stop was the storeroom, where the banal task of inventory was waiting for her. Before she could get started, though, her cellphone rang. Fishing it out of her back pocket, she checked the number. What could Di want?

"Where's Jack?"

She eyeballed the boxes containing bottles, mentally calculating. "At the main house, I assume."

"No, because I'm at the main house. His car's gone."

Brenna's heart jumped in her chest, then sank. Which is it? she asked herself. Am I happy or not? "Gone?"

Di sounded exasperated. "I can't believe he'd take off without telling anyone. That's just plain rude. And after what you said about last night…"

It *was* a bit of a slap in the face. "Jack can come and go as he pleases. He doesn't owe anyone any kind of explanation."

"Maybe he just went into town for something. Want me to check his room and see if his stuff's gone? It would give us a clue if he's planning on coming back or not."

"Di, no. If he's not coming back he'll call. Or have his lawyer call. It's not like anything is settled. We should enjoy the break while we can."

Then why didn't she feel any relief? She still felt the tightness around her chest that hurt when she breathed. *Good thing I didn't sleep with him.*

"But Brenna…"

"Don't you have something you need to do? Something useful?"

"Fine." Dianne grumbled. "But I wonder where he went? And why?"

Me, too. "It's not our business."

She wasn't naïve enough to believe Jack had simply given up and gone home, and the knots in her stomach tightened. No, Jack had something cooking, and she wasn't going to like it.

"You're off your game. That's the closest I've come to beating you in five years." Roger bounced the blue ball in his direction and Jack caught it easily. "Whatever it is, keep it up. I could get used to not having my ass handed to me twice a week."

Roger's words echoed in the enclosed court as he wiped a towel across his sweaty face. Jack took aim, then sent the ball flying down the court to bounce off the wall and hit Roger in the leg. "I'll never be *that* off my game."

But Roger was right. He was distracted. Two days of dealing with Brenna and he couldn't even keep his mind on a racquetball game. He couldn't decide which was more of a distraction, though: remembering the feel of her skin and the way she'd reacted to his touch, or the look on her face when she accused him of breaking her heart.

"I have three ex-wives, remember?" Roger continued as he packed up his gear. "As your attorney and your friend, I can tell you it never gets any better. The path of least resistance is your best bet. Expensive, but expedient. If you want to stay sane, that is."

"I think I've figured that out for myself." Jack opened the door and stepped out into the cool air of the gym. Brenna had been up and gone before he'd left the house this morning, so he had no idea how she was handling everything that had happened last night.

He'd finally figured out what he wanted around three o'clock this morning, and having a plan had allowed him to finally sleep a little. The erotic dreams of Bren awaiting him had been nice, but the memory of those dreams was definitely a distraction this morning.

"That's a shame. I was looking forward to stomping on you in the near future."

Jack shrugged as Roger fell into step beside him and they headed for the locker room. He had a three o'clock meeting, and he needed to put in a couple of hours at the office before he headed back to Sonoma.

"You know, investing in a winery sounds interesting."

Jack stopped. "Good Lord, not you, too? It's like an epidemic. Everywhere I turn, someone wants to own a winery."

Roger grinned. "Except you, for some reason."

"Because I have no romantic notions about winemaking." Jack returned the greetings of the socialites at the juice bar, and got moving again before any of them decided to come over and say hello in person. He didn't have time—or the inclination at the moment— to deal with that.

Roger trotted to catch up. "Come on, how difficult could it be? Stomp a few grapes, mingle with the tourists, drink a lot. Sounds like a sweet job to me."

Jack spared a glance to see if Roger was kidding. Shockingly, Jack didn't think he was. "When was the last time you were in a vineyard?"

"I took the tour a couple of years ago, when the last set of in-laws visited."

Maybe Bren was right about not selling to just anyone. "And that makes you an expert, of course. Trust me, Brenna would cheerfully and painfully remove your feet if you put them anywhere near her precious grapes."

Roger spun the dial on his locker casually. "I'm surprised you're being so generous. Brenna Walsh must really love you."

That stopped him in his tracks. "What?"

Backtracking, Roger sputtered. "I mean, you're the best ex-husband a woman could ask for. She can't be cursing your name too often."

He doubted that. Brenna was probably burning him in effigy right now.

"You're setting a bad precedent for the rest of us," Roger continued.

Jack closed his locker with a satisfying bang. "Tell you what. You deal with your ex-wives, and I'll deal with mine."

Roger put his hands up and backed away. "Fine. I'll have the papers on your desk this afternoon."

Good. He'd have them in hand when he went back to Amante Verano tonight. He'd use the weekend to go through the rest of Max's things and get Brenna on board with the new plan. By Monday this whole situation would be off his plate and his life could go back to normal.

As the hot water of the shower kneaded his muscles, he realized there was still one last possible problem with his plan. Was Brenna over last night's debacle yet, or was she nursing her anger today, building steam to go another round or two? The fight, the rehashing of the past—it all left a bad taste in his mouth, but it didn't dampen the fire in his blood. Remembering Brenna's physical response only fanned it. He'd reacquainted himself with the way she smelled and the feel of her skin. If he'd just kept his big mouth shut…

Grimacing, he turned the water to cold and pushed the image of Brenna—deliciously wet and covered only in a scrap of fabric—from his mind. He had a lot of real work to do today, and a raging erection wasn't going to help.

Concentrating on the zoning issues for the new property in Sacramento *did* help, and while he might have been slightly distracted during the endless meetings, he managed to keep Brenna off his mind for the better part of the afternoon.

As promised, Roger's courier had the documents on his desk before the end of the business day, and Brenna was once again front and center in his thoughts. Only this time it was the image of Brenna, teary-eyed and trying to hold it together, that kept appearing.

Brenna had said she was finished crying for him. And she'd said it so candidly, without any other pretense; he was leaning toward believing it. Had she cried alone? Without him knowing?

That would make him a first-class bastard who deserved to have her walk out on him.

Yet another reason he needed out of this mess. Quickly. He should let Roger handle it from here. It would be easier on him and Brenna both.

Then why the hell was he on his way to Sonoma?

Because I want her. Brenna was like a bad habit he'd thought he'd kicked years ago, but one tiny taste was enough to awaken the craving. Last night had cleared the air a little about their past, and the papers he had on the seat next to him should take care of their present problem. If Brenna wasn't holding a grudge, he planned to finish what they'd started last night.

As he made the turn onto Amante Verano property he was cautiously optimistic about the night ahead. But, like a junkie who knew his fix was just moments away, the craving intensified as he parked next to Brenna's Jeep.

The low hum of the television greeted him as he opened the door, and he saw Brenna on the couch, her long legs stretched out across the cushions. A magazine lay open on her lap; her face was serious as she read. She toyed with a lock of hair that had escaped the loose twist on the back of her head, more relaxed than he'd seen her in a long time. The image disappeared, though, when she heard his steps on the marble floor and the thud of his briefcase landing on the table. Startled, she turned to find the source of the noise, and the magazine slid to the floor.

"Jack! I—I—didn't realize you'd be back tonight." She pushed a button on the remote and the TV went black.

"Is that a problem?"

"No, not at all. I've already told you you're welcome here." Brenna sounded friendly enough, but he still approached with caution, picking the magazine up off the floor and handing it back to her. It was a wine magazine. No surprise there.

"Interesting reading?"

"Very much so." She grinned at him and his stomach tightened a bit. "There's a fascinating article on cap management regimes, if you are looking for some light reading."

Bren wasn't poised for attack; in fact he almost believed her attitude was genuine. Was she looking for a ceasefire as well? That would make this evening—and all his plans—much easier. "I'll pass, thanks." He took the chair opposite the couch and noticed the glass on the table between them. No stem. Straight sides. A dark amber liquid with a small film of white bubbles across the surface. "Is that a *beer*?"

Brenna laughed. "Yes, it's beer. Dianne and I went to town this afternoon, and I was able to replenish the supplies. Help yourself. There's actual food in there, too, if you're hungry," she called at his back as he headed to the fridge.

Brenna's amazing attitude adjustment seemed too good to be true. His optimism grew.

"A beer is all I need. It's been a hell of a day." He twisted off the cap and held the bottle by the neck as he slid the new agreement out of his briefcase.

"Sorry to hear that. Something wrong at the office?"

Her attempt at small talk brought a smile to his face, and it was tempting to just take his beer back to the living room for the simple, normal activity of human company and conversation after a long day. But that would only be a stalling tactic, and he wanted to get business out of the way first.

Brenna still wore her open, friendly look as he returned to the living room, but it faded as she saw the papers in his hand. Her eyes narrowed. "I'm not signing that."

"You should really read it before you decide." He handed it to her and reclaimed his seat, stretching his legs out in front of him and drinking from the bottle as she flipped through the pages.

"This looks like it could take a while. How about you give me the abridged version instead?" She reached for her own glass, placing the papers on the table and leaving them there as she settled back against the cushions and looked at him expectantly.

"All right. Short version it is. This gives you an additional twenty-five percent share in the business." Her eyebrows went up. "Free and clear," he assured her. "That gives you a majority stake, no matter what happens. In return, you agree to the sale of my remaining twenty-five percent to Garrett Properties, and the company will back you as a silent partner for the next year. At the end of that year you agree to allow the company to sell its interest to whatever buyer it finds— you, of course, will have the right of first refusal at that time, but you cannot block the sale."

"You'd give me another twenty-five percent?" She sounded as if she was waiting for the trap to snap shut. She picked up the papers and began scanning, obviously looking for the catch. "Why?"

Roger had asked him the same question, so he recycled his answer. "Consider it part of your divorce settlement. Half of my half."

"But I didn't get a divorce settlement. We weren't married long enough."

"Then this gives me the opportunity to rectify that lack." Brenna shot him a distrusting look. "Don't look at me like that. It's a gift. No strings beyond what I've already said."

She flipped through a few more pages before placing them back on the table. Picking her glass up again, she stared at the liquid, her eyebrows knitting together as she thought. He could almost see the wheels turning in her head, but he had no idea what conclusions she was drawing.

"I know it's not what you want, but it's the best I can do for you, Bren."

She nodded and drummed her nails on the side of the glass. Then she swallowed hard and lifted her brown eyes to his. "I know it is. And it seems more than fair."

CHAPTER SIX

BRENNA'S throat felt tight. It was *very* fair. More than she could have hoped for, actually. Jack looked shocked. What had he expected? It wasn't as if she had much room to bargain. In fact *she* was shocked he'd been so accommodating. He could have just continued to hound her until she gave in. Because, though she hadn't admitted it to anyone, deep down she'd known she would have eventually buckled under the pressure.

"You agree to those terms?" Jack seemed a little surprised at her easy acceptance.

She nodded and drank deeply from her glass, hoping the beer would loosen the constriction around her vocal cords. It didn't.

Jack sat back in his chair and folded his hands across his stomach. "I'm glad to hear it. There's no sense dragging this out endlessly."

He was being mighty friendly for someone who'd gone ten rounds with her the night before. And this offer, coming out of nowhere like a gift from the gods… What was the catch? Stealth maneuvers and shady business weren't Jack's style at all, though. Maybe there wasn't a catch. "I agree. I assume, though, you won't object if I have my attorney read this before I sign."

"Don't you trust me?" His lips twitched in amusement.

She snorted. "Based on what? Our long, happy history?"

Jack tilted his head, acknowledging the truth to her statement, and shrugged.

"What's the saying? 'Trust, yet verify'? I think on something this important, I should be sure I know exactly what I'm signing."

"That's a sound plan, Bren. But since there's no trapdoors to worry about, I look forward to hearing from your lawyer sometime next week." He raised his bottle in a small toast. "To equitable solutions."

"I'll drink to that." She drained her glass with the toast. Oddly enough, the knots of tension in her stomach finally released a little. After being tied up for so long, the relief felt alien.

Although she did fully intend to go over that agreement with a microscope to be sure, she realized she trusted Jack enough to believe it said what he claimed. She was just glad to have the end of this nightmare in sight.

And it felt really good, even if her hands were still shaking from making a stand.

Jack turned up his bottle and drained it as well. "Another?" he asked as he stood and crossed behind her to the kitchen.

"Please." She heard glass clinking, and the tiny *psfft* as Jack opened the bottles. Maybe she should choose something a bit stronger. It wasn't late, by any stretch of the imagination, but if Jack was starting his second beer it meant he didn't plan on heading back to the city tonight. As he settled back into his seat Brenna realized he might decide to spend the evening in here. With her.

Last night's events were too fresh to ignore, and the memories came back in a disturbing rush of sensation and emotion. Goosebumps formed on her skin as she remembered the feel of his fingers teasing over her stomach, and the sincere shock in his eyes when she had accused him of not loving her. She closed her eyes, only to be met with a vision of water tracing down Jack's chest in the dim patio lights. She quickly opened her eyes and focused on the painting on the far wall as she took deep breaths. The room felt overly warm, and the beer she gulped didn't help cool her any.

Maybe she should go grab the bottle of port. Dull the edges a bit with something more fortified—and fortifying—than beer.

"No big plans for your Friday night?" Jack asked, snapping her back to the present.

Conversation. Focus on the conversation. "This is it. We lack a happening club scene out here. Much to my dismay, of course." Jack snorted, and took another sip of his beer. "But I could ask you the same thing." She was a happy homebody, while Jack was a social creature—and a popular one, she knew. His life was usually one exciting event after another; surely he had something better to do on a Friday night.

"Well, I'd planned to have a shouting match with you tonight, but it seems like that's been shot down." He winked at her. "Not that I mind, of course, but it has freed up my evening unexpectedly."

"I could throw some insults at you anyway, if you'd like," she offered, in what she hoped was a helpful, teasing tone. It would certainly help *her* keep her mind away from dangerous places. At the same time, though, it was nice not to be at daggers drawn with him.

"Pass." Jack stared out through the French doors at the dark vineyard, and she wondered what he was thinking about. It was easier, though, than having him look at her, and she was glad for the reprieve. The house normally seemed so big and empty, but with Jack here she felt slightly claustrophobic.

How could he look so relaxed? Feet propped up, settled back comfortably in her second favorite chair, he looked very much like the monarch of the glen as he casually lifted the bottle to his lips. His throat worked as he swallowed, calling her attention to the unbuttoned collar of his shirt, where the crisp white cotton looked stark against his tanned neck and the dark hair that just brushed the collar.

She knew what it felt like to run her fingers over the hard muscles at the nape of his neck and thread them through the inky softness—he'd worn it longer when he was younger, and she remembered how it had tickled her skin like a silky caress...

"Don't you get lonely out here, Bren?"

She jumped as he spoke, and felt the guilty flush rise up her neck again. Thankfully, Jack was still focused on the vineyard; maybe he hadn't noticed her inappropriate stare. "Don't you mean bored?" she challenged, out of habit.

"No, I meant lonely." There was no sarcasm in his voice, and when he did turn to look at her she only saw sincere curiosity on his face.

She regretted her snark instantly. "A little. It's been tough since Max died—being alone, that is. The house is awfully big for just one person." She shrugged and stared into her glass, wishing for another beer. "I've been thinking about getting a puppy, though. I could use the company."

Jack seemed to read her mind, and he made the short trek to the kitchen and returned with another bottle for them both. She skipped the glass this time, and held her own bottle by the neck as she drank. Drinking this much this fast was going to give her one hell of a headache tomorrow, but she needed the balm for her nerves.

Instead of returning to his seat, Jack pulled a cushion off the chair and tossed it to the floor beside the couch. As he lowered himself to the floor, he asked, "Do you mind? My back's a little tight from my racquetball game today and the drive back."

"Be my guest." She shifted on the couch, turning to her side to face him more easily in his new position. Jack closed his eyes and stretched, and Brenna's pulse kicked up as she watched. *Keep the conversation going.* She cleared her throat. "Yeah, a puppy. Something big, like a Boxer or a Rottweiler."

Jack smiled without opening his eyes. "And to think you wanted that little Corgi puppy before."

"We lived in a suite in a hotel." A dark eyebrow went up. "Okay, so it wasn't exactly a shoebox apartment, but still, it didn't seem fair to a bigger dog to not have a yard." Jack's grin was heartstopping. She'd forgotten what it was like. "Maybe I'll get two. They can keep each other company. Play together."

"Then who will play with you?" he asked softly.

Her heart skipped a beat and she reached for her drink again. "It's not like I'm a hermit out here. I've got Dianne and Ted and the baby—not to mention the people who work here every day."

"And that's enough for you? You don't have any other…uh…company?"

She nearly choked on her drink. She swallowed and coughed painfully. "Are you seriously asking me about my love-life?"

Jack shrugged—a strange movement, considering his position. "I have to admit, I'm a bit curious."

"You should have asked me that before you propositioned me last night."

Jack's eyes popped open, and she saw a strange light there in the dark blue depths. "Probably," he answered, and she realized too late she'd said that last thought aloud.

Damn it, she should have stopped after her second beer. Now her liquor-loosened tongue had taken her smack into the middle of the one topic she'd desperately wanted to avoid. "Just forget it."

He levered himself into a sitting position, putting him a little too close for Brenna's comfort. Those broad shoulders were only inches from her. "I'm finding that difficult to do."

She mustered her bravado, but it was still shaky from Jack's simple proximity. "Guilty conscience?"

"Not at all. I didn't say anything that wasn't true."

She thought of his fingers trailing over her collarbone. *We've always had this.* She fought back the shiver. "And you don't think your little 'bargain' was crass in any way?"

He didn't even have the decency to look the least bit chagrined. Instead, he seemed to be fighting back a smile. "It may have lacked finesse, but my motives were clear."

"Once more for old times' sake?" Her voice shook, completely destroying the casual tone she was hoping for.

"Is that really such a shocker, Bren? The pool, the moonlight… Are you denying it stirred up some fond memories for you, too?"

"Emphatically." She just needed to keep reminding herself of that.

"You're a bad liar. I was there, remember? I had my hands on you. I felt the way you shivered when you re-membered exactly how good we were together."

"In bed, maybe. But I also remember the rest of our, ahem, 'conversation' last night. That also brought back memories—not all of them fond ones."

"We had some good times. You can't deny that." His hand came up to play with her hair.

"Not enough to tip the balance." She shuddered as his hand moved to her face. "We said—and did—some pretty horrible things to each other."

He shrugged away months of arguments and years of pain with "We were young. I'm not carrying a grudge. Are you?"

"From then? Or now?" she countered, mainly to

keep him talking. She couldn't pull away, but this was moving into dangerous territory.

"Ten years is a long time to carry a grudge." His eyes searched her face and she shivered. "Me? I'm grudge-free."

"Then, here's to putting the past behind us. Should we drink to that?" *Anything* to put a little distance between them.

Jack shook his head slightly. He tucked a lock of hair behind her ear, then traced his fingers over the curve of her jaw. "Beautiful. Tempting. Stubborn."

He was close—too close—his face only inches from hers. The gentle caress over sensitive skin and his husky, seductive voice sucked her in, while those blue eyes captured her and led her straight into temptation.

And she desperately wanted to go. Every nerve in her body screamed for Jack to touch her. Her skin begged for it. She'd suffered the aftermath of last night all day—the achy need, the smoldering want. Her mouth went dry as Jack's hand curved around the nape of her neck and his thumb smoothed over the tense muscles.

Just one more time. Do you think you'll ever get this chance again? Once her signature was on those papers, she'd have no reason to see Jack again. That thought put a strange hollow feeling in her chest—one that felt oddly familiar, yet strange, because until yesterday she would have sworn she was long over him.

Jack reached up to remove the clip holding her hair back, and his fingers threaded through the mass to massage her scalp. She closed her eyes in bliss as the tension drained out of her, only for it to be replaced with an aching need. When she opened her eyes again she met Jack's stare, and gasped at the hunger and promise she saw there.

She was lost and she knew it. She always was when Jack looked at her like that. Anger, bruised pride, indignant huffs—none of it was able to stand firm against the need and desire he could fire in her.

Jack seemed to know the moment she made up her mind, and he surged to his knees, pulling her to him and covering her mouth with his.

Yesss. Oh, *yes.*

It wasn't gentle. Or nostalgic or sweet. Jack met her hunger head-on and returned it, his mouth devouring hers. His fingers tightened in her hair, holding her head still as his tongue slid over hers, and she shivered in response.

Jack broke the kiss, sliding his mouth over her jaw to the sensitive skin of her neck. She panted, gasping for air as his teeth grazed her, and she tilted her head back to allow him greater access even as her fingers threaded through his hair to hold him there.

She hadn't forgotten this, but the memory was bland compared to the reality. She groaned, and Jack echoed the sound before his arms locked around her waist and he pulled her off the couch and into his lap.

The feel of Jack's hard body against hers as she straddled his thighs sent tremors through her insides, and she pressed into him, craving the heat and pressure. She pulled at his shirt, bunching it into her hands until she could reach underneath to feel the smooth planes of muscle on his back.

Jack's hot mouth traced her collarbone as his hands slid over her hips to her waist, and finally her ribs, where his thumbs could stroke teasingly against the undersides of her breasts. Her nipples tightened with anticipation and she arched back in invitation.

Instead, Jack pulled her close, his mouth covering hers again, his hands snaking under the hem of her shirt and sliding it up with agonizing slowness. He broke the kiss to sweep the fabric over her head, then gently leaned her back, supporting her with one hand while the other grazed gently over the expanse of her chest and in the valley between her aching breasts.

Brenna shivered, enjoying the tease of his touch yet hating the delay. She was on fire, needing more of him—*all* of him—before the anticipation killed her. One finger circled her nipple, causing her to clench her thighs around his as the pleasure rippled through her. The corner of Jack's mouth turned up in pleasure at her response as he drove her slowly insane with his feather-light touch.

Brenna concentrated on her shaking hands, reaching for the buttons of his shirt. Clumsily, she managed to work them through their holes, pausing occasionally to bite her lip when Jack's slow, deliberate torture became too much. Finally, she pushed the shirt off his shoulders, and his chest was hers to touch.

She echoed his movements, running her fingertips over the ridge of his pecs, teasing his nipples with her nails. His fingers tightened on her waist when he shuddered in pleasure.

A split second later Jack flipped her to her back, her

head landing on the cushion he'd used earlier, and his body finally covered hers. She moaned at the sensation of skin against skin, at the heat and weight of his body nestled in the vee of her legs. How could she have forgotten this? The memories paled in comparison to the reality. How had she ever walked away from this? Jack's kiss sent her head spinning, but when his head dipped lower to capture her nipple between his lips fireworks exploded behind her eyes and she groaned his name.

The sound seemed to spur him, and he suckled harder, causing her to nearly arch off the floor as pleasure shot through her. When his weight shifted off her, she reached for his waist to pull him back, but let her hand fall away when she felt the snap of her shorts release and the zipper give way.

Her stomach tightened under his hand as it slid low and his fingertips tickled along the edge of her panties, while Jack's mouth returned to hers for a shattering kiss. But one rational thought surfaced and made a weak, last-ditch effort: *This is the point of no return. Are you sure?*

Her body answered first, twisting toward him, granting access, but Jack seemed to hesitate briefly, his kiss gentling as if he knew she was fighting one last battle against herself.

Yes.

She knew what Jack could do to her body; the guaranteed pleasure awaiting her. But she'd been faced with the hard fact today that she wasn't as immune to him as she'd long assumed, and deep down she knew she'd be setting herself up for a bad fall in the morning, when Jack walked out of her life again.

Was it worth the risk?

Then Jack pushed the thin silk aside, and his fingers found her heated, needy center. Flames licked through her, leaving her panting against his kiss.

Oh, yes.

Jack felt the last of the uncertainty leave her body just as her thighs clamped around his hand and she shuddered in pleasure. He felt as if he was holding a live wire, and each little sound, every gasp, every tremor, zinged through him like raw electricity.

The need to taste her, to take her, bordered on painful—even more so than the pressure against his zipper—but Brenna was already on the brink. She tore her mouth away and buried her face in his shoulder, muffling low, guttural noises. Brenna's nails bit into his arms, holding him in place while she moved restlessly against his hand and he took her over the edge.

She was still throbbing around his finger when she lifted her face to his. Her cheeks were flushed, but her brown eyes were clear and burning—for *him*. Oh, no, his Bren wasn't done yet; she was still on fire. And, while he'd seen that look before and had even expected it, the raw hunger there slammed into him, causing his breath to catch.

Brenna held his gaze as she released his arm and smoothed her fingers over the half-moon marks her nails had left. Then she lifted her hips, sliding her shorts and panties off and kicking them away quickly. A second later she released his zipper and grasped his straining erection.

She moved so quickly she was an erotic blur, but at the feel of her hot hand on him he exhaled sharply, and closed his eyes to savor the sensation. Brenna had never been a meek partner, but there was an urgency behind her desire this time. He could feel it—in her heated touch, in the desperate movement of her lips, and through the maddening press of her body against his.

He could relate. The same knife-edge cut through him.

When his hand cupped her breast again she hissed and rolled to her back, pulling him over her.

"Now, Jack," she whispered, her breath hot against his ear.

He wanted to slow her down, to savor the feel and taste of her, relearn her skin, but the desperate *"Please…"* she added had him adjusting her hips, parting her thighs, and driving into her so hard he saw stars.

Brenna's back bowed, nearly lifting her completely off the rug, and her fingers dug into his biceps for support. A sheen of moisture covered her body, and he could see the tiny trembles already moving through her. Her tight, throbbing warmth was sanity-snatching, and his hips moved of their own accord.

As he eased slowly out Brenna's head snapped up, her eyes connecting with his as her legs locked around his waist. Gathering her close to his body, he shifted his weight to his elbows and met her halfway as she thrust against him.

He held Brenna's stare as they rocked together, until her eyes glazed over and she buried her face in his shoulder again. He felt the nip of her teeth against his skin as short, sharp cries told him she was falling over the edge. Then Brenna tensed against him, shaking violently with the power of her orgasm. The sensation took him over with her and he groaned as he collapsed on top of her.

It took a long time for reality to return, and when it did it came in pieces. The delicious weight of Jack covering her. The scratch of the wool rug against her back. The sound of Jack's breathing evening out next to her ear. The thump of Jack's heart against her chest. The lovely languorous feeling only a truly mind-scrambling orgasm could provide.

And Jack was the only one who'd ever been able to scramble her mind like that.

Jack had been right about one thing: no matter what else, they'd always had this. She stroked the back of his head absently, loving the silky feel of his hair between her fingers.

Jack stirred. Pushing himself up onto his elbows, he brushed the hair back from her face before leaning in to give her a slow, stirring kiss. Then his lips curled into a breath-stopping smile. "Better?"

She felt her face heat. He'd seen—and felt—that edge of her desperation. She tried to match his smile and act casual. "Oh, yeah. I'm feeling much better now."

"Good." He kissed her forehead, rolled off, and pushed to his feet. He looked like a god standing over her—all golden-skin and lean muscle. She could stare at him forever and never get tired of the view. She let her eyes trail appreciatively over his body before meeting his amused eyes.

He extended his hand and she took it, letting him pull her up. A moment later her feet were swept out from under her, and she found herself pressed against Jack's chest.

But Jack didn't turn in the direction of the hallway to her room, or toward the kitchen and the far side of the house where his room was. Instead, he moved toward the French doors.

"Where are you taking me?" she asked.

"The hot tub."

CHAPTER SEVEN

WAKING up with a warm male body snuggled around her should feel…alien, or wrong somehow. But it didn't. Neither did the strong hand idly caressing her breast, nor the erection pressing insistently against her backside. It felt almost right.

The idle caress turned purposeful, with Jack's thumb grazing across her nipple and sending a shiver through her. Correction, she thought, it felt amazing.

"'Bout time you woke up," Jack murmured against her shoulder. His hand changed course, sliding over her stomach and between her legs.

She hummed in pleasure and parted her thighs to give him better access. Was there a better way to greet a Saturday morning? Weekend mornings had always been her favorite time when they were married. Jack hadn't had to jump up and rush off to work or class, and the whole morning had been theirs to laze in bed, drink coffee, and make love without any pressure to do anything else. She smiled as the first small shudder moved through her. How many times had he awoken her just like this?

Jack's fingers were magic, slowly building the pressure until her hands were fisted in the sheets and her breath became labored. She moaned his name as she started to shatter, and she vaguely heard him encouraging her on with hot words in her ear.

She reached for him then, pulling his head down to hers for a blazing kiss as she came apart. Jack's tongue moved over hers like a wicked promise as he pulled her under him and kneed her thighs apart. The last tremor of her orgasm still vibrated through her as he slid slowly into her, causing the pleasure to continue instead of abate.

She held Jack's intense blue stare as he moved with agonizing slowness, setting a leisurely pace she knew would drive her insane. She bucked and writhed, trying to meet his thrusts, but Jack gripped her hips and kept her steady. Sensation built until she couldn't take it anymore, and she grabbed the headboard as she arched against him and practically screamed his name. Only then did Jack speed up, slamming into her as she clung to him and climaxed again. Vaguely she felt Jack stiffen against her, and heard him shout her name in response.

How long she lay there, waiting for her breathing to even out and her brain to restart, she didn't know. Jack had moved to her side at some point, leaving one heavy thigh draped over hers, and his breath was evening out as well.

Brenna cracked one eye, looked at the clock and groaned. People would be wondering where she was soon if she didn't get moving. And she certainly didn't need Di pounding on her door while Jack was still naked in her bed. She flipped back the sheet and tried to sit up, but Jack's hand on her arm and his leg over hers held her in place.

His eyes were still closed, but he smiled lazily. "Where are you going?"

"To work."

"It's Saturday. Wouldn't you rather stay here? With me?" Jack trailed a hand over her suggestively. Promisingly.

"It's tempting." Her body was primed for a long, lazy morning in bed, but she wiggled out of his grasp before she could give in. "But not all of us are lucky enough to be hotel tycoons. Some of us must go labor in the fields."

One eye opened slightly. "You did that already, remember?"

"And now I must go check the fruits of my labor. Or actually the juice of the fruits." She found her robe on the back of the bathroom door and pulled it on. "Don't you have to go back to the city? Get some work done?"

Jack rolled to his side and propped on his elbow. "I don't *have* to. One of the many perks of being a tycoon, you know, is having people on staff." He crooked a finger at her. "Come here."

Oh, he *was* tempting. His hair stood up in adorable spikes—either from her hands or sleep. Wrapped in a sheet to his waist, with a dark shadow of stubble across his jaw, *this* Jack was one she remembered, and the lure to crawl back into bed was strong.

"Tanks," she muttered.

Jack's eyebrows went up. "You're welcome. I think."

She shook her head at him and went to splash cold

water on her face. *And her libido.* "I said 'tanks'—as in fermentation. I need to go check the temperatures and the sugar levels. I won't be gone long. Maybe a couple of hours."

"Have Ted do it."

"And what excuse would I give him for adding another task to his to-do list today?" Jeans. Bra. Panties. T-shirt. She pulled clothes out of drawers, tossing them onto the bed as she talked.

"You're the boss. You don't have to give reasons."

"Maybe that works at Garrett Properties, but we're a smaller operation here." She bent at the waist to flip her hair over her head as she tackled the mass of tangles. Sex on the floor, sex in the pool, sex in the bed, going to sleep with wet hair—the knots had knots in them.

"I admire your dedication, but seriously, Bren, you have employees for a reason. You don't have to do it all."

"You're one to talk."

"I'm not the one rushing off to work this morning."

From her upside down position, she could see Jack sitting cross-legged on her bed, the sheet tented over his knees. She tugged the comb through one last tangle and stood up straight again, the blood-rush from her head making her wobble a bit as she did so. Jack crooked a finger at her and gave her a look that made her knees wobble for real. At that moment she wanted nothing more than to crawl back under the covers and lose herself in him again.

What was she thinking? Less than twelve hours after

becoming the majority owner of a winery—not to mention the fact she was the vintner as well—and she was already considering shirking her responsibilities because Jack had a magnetism that was near impossible to resist. And what would happen when Jack went back to the city? She'd be left with nothing but a batch of ruined wine.

Jack was temporary. He wasn't for her—she'd learned that the hard way. The sharp stab of regret she felt at that thought only confirmed what she'd admitted yesterday. Jack did still have a piece of her heart. And she was setting herself up for another massive heartbreak.

She must have stood there too long, arguing with herself, because Jack tossed back the covers and crossed the room quickly to catch her hand. He gave a small tug, but she resisted. His eyebrows went up in question.

"What are you doing, Jack?"

That grin of his would be her undoing one day. "Isn't it obvious? Bringing you back to bed."

The fact he was gloriously naked wasn't helping either. But she couldn't let either his grin or his body distract her. "No. I mean what are *we* doing? You and me. Here. Like this."

Jack rolled his eyes. "Do we have to analyze it?"

"Yeah, I think we do." She stepped back and sat on her vanity stool. "I have to admit, my head is still spinning."

"Then why ruin that feeling?"

"Because… Because…" She couldn't find the right words. "All things considered, I think we should quit while we're ahead."

"Meaning?"

Meaning this is a dangerous game I don't want to play. Because I'll lose. "Meaning, I'm glad we've managed to call a ceasefire of sorts, and that we're not sniping at each other anymore. It will make things much easier in the future and last night was great…" She was rambling now, not making a lot of sense, and she knew it. The look Jack was giving her wasn't helping any.

She was making a mess of this, and in another minute or two she'd end up making a fool of herself. She grabbed her clothes and put them on quickly. "Look, um, I really need to get to the winery."

"Brenna…" Jack started.

She backed toward the door, hating the feeling of retreat. *Lord, I'm such a wuss.* But she desperately needed some distance to make sense of this situation and figure out what she was going to say to him. Without babbling next time. "We'll talk later, okay? There's, um, plenty of food and stuff in the fridge. Just make yourself at home. Bye."

Jack called her name as she bolted, the exasperation in his voice very clear even from a distance.

But retreat—no matter how cowardly or graceless—really was the best option right now. Otherwise she was going to make a big fool of herself over him.

Again.

Jack was tempted to go after Brenna, but the scared-rabbit look in her eyes kept him standing still. No need to back her into a corner right now.

He'd been awake less than an hour and his day was

already turning surreal. Brenna certainly had a way of spinning his world off its axis. He'd forgotten what it was like, but oddly enough he didn't feel half as frustrated as he figured he should. Instead, dealing with Brenna seemed to have blown the cobwebs out of his brain, energizing him.

Her retreat this morning—whatever had triggered it—had left his body still burning for her. But now that he wasn't thinking only with his libido, he realized Bren might have a point. The events of the past few days had his head spinning, too, and maybe he should decide what, exactly, his next plan would be.

Amante Verano wouldn't be his problem much longer, but what about Bren?

He really hadn't been awake long enough for his brain to be working properly. He needed coffee. And a shower and a shave.

Then he'd spend some time in Max's office, as he'd originally planned.

That would give Bren time to calm down *and* give him time to decide what he was going to do about her.

She was going to ruin this entire batch of wine, and it would be all Jack's fault. Brenna checked her numbers again, willing them to make sense. It would be nice if *something* made sense today.

In the safety of her office, she'd hoped to find the answers she needed. Three hours later she still didn't have a clear idea of what she wanted, much less what she thought was the right thing to do. The last couple of days with Jack had awakened so many of her old feelings, but new ones were fighting for recognition as well. On the one hand, it seemed as if they were simply picking up where they'd left off, but at the same time it felt different. Like a new start.

But it probably wasn't. This was just an interlude, a hiatus from real life, her mind kept telling her. The idea of starting again, starting over, was just wishful thinking on her part.

Of course none of this was helping her get any work done. For the umpteenth time the scribbles on the paper in front of her swam out of focus and Jack's blue eyes filled her mind. "Damn it." The curse bounced off the fermentation tanks and echoed around the room. This was ridiculous. She glanced over her shoulder, checking the door to the fermentation room was shut firmly, and gave in to her frustration.

Childishly, she flung the notebook to the floor and stomped on it. Then she jumped on it. It didn't help anything, but she felt a tiny bit better after the outburst. She blew her breath out in a huff and picked up the crumpled notebook to smooth out the pages.

"Focus, Brenna, focus," she muttered.

"Am I interrupting something?"

Jack's amused voice spun her around, and she found him leaning against the door and biting back a smile. His hands were in the back pockets of his battered jeans, causing the gray T-shirt he wore to strain over his broad shoulders. From the scuffed work boots to the lock of black hair that fell over his forehead the entire effect was enough to make her heart skip a beat.

This was the Jack she remembered.

She cleared her throat and reached for the pencil stuck through her ponytail. "Just making some notes."

The corner of his mouth quirked up. "With your feet?"

So he'd seen her little temper tantrum. Great. As if it wasn't awkward enough right this second, she also got to add "caught acting like a three-year-old" to her list of cringe-worthy topics of conversation. "It's traditional," she bluffed. "Secret winemaking superstitions handed down through the generations. It's essential to the wine mojo."

Jack nodded sagely. "I see. You don't stomp the grapes anymore, so you stomp the office supplies instead. Interesting."

She straightened her spine. "I don't question *your* business methods…"

His hands came up in appeasement. "Not questioning your methods at all."

She held the notebook close to her chest like a shield, and wrapped her hands tightly around the edges to steady them. "Not to sound, um, rude, but what brings you down here?"

"A sudden interest in deceptively simple Chardonnays?"

There was that smile. The one that usually meant he was thinking about… Her knees wobbled a little, but she gripped the edges of her notebook tighter and forcefully steadied herself. "That isn't Chardonnay."

"Huh? Well, I'm not really—"

"Interested. I know." She sighed, causing Jack to laugh.

"Sorry." He didn't sound the least bit apologetic.

"How about I promise not to tell you what's actually in those tanks, and you promise not to ramble on about stocks or square footage or zoning laws?"

"Deal."

That was easy. Too little, too late, but nice nonetheless. Jack hadn't moved from his casual lean, but her stress level began to increase with his continued presence and increasingly interested look. Why was he here? What was he after? "Jack? Was there something you needed from me?"

"Not really. You said this would only take a couple of hours, and when you didn't come back I came to check everything was okay."

"Sometimes things don't go according to plan. You know how it is." There was an understatement. She didn't even have a plan to deviate from. "Everything okay at the house? Did you find everything you need?"

Jack looked at her oddly. "I got a little bit of work done. I've been going through some of Max's things, and I need to know if there's anything specific you want."

Her heart twinged a little. With everything Jack had stirred up in her recently, she hadn't thought about Max actually being gone in days. "Probably nothing that you want. A couple of photos, Max's sketchbook, the decanter set in the office. Why don't you pack up whatever you want to take, and I'll deal with the rest?"

"All I need is some of Max's paperwork, a few old files."

"Whatever, Jack. Really." Her voice broke a little. It hurt to think of Max's things being divvyed up, but the underlying thought of Jack taking those things *when he left* confirmed her earlier thoughts.

He was beside her in an instant, his face concerned and his hand gentle on her arm. "Are you okay? I'd forgotten this might be tough on you—as close as you and Max were."

Her eyes burned, but she took a deep breath. "How is it not tough for *you*?"

Jack's face clouded briefly. "Max and I had our problems. Our differences. You know that. I'm not saying it doesn't bother me, but I know it's a lot worse for you." He sighed. "I understand, really. If you'd like to wait a while before… There's no real rush, Bren."

"No. It's—it's…" She paused and pulled herself together. "I'm okay. We can do this." Closure all the way around. She patted his hand absently as she spoke, but Jack's hand closed over hers and squeezed. She looked up in surprise.

He was too close. She could count his eyelashes, smell the faint scent of his soap. The concern was still there in his face, but it was tempered by something else. The *something* she'd spent the last hours trying to convince herself wasn't actually there. All the rational pep talks she'd given herself spun away and she felt dizzy.

"Bren…" Jack whispered as he moved another inch closer to her. His fingers twined in hers, and he pulled her hand up to his mouth and traced her knuckles with his lips. "Come back to the house with me."

"I don't think that's a good idea, Jack." Jack's lips snaked across her wrist. Her eyelids felt heavy as they slid shut.

"You're right," he murmured, and her heart sank. This was it. She'd known it was coming. It was for the best.

Then why did it hurt like hell?

He closed the last bit of space, the notebook she still held against her chest the only thing keeping her from being pressed completely against him. She could feel the heavy thud of his heartbeat against her hand. But the words she was bracing herself for didn't come. Instead, his mouth landed on the sensitive skin of her neck.

"What are you doing?"

"Remembering how that sound you make just before you come echoes in this room."

She remembered, too. In blinding detail. The contrast of the cool steel against her back and the hard heat of Jack against her chest and between her legs. Liquid heat pooled in her stomach, and she dropped her notebook in shock. Jack took advantage of both, pressing his body completely against hers and leaning her against the closest tank. Her gasp echoed off the tanks, and she felt his lips curve into a smile at the sound.

Her fingers closed around the soft cotton of his shirt, bracing herself as his free hand slid over the small of her back into the waistband of her jeans. The warmth of his hand after the chill of the tank had her gasping as he pulled her closer still and covered her mouth with his.

The first time Jack had kissed her, they'd been in this room, not far from where they were now. The kiss had left her so dizzy she'd thought something was wrong with the

CO_2 fans. That same feeling swept over her now, as Jack's tongue made a leisurely exploration of her mouth.

A sharp tug at her waist released the snap of her jeans, and a second later Jack's finger dragged a groan from deep in her throat.

A clatter outside reminded her where she was. The huge door to the fermentation room didn't have a lock, and any of her staff could wander in at any moment. She broke the kiss, panting. "Jack. Not here. Someone could—"

Jack kissed her again, cutting off her protest, but then his arm tightened around her waist, lifting her off her feet and maneuvering her behind the largest of the tanks, out of sight of the door.

In the relative privacy they'd found, Jack's kisses became more demanding, his hands more purposeful as clothing was pushed aside, stripped off. Soon she was clinging to him for support, unsure she could handle the onslaught.

Oddly, though, she gained clarity on one thing: the decision she'd been fretting over all morning. The one she'd made but didn't want to admit—not even to herself.

If Jack was going to leave—this time for good—she wanted one last good memory to keep with her. She'd take what he was willing to give.

Would she regret this? Probably. Did she care? Not in the least. For just a little while she wanted to feel like she had when she was eighteen and Jack had wanted her more than anything.

Strong hands closed around her waist, lifting her.

She wrapped her legs around him, and then she couldn't think at all.

She heard her cries of pleasure echoing around her, mixing with the rasping sounds of Jack's breath. She wanted more. Wanted what only Jack could give her.

It wouldn't be enough, but it would have to do.

CHAPTER EIGHT

BRENNA had the most beautiful back. Jack traced his fingers along the indentation of her spine until the sheet draped over her hips stopped his lazy exploration. The sunlight played over her body, bathing her in a golden glow as she lay on her stomach on his bed. Last time he'd checked her eyes had been closed, and their nonsense conversation was easy and relaxed.

But he couldn't keep his hands off her. It was as if his body wanted to make up for lost time—all the years he hadn't had Brenna in his bed.

And suddenly he couldn't remember why that was.

Brenna stretched lazily under his hand and hummed lightly in pleasure. She shifted, turning slightly on her side to face him and resting her head next to his arm. Her fingers traced idly along the arm supporting his body and she sighed deeply in satisfaction.

He pushed her hair over her shoulder to trace the line of her collarbone. "The symphony is hosting a reception Wednesday night, honoring Max's support over the years."

Brenna nodded. "I know. We sent wine."

"But you're not planning to go?"

"Nope."

"Why not?"

She scrunched her nose in displeasure. "The crowds, the small talk—I'm not very good in those situations. You know that."

He did know that. Just another thing they'd fought about more than once. "Still shy in a crowd, huh?"

"I'm not *shy*," Brenna rebutted, "just not good at mingling with people." She shrugged as her fingers moved aimlessly to his chest. "Plus there's the drive down, and since it would be so late I'd have to find a place to stay for the night…"

He laughed. "A place to stay? That's a weak excuse. I own a hotel not four blocks from the concert hall."

Brenna's hand stopped. "Yeah." She narrowed her eyes at him. "And there's that."

Understanding dawned. "Oh. I see. You didn't want to run into me at the party."

"Not to put too fine a point on it, but, yes. I'm avoiding you." She snorted. "Or at least I *was*."

"And now that you're not?"

"Still in the 'not going' camp. There's no one there I really want to see—"

"Except me," he teased.

Brenna pursed her lips and made a face at him. "I know you like these kinds of events, but I don't."

"No one likes these kinds of events. You go because you have to."

"Really?" She pushed up onto her elbow. "You always seemed so keen on them."

"Only in comparison to you and your absolute dread of parties."

Brenna stuck out her tongue and lay back down on her stomach, bunching the pillow under her head.

"You should come, though," he added. When she didn't answer, he pulled out a bigger incentive. "For Max."

"Don't lay a guilt trip on me," she mumbled into the pillow. "The event isn't for Max. It's for Max's money. Max wouldn't care either way."

"True, but as the proprietor of Amante Verano you should be there. You *are* the winery now. It's part of the gig."

She rolled back to face him again, giving him a delicious view. "Ugh. Really?" She looked genuinely displeased at the thought.

"Really." Stroking her stomach lightly, he added, "But you could come with me."

Brenna's eyes widened, and he had to bite back laughter at her horrified yet confused look. "With you?"

"Yes, with me. Do you have a dress?"

"Of course I have a dress." She paused, face crinkling in thought. "Or Di does, at least. But it's still…"

"Come on, Bren. It won't be fun, but it won't suck either."

She flopped back onto the pillow and stared at the ceiling. "Oh, *that's* the way to convince me. I'm not exactly a big symphony fan, you know."

"Then it's a good thing it's not a performance. Simply a meet-and-greet."

Brenna opened her mouth, then closed it and bit her lip. After what looked like an interesting internal conversation, she lifted her head to look at him again. "Are you asking me out? Like on a date?"

He nearly choked, but caught himself and cleared his throat while Brenna stared at him in mild shock. "Well, I am planning to ply you with alcohol and chocolate in an attempt to get you to come back to my place for the evening."

She nodded. "I see. And then?"

The question was casual, but he didn't want any misunderstandings between them. "What are you asking, Bren?"

"I spent years trying to forget about you. And then all the stuff with the winery happens and you're back." She pushed herself to a sitting position. "I find out that not only haven't I forgotten you, I also don't hate you as well. Now we're back here—" she indicated the bed "—and I'm not sure which way to turn."

She wanted an answer, but he didn't have one to give her. "And I don't know what to tell you, Bren. Can't this be enough for now?"

She laughed. "Hell, I'm not sure it's not too much already. Maybe we should just quit while we're ahead. Before things go bad again."

Brenna wasn't wrong about that, but it didn't mean he wanted to take her up on it. "That's the second time today you've played that card."

"Maybe it's worth thinking about."

"Are you kicking me out?"

Her half-smile gave him his answer. "This place is still half yours, you know. For the moment."

He ran a hand down the smooth skin of her arm. "Then I think I'll stay tonight."

"About the symphony thing…"

He lifted a hand to stop her. "I'll send a car. You don't have to get in if you decide you don't want to."

"That sounds fair."

"In the meantime…" He reached for her, and Brenna slid neatly into his arms, molding her body to his. He let her push him onto his back, and the curtain of her hair fell around them, seeming to block out everything else.

This wasn't his average Saturday night. Jack leaned back in his chair at Dianne and Ted's kitchen table and reached for his beer.

With his and Brenna's new truce secure, he'd fully planned to spend the evening in bed, making up for lost time. Around six, though, Brenna had informed him she was due at Dianne's for dinner, and that he was welcome to come along.

He tried to remember what had been on his calendar for tonight—before he'd cleared it to come to Amante Verano. A business dinner? Another charity event? Probably something black-tie.

Instead, he sat at an only partially refinished antique table after a simple family meal, nibbling on cashews and getting soundly beaten in Scrabble.

And, surprisingly, he was enjoying himself.

Brenna held Chloe in her lap, unsuccessfully attempting to keep the tiles out of the baby's reach. "Where's my E?" Brenna asked. "I know I have one.

Aha!" She pried the tile out of Chloe's chubby fist and placed it on the board.

Jack looked at what she played. "Olpe? That's not a word."

Brenna counted her points. "Yes, it is. An olpe is a wine pitcher or flask. Ted?"

Ted nodded. "She's right. It's a word."

Brenna shot him a triumphant look. He countered the look with, "Is it English?"

Dianne returned from the kitchen at that point and leaned against the arm of Ted's chair. "I told you not to play with them. They cheat."

Ted pulled his wife into his lap. "We do not cheat. We just have bigger vocabularies."

Dianne and Ted had been surprised when he'd arrived with Brenna earlier tonight, but after a few interesting looks he didn't quite understand had passed between them and Brenna, they'd set another place at the table for dinner. The conversation had been stilted at first, but they'd warmed up and now treated him like a long-lost family member.

Which, in a way, he guessed he kind of was.

Brenna rescued another tile from Chloe's mouth and handed her a soft toy to play with instead. "There's no need to be a poor loser, Jack."

He looked at the board and at his tiles. Nothing he could play now that Brenna had used the L for her non-existent word. He shook his head and passed. "I'm wondering why Dianne doesn't get a dictionary and shut you both down."

Her cheeky grin snared him. "Because then it

wouldn't be any fun. Would it, Chloe?" she asked the baby, burying her face in Chloe's neck and making them both giggle.

It was a nice picture. Brenna laughing, relaxed and glowing. Not something he could say he'd seen in a very long time. She was obviously happy, and he was glad he hadn't listened to either his attorneys or his accountants when they'd expressed shock over his plans to give control of the vineyard to Brenna.

"Brenna, I got a call from Charlie today. He says his Chardonnays are almost ready."

That perked Brenna's interest, and she leaned toward Ted. "Wow, that's sooner than expected."

"I'm going to go over tomorrow and test myself, but we could be getting grapes from him early next week."

"Charlie often wants to jump the gun," Brenna cautioned.

"I know, and I'd planned to get ours in first, but…"

Ted and Brenna were just starting to get excited about their conversation when Dianne interrupted. "Stop it, both of you." Dianne rolled her eyes and moved out of Ted's lap. "Can we talk about something else for one night?"

Jack rushed to back her up. "I'm with you, Dianne."

"Thank you, Jack. For once I'm not outnumbered by grape geeks at the table, and I'd like to take advantage of that."

Ted mumbled something under his breath and toyed with his glass. Bren flushed a shade of pink that clashed with her hair. They both looked like children who'd been caught playing with a favorite but off-limits toy.

Ted looked so disappointed Jack almost relented to the conversation.

But it was all he could do not to laugh out loud at them both.

Ted cleared his throat. "Rumor has it a new winery is opening in Napa…"

"Ted!" Dianne chastised.

"What?" Ted spread his hands in innocence. "It's not about *our* wine…"

Brenna caught his eye then, and when he winked at her she smiled in return.

Two hours later Ted carried a sound asleep Chloe to her room as Dianne wished them goodnight and he and Brenna started the walk back to the main house. A full moon lit the vineyard, and crickets chirped all around them. It was quiet otherwise, almost idyllic, and then Brenna slipped her hand into his as they walked. This was more than just a truce—it seemed he and Brenna had something *else* started. And, despite his words earlier, that idea was growing on him a bit.

Brenna squeezed his hand. "You were a good sport tonight."

"Because I let you cheat at Scrabble?"

"I don't cheat." Brenna smacked his arm playfully. "But that's not what I meant. I know tacos and Scrabble aren't your idea of a fun Saturday night, but…"

"I had a good time, Bren."

"Really?"

"Really." Brenna fell quiet and he wondered what she was thinking. "But this is nice, too. I'd forgotten how quiet it gets out here at night."

"It's not San Francisco, that's for sure."

He stopped and pulled her close. "It has its own charms."

Brenna stood on tiptoe to brush a quick kiss across his lips. "It *is* a nice night. Feel like going for a swim?"

A vision of Brenna, wet and slippery, flashed through his mind. He returned the kiss—a hungry one this time, that left Brenna swaying against him—and led her toward the house. "Later."

Brenna's vineyard had one thing San Francisco didn't: Brenna.

CHAPTER NINE

"You know, Brenna, I don't know if this is such a good idea." Dianne carefully unwound a lock of Brenna's hair from around the curling iron and the hot curl landed against Brenna's neck.

Brenna met Di's eyes in the mirror. Dianne shrugged and reached around her for a comb to section off another piece. Brenna sighed. "I know. I mean, me and Jack again? It's crazy and it doesn't make any sense at all, but I just can't help it."

Dianne cleared her throat. "I was actually referring to this up do. I'm not sure your hair will hold the curl."

Brenna flushed. "Oh."

"However," she said, as she twisted and pinned up another lock, "if you'd like to talk about this thing with Jack, I'm certainly willing to listen."

Brenna went back to filing her nails while she thought. Dianne didn't say anything. Finally, unable to meet her eyes again, Brenna asked, "Do you think I'm making a mistake? Getting involved with him again?"

"*Are* you two involved again? I mean, are we talking

about just a little temporary thing or are you thinking this might be long-term?"

Brenna tossed the file onto the vanity. "I wish I knew. This weekend was amazing. After we quit fighting, at least. It's like all the old baggage is gone, and we're kind of starting over." That much was true, and the giddy, light-hearted feeling she remembered so well had her grinning so much most of her employees were giving her strange looks. If only she could shake that other, not-so-giddy feeling that sat low in her chest like a shadow of doom...

"In bed?" Dianne twisted and pinned another piece of hair into place.

"What?" She had to scramble to catch up with the conversation. "Oh. Well, that kinda *is* where we started from the first time."

"And *that* ended well." Dianne snorted.

"We were younger then. This time we're actually talking, too. Ouch! Easy, there."

"Sorry," she muttered. "Hold still, okay?"

Brenna squared her shoulders. "There's a lot to Jack—more than meets the eye—and he seems to understand me now."

"Well, it's good someone does."

She made a face at the mirror. "You're so funny. I'm not that complicated."

"So you say. *I'd* say the fact you're running off to San Francisco to hook up with a guy you couldn't tolerate last week falls smack into the 'beyond-screwed-up' category."

That same thought had occurred to her as well, even if she hadn't wanted to admit it. "So you do think this is a bad idea?"

Di shrugged and reached for the curling iron again. "I don't know what I think. I don't know Jack as well as you do, but I know you don't have a history of making good decisions when it comes to him." Her voice dropped a notch. "I just don't want you to get hurt again."

Me neither, she thought, then shook it off. *People change. Things change.* They could both learn from the past. "I'm an adult. I know what I'm getting into."

"Do you?" Dianne stared sharply at Brenna's reflection. "What's changed? What's so different about *this* time that will keep it from going horribly wrong?"

She'd been asking herself the same question for two days now. "We're older. Wiser. Less volatile. We understand things better now. You saw him Saturday night. Tell me he's not different than he used to be."

"He does seem to be calmer than he used to. And he gets major points for playing along at taco and Scrabble night."

"See? We were just too young to cope with the reality of a relationship. Now we're not."

"That's great, Brenna. Really." Di's words sounded forced.

"You think I should quit while I'm ahead?"

Dianne rested her hands on Brenna's shoulders and squeezed gently. "I just want you to be happy, Brenna. If Jack can do that, then great—I'm on board. But don't let one fabulous weekend in bed and those flowers blind you to everything else. Use your head this time, too, okay?"

Brenna thought of the enormous arrangement of peonies and hydrangea on her desk in the office.

"How'd you know about my flowers?" The flowers had arrived Monday afternoon, but Brenna had intercepted the delivery up by the entrance to the vineyard. No one had seen them arrive—or at least that was what she'd thought—and she'd stashed them where no one— Dianne specifically—should have seen them. At least Di didn't know about the late-night phone calls…

"That's what you pay me for, right?" Dianne pushed one more pin into the mass of Brenna's hair and eyed it critically. "That should do it. Close your eyes."

Brenna did, and Dianne sprayed her handiwork liberally with hairspray. Coughing, Brenna waved the mist away from her face.

"What do you think?" Di asked.

Long, loose ringlets framed her face, while the rest of her hair was up in an artfully arranged chignon. "You're a genius, Di. Now for the dress…"

Brenna held her breath as Dianne worked the zipper. The simple black sheath hugged her curves, making her feel feminine and elegant, and the beading around the neck and hem caught the light of the afternoon sun and sparkled. She slid her feet into Dianne's prized pair of slingbacks, and twirled in front of the mirror. "Wow," she said to her reflection.

Dianne eyed her critically and tugged at the hem of the dress, straightening it. "Wow is right. You clean up nicely, Brenna."

"In your clothes." She laughed as Dianne handed her jewelry and a handbag. "I'd be going to this shindig in jeans if not for you."

"That's my lucky dress. It's what I was wearing the

night I met Ted." Di collapsed into the chair Brenna had only recently occupied and smiled at the memory.

Brenna winked at her. "Sounds more like a get lucky dress. All the better."

"You don't need my dress to get lucky tonight. Just be careful, okay?"

"Your dress is safe. I doubt Jack will be ripping it off my body."

Dianne stared at her evenly. "I'm not worried about the dress."

A movement of something black outside her window caught Brenna's attention, and she moved the curtains fully aside to check. "Jack sent a limo. He doesn't do anything halfway, does he?" She grabbed her overnight bag and shawl.

"Brenna…"

"I hear you, Di. And I will be careful. I'm not some naïve kid anymore." She wrapped Dianne in a one-armed hug. "Thank you. For everything."

"Have fun. You'll be home when? Tomorrow? Friday?"

"I'll be back by Friday for sure. Jack leaves for New York that morning. Hold down the fort for me."

"I will."

"Just don't forget to check—"

"It's under control. Go. Have fun."

She didn't recognize the chauffeur who took her bags and offered a hand to help her in the car, but he had a friendly smile as he introduced himself as Michael.

"And may I say how lovely you look, Miss Walsh?"

"Thank you." She settled back against the butter-soft seats and sighed. The last time she'd been in a limo Jack had been with her. They'd been out somewhere, but left early because they were fighting again. They'd reconciled in the privacy of the back seat, and she'd knocked the decanter of Scotch to the floor with her enthusiasm. They'd been drunk off the fumes by the time they'd arrived home…

That was the story of her life with Jack. Fight. Make up. Fight. Make up. The when, the where and the what might change, but the pattern was part of the whole. Funny how she couldn't quite remember what that fight had been about, but she could remember exactly how Jack had held her, and the things he'd whispered in her ear…

Man, it was stuffy in here. She fumbled with the air vent, directing the cool air at her heated cheeks. Di's concerned face swam into focus. She had a point: why should this time be any different? And what, exactly, was she hoping for? A new start with Jack? Just a good time? And for how long?

Miles of vineyards flew past her window in a blur as the limo passed through the Sonoma Valley toward the city. Much more than fifty miles separated Amante Verano from San Francisco. It was a whole different world—one that she'd failed miserably to join or even enjoy the last time.

Was Dianne right? Was she walking right back into a disaster? Had this weekend been just Jack humoring her, or could he really want her—Scrabble and all—again?

It *could* be different, she told herself. She and Jack

didn't have any misconceptions about each other any-more. They knew where they stood, and she was a big enough girl to know when to pull the plug on this experiment. But she'd never forgive herself if she didn't at least *try*. She'd always wonder otherwise…

Belatedly, she noticed the small bouquet of flowers tucked into a vase on the bar. White orchids tied with a red ribbon, with a small envelope peeking out of the blooms. As she pulled it free she saw her name written across the front in Jack's bold handwriting. It felt lumpy in her hand as she released the flap and pulled out the note inside.

Glad you decided to come after all. See you soon.

Jack's initials, MJG, were scrawled in the corner, almost illegible if she hadn't seen them a million times before. She shook the envelope and something sparkly landed in her hand.

A bracelet. No, an anklet. The sunlight, muted slightly through the tinted windows, caused the rubies set in a thin gold chain to flash. Rubies—because she'd told him once that diamonds were too cold and rubies reminded her of her wines.

Jack had a good memory. Orchids and peonies, not roses. Rubies, not diamonds. An anklet because she didn't like bracelets because they caught on things. Little things that should have faded from his memory long ago, but touched her now simply because they hadn't.

She propped her foot on the seat and fastened the chain around her ankle. The slowing of the car caused her to look up, and she saw the orange railings of the

Golden Gate Bridge. How had she got here so fast? This really was the point of no return.

The limo crawled through the city traffic at an infuriating pace. Now that she'd made the decision, got in the car and clasped Jack's gift around her ankle, she was eager to see him. Her heartbeat picked up as the limo pulled to a stop. But it wasn't the multi-colored awning of Garrett Towers outside her window.

It was the concert hall.

Michael opened her door and extended a hand to her. "Don't we need to go get Jack first?" She didn't want to imply Michael had forgotten to stop at Garrett Towers…

"No, Miss Walsh, Mr. Garrett asked me to bring you directly here."

"So he's inside?"

"Mr. Garrett has been delayed in a meeting. He will meet you here shortly." Michael extended his hand again to help her out.

She definitely didn't want to go inside alone. "Can't you take me back…?" She stopped as Michael's eyebrows went up a fraction of an inch. Of course not. That would be silly.

She was an adult; she could walk into a party by herself. More importantly, she was the owner of Amante Verano, Max's pride and joy, and this party was in his honor. She allowed Michael to help her from the limo, and took a deep breath to steady herself as a doorman opened the massive entry doors for her.

She could do this. No problem.

She was also going to kill Jack Garrett later.

* * *

An hour later, Brenna was plotting inventive and painful ways for Jack to die as she made awkward small talk with strangers. The fake smile was starting to hurt her cheeks, and she wished she'd stuck to her earlier resolution not to come at all.

Everyone had known Max, so he was a safe and easy topic of conversation for her, but without fail the conversation would turn quickly to Max's other interests in San Francisco—which she knew little to nothing about—and then on to people she didn't know and places she'd never been. She had nothing to add to the conversation, and she could only ask so many questions before she began to look like some hayseed hick from the boonies.

She certainly felt like one.

A server offered her another glass of wine, and for the first time in her life she declined. The caterers had the Cabernet too cold and the Chardonnay too warm, totally ruining them both. But several people, on learning she was the vintner at Amante Verano, complimented her on the wines. One older gentleman, who owned a chain of popular restaurants across the state, seemed very interested in adding her wines to his wine list. Jack had been right about that much: this was as much a business affair as a social one. She didn't feel bad, since it was Max's celebration anyway and he'd be happy to see his wines' reputation grow, but if she was making business contacts here it meant everyone else was, too, and that just felt wrong.

Escaping to the ladies' room, she touched up her lipstick and checked to see Di's up do was staying put.

For once, Di was wrong: her hair was holding the curls just fine, and none had escaped the mass of pins she'd used to hold them in place.

She stared at herself in the mirror, oddly pleased with herself. In spite of everything, she'd handled this event just fine. A small smile tugged at the corner of her mouth: she, of all people, had just mingled her way into what could lead to a lucrative business contact. A small surge of pride moved through her.

She hesitated, though, before heading back out into the party proper, and glanced at her watch one last time.

Jack was now an hour and a half late. *Damn it*. What was keeping him?

"Excuse me. Have we met?"

Brenna turned to see a woman about her age; while her face looked vaguely familiar, she couldn't place her. She plastered a smile on her face regardless. "Possibly. I'm Brenna Walsh, from Amante Verano Cellars." At the woman's blank look, she added helpfully, "Max Garrett's vineyard?"

"Oh, you're Jack's ex."

She'd known this moment would come. "Yes, that, too."

"Is Jack here?"

"Not yet, but he is planning to come."

"Oh, good. It's been ages since I've seen him." The woman opened her purse and pulled out a lipstick.

"And you are…?" Brenna prompted.

"Libby Winston. We met years ago at another event. I think it was shortly after you and Jack got married."

Brenna still couldn't place her, and it must have shown on her face.

"You probably met so many of Jack's friends, and it was so long ago…"

Embarrassed, she tried to explain. "I'm terribly sorry. I'm really bad at…"

Libby brushed the apology away. "Don't worry about it. You were so shy and quiet. I'm not surprised you don't remember many of Jack's friends." Libby smiled, but it held no warmth at all. "Everyone remembers you, of course. Jack really surprised us all, getting married like that. And we certainly weren't expecting *you*, either."

What was that supposed to mean? She tried to sound flippant. "That's the thing about whirlwind romances. They surprise everyone."

"Thank goodness you came to your senses, then. I never could figure out what brought you two together."

Brenna officially no longer liked Libby Winston.

Libby's eyes narrowed in curiosity. "You and Jack aren't back together again, are you?"

Brenna nearly choked. She had a feeling Libby might be overly interested in the answer, and after Libby's earlier comment she was tempted to say yes. But Brenna herself wasn't even completely sure *what* she and Jack were right now. "Jack and I are business partners." It wasn't a complete lie. Technically, they still were. She hadn't signed the sale agreement yet.

"That must be interesting, considering your past."

"Actually, it's working out quite well." Thankfully her phone beeped, alerting her to an incoming text message. Jack. About damn time. "Excuse me. I need to take care of this."

She slipped out the door before Libby could bring up any other uncomfortable subjects and read Jack's message: *"By the bar. Where are you?"*

A quick glance toward the bar, and she spotted his dark head scanning the crowd. When he spotted her, she waved, and his answering smile gave her a jolt even through her ire at his tardiness.

"Bren, you look incredible."

He leaned in to kiss her gently on the cheek and she muttered through her teeth, "You're late."

"Unavoidable," he whispered.

"You're dead meat."

"I'll make it up to you." He pulled back, still wearing that same smile for anyone watching. Stepping back, he let his eyes roam appreciatively down her body. "You look better than incredible."

The look sent a zing of electricity through her. Damn it, he wasn't getting off that easy. He'd asked her to come, and she had. The least he could have done was *be* here. "Flattery will get you nowhere."

Tugging on her hand, he pulled her close again and said quietly, "Then let me start making it up to you now."

"What? How?" Jack was leading her behind the crowd, out a side door by the kitchen, and down a back hallway as she sputtered her questions. "Where are you taking me?"

In answer, he pushed open a door marked "Private. Rehearsal Room One." The door closed behind them, and she heard the lock snap into place. "I apologize for being late. There was a problem with the New York property I had to sort out."

"And you had to bring me here to apologize?" The small room held a baby grand piano and a music stand, but little else.

"No, I brought you here because I've missed you." Jack sat on the piano bench and pulled her into his lap. "And this room is soundproof."

That was all the warning she got before his mouth landed on hers.

CHAPTER TEN

INDICATING the man to his right, Jack said, "Brenna, I'd like to introduce you to the Mayor."

Brenna's knees were still weak from their frenzied trip to the rehearsal room, and she knew her cheeks were still flushed. Meeting the Mayor, the Artistic Director, and the First Violin ten minutes after a mind-blowing orgasm…surreal. She might not have forgiven Jack completely for being over an hour late, but she was less upset about it now, at least. It still bothered her to think where she ranked on his priority list, but he had searched her out immediately once he did arrive.

And pulled her away for a quickie. As the afterglow faded and Jack glad-handed his way around the room—leaving her alone again quite a bit—her view on that experience began to change a little, too. She felt like a convenience—or an inconvenience, depending how she looked at it.

But standing at Jack's side while he mingled wasn't much better either. She got to talk to the same people she'd met earlier. Or at least she got to listen to them. If the conversation had been difficult earlier, it was worse now. The hayseed hick feeling came back in full force, because Jack *did* know all the people and *had* been to all the places. And she still had nothing to add to the conversation.

Two and a half hours down. She might make it through the last thirty minutes, but her patience was wearing thin. She kept the smile on her face, though. After all, these were Jack's friends and associates. She owed him a sincere attempt after he'd done so well with *her* friends.

More people had connected the mental dots now, and she received several curious stares as folks tried to figure out why Jack was here with his ex-wife. The more forthright just asked directly. While she tried to explain her connection to Max through Amante Verano, it rarely satisfied anyone. If one more person referred to her as "Jack's ex," she'd pull her own hair out. And Jack wasn't exactly correcting them either. Not that she necessarily *wanted* to spread the word prematurely that she and Jack were seeing each other again, but she figured that trip to the rehearsal room at least took her out of the "ex" category.

"Jack! You're finally here." Libby Winston leaned in a little too close as she greeted Jack with air kisses. Wrapping her manicured hand around Jack's arm, Libby anchored herself to his side. If Jack minded the obvious fawning, he certainly didn't put a stop to it, and it made Brenna a bit nauseous to watch.

"Libby, you remember Brenna?"

"Of course. Brenna and I actually ran into each other earlier in the Ladies'. You two have certainly got speculation flying, being here together like this." Libby batted her eyelashes at Jack insipidly.

Oh, please. That had to be the most unsubtle attempt to pry out information she'd ever heard.

"Brenna is running Max's winery now," Jack answered smoothly.

"She said you two were business partners?"

I'm standing right here, you know. Of course it wasn't the first time she'd felt invisible tonight, but coming from Libby it was really grating her nerves.

Jack inclined his head, acknowledging the statement without further response, and Brenna wanted to smack him.

Libby forged ahead. "We missed you at Harry and Susan's Saturday night."

"I spent the weekend at the vineyard."

Libby's eyebrows moved the millimeter allowed by botox. "*You*, Jack? Rusticating in wine country? The wonders never cease."

How much longer would she have to stand here and listen to this?

"There's a first time for everything." Jack flashed Libby his ladykiller smile, and Libby practically swooned.

"I trust it won't be a regular occurrence, then? Weekends in the country?"

"Surely you know me better than that, Libby?"

Libby narrowed her eyes at Brenna, but Brenna held the same smile she'd worn all evening. She wouldn't give Libby the satisfaction. She, better than anyone, knew Jack's feelings about wine country.

Libby batted her eyelashes at Jack again before

turning to Brenna. "I promised Tom and Margaret I'd round Jack up—" Libby paused and blinked. "Do you know Tom and Margaret, Brenna?"

Of course she didn't, and she'd bet next season's Chardonnay Libby knew that. "Can't say I've had the pleasure."

"That's a shame. But," she continued, "I *did* promise them I'd drag Jack over so they can finalize those plans for the golf tournament. Do you mind, Brenna?"

"Not at all." *Twenty more minutes. That's it.*

"Bren, would you…?" Jack started, but she waved him silent.

"Actually, I think I'll just get a refill while you all talk business."

Jack looked at her strangely. "I'll only be a minute."

"No problem."

Libby dragged Jack away before the words were fully out of her mouth. Jack didn't even play golf. Or did he? He might have picked up the hobby sometime in the last decade.

Draining the last of her soda, she handed the empty glass to a passing waiter and went to find a place to sit. She slid her feet out of Dianne's shoes and wiggled her toes in relief. The feeling didn't extend to her mind, though.

Brenna felt as if she was having a flashback to their marriage. Hell, the whole damn night felt like a re-run. The awkward conversations with his friends, being an outsider… They'd go home, fight, and have make-up sex. But the next outing would bring more of the same. She snorted. They'd already *had* the fight and the make-up sex tonight. The cycle was complete. History repeated itself. She'd given it her best shot and still fallen short.

A high-pitched laugh caught her attention over the music, and she looked over to see Libby Winston's head thrown back in over-dramatic style as she found whatever Jack was saying to be hilarious. Libby swatted Jack's arm playfully, then pulled him close to whisper something in his ear. Jack wore a look of mild amusement as Libby practically shoved her breasts in his face.

It was sickening to watch.

She knew she shouldn't care, but she couldn't help the feeling coiling in her stomach. Even more, she didn't like what that might mean for her.

She shouldn't have come tonight. She'd been right in her first decision not to come, but for all the wrong reasons. She could be the face of Amante Verano, shake hands and network just fine. It was everything else that was horribly wrong.

But the trip wasn't in vain. She'd made some good business connections. Hell, she'd even met the Mayor. But this event had also brought home the truth she'd been fighting against all along.

At least she'd been reminded *before* she got in too deep this time. She and Jack were from different worlds—Libby Winston had just driven that point home for her—and getting involved with him again wouldn't end any better this time.

Something was bothering Brenna. On the surface she seemed fine, smiling and chatting with some of the biggest names in the community. He'd had many compliments on the wine, and he hoped Brenna was taking advantage of the opportunity to network.

Even though she smiled and nodded and charmed who she could, he could tell something wasn't right. Tension hummed under everything she said to him, and he could see the uncomfortable set to her shoulders. Even her smile had lost its sparkle.

She slid into the limo with an audible sigh of relief. "Thank God that's over."

Why was she sitting on the opposite seat? "You did great."

"That doesn't mean it wasn't horrible."

"Well, it's over now, and the night can only get better from here, right?"

"I wouldn't count on that." Brenna reached for one of the decanters, sniffed the contents, then poured herself a glass. The tension he'd sensed earlier must have been repressed hostility, because it now filled the air around them.

"Are you still mad because I was late?"

Crossing her arms across her chest, she shot him a dirty look. "It's certainly a place to start."

"I told you, it was unavoidable."

She rolled her eyes. "It always is with you. You *wanted* me to come to this party, and then you couldn't be bothered to even show up on time."

He sighed. "How many times do I have to apologize for that?"

"Don't bother. We've had *that* fight before. I know how it ends."

Exasperation set in. Brenna wasn't making sense. "Then what?"

That lit her fire, and the look she leveled on him nearly scorched him. "I don't even know where to begin. The wham-bam-thank-you-ma'am in the rehearsal room?"

Wham-bam…? What the hell…?

"Or the fact that right after that I got to watch you flirt with half the female population of San Francisco?"

That was what had her upset? "I was simply being nice."

She snorted, and turned to stare pointedly out the window.

"Are you jealous, Bren?" He couldn't keep the amazed amusement out of his voice.

That snapped Brenna's eyes back to his. "No. Not in the least. I just think it's rude to expect me to stand there and watch you eat up all that simpering."

"So you'd rather I be rude to them?"

"Polite party conversation doesn't require your head in Libby's cleavage. And it certainly—" She choked on her ire and turned back to the window. "You could've put a stop to it, but you didn't. It's like I wasn't even there."

The twelve blocks back to Garrett Towers took only a few minutes at this time of night, and they were already pulling to a stop under the awning. The night doorman had the door open seconds later, and Brenna was out of the limo before Jack could even respond to her last comment.

But her game face was back in place as she smiled at the doorman and they walked calmly to the elevator.

Brenna's jealousy was a new experience for him, and, while he didn't look forward to trying to talk her out of her anger, the fact she was jealous at all did bring him a small bit of satisfaction.

Once the elevator doors closed, he tried to talk her down. "I would think that trip to the rehearsal room proved you have no reason at all to be jealous. In fact, I'm willing to spend all night proving it to you."

"Not a chance," she scoffed. "I'm just going up long enough to get my suitcase. I'm going home."

"Home?" he repeated dumbly. "Now?"

"Yes, now." She shot him a level look as the elevator doors opened. "You don't even have to order a car for me this time. I can do it myself."

The chauffeur had left Brenna's bag sitting right inside the door, and she grabbed the handle, obviously intending to get right back on the elevator. He stopped her by closing the door and standing in front of it. With all he knew now, he wasn't going to let Brenna retreat again. "Are you really going to storm out of here just because you're jealous of Libby and her posse?"

"I'm going home because I realized tonight that I was crazy to think anything would be different this time. Libby Winston's swooning is only part of it. I won't just be your accessory again."

Ah, finally they were at the heart of the matter. Unfortunately, he wasn't quite sure what that was. He approached her carefully. "Again?"

"Jack…" Brenna's jaw clenched.

"Spit it out, Bren. If you're not just jealous of Libby, then what is the problem?"

Brenna dropped the handle of her suitcase. That was good news. At least he'd kept her from running out on him.

She crossed her arms and cocked an eyebrow at him. "The problem is you."

"Me?"

"Yes, you. You want a list?"

The gauntlet was down now; he couldn't wait to hear this. "Please. No need to hold back."

"Fine." Brenna stomped across the room and sank gracefully onto the couch, her spine ramrod-straight with anger. Her voice dripped with icy, sarcastic politeness as she started on her litany. "We'll skip over the lateness, since that's just par for the course."

Personally, he felt that statement deserved addressing, but Brenna moved on before he could.

"We'll also skip past the fact you let everyone dismiss me as just your ex, since technically I am. The five minutes in the rehearsal room notwithstanding, of course."

He nearly choked at the insult. Five minutes? It had been closer to twenty really good, intense minutes, and he was tempted to remind her how she hadn't been complaining at the time, but he bit his tongue for the moment.

"Half the time you treated me like I wasn't even there. And you let everyone else do it, too. Just because I don't travel in the same circles and I don't know the same people, that doesn't mean I'm invisible."

He was damned no matter what he tried to do. "I know you don't like these kinds of events, and after leaving you on your own for so long I thought you'd *like* not having to be on the spot for the rest of the evening."

Her eyes narrowed. "You thought I couldn't handle it? After I'd been handling it for the last hour just fine? Why the hell did you want me to come in the first place?"

Brenna wasn't known for her reasonableness when she was angry, but now they were going in circles. He tried to keep his frustration in check. "I know you can handle it, Bren, I just thought you didn't *want* to."

"And you didn't see how we'd time-warped back ten years?"

Brenna was getting more worked up instead of calming down. This was *not* his plan for tonight.

Brenna shook her head when he didn't respond. "Hell, you and Libby seemed to forget I was even standing there."

Back to Libby. So Brenna *was* jealous. Not that her other complaints weren't valid, and they probably did deserve addressing at a later time, but Brenna's jealousy—obvious now, even though she tried to hide it—was definitely more interesting and pertinent to the matter at hand.

"Libby Winston might be a terrible flirt," he said as he crossed the space between them and joined her on the couch.

"In many ways," Brenna muttered.

He bit back a smile. "But she's no threat to you."

Jack's sincerity shook her. As did his proximity. The tension simmering between them had moved from hostility to something more, and taken on a sharper edge. This was exactly why the make-up sex was always so intense. One type of heat led to another. Even now.

"I am *not* threatened by Libby and her surgically enhanced self," she countered, but even she could hear the outright bluff in her voice and she hated it. She scooted back a little, trying to put distance between the meaningful glow in Jack's eyes and her already weakening resolve.

She didn't want to be jealous of Libby Winston. She didn't like what that implied about her and her inability to fit into that part of Jack's life. Again.

And she definitely didn't want Jack's assurances that he wanted her, not Libby, to affect her the way they did.

It meant she was already too far in. She was going to get hurt, and neither her heart nor her ego could take that punch. While part of her wanted to end this right now, to take her pride while she still had it and head back to the safety of Amante Verano, she couldn't seem to gather the energy to get off the couch.

"Bren…" Jack's hand was on her knee, his fingers tracing a small circle and causing goosebumps to rise all over her body. Damn him. No, damn *herself*. She was mad at him. Really mad, yet her body had already forgotten everything else, and her blood was beginning to surge through her veins in anticipation.

"Jack…" She tried to protest.

"If I'd known you didn't mind the whole of San Francisco knowing exactly how we spent the weekend, I would have gladly corrected anyone who tried to categorize you as simply my ex."

His hand moved higher, distracting her from his words. She forced herself to concentrate.

"And if Libby Winston or anyone else in that room

was even the smallest bit deserving of your jealousy I wouldn't have needed to coerce you to come tonight— or dragged you off to the rehearsal room."

There went the rest of her anger, smothered by the seductive promise in his voice. Breathing became difficult as he leaned closer.

"Do you doubt me, Bren?"

God, the man oozed pure sex appeal out of every pore. Even as he calmed her with his words, she could feel the desire he was holding carefully—if temporarily—in check vibrating in the air.

"I don't doubt that you want me. But I—I…" She couldn't quite get the words out. Clearing her throat, she made her stand. "That's not enough this time. I want more than that."

A look she hadn't seen in years crossed his face. She'd almost forgotten it, but she recognized it the moment it appeared. And her heart skipped a beat at the sight. There. *That* was her Jack. A small smile tugged at the corner of his mouth. "More, huh?"

"More."

He tugged slightly on her hand, and she slid across the leather until they were only inches apart. "More sounds like an interesting idea."

Jack's hand trailed up her arm to smooth across the curve of her shoulder before it moved to her back.

Focus. "I don't know if we're capable of that. We always end up fighting. Just like tonight." Her voice trembled a little as her body fell into habit: they'd fought, and now it was time to make up. Her muscles loosened and her pulse kicked up in anticipation.

"Some things are important enough to fight for. And you're worth fighting with." The husky undertone affected her almost as much as the words. She felt the zip of Dianne's lucky dress give way as he eased it down.

She was a goner and she knew it. She couldn't fight it any longer, and she didn't want to either. God help her, she was still in love with Jack.

CHAPTER ELEVEN

HER phone was ringing.

The chirpy noise filtered into her dream and pulled her to semi-consciousness. No light filtered through her eyelids, so it had to be very late. Or maybe very early.

Jack's arm had her pinned to the bed. His body curved around hers, and her feet were tangled in the sheets. Getting out of bed wasn't tempting at all—much less for what was probably a wrong number anyway.

The noise stopped, and Brenna let sleep start to tug her back under. She was exhausted, thanks to Jack. Make-up sex had never been like that. Although neither one of them had said anything outright, the dynamic had shifted somehow, and they'd have to address that eventually.

She was looking forward to it.

When the chirping started again, she sighed. Even Jack stirred this time.

"Is that your phone?" he mumbled.

"Yes. It's probably just a wrong number."

"Then you're not going to answer it?"

"No."

"Good." Jack pulled her closer and adjusted his hold

on her, snuggling her in against his chest. His deep sigh of satisfaction seemed to slide through her, warming her soul. She could feel the smile on her face as she closed her eyes and—

Jack's phone blared like a Klaxon, jarring them both wide awake. As Jack cursed under his breath and pushed to a sitting position alarm bells started clanging in her head. The chances of both of them getting wrong number calls so close together… Something wasn't right.

Jack retrieved his pants from the floor and fished in the pocket for his phone, while Brenna made her way to the other room to find her purse. She pulled out her phone and flipped it open. She could hear Jack's voice as he answered, but couldn't make out any of the words as she scrolled through the menu on her phone. Two missed calls from Amante Verano's main line. Her heart stopped beating.

She didn't seem to have any voicemail waiting, but deep down she knew Jack was getting whatever news there was right now. She should go in, eavesdrop on Jack's side of the conversation and see what she could figure out, but something held her back. It couldn't be good news. Not at this time of night.

Then Jack appeared in the doorway, his phone still in his hand. The look of concern and pity on his face confirmed her earlier thought: the news—whatever it was—wasn't good. Her knees shook a little.

He seemed to be searching for words. "That was Ted."

Oh, God. "Was someone hurt? Di? Was there an accident?"

"No one was hurt. Everyone is fine," he reassured her, and the relief that washed over her staggered her. But the relief was painfully short-lived; she could tell the worst was yet to come.

"*What*, Jack. Tell me."

He took a deep breath. "There was a fire."

"*Fire?*" Of all the possibilities… "Oh, my God. Where? When?" She was already in the bedroom, searching through her suitcase, pulling out clothes and trying to dress with shaking hands.

Jack caught her arms and held her—forcing her to look at him directly, yet still offering his support. "In the winery itself. Bren…" He blew out his breath in a long, noisy sigh. She braced herself. "The building is a total loss."

"Tot—" She couldn't get the word past the lump in her throat. "Oh, God."

"I'm so sorry, Bren."

Total. She couldn't process it. Her winery was gone? "I need to…need to…" She looked at the clothes in her hand and had no idea what to do with them.

"Finish getting dressed. We'll leave whenever you're ready."

She'd never been so tired in her life, but there was no way she could sleep. There was too much to do, and while her brain spun at top speed, she couldn't shake the weight that kept her moving sluggishly and mechanically.

They'd arrived at Amante Verano at sunrise, but the beautiful picture that normally greeted her had been scarred by the charred, blackened ruins of the winery.

Everything else looked the same as it had when she'd left yesterday—*God, had it really been less than twenty-four hours?*—and the surreal disconnect only added to the problems she was having making her thoughts fall into logical order.

Jack had been there for her, holding her hand while Ted filled her in on the details. When it came to what needed to be done next—calling the insurance company, talking to the Fire Marshal—he'd taken over, with her blessing and heartfelt thanks.

In fact, Jack was in her office right now—where she should be, *would* be as soon as she could muster the strength to stand. Instead, she sat cross-legged on the ground, unable to stop staring at what was left of her winery. The walls leaned at drunken angles, barely holding up what was left of the roof. The giant hole in the side wall—caused when the tank full of neutral grape spirits exploded, Ted said—mirrored the feeling in her stomach.

She needed to quit wallowing. Ted was burning up the phone lines, trying to find someone to take the grapes off their hands. They still needed to harvest next week, or else lose the crop entirely, but they needed somewhere to send those grapes once they did. She should be helping with that chore, or doing any of the dozen other things waiting for her, and she would.

In just another minute.

If Max were alive, Jack would gladly read him the riot act over the astounding lack of proper insurance this place had. This was a giant mess. Max had certainly known the implications of underinsuring, so Jack could only assume Max had figured he'd play the odds and use his own money should those odds ever not work out in his favor. It looked as if Brenna also knew the winery was underinsured, and had planned to remedy that, but for whatever reason hadn't done so yet. The road to recovery would be rough, to say the least. Without a serious infusion of cash, Amante Verano might not recover at all.

And he had a feeling Brenna understood that on some level.

He hadn't seen much of Brenna since shortly after they'd arrived. In a sort of unspoken agreement Brenna had taken charge of the "wine side"—conferring with Ted and Dianne on grapes and stock issues—while he had done what he did best and buried himself in paperwork and crunched numbers as night fell.

In the wake of that thought he heard footsteps in the hall, and Brenna entered the office. She'd been pale and haunted-looking in the car on the way out this morning, and the events of the day hadn't helped her any. For lack of a better word, Brenna looked fragile—a sharp contrast to her normal energy and strength—and dark circles shadowed her eyes.

"How's it look?" she asked as she collapsed into her chair opposite Max's desk.

"Honestly, Bren, it's not great." He wanted to cushion the blow if he could. "There are options, but…"

"But they're not great. I figured as much." She sighed, and scrubbed her hands over her face.

He noticed the soot on her hands. He should have

known Brenna wouldn't be able to stay away from the building entirely, as the Fire Marshal had recommended. "How are you holding up?"

She laughed bitterly. "Not great. Ted's having a little luck finding buyers for some of the fruit." She sighed. "Box wine. My grapes are going to be made into cheap box wine. My mother is rolling in her grave."

"You're doing the best you can under the circumstances, Bren."

"I know. It doesn't lessen the feeling, though." Another deep sigh, and Brenna shook her head as if to clear it. "Any other news I need to know about? What did the Fire Marshal say?"

"Other than 'Stay away from the building,' you mean?" Brenna dropped her eyes. "It's all preliminary, but he thinks he knows what started the fire."

That got Brenna's attention. "Really? Already?"

"Yeah. It was electrical in nature; that much he's pretty sure of. It looks like a short in the main pump sparked it."

He didn't think it could be possible, but Brenna went even paler behind her freckles as she pulled in her breath sharply. "The pump?" she whispered.

She looked as if she was about to pass out. He came out from behind the desk and squatted in front of her as she took deep breaths. "Are you all right, Bren?"

"Oh, my God. This is *my* fault."

"How could it possibly be your fault?"

Brenna stood and wrapped her arms around her stomach. "The pump's been acting up lately. I took it apart last week. Twice, actually." When she looked at him, the horror in her eyes shocked him. "This is my fault. *I* burned down my winery."

"It's not your fault. The findings are still preliminary, and they could change." She started to protest, but in her current state he needed to talk her down. "Even if it was the pump, it's still not your fault. I know you, Bren, and you could take that thing apart in your sleep. You didn't cause this."

She didn't seem comforted. If anything, she became more agitated. "Half a dozen owners, Prohibition, droughts, phylloxera—no problem. My family has produced the best fruit and the best wine in the valley regardless of the circumstances. But *I* take over, and I destroy everything in a month because I can't put a stupid pump back together properly."

"Bren…" He reached for her, but she flinched away from his hand.

"Don't!" Her voice shook as she took two steps back. In a slightly calmer, although still shaking voice, she whispered, "Please don't touch me. I can't handle it. I'm barely holding myself together as it is."

All the more reason to give her someone to hold on to, as far as he figured, but Brenna was already out of reach. "You look exhausted. Why don't you go rest for a little while? Or we could get something to eat if you want. Later we'll sit down and come up with a plan."

She swallowed hard. "You're right. I could use a break. I think I will go lie down. I'll see you later." She walked from the room, still muttering to herself. *Probably still beating herself up over that damn pump.*

A ping from the computer brought him back to the other business clamoring for his attention. He couldn't leave Brenna and the vineyard right now, so he'd emailed Roger earlier and informed him of the change of plans. He couldn't postpone the meetings in New York on such short notice, so Roger would have to go in his place. Unfortunately, bringing him up to speed was taking a bit more time than he'd hoped.

After an hour of back and forth emails and a phone call he finally had it sorted out. Brenna hadn't reappeared, and all seemed quiet, so he went to the kitchen for a beer.

A moment later Brenna stuck her head around the door. Her color was a bit better now, but she still wore that tired, haunted look. Her hair hung in a slightly damp curtain around her face. Obviously fresh from a shower, she wore a baggy T-shirt and pajama pants. Red toenails peeked out from under the floppy hems.

She cleared her throat. "I'm sorry about earlier. I shouldn't have snapped at you like that."

"It's understandable."

"Thanks. It's not been a good day. I feel like I've come loose from my trellis and I'm just flapping in the breeze."

"You'll get through this. It may sound trite, but it's true."

"The thing is…" She paused and took another of those deep breaths. "It really means a lot to me that you're here. You didn't have to come—"

"Of course I did."

She shook her head. "Actually, you didn't. And I overheard you talking on the phone earlier. I know you've canceled your trip to New York so you can stay here during all this. I really appreciate it."

Her hands pleated the hem of her T-shirt, telling him she had something more to say. "You know, I've been feeling kind of lonely out here, and when I saw the—" Her voice cracked. She swallowed and tried again. "When I saw what was left, I thought I'd hit bottom. I've never felt so alone and scared as I did at that moment. But you were there, and I realized I wasn't alone. That I didn't have to be." Her eyes met his. "And that I don't *want* to be."

Her words slammed into him like a hurricane, causing his breath to catch in his chest. The right response escaped him at that moment, and all he could manage was "Come here."

She crossed the short distance and threw herself against him. Brenna buried her face against his chest and breathed deeply while her arms gripped him like a life rope. He could feel the tension leaving her in increments, each slow breath seeming to ease her. Occasionally her breath stuttered suspiciously, like a sob, but the trembles that moved over her slowly dissipated.

He didn't know how long they stood there, the warmth of Brenna seeping into his bones as he breathed in the sunshine citrus scent of her hair and stroked the soft strands. The iron grip of her hands finally loosened, and then began to smooth a gentle path up and down his sides and over his chest. When she lifted her head and met his eyes again, he could see a bit of his Brenna emerging from behind the fatigue and worry.

Rising up on her tiptoes, Brenna wrapped a hand

around his neck and pulled his mouth to hers. The fire, the passion, the raw desire—it was all there, and it moved though him like an electrical current. But it was tempered by something else in her kiss.

That feeling shook him, and he groaned as he lifted her off her feet, loving the way she clung to him, moving them both the short distance down the hall to his bed, where he pulled her down on top of him.

Brenna deepened the kiss, threading her fingers through his hair, scratching her nails gently against his scalp. She sighed his name against his neck as his arms tightened around her and molded her body to his, and he felt another tremor—of pleasure this time—shake her gently.

Brenna didn't want to be alone. Didn't have to be alone.

Neither did he.

The headache throbbing behind her eyes was growing steadily worse. She should have gone back to bed after the first phone call of the morning. The nice woman in North Napa who'd heard Brenna was selling off her grapes and wanted to buy a couple of bins' worth to make jam had been a blow to her ego. Her mother's Pinot Noir grapes, being made into *jam*. Ugh. At the time she'd thought with a starting note like that the day could only get better.

Then Ted had brought her more bad news. Her head was still spinning from *that* information, but she was holding it together. Tears would not help the situation any.

Now she was up to her ears in numbers—including the ones Jack had crunched yesterday—and the bottom line was just plain depressing. As the weight settled more firmly on her shoulders, she seriously re-thought her earlier resolution not to cry. A good let-it-all-out bawl might make her feel a little better, at least.

No. She took a deep cleansing breath and let it out slowly. As Jack had said last night, she would get through this. If she just kept repeating that to herself, she might actually begin to believe it.

Jack wasn't an early riser, and he'd been sleeping soundly when she crawled out of bed at dawn. Now she heard rattling in the kitchen, the unmistakable sounds of someone after a cup of coffee. When Jack entered the office a few minutes later he held two cups, one of which he placed in front of her as he bent to kiss the top of her head. "Did you get any sleep?"

"Only a little," she confessed. "It's hard to turn my brain off."

"What's that?" Jack asked, reading the notepad in front of her.

She didn't need to look at it again. "Only the latest bad news."

"And?"

"Ted's worried about soil contamination—from the runoff from the fire. All the chemicals and the ashes in the water have drained into the vines. There's no telling what it will do. We're going to lose the acre behind the winery. Maybe a little more than that."

Jack's mouth twisted a little. "Sorry to hear that. How long will it take to replace them?"

"After we replace the soil and replant it will still be three to five years before we can get any fruit off the new vines."

"Ouch. At least I know your insurance policy *does* cover that loss."

She could tell Jack was trying to be upbeat for her sake, but, while she appreciated the gesture, he seemed to be missing the point entirely. "The money's not the issue," she explained.

He glanced at the sheet of figures in front of her. "That kind of money should be."

He just didn't get it. "Jack, my great-grandfather planted those vines, almost sixty years ago. They're healthy, productive vines—the fruit is amazing—and I'm going to have to rip them of the ground. Trust me, the money isn't the problem."

"But they *can* be replaced."

Hadn't he been listening? "No, they can't."

"Only you could have a sentimental attachment to a plant." There was a small chuckle in his voice that sent her hackles up.

She spun in her chair to face him squarely. "What's that supposed to mean?"

"Don't get your back up, Bren. I'm just saying that you're emotionally invested in this place—"

"Well, *yeah*," she interrupted. But he knew that. He knew how she felt about Amante Verano.

He continued as if she hadn't said anything. "To the

extent that you don't always see the big picture. They're just vines. We'll replace them with something better."

His words cut her, and the hurt ran deep. "They're slightly more than 'just vines' to me. They can't be replaced that easily—much less with something 'better.' Those vines are the backbone and history of Amante Verano. I'm sorry if that offends your MBA, but that's the truth." She could hear the snap in her voice, and she tried unsuccessfully to tone it down.

"'Backbone and history'? Bren, you have to keep your emotions separate from your business."

He didn't know her at all. "That's your answer for everything. 'Keep your business and your personal life apart.' Sorry, but it's not so clear-cut for me. This is my *home* as well as my livelihood. I can't really separate the two."

"Then it's a good thing I'm here, isn't it?"

Not necessarily. His grin wasn't working on her this time. "Are you implying…?"

"I'm not implying anything. You said it yourself— you're too close to be objective."

She could quite happily strangle him at that moment. "Wine-making is a very *sub*jective business. I don't have to be completely objective."

"Then it's a good thing I still own half of this place, isn't it?"

Anger erupted in her chest. The nerve… *That* was the last straw. Almost blinded by the red haze in front of her eyes, she jerked open desk drawers until she found the manila folder she was looking for. Inside it was the sale agreement. Grabbing a pen off the desk, she flipped to the last page and scrawled her signature at the bottom.

In two steps she was around the desk. She slapped the agreement against his chest, where he grabbed it reflexively. "There. Now you don't own any of it."

"Bren…"

"Amante Verano may be a mess, but it's my mess. And I won't have you patronizing me or telling me the proper way to run *my* business. I'll get through this, remember?"

"I'm trying to help you here, Bren."

"I don't want or need your help. Now, get the hell off my property."

Not waiting for Jack's response, she let her ire carry her back to Max's desk—*her* desk—where she turned her back on him and stared blindly at the numbers on the paper in front of her.

She heard his sigh, but his words were clipped, angry. "If that's the way you want it, Bren, *fine*. Good luck."

On that note, Jack left the room. A minute later she heard the back door close and Jack's car start up. She sat quietly until the noise faded into the distance, then sagged back against the chair. Closing her eyes, she felt the finality of what had just happened wash over her.

Once again she'd lost Jack. Driven him away. The pain that sliced through her put anything she'd felt in the last two days to shame. The bands tightening around her chest made it hard to breathe, and her heart sat like a stone in her chest.

She could feel the tears burning her eyes; she could

feel the sobs trapped in her throat just waiting to be set free. *Tears won't help*, she reminded herself.

But it was too late. She laid her head on her desk and cried.

CHAPTER TWELVE

IN THE two weeks since Brenna had thrown him off her property he'd had no word from her or Amante Verano. Not that he'd expected it; her intent had been very clear, and, if he'd had any doubts, the arrival by courier of the anklet he'd given her a few days later would have clarified it. He and Brenna were back where they'd started a few weeks ago. *Ex*.

That bothered him. A lot more than he'd thought it would.

His life had quickly settled right back into its normal routine, and he was bored stiff by it. He missed the energy and spark Brenna brought just by being in the same room. Everything moved along like before, but it felt monotonous and bland. Plus, he was getting damned tired of everyone agreeing with him all the time.

Business was good. The New York deal had gone through without a hitch, and Garrett Properties was now established on both coasts. Profits were up. His employees and his stockholders were equally happy with him. He'd received notice just yesterday he'd be receiving an award for "Outstanding Philanthropic Efforts" in the city of San Francisco.

He was having a hard time dredging up enthusiasm for any of it, and he could trace his general dissatisfaction with life straight back to Brenna.

Even though Brenna was ignoring him, that didn't mean he didn't have access to what was going on at Amante Verano. His company still had a twenty-five percent interest in the vineyard, so he was fully up-to-date with Brenna's recovery efforts.

They weren't going well. Amante Verano just didn't have the funds on hand to tide them over until settlements could be reached with the insurance companies and the building could be replaced. Now the bank had turned down her request to have her line of credit increased. He fully understood why: the vineyard was a very bad risk at the moment.

Brenna was hemorrhaging money as she tried to get her feet back under her, but it would be a full year before she'd even get another crop in, even longer before she'd have wine ready to sell.

She was teetering on the edge of bankruptcy already. The loss on Jack's books would be negligible. He could tell, though, by the update he'd received from his people, that Brenna knew she was on the precipice.

It had to be killing her, but he knew Brenna would never come to him for help now. Her stubborn pride wouldn't let her—not after the way they'd left things. She'd accused him of not fully understanding her, but he did. Probably better than anyone else. While he might not understand her emotional attachment to

Amante Verano, he did understand it was as much a part of her as her red hair and her temper.

And he loved her in spite of it.

He sighed and swiveled his chair around, taking in the view of the Golden Gate Bridge, where buses full of tourists were making their way out to wine country. A month ago some of them would have been headed to Brenna's, but now there wasn't much there to interest the tourists. The great irony was that now there was something at Amante Verano of great interest to *him*.

He was in love with his ex-wife… Lord, could his life be any more screwed up?

But he still didn't know exactly how he could help her right things at the winery. He had plenty of the one thing Brenna needed most right now—money—but the chances of her accepting it if he offered…? Slim.

He hadn't wanted anything to do with owning a winery, or investing in one, and he'd succeeded. He'd wanted out, and Brenna had thrown him out.

Be careful what you wish for.

But all routes weren't closed to him. As Brenna had said, the Garrett name alone could open many doors. She might not want his help, but she was going to get it.

It was the least he could do for her.

As he picked up the phone, he knew somewhere Max was laughing his head off.

The idleness was driving Brenna crazy. She'd never had so much free time on her hands. Every morning when she woke up and realized she didn't have a ton of work waiting for her in the winery, the blow was just as fresh.

And spending the day fielding frustrating phone calls and watching her bottom line sink deeper and deeper into the red wasn't any better than having nothing to do at all.

But the disaster of her professional life had only highlighted something else: how little personal life she actually had. No hobbies. Few friends beyond Di and Ted, and those she did have buried under their own post-crush work in *their* wineries. Somehow, that used to seem like enough, but now it didn't. Playing Solitaire on her laptop was a poor excuse for a life.

Jack was right: she needed to get off the property more.

Jack. The thought of him brought a chest-crushing wave of pain that hadn't subsided any over the last couple of weeks. Without the busy work Amante Verano used to provide she had ample time to think about Jack, and everything that had transpired, until the pain and emptiness overwhelmed her.

She'd let her temper get the best of her. Even if she tried to blame her last outburst on a really bad day, she had to admit that it had been more than just stress egging her on. The amount of time she'd had to think had given her clarity on a couple of topics. She had used the vineyard as a safety blanket all these years: no need to mourn the loss of Jack when she had Amante Verano to immerse herself in. It had still been a connection to Jack—however tenuous—but now that was gone.

Losing Jack a second time had sucked all the blood out of her heart, and she felt like a zombie wandering though what was left of her life. Facing the destruction of the winery had been much easier when Jack was here; now it seemed insurmountable.

Late at night, when there was even less to occupy her, Jack's absence was harder to bear. Jack had been a safe harbor when she'd hit bottom, and she missed that feeling of strength he gave her by just being there.

Oh, who was she trying to fool? She just missed *him*. The pain she'd felt when she'd signed the divorce papers was nothing compared to this—because this time she'd gone in eyes open, without all those teenage romanticized ideas.

And she'd fallen even harder than before.

She'd quit crying herself to sleep simply because she'd run out of tears.

Brenna blew her hair out of her face and stared blankly at her computer screen, trying to remember what she was supposed to be doing. Good Lord, she couldn't even concentrate on the disaster in front of her because of Jack.

From her seat on the couch she saw Di through the French doors, shortcutting her way into the house through the vines. Dianne was moving faster than normal, and she practically burst through the doors. "'Every day is a great day at Amante Verano', right?"

"I wouldn't say *great*, Di," Brenna answered, but the excited grin on Dianne's face was enough to toss a shot of hope into the bleakness.

"Well, this should definitely make this day a little better for you." Dianne waved a letter at her.

"Because…?" she prompted.

"The bank has approved your application to extend our line of credit."

"What? They shot us down as too big a risk."

"Obviously they've reconsidered. Look, Brenna." Di handed her the letter. "Money. Look at all those zeros. Enough to tide us over until the insurance pays out and we get back on our feet." Di was almost dancing with excitement.

It didn't make any sense, but there, in black and white, was the lifeline she needed. It seemed too good to be true. "Hand me the phone, will you?"

Dianne did as she asked, but as she handed it over added, "Who are you calling?"

"Mia Ryan at the bank. I want to be sure this isn't a computer glitch before I start spending money I don't really have."

Dianne raised an eyebrow, then shrugged as Brenna dialed.

"Mia, it's Brenna Walsh. Can you tell me what's up with our line of credit?"

"Of course, Brenna." She could hear Mia's fingers on her keyboard. "How are things?"

"If the letter I got today is for real, then things are about to be much better."

"I'm glad to hear it. Here we go. Let me see…" There was a long pause as Mia consulted something, then Brenna heard the keyboard again. "Interesting…"

"Interesting? How?"

"Your LOC request was reopened two days ago and approved based on an increase in your cash on hand and a guarantee on the debt."

"Cash on hand?" She didn't *have* any cash on hand.

Money was flowing out of Amante Verano like a river, not in. "Are you sure?"

"That's what it says." Mia read Brenna her account balance, and Brenna's good mood evaporated.

"That's a mistake."

"I don't think so, Brenna. Let me check something."

Brenna tried to be patient as Mia put her on hold, but Dianne's questions in the interim were only increasing her confusion and agitation about the situation. She held up a hand to silence her as Mia came back on the line.

"Okay, Brenna. I found it, and it's all correct. Jack Garrett deposited the money into your account at the same time he guaranteed the LOC."

"Jack?" Her throat seemed to be closing and words were hard to get out. "Surely you mean Garrett Properties. They're the other partner. Not Jack."

"No." Mia sounded as if she thought Brenna was a marble or two shy of a game. "It was Jack Garrett personally. I can see the scan of the check and the LOC agreement. Are you okay, Brenna?" she added, as Brenna started to choke.

Di's eyes widened and she handed Brenna her glass of water.

Brenna waved her away. "I'm fine," she said, to Di and Mia both. "Thanks for checking, Mia."

"Anytime. And good luck."

Brenna hung up the phone and met Dianne's amazed stare. Her world had just turned slightly sideways. The hope of financial rescue was tempered by the surety there was a mistake, a catch somehow. But that funny feeling in her stomach at the thought of Jack…

"Did I hear that right?" Di asked. "*Jack* had something to do with this?"

"Mia says he personally guaranteed our line of credit *and* deposited a nice chunk of cash into our account." The words sounded too unreal to believe, even to her, and yet she had confirmation from the bank.

From the look on Dianne's face, Brenna knew Di was finding it hard to believe, too. "And you didn't know? He didn't tell you?"

"Do I look like I knew Jack was going to do this?"

Di shrugged. "So what does this mean?"

"I don't know. I find it hard to believe Jack's had a sudden desire to invest in a winery. Much less one that's teetering on the edge of disaster."

"Me, too. He was so adamant about…"

"Yeah, I know." *But he was starting to come around—at least until I kicked him off the property.*

"Then this is about you." Di's smile turned smug.

"Me?" she squeaked as her heart did a flip-flop in her chest. "No, it must have something to do with protecting Garrett Properties' share. Or something…" Brenna pushed herself off the couch and headed down the hall. "I'll see you later, Di."

"Where are you going?"

Where else? "San Francisco. To talk to Jack."

While she had the nerve.

Golf tournaments. He'd sponsor them, but he wasn't going to play in them. He responded to Libby Winston's email invite with a vague claim of other plans. Garrett Properties would send a check, and that would have to do. Libby's not-so-subtle request that he accompany her was better left ignored.

The intercom on his desk beeped. "Mr. Garrett, there's a Brenna Walsh here to see you. She doesn't have an appointment—"

His pulse kicked up. He didn't wait to hear the rest. "Send her in." *Brenna, here?* He stood and rounded his desk as his office door opened and Brenna walked in.

"Hi, Jack." She looked much better than she had two weeks ago—a little more color to her cheeks, no shadows under her eyes—but her face was still pinched with stress. "Sorry to barge in."

He hadn't expected to be so happy to see her. Or that he wouldn't know what to say to her. Casual small talk seemed ridiculous, considering everything. "It's not a problem, Bren. How are things at Amante Verano?"

She raised an eyebrow. "You mean you don't know?"

So she knew already. The bank must have moved quickly. But her voice lacked any heat behind the sarcasm, so it was hard for him to tell how she was choosing to take the news—that raised eyebrow wasn't offering much help.

"Touché. Yes, I know how things are businesswise at Amante Verano. How are you and Dianne and Ted doing?"

A shrug. "We're getting by. It's a struggle, but we're doing what we can."

God, he was tempted to reach for her, but…

"Look, I'll cut to the chase." Brenna moved to the

chair in front of his desk and sat. "I want to know why you are the guarantor on my line of credit."

Business it was, then. He went back to his chair and faced her across the expanse of his desk. "Because the bank wouldn't extend it without one. Not even for me. You're too high a risk at the moment."

"You can say that again," she muttered. "And the money that's appeared in my account?"

It was his turn to shrug. "Consider it a gift."

Brenna's mouth fell open. "That kind of money is not a gift. There's no way I can accept it. Surely you know that? I don't need your charity."

Obviously she'd forgotten he knew the state of her finances at the moment. "Then consider it a loan. You can pay it back when you get back on your feet."

That seemed to surprise her. "Just like that? You don't even want me to sign an IOU?"

"I don't think we need one. Do you?"

Brenna eyed him carefully. "Are you drunk?"

"No."

"Did you take up drugs? Hit your head against something hard?"

He was hard-pressed not to laugh. "No and no."

"Then you've gone insane."

Bren did have that effect on him. "Possibly. Why?"

"Because sane people don't go sticking money into their ex-wives' accounts or guaranteeing their loans."

"Maybe I believe Amante Verano is a good investment."

He saw the way her spine straightened with pride before she caught herself. "You really have lost your mind. You don't want to be in this business. You didn't want to own part of a winery when times were good, so why would you want to invest in one now? Considering the shape we're in…"

"I just want you to be happy, Bren, and I know getting Amante Verano back on track will make you happy."

He could see the suspicion in her eyes. "I don't get it. What's in it for you, Jack?"

This was it. Time to put up or shut up. He let the question hang there for a moment, until Brenna started shifting uncomfortably in her seat, her impatience starting to fuel her temper.

"Well, Jack? Tell me what's in it for you."

"You."

The word seemed to hang in the air between them, bringing their conversation—if that was what it could be called—to a screeching halt. All the breath seemed to rush out of her lungs, and she couldn't quite make her body remember to inhale again.

"I don't— I mean—I don't quite understand. What do you mean *me*?" *What happened to keeping business and personal lives separate?*

Jack met her eyes levelly. "You wouldn't be you without Amante Verano. I'm not saying I fully understand the connection—but then I don't understand the attraction to golf either. But I *do* understand that it's important to you and that it makes you happy." He sighed. "If I have to pump money into your winery to make you happy again and make you *you*, I will."

That was a lot to process all at once. "You'd do that? For me?"

Exasperated, Jack rolled his eyes. "Yes, you infuriating woman."

The disconnect was too much. "But you don't *want* a winery."

There was that even stare again. "But I want you."

Her heart jumped in her chest as his words brought tears to the corners of her eyes. "Really?"

"Bren…"

She stood, stalling for a moment while she tried to make sense of everything. "I thought you just felt sorry for me. Or that you were trying to protect your company's bottom line. I couldn't believe you'd…not after the way I treated you."

Jack came around the desk and leaned against it. "You've got a temper, Bren. I know that. But you should know by now that I do, too." He caught her arm and pulled her around to look at him. "I'm telling you that I understand how much your vineyard means to you, and I shouldn't have discounted that."

"But that's the thing, Jack. I've had plenty of time to think over the last few weeks." Now that she knew what she wanted to say, she couldn't get the words out fast enough. "Yeah, it's bad at the vineyard right now, but that's only been a part of the general suckiness of my life. I realized I've used Amante Verano as an excuse for far too long. I used it as a safety net after the divorce, and it's become a habit. But what I've been going through with the vineyard is nothing compared to what I've gone through not having you."

It was his turn to look surprised, but the look quickly gentled into something beautiful. It gave her the courage to say the rest.

"I told you that night after the fire that I realized I didn't want to be alone. But it's more than just not being alone. I want to be with *you*."

His eyes began to glow with warmth—and desire. It sent a shiver through her. "Really, Bren."

"Yeah. And I want more than that."

He nodded as he crossed his arms over his chest. "Ah, back to more…"

Now was not the time to back down. "Yes. It's going to take more than just throwing money at my business to make me happy. And you did say you wanted to make me happy."

"I'll bite, Bren. What more do you want?"

"You."

The brilliant smile that crossed his face made the last few weeks of hell all worthwhile. This time, when Jack reached for her, there was no hesitation at all as she walked into his arms. As he pulled her against him she felt the warmth of his body seep into hers, thawing the chill that had gripped her since he'd left. Finally her heart seemed to be beating at a normal rhythm again. *This* was right. She'd been crazy to fight it.

Then he kissed her, and her heartbeat was no longer normal at all.

"I love you, Jack. I always have."

Jack pressed his forehead to hers. "And I love you. Let's go home."

Home. The thought thrilled her and twinged her

heart at the same time. It must have shown on her face, because Jack pulled back and his brows knitted together in concern.

"What's wrong, Bren?"

She was not going to let anything ruin this moment. "Nothing." She raised up on her tiptoes to kiss him again, but Jack held her at arm's length.

"You might as well tell me now. Our brilliant lack of communication skills is what got us divorced last time. I don't want to go there again."

Again? Was Jack already thinking…? She paused that happy thought. He was right. "It's hard for me to consider a hotel home. No matter how nice it is," she qualified.

Jack nodded. "But Amante Verano isn't home for me, you know?"

She had no illusions. "I know. I'll just—"

"How do you feel about Bel Marin Keys?"

"Excuse me?"

He cocked his head. "Or Novato, maybe? That's not too crowded. You don't have to live directly on the property, do you?"

His meaning finally registered. "You'd leave San Francisco?"

Jack slid his hands up and down her arms. "We'll compromise, Bren. Find someplace between here and there to live."

"I can't believe you'd leave the city?"

"If I have to, to keep you happy, yes."

"You make me happy, Jack." She paused. "Even if you do annoy me sometimes."

He laughed. "You can annoy me whenever you want. I've felt half-dead without you around."

"Me, too." She tugged on his hand. "So let's go."

Jack resisted the tug. "One last thing. About the money I put in your account. I think we should come up with some kind of arrangement."

Business and personal life separate. *Right.* "I understand. How about—?"

He held up a hand to stop her. "Remember my first offer? The one I made that night by the hot tub?"

Ugh. "It's not my favorite memory, but, yes."

"I want to amend that offer. You can have Amante Verano—and whatever you need to get it back on its feet—but it will cost you more than just one night. Possibly a lifetime."

She should smack him, but instead she mirrored his cheeky grin. "Where do I sign?"

EPILOGUE

BRENNA winced as Jack's construction crew knocked down the wall of what used to be her kitchen. "Max would not be happy about this."

Jack put his arm around her shoulder and squeezed. "Max would be thrilled. Trust me on that. His two favorite things—hotels and wine—in one convenient location."

Jack was right, but it was still difficult to see her home gutted and rearranged. What *used* to be her home, she amended. She didn't live here anymore, hadn't lived here in almost two years. It was wrong to let the building continue to sit empty, but it still hurt to see that gaping hole.

He placed a finger under her chin and lifted her face to his. "You do know the building can't feel anything, right?"

She elbowed him in return, then pulled the collar of her jacket up around her neck as the March wind picked up. She looked around the patio, which looked as bad as the rest of the place. Power tools, saw-horses, bags of concrete and all the other debris of destruction and construction littered what had used to be her quiet, serene escape. At least the plants were still alive, but they looked odd, sitting around the drained hot tub and swimming pool. "It just feels weird."

"It's going to be very profitable, though. Dianne is already getting calls—she's booking out rooms and we're still six weeks from the Grand Opening."

"I know. She's giddy about it. I never dreamed she'd take the idea and run with it like this." Dianne had embraced Jack's idea to open up Amante Verano for wine seminars, using what had used to be Brenna's house as a bed-and-breakfast for people who wanted to learn more about the process of making wine than the usual hour-long tour provided. Before she knew it, her simple little vineyard had suddenly exploded into a full-on tourist destination.

And now that word was out that Garrett Properties was opening a boutique hotel on the vineyard property, everyone from wine aficionados to brides looking for a unique wedding venue was knocking down her doors.

Metaphorically, at least. The house currently didn't *have* any doors—unless she counted the ones leaning against the side of the building, waiting to be installed.

Brenna had taken to hiding in her lab or her office most of the time she was on the property these days, but she'd made the mistake of surfacing just in time to see this blow dealt to the house. The place looked like… "Will it actually be finished in six weeks?"

"It'll be finished in five." Jack winked at her. "By the way, that wine magazine you like so much is sending someone out to cover the Grand Opening reception."

"Interesting. Two years ago they wouldn't give me the time of day. They weren't interested in Brenna Walsh. Brenna Garrett is a different story, it seems."

"See? there are all kinds of perks to being a Garrett."

"Many," she agreed, rising up on her tiptoes to kiss him. Stepping back, she shaded her eyes from the sun and looked up at him. "What are you doing here today anyway? I thought you were going to Sacramento for a meeting."

Jack shrugged. "I didn't feel like it. I sent Martin instead."

"Tsk, tsk," she scolded. "Blowing off work like that…"

He was unrepentant. "It's just another one of the perks of being a Garrett. Anyway, I needed to come check on the progress here." He looked around and shrugged. "Seems to be moving along fine. I guess I'm done for the day."

Jack slid his fingers through hers and pulled her close again. "What say we go home early?"

She mentally ran down her to-do list. "Are you insane? Some of us don't have half a dozen minions on hand to run our businesses for us."

"Then hire some."

"You run your business and I'll run mine. You're a silent partner, remember?"

"Silent, but not mute."

"Mute would be delightful," Brenna grumbled.

"Ah, but then I couldn't tell you what I have planned

for this afternoon…" Pulling her close, he whispered ideas that had her toes curling and her heart pounding in anticipation.

"You are evil, Jack Garrett. It was your idea to start all this expansion and construction, and *now* you want me to play hooky?"

"I just want you, period." He shrugged. "Seriously, Bren, this place is getting too big for you to do everything. Even Dianne has a fleet of assistants now. You can't keep doing everything on your own. You're wearing yourself out. You're so tired lately."

It was the opening she needed. The one she'd been waiting for the last few days. Now seemed to be the right time. "You're right. I should hire some people. Including an assistant vintner or two."

Jack eyebrows flew up in surprise. "It's about damn time. I never thought I'd hear you say that."

She needed to sit for this conversation, but all her patio furniture was either stacked in the yard or being used to hold construction paraphernalia. She walked to the edge of the hot tub and sat, dangling her feet into the emptiness. "Yeah, well, I'm going to need the help soon enough. This year's crush is going to be a bit difficult for me."

Jack joined her, studying her face curiously. "Because…?" he prompted.

"Did Max ever give you the lecture on the three things he wanted most?"

Jack shook his head and looked at her questioningly.

"Number one was a five-star hotel in Manhattan."

He smiled smugly. "Done."

"Number two was a gold-medal wine."

"Done—thanks to you." He reached for her hand again and squeezed her fingers.

She nodded at the compliment, then took a deep breath. "Number three was a grandchild."

A small smile began to form on his face. "And...?"

"Well, he's going to get one of those, too."

Jack pulled her close, one hand against her back, the other splayed over her still-flat stomach. The small smile had grown into an all-out grin, and it told her how happy he was with her news. "See? I told you Max didn't like to be thwarted."

Huh? "When did you tell me that?"

"Right after Max died. We were out here, remember? In the hot tub."

It took a second, but the memory came. She snorted. "How could I forget that night? Among *other things* we won't mention—" she narrowed her eyes at him "—you called me a wine snob."

Jack laughed. "And you called me a jerk."

"I wasn't wrong," she countered.

"Neither was I—about that part, at least."

She feigned shock. "You're admitting you were wrong about something? That's a first."

Jack made a face at her. "You asked me what made me happy."

She'd almost forgotten. "Oh, yeah. You said something about cars and Scotch, or something ridiculous."

He nudged her arm with his elbow playfully. "Ask me again."

She'd bite. The twinkle in his eye was irresistible. "What makes you happy, Jack?"

He kissed her, sending a thrill through her, then smiled as he cupped her face.

"You."

UNFINISHED BUSINESS
WITH THE DUKE

BY
HEIDI RICE

Heidi Rice was born and bred and still lives in London. She has two boys who love to bicker, a wonderful husband who, luckily for everyone, has loads of patience, and a supportive and ever-growing British/French/Irish/American family. As much as Heidi adores "the Big Smoke", she also loves America, and every two years or so she and her best friend leave hubby and kids behind and *Thelma and Louise* it across the States for a couple of weeks (although they always leave out the driving off a cliff bit). She's been a film buff since her early teens, and a romance junkie for almost as long. She indulged her first love by being a film reviewer for ten years. Then, two years ago, she decided to spice up her life by writing romance. Discovering the fantastic sisterhood of romance writers (both published and unpublished) in Britain and America made it a wild and wonderful journey to her first Mills & Boon® novel, and she's looking forward to many more to come.

A special thanks to my Florentine specialists,
Steve and Biz,
to Katherine at the terrific Kings Head Theatre
in Islington, and Leonardo,
who answered my daft questions about architecture.

CHAPTER ONE

THE six-inch stiletto heels of Issy Helligan's thigh-high leather boots echoed like gunshots against the marble floor of the gentlemen's club. The sharp rhythmic cracks sounded like a firing squad doing target practice as she approached the closed door at the end of the corridor.

How appropriate.

She huffed and came to a stop. The gunshots cut off, but her stomach carried right on going, doing a loop-the-loop and then swaying like the pendulum of Big Ben. Recognising the symptoms of chronic stage fright, Issy pressed her palm to her midriff as she focussed on the elaborate brass plaque announcing the entrance to the 'East Wing Common Room'.

Calm down. You can do this. You're a theatrical professional with seven years' experience.

Detecting the muffled rumble of loud male laughter, she locked her knees as a thin trickle of sweat ran down her back beneath her second-hand Versace mac.

People are depending on you. People you care about. Getting ogled by a group of pompous old fossils is a small price to pay for keeping those people gainfully employed.

It was a mantra she'd been repeating for the past hour—to absolutely no avail.

After grappling with the knot on the mac's belt, she pulled the coat off and placed it on the upholstered chair beside the door. Then she looked down at her costume—and Big Ben's pendulum got stuck in her throat.

Blood-red satin squeezed her ample curves into an hourglass shape, making her cleavage look like a freak of nature. She took a shallow breath and the bustier's underwiring dug into her ribs.

She tugged the band out of her hair and let the mass of Pre-Raphaelite curls tumble over her bare shoulders as she counted to ten.

Fine, so the costume from last season's production of *The Rocky Horror Picture Show* wasn't exactly subtle, but she hadn't had a lot of options at such short notice—and the man who had booked her that morning hadn't wanted subtle.

'Tarty, darling. That's the look I'm after,' he'd stated in his cut-glass Etonian accent. 'Rodders is moving to Dubai and we plan to show him what he'll be missing. So don't stint on the T and A, sweetheart.'

It had been on the tip of Issy's tongue to tell him to buzz off and hire himself a stripper, but then he'd mentioned the astronomical sum he was prepared to pay if she 'put on a decent show'—and her tongue had gone numb.

After six months of scrimping and saving and struggling to find a sponsor, Issy was fast running out of ways to get the thirty grand she needed to keep the Crown and Feathers Theatre Pub open for another season. The Billet Doux Singergram Agency had been the jewel in the crown of her many fund-raising ideas. But so far they'd had a grand total of six bookings—and all of those had been from well-meaning friends. Having worked her way up from general dogsbody to general manager in the last seven years, she had everyone at the theatre looking to her to make sure the show went on.

Issy sighed, the weight of responsibility making her head hurt as the corset's whalebone panels constricted around her lungs. With the bank threatening to foreclose on the theatre's loan any minute, feminist principles were just another of the luxuries she could no longer afford.

When she'd taken the booking eight hours ago she'd been determined to see it as a golden opportunity. She'd do a tastefully suggestive rendition of 'Life Is a Cabaret', flash a modest amount of T and A and walk away with a nice healthy sum to add to the Crown and Feathers's survival kitty, plus the possibility of some serious word-of-mouth business. After all, this was one of the most exclusive gentlemen's clubs in the world, boasting princes, dukes and lords of the realm, not to mention Europe's richest and most powerful businessmen among its membership.

Really, it should be a doddle. She'd made it quite clear to her booker what a singing telegram did—and did not—entail. And Roderick Carstairs and his mates couldn't possibly be as tough an audience to crack as the twenty-two five-year-olds tripping on a sugar rush she'd sung 'Happy Birthday' to last week.

Or so she hoped.

But as Issy eased the heavy oak panelled door to the East Wing Common Room open, and heard the barrage of male hoots and guffaws coming from inside, that hope died a quick and painful death.

From the sound of it, her audience were primed and ready for her—and not nearly as old and fossilised as she'd assumed. The corset squeezed her ribcage as she stayed rooted in the doorway, shielded from view.

Putting on 'a decent show' didn't seem such a doddle any more.

She was staring blankly at the rows of bookcases lining the wall, mustering the courage to walk into the lions' den, when she caught a movement on the balcony opposite. Silhouetted by the dusky evening light, a tall figure strode into view, talking into his mobile phone. It was impossible to make out his features, but *déjà vu* had the hair on the back of Issy's neck standing to attention. Momentarily transfixed by the stranger's broad-shouldered build, and the forceful, predatory way he moved in the small space, Issy shivered, thinking of a tiger prowling a cage.

She jumped at the disembodied chorus of rowdy masculine cheers and dragged her gaze away.

Focus, Issy, focus.

She straightened her spine and took a step forward, but then her eyes darted to the balcony again. The stranger had stopped moving. Was he watching her?

She thought of the tiger again. And then memory blindsided her.

'Gio,' she whispered, as her breath clogged in her lungs and the corset constricted like a vice around her torso.

She gasped in a breath as heat seared up the back of her neck and made her scalp burn.

Ignore him.

She pulled her gaze away, mortified that the mere thought of Giovanni Hamilton still made all her erogenous zones do the happy dance and her heart squeeze painfully in her chest.

Don't be ridiculous.

That guy could not be Gio. She couldn't possibly be that unlucky. To come face to face with the biggest disaster of her life when she was about to waltz into another. Clearly stress was making her hallucinate.

Issy pushed her shoulders back and took as deep a breath as the corset's stays would allow.

Enough with the nervous breakdown, already. It's showtime.

Striding into the main body of the room, she launched into the sultry opening bars of Liza Minnelli's signature song. Only to come to a stumbling halt, her stomach lurching back into Big Ben mode, as she rounded the door and got an eyeful of Rodders and his mates. The mob of young, debauched and completely pie-eyed Hooray Henries lunged to their feet, jeers and wolf whistles echoing off the antique furnishings as the room erupted.

Issy's throat constricted in horror as she imagined Little Red Riding Hood being fed to a pack of sex-starved, booze-sodden wolves while singing a show tune in her underwear.

Suddenly a firing squad looked remarkably appealing.

Go ahead and shoot me now, fellas.

What in God's name was Issy Helligan doing working as a stripper?

Gio Hamilton stood in the shadows of the balcony, stunned into silence, his gaze fixed on the young woman who strutted into the room with the confidence of a courtesan. Her full figure moved in time with her long, leggy strides. Sequins glittered on an outfit that would make a hooker blush.

'Gio?' The heavily accented voice of his partnership manager crackled down the phone from Florence.

'*Si, Gio.*' He pressed the phone to his ear and tried to

get his mind to engage. 'I'll get back to you about the Venice project,' he said, slipping into English. 'You know how the Italian authorities love red tape—it's probably just a formality. *Ciao*.' He disconnected the call—and stared.

That couldn't be the sweet, impulsive and impossibly naïve girl he'd grown up with. Could it?

But then he noticed the pale freckled skin on her shoulder blades and he knew. Heat pulsed in his groin as he recalled Issy the last time he'd seen her—that same pale skin flushed pink by their recent lovemaking and those wild auburn curls cascading over bare shoulders.

The smoky, seductive notes of an old theatre song, barely audible above the hoots and jeers, yanked Gio out of the past and brought him slap-bang up to date. Issy's rich, velvety voice sent shivers rippling up his spine and arousal flared—before the song was drowned out by the chant of 'Get it off!' from Carstairs and his crowd.

Gio's contempt for the arrogant toff and his cronies turned to disgust as Issy's singing stopped and she froze. Suddenly she wasn't the inexperienced young temptress who'd seduced him one hot summer night, but the awkward girl who had trailed after him throughout his teenage years, her bright blue eyes glowing with adoration.

He stuffed his phone into his back pocket, anger and arousal and something else he didn't want to acknowledge coiling in his gut.

Then Carstairs lunged. Gio's fingers clenched into fists as the younger man grabbed Issy around the waist. Her head twisted to avoid the boozy kiss.

To hell with that.

The primitive urge to protect came from nowhere.

'Get your filthy hands off her, Carstairs.'

The shout echoed as eleven pairs of eyes turned his way.

Issy yelped as he strode towards her, those exotic turquoise eyes going wide with astonishment and then blank with shock.

Carstairs raised his head, his ruddy face glazed with champagne and confusion. 'Who the…?'

Gio slammed an upper-cut straight into the idiot's jaw. Pain ricocheted up his arm.

'Ow! Dammit,' he breathed, cradling his throbbing knuckles as he watched Carstairs crumple onto the carpet.

Hearing Issy's sharp gasp, he looked round to see her eyes roll back. He caught her as she flopped, and scooped her into his arms. Carrying her against his chest, he tuned out the shouts and taunts coming from Carstairs's friends. Not one of them was sober enough—or had enough gumption—to cause him a problem.

'Kick this piece of rubbish out of here when he comes to,' Gio said to the elderly attendant who had scurried in from his post in the billiards room next door.

The old guy bobbed his head. 'Yes, Your Grace. Will the lady be all right?'

'She'll be fine. Once you've dealt with Carstairs, have some ice water and brandy sent to my suite.'

He drew a deep breath as he strolled down the corridor towards the lifts, caught the rose scent of Issy's shampoo and realised it wasn't only his knuckles throbbing.

He gave the attendant a stiff nod as he walked into the lift, with Issy still out cold in his arms. She stirred slightly and he got his first good look at her face in the fluorescent light.

He could see the tantalising sprinkle of freckles on her nose. And the slight overbite which gave her lips an irresistible pout. Despite the heavy stage make-up and the glossy coating of letterbox-red lipstick, her heart-shaped face still had the tantalising combination of innocence and sensuality that had caused him so many sleepless nights a lifetime ago.

Gio's gaze strayed to the swell of her cleavage, barely confined by dark red satin. The antique lift shuddered to a stop at his floor, and his groin began to throb in earnest.

He adjusted her dead weight, flexing his shoulder muscles as he headed down the corridor to the suite of rooms he kept at the club.

Even at seventeen Issy Helligan had been a force of nature. As impossible to ignore as she was to control. He was a man who loved taking risks, but Issy had still been able to shock the hell out of him.

From the looks of things that hadn't changed.

He shoved opened the door to his suite, and walked through into the bedroom. Placing his cargo on the bed, he stepped back and stared at her barely clad body in the half-light.

So what did he do with her now?

He hadn't a clue where the urge to ride to her rescue had come from. But giving Carstairs a right jab and knocking the drunken idiot out cold was where any lingering sense of responsibility both started and stopped. He was nobody's knight in shining armour.

He frowned, his irritation rising right alongside his arousal as he watched her shallow breathing.

What was that thing made of? Armour-plating? No

wonder she'd fainted. It looked as if she was struggling to take a decent breath.

Cursing softly, he perched on the edge of the bed and tugged the bow at her cleavage. Issy gave a soft moan as the satin knot slipped. He loosened the laces, his eyes riveted to the plump flesh of her breasts as the corset expanded.

She was even more exquisite than he remembered.

The pain in his crotch increased, but he resisted the urge to loosen the contraption further and expose her to his gaze. Then he spotted the red marks on her pale skin where the panels had dug into tender flesh.

'For heaven's sake, Issy,' he whispered as he smoothed his thumb over the bruising.

What had she been thinking, wearing this outfit in the first place? And then prancing around in front of a drunken fool like Carstairs?

Issy Helligan had always needed a keeper. He'd have to give her a good talking-to when she came round.

He stood and walked to the window. After flinging open the velvet drapes, he sat in the gilt chair beside the bed. This shouldn't be too hard to sort out.

The reason for her disastrous charade downstairs had to be something to do with money. Issy had always been headstrong and foolhardy, but she'd never been promiscuous. So he'd offer her an injection of capital when she woke up.

She'd never have to do anything this reckless again— and he'd be free to forget about her.

His gaze drifted to the tantalising glimpse of one rosy nipple peeking over the satin rim of the corset.

And if she knew what was good for her, she'd damn well take the money.

Issy's eyelids fluttered as she inhaled the fresh scent of clean linen.

'Hello again, Isadora.' The low, masculine voice rumbled across her consciousness and made her insides feel deliciously warm and fuzzy.

She took a deep breath and sighed. Hallelujah. She could breathe. The relief was intoxicating.

'Mmm? What?' she purred. She felt as if she were floating on a cloud. A light, fluffy cloud made of delicious pink candyfloss.

'I loosened your torture equipment. No wonder you fainted. You could barely breathe.'

It was the gorgeous voice again, crisp British vowels underlaid with a lazy hint of the Mediterranean—and a definite hint of censure. Issy frowned. Didn't she know that voice?

Her eyes opened, and she stared at an elaborate plaster moulding on the ceiling. Swivelling her head, she saw a man by her bedside. Her first thought was that he looked far too masculine for the fancy gilt chair. But then she focussed on his face, and the bolt of recognition hit her, knocking her off the candyfloss cloud and shoving her head first into sticky reality.

She snapped her eyelids shut, threw one arm over her face and sank back down into the pillows. 'Go away. You're a hallucination,' she groaned. But it was too late.

Even the brief glimpse had seared the image of his harsh, handsome features onto her retinas and made her heartbeat hit panic mode. The sculpted cheekbones, the square jaw with a small dent in the chin, the wavy chest-nut hair pushed back from dark brows and those thickly-lashed chocolate eyes more tempting than original sin. Pain lanced into her chest as she recalled how those eyes had looked the last time she'd seen them, shadowed with annoyance and regret.

Then everything else came flooding back. And Issy groaned louder.

Carstairs's sweaty hands gripping her waist, the rank whiff of whisky and cigars on his breath, the pulse of fear replaced by shock as Carstairs's head snapped back and Gio loomed over her. Then the deafening buzzing in her ears before she'd done her 'Perils of Pauline' act.

No way. This could not be happening. Gio had to be a hallucination.

'Leave me alone and let me die in peace,' she moaned.

She heard a husky chuckle and grimaced. Had she said that out loud?

'Once a drama queen, always a drama queen, I see, Isadora?'

She dropped her arm and stared at her tormentor. Taking in the tanned biceps stretching the sleeves of his black polo shirt and the teasing glint in his eyes, she resigned herself to the fact this was no hallucination. The few strands of silver at his temples and the crinkles around the corners of his eyes hadn't been there ten years ago, but at thirty-one Giovanni Hamilton was as devastatingly gorgeous as he had been at twenty-one—and twice as much of a hunk.

Why couldn't he have got fat, bald and ugly? It was the least he deserved.

'Don't call me Isadora. I hate that name,' she said, not caring if she sounded snotty.

'Really?' One eyebrow rose in mocking enquiry as his lips quirked. 'Since when?'

Since you walked away.

She quashed the sentimental thought. To think she'd once adored it when he'd called her by her given name. Had often basked for days in the proof that he'd noticed her.

How pitiful.

Luckily she wasn't that needy, eager-to-please teenager any more.

'Since I grew up and decided it didn't suit me,' she said, pretending not to notice the warm liquid sensation turning her insides to mush as he smiled at her.

The eyebrow rose another notch and the sexy grin widened as he lounged in his chair. He didn't look the least bit wounded by her rebuff.

His gaze dipped to her cleavage. 'I can see how grown up you are. It's kind of hard to miss.'

Heat sizzled at the suggestive tone. She bolted upright, aware of how much flesh she had on display as the bustier drooped. She drew her knees up and wrapped her arms around her shins as the brutal blush fanned out across her chest.

'I was on a job,' she said defensively, annoyed that the costume felt more revealing now than it had in front of Carstairs and all his mates.

'A job? Is that what you call it?' Gio commented dryly. 'What sort of *job* requires you to get assaulted by an idiot like Carstairs?' His eyes narrowed. 'What exactly do you think would have happened if I hadn't been there?'

She heard the sanctimonious note of disapproval—
and the injustice of the accusation made her want to
scream.

In hindsight, she should never have accepted the
booking. And maybe it had been a mistake to walk into
that room once she'd known how plastered her audience
was. But she'd been under so much pressure for months
now. Her livelihood and the livelihood of people she
loved was at stake.

So she'd taken a chance. A stupid, desperate, foolish
chance that had backfired spectacularly. But she wasn't
going to regret it. And she certainly wasn't going to be
criticised for it by someone who had never cared about
anyone in his entire life but himself.

'Don't you *dare* imply I'm to blame for Carstairs's
appalling behaviour,' she said, fury making the words
louder than she'd intended.

Surprise flickered in Gio's eyes.

Good.

It was about time he realised she wasn't the simpering little groupie she'd once been.

'The man was blind drunk and a lech,' she continued,
shuffling over to the other side of the bed and swinging
her legs to the floor. 'Nobody asked you to get involved.'
She stood and faced him. 'You did that all on your own.
I would have been perfectly fine if you hadn't been
there.'

Probably.

She marched across the lavishly furnished bedroom—
keeping a death grip on the sagging costume. What she
wouldn't give right now to be wearing her favourite jeans
and a T-shirt. Somehow her speech didn't have as much

impact while she was dressed like an escapee from the Moulin Rouge.

'Where do you think you're going?' he said, his voice dangerously low.

'I'm leaving,' she replied, reaching for the doorknob.

But as she yanked the door, all set to make a grand exit, a large, tanned hand slapped against the wood above her head and slammed it shut.

'No, you're not,' he said.

She whipped round and immediately realised her mistake. Her breath caught as her bare shoulders butted the door. He stood so close she could see the flecks of gold in his irises, taste the spicy scent of his aftershave, and feel the heat of his body inches from hers.

She clasped her arms over her chest as her nipples puckered, awareness making every one of her pulse-points pound.

'What?' she snapped, cornered. The last time she'd been this close to Gio she'd been losing her virginity to him.

'There's no need to go storming off.' The rock-hard bicep next to her ear tensed before his arm dropped to his side. Her breath released in an audible puff as he eased back.

'You misunderstood me,' he said, heaving an impatient sigh.

'About what, exactly?' She tilted her head, thrust her chin out.

How infuriating.

At five foot six, and with six-inch heels on, she ought to be able to look him in the eye. No such luck. Gio had always been tall—tall and lanky—but when had he got so…solid?

She tried to look bored. No easy feat, given her limited acting skills and the fact that her heart felt as if it were being ripped out of her chest all over again. She pushed the memory back, locking it back in the box marked 'Biggest Mistake of your Life', while his gaze roamed over her, the chocolate-brown giving nothing away. To think she'd once believed that bleak expression was enigmatic, when all it had ever been was proof Gio had no soul.

'Carstairs deserved everything he got, and I enjoyed giving it to him,' he said coldly, shoving a fist into the pocket of his trousers. 'I'm not blaming you. I'm blaming the situation.' His eyes met hers and she saw something that stunned her for a second. Was that concern?

'If you needed money you should have come to me,' he said with dictatorial authority, and she knew she'd made a stupid mistake. That wasn't concern. It was contempt.

'There was no need for you to become a stripper,' he remarked.

Her heart stopped and the blush blazed like wildfire.
Did he just say stripper?

He cupped her cheek. The unexpected contact had her outraged reply getting stuck in her throat.

'I know things ended badly between us, but we were friends once. I can help you.' His thumb skimmed across her cheek with the lightest of touches. 'And, whatever happens, you're finding another job.' The patronising tone did nothing to diminish the arousal darkening his eyes. 'Because, quite apart from anything else, you're a terrible stripper.'

CHAPTER TWO

Issy wasn't often rendered speechless. As a rule she liked to talk. And she was never shy about voicing her opinion. But right now she couldn't utter a single syllable, because she was far too busy trying to figure out what outraged her the most.

That Gio thought she was a stripper. That he thought she was terrible. That he actually thought it was any of his business. Or that he should have the audacity to claim he had been her friend...

'We're not friends,' she spluttered. 'Not any more. I got over that delusion a long time ago. Remember?'

His hand stroked her nape, making it hard for her to concentrate. 'Perhaps friendship's not the right word.' His eyes met hers, and what she saw made her gasp. His pupils had dilated, the chocolate-brown now black with desire. He was turned on. Seriously turned on. But what shocked her more was the vicious throb of arousal in her own abdomen.

'How about we kiss and make up?' he said, purpose and demand clear in the husky voice.

Before she could respond he brushed his lips across hers, then dipped his head and kissed the swell of her left breast. Raw desire assailed her, paralysing her tongue as he nipped at the sensitive flesh. Her breath gushed out and her head bumped against the door, shock and panic obliterated by the swift jolt of molten heat.

Stop him. Stop this.

The words crashed through her mind. But the only thing that registered was the brutal yearning to feel his mouth on her breast. She could still remember the way his insistent lips had once ignited her senses. Her arms relaxed their death grip on the corset, and the ripe peak spilled out.

She sobbed as he circled the rigid nipple with his tongue, then captured it between his lips and suckled strongly. Vivid memory and raw new sensation tangled as she arched into his mouth. Her thigh muscles clutched and released as she surrendered. He pushed the sagging bodice down, cupped her other breast. She moaned as he tugged at the swelling peak.

The firestorm of need twisted and built. Dazed, she clasped his head, gripping the silky waves—and felt the sharp knock on the door rap against her back.

Her eyes popped open as he raised his head.

'Hell, ten years isn't enough,' he murmured, the sinful chocolate gaze hot with lust and knowledge.

She scrambled away, shame shattering the sensual spell. Drawing in a ragged breath, she grasped the sagging corset, covered herself, wincing as the cool satin touched tender flesh.

The knock sounded again, and panic skittered up her spine.

What had just happened? What had she let happen? How could he still have this effect on her?

'Excuse me, Your Grace.' The tentative voice, muffled by the door, broke the charged silence. 'Would you like me to leave the tray here?'

'Just a minute,' Gio shouted, his eyes fixed on hers. 'Stand over there,' he murmured, nodding to a space behind the door that would keep her out of sight.

She bristled at the note of command, but stepped back. She had to get out of here. Before this got any worse.

'I have your brandy and iced water, Your Grace,' the footman announced as Gio swung open the door. 'And the lady's coat. It was on the hall chair downstairs.'

'Great,' Gio said curtly as he took the coat from unseen hands. Glancing her way, he passed it to her.

She stuffed her arms into the sleeves. Hastily tying the corset laces, she belted the mac as she watched Gio hand over a large tip and take the tray from the invisible footman.

He scowled as he pushed the door shut. 'Let's talk,' he said, sliding the tray onto the table beside the door.

'No, let's not,' she said, pleased that she'd stopped shaking long enough to cover some of her modesty.

She stepped forward and gripped the door handle, but she had wrestled it open less than an inch before his hand slapped against the wood, holding it closed.

'Stop behaving like a child. Surely after ten years you're over that night?'

She flinched at the impatient words. Then straightened, his casual reference to the worse night of her life forcing her pride to finally put in an appearance. Better late than never.

'Of course I'm over it,' she said emphatically, ignoring the ache under her breastbone. 'I'm not a child any more. Or an imbecile.'

She'd rather suffer the tortures of hell than admit

she'd cried herself to sleep for over a month after he'd gone. And lived with that pointless spurt of hope every time the phone rang for much longer. It was pathetic. And all completely academic now.

She might still have a problem controlling her body's reaction to him. But thankfully her heart was safe. She wasn't that overly romantic child any more—who'd believed infatuation was love.

But that didn't mean she was going to forgive him.

'I may have been young and foolish.' She tried not to cringe at the memory of *how* young and foolish. 'But luckily I happen to be a fast learner.'

Fast enough to know she would never fall that easily again. And especially not for a man like Gio, who didn't understand love and had no idea what it was worth.

'What's the problem, then?' He shrugged, as if that night had never happened. 'There's still a powerful attraction between us.' His eyes lowered to her lips. 'The way you just responded to me is proof of that. So why get upset because we acted on it?'

'I'm not upset!' she shouted. She paused, lowered her voice. 'To get upset, I'd actually have to give a damn.'

She turned to make her getaway again, but his hand slammed back against the door.

'Will you stop doing that?' she said, exasperated.

'You're not leaving until we sort out your situation,' he said, with infuriating patience.

'What situation?'

'You know very well what situation.'

His mouth had flattened into a grim line. What on earth was he on about?

'In case you haven't noticed, Your Dukeship, this is a free country. You can't hold me here against my will.'

'Nothing's free—and you know it.' His eyes raked over her outfit. 'Let me spell it out. I'm here in the UK having Hamilton Hall renovated, which means I can transfer the money you need by the end of today.'

What?

Her tongue went numb. Good God, he'd rendered her speechless again.

'And don't tell me you *like* working as a stripper,' he continued, clearly oblivious to her rising outrage, 'because I saw how petrified you were when Carstairs put his paws on you. My guess is this was your first job. And I intend to ensure it's also your last.'

'I'm not a stripper,' she all but choked. Of all the arrogant, patronising, overbearing… 'And even if I were, I would never be desperate enough to ask *you* for help.'

She'd always stood on her own two feet, had worked hard for her independence and was proud of what she'd achieved—even if it *was* all about to belong to the bank.

'If you're not a stripper,' he said, scepticism sharpening his voice, 'then what on earth were you doing downstairs?'

'I was delivering a singing telegram.'

His brow furrowed. 'A what?'

'Never mind.' She waved the question away. Why was she explaining herself to him? 'The point is, I don't need your help.'

'Stop being stupid.' He gripped her arm as she tried to turn. 'Whatever you were doing, it's obvious you must be desperate. I'm offering you a way out here. No strings attached. You'd be a fool not to take it.'

She tried to wrestle free, glaring at him when his fingers only tightened. 'I'd be an even bigger fool to take anything from you.' Anger and humiliation churned, bringing back the feeling of defeat and inadequacy that had dogged her for years after he'd walked away. And she hit back without thinking. 'Haven't you figured it out yet, Gio?' she said, hating the bitterness and negativity in her voice. 'I'd rather do twenty stripteases for Carstairs and his whole entourage than accept a penny from you. I happen to have a few principles, and I would never take money from someone I detest.'

His fingers released as the words struck home.

She fumbled with the door and darted out of the room, determined not to care about the shock on his face.

'Your body may be all grown up, Isadora.' The deep voice taunted her as her booted heels clicked on the polished parquet. 'What a shame the rest of you still has a way to go.'

She squared her shoulders as the door slammed at her back, and plunged her fists into the pockets of the mac, battling the blush burning her scalp. As she rushed down the hallway she played her parting shot over in her mind.

If only she *did* detest him.

Unfortunately, where Gio was concerned, nothing was ever that simple.

Gio strode into the living room of the suite and dumped the tray on the coffee table. Sitting on the fussy Queen Anne chaise-longue, he kicked off his shoes, propped his feet on the equally fussy antique table, and for the first time in years fervently wished for a cigarette.

Reaching for the generous glass of vintage cognac, he chugged it down in one punishing swallow. The burn in his throat did nothing to alleviate the pain in his groin, or the frustration making his head start to throb.

Issy Helligan was a walking disaster area.

He stared at the thick ridge in his trousers.

If that didn't go down in a minute he'd be forced to take a cold shower. Dropping his head against the sofa's backrest, he gazed at the ceiling. When had he last been stuck with an erection this persistent?

The vivid memory of Issy, her lithe young body moulded to his as he rode his motorcycle through the leafy country lanes to the Hall, instantly sprang to mind. And the blood pounded even harder.

Unbelievable. He could still recall every detail of that twenty-minute trip. As if it had happened ten seconds ago instead of ten years. Her full breasts flattening against his back, her thighs hugging his backside, her arms clinging to his waist—and the earlier shock to his system when she'd first strolled out of the school gates and climbed aboard the reconditioned Harley.

He'd expected to see the plump, cute tomboy he remembered—not a statuesque young woman with the face and figure of a goddess.

At twenty-one, he had been far more experienced than most men his age, and lusting after a girl of seventeen—a girl who had once been his only friend—had seemed wrong. But he hadn't been able to control his reaction to her then any more than he had today.

He cursed. If it hadn't been for the footman's well-timed interruption five minutes ago things would have gone a great deal further.

The second his lips had tasted her warm, fragrant flesh, and he'd heard her breath catch and felt her shudder of response, instinct had taken over—as it always did with Issy. His mouth had closed over her breast and he'd revelled in the feel of her nipple swelling and hardening under his tongue.

He blew out a breath and adjusted his trousers.

But Issy had changed. She wasn't the sweet, passionate teenager who had once adored him, but a vibrant, self-aware and stunningly beautiful young woman—who detested him.

Gio placed the brandy glass back on the tray, frustrated by the strange little jolt in his chest. He pressed the heel of his hand against his breastbone. He didn't care what she thought of him. Why should he?

Women tended to overreact about this stuff. Look at most of the women he'd dated.

He always made it crystal-clear he was only interested in recreational sex and lively companionship but they never believed him. And recently the triple whammy of career success, reaching his thirties and inheriting a dukedom had only made them harder to convince.

Angry words had never bothered him before when the inevitable breakup occurred. So why had Issy's?

Gio frowned and pushed the hair off his brow.

Why was he even surprised by his odd reaction? Nothing made sense where Issy was concerned, for the simple reason that he stopped thinking altogether whenever she was around. He was probably lucky the sudden rush of blood from his head hadn't left him with permanent brain damage.

Gio brought his feet off the table and rested his elbows on his knees. He poured himself a glass of the iced water and gulped it down. Much more concerning was his idiot behaviour this afternoon.

He'd decided at an early age never to be controlled

by his lust or his emotions—yet he'd been controlled by both as soon as he'd spotted Issy downstairs.

But then, this wasn't the first time Issy had torpedoed his self-control.

Images swirled of Issy at seventeen, her eyes brimming with adulation, her beautiful body gilded by moonlight, the scent of fresh earth and young lust in the air.

She'd caught him in a moment of weakness ten years ago, but he still didn't understand why he'd given in to her innocent attempts to seduce him. The way things had ended had been messy and unnecessary—and he had to take the lion's share of the blame.

He rolled the chilled glass across his forehead. Damn Issy Helligan. At seventeen she had been irresistible. How could she be even more so now?

Standing, he crossed to the window and peered out at the tourists and office workers jostling for space on the pavement below.

Why was he even worrying about this? He would never see Issy again. He'd offered her money, and she'd declined. End of story.

But then his gaze caught on a familiar shock of red curls weaving through the crowd. With her raincoat barely covering her bottom, and those ludicrous boots riding halfway up her thighs, she stood out like a beacon.

As he studied her, striding away disguised as a high-class hooker, a picture formed of Issy ten years ago, with the vivid blue of her eyes shining with innocence and hope and a terminal case of hero-worship. He heard the echo of her voice, telling him she would love him forever.

And the jolt punched him in the chest again.

* * *

'Iss, I've got dreadful news.'

Issy glanced over as her admin assistant Maxi put down the phone, peering over the teetering pile of papers on her desk. Maxi's small pixie-like face had gone chalk white.

'What is it?' Issy asked, her heart sinking. Had one of the company broken a leg or something equally catastrophic? Maxi was exceptionally calm and steady. Panicking was Issy's forte.

Issy steeled herself for very bad news. But, really, how much worse could it get?

After her aborted singergram a week ago, the singing telegram business had dried up completely. The three grants they'd applied for had been awarded elsewhere, and all her sponsorship requests had come back negative. She'd spent the week frantically cold-calling a new list of potential but even less likely donors, while also arranging the schedule for a season of plays that would probably never go into production. And the boiler had sprung another leak. Not a problem in the height of summer, but come autumn it would be another major expenditure they couldn't afford. Assuming they still had a theatre to heat.

'That was the bank manager,' Maxi muttered.

Issy's heart sank to her toes. Okay, that was worse.

'He's demanding payment of the interest in ten working days. If we don't find the thirty thousand to cover the payments we've missed, he's calling in the bailiffs.'

'What the—?' Issy shouted.

Seeing Maxi flinch, she held on to the swear word

that wanted to fly out of her mouth and deafen the whole of Islington.

'That toerag,' she sneered. 'But we *paid* something. Not the full amount, I know, but something.' Her fingers clenched so tightly on her pen she felt as if she were fighting off rigor mortis. 'He can't do that.'

'Apparently he can,' Maxi replied, her voice despondent. 'Our last payment was so low it amounts to defaulting on the loan. Technically.' She huffed. 'Toerag is right.'

'Remind me not to send Mr Toerag any more complimentary tickets,' Issy replied, trying to put some of her usual spirit into the put-down. But her heart wasn't in it, her anger having deflated like a burst party balloon.

This wasn't the banker manager's fault. Not really. The theatre had been skirting the edge of a precipice for months; all he'd done was give it the final nudge into the abyss.

Issy crossed to the office's single dust-covered window and stared at the back alley below, which looked even grottier than usual this morning.

Maybe a broken leg wouldn't have been so bad. Three weeks laid up in bed on a morphine drip with excruciating pain shooting through her entire body couldn't make her feel any worse than she did at this moment.

She'd failed. Utterly and completely. How was she going to break the news to everyone? To Dave their principal director, to Terri and Steve and the rest of their regular crew of actors and technicians, not to mention all the ushers and front-of-house staff? They'd worked so hard over the years, many of them offering their time and talent for free, to make this place work, to make it a success.

They'd have to stop all the outreach projects too, with the local schools and the church youth group, and the pensioners' drop-in centre.

She pressed her teeth into her bottom lip to stop it trembling.

'Is this finally it, then?'

Issy turned at the murmured question to see a suspicious sheen in her assistant's eyes.

'Are we going to have to tell Dave and the troops?' Maxi asked carefully. 'They'll be devastated. They've worked so hard. We all have.'

'No. Not yet.' Issy scrubbed her hands down her face, forced the lump back down her throat.

Stop being such a wimp.

The Crown and Feathers Theatre wasn't going dark. Not on her watch. Not until the fat lady was singing. And until Issy Helligan admitted defeat the fat lady could keep her big mouth shut.

'Let's keep it quiet for a bit longer.' No point in telling anyone how bad things were until she absolutely had to. Which would be when the bailiffs arrived and started carting away crucial parts of the stage. 'There must be some avenue we haven't explored yet.'

Think, woman, think.

They had two whole weeks. There had to be something they could do.

'I can't think of any,' Maxi said. 'We've both been racking our brains for months over this. If there's an avenue we haven't tried, it's probably a dead end.' Maxi gave a hollow laugh. 'I even had a dream last night about us begging Prince Charles to become our patron.'

'What did he say?' Issy asked absently, eager to be distracted. Her head was starting to hurt.

'I woke up before he gave me an answer,' Maxi said dejectedly, giving a heartfelt sigh. 'If only we knew someone who was loaded and had a passion for the dramatic arts. All our problems would be over.'

Issy swallowed heavily, Maxi's words reminding her of someone she'd been trying extra hard to forget in the past seven days.

Not that. Anything but that.

She sat back down in her chair with an audible plop.

'What's the matter?' Maxi asked, sounding concerned. 'You've gone white as a sheet.'

'I do know someone. He's a duke.'

'A duke!' Maxi bounced up. 'You're friends with a duke, and we haven't approached him for sponsorship yet?' She waved the comment away as she rushed to Issy's desk, her eyes bright with newfound hope. 'Does he have a passion for theatre?'

'Not that I know of.' And they weren't exactly friends either.

Heat rose up her neck and her nipples pebbled painfully as the memory she'd been trying to suppress for a week burst back to life.

No, they definitely weren't friends.

'But he is loaded,' she added, not wanting to extinguish the excitement in Maxi's gaze.

Or she assumed Gio was loaded. She had absolutely no idea what he did for a living, or even if he did anything. But he was a duke. And he kept a room at the swanky gentlemen's club. And hadn't he said something about renovating Hamilton Hall? Surely it made sense to assume he must be loaded?

Issy crossed her arms over her chest as her breasts began to throb. Something they'd been doing on a regular basis for days, every time she thought about Gio and his hot, insistent lips… She shook her head. Those thoughts had been coming a lot thicker and faster than she wanted to admit. And not just those thoughts, but other ones—which involved his lips and tongue and teeth and hands on the whole of her naked body, driving her to untold…

Issy squeezed her pulsating breasts harder as all her nerve endings started to tingle.

'When are you going to see him again? Can you contact him today?'

She tensed at Maxi's eager question.

'What's wrong?' Maxi asked, the light leaving her eyes. 'You don't look all that enthusiastic.'

'It's a long shot, Max. At best.'

More than a long shot, if she were being totally honest. She'd told Gio she detested him, for goodness' sake. Like a spoilt child. And, while it had given her some satisfaction at the time, and she doubted he cared *what* she thought of him, it wasn't going to make begging him for money any easier.

Maxi cocked her head to one side, looking concerned. 'Exactly how well do you know this duke? Because you've gone bright red…'

'Well enough.' Maybe too well.

She needed a strategy before she saw Gio again. A foolproof strategy. If she was going to have any hope of winning a stay of execution for the theatre—and keeping even a small part of her dignity intact.

Issy felt as if she'd travelled back in time as she stepped off the train at the tiny Hampshire station of Hamilton's

Cross and walked down the platform. It was a journey she'd done dozens of times during her childhood and adolescence when her widowed mother Edie had been housekeeper at the Hall.

Seeing her reflection in the glass door of the ticket office—which never seemed to be open then and wasn't now—Issy congratulated herself on how much her appearance had changed from that dumpy schoolgirl with the fire-engine red hair. The chic emerald silk dress with matching pumps, accented with her favourite chunky necklace and designer sunglasses, looked a good deal more sophisticated than the ill-fitting school uniform, for starters. Teased into a waterfall of corkscrew curls instead of the unruly fuzzball of her childhood, even her vivid red hair now looked more Rita Hayworth than Little Orphan Annie.

The thought gave her a confidence boost as she headed for the newspaper booth which doubled as a mini-cab office. A boost she desperately needed after spending half the night struggling to figure out a workable strategy for her meeting with Gio.

If only she hadn't told him she detested him!

Unfortunately the strategy she'd settled on—to be businesslike and efficient and not lose her cool—seemed disappointingly vague and far from foolproof as zero hour approached.

She tucked the stray curls behind her ear and gripped the shoulder strap on her satchel-style briefcase. Full of paperwork about the theatre—including details of the loans, financial projections, the stunning reviews from their summer season and her plans for next season—the briefcase put the finishing touch on her smart, savvy career-woman act.

Not that it was an act, *per se*, she corrected. She *was* smart and savvy and a career woman—of sorts. Unfortunately she was also a nervous wreck—after a sleepless night spent contemplating all the things that could go wrong today.

Having discarded the idea of informing Gio of her visit beforehand—fairly certain he would refuse to see her—she had surprise on her side. But from what she'd learned about Gio after scouring the internet for information, surprise was about all she had.

The startling revelation that Gio was now a world-renowned architect, with a reputation for striking and innovative designs and a practice which was one of the most sought-after in Europe, hadn't helped with her nervous breakdown one bit.

Okay, Gio was definitely rich. That had to be a plus, given the reason why she was here. But the discovery that the wild, reckless boy she had idolised had made such a staggering success of his life had brought with it a strange poignancy which didn't bode well for their meeting.

And that was without factoring in the way her body had responded to him a week ago. Which, try as she might, she still hadn't been able to forget.

She was here for one reason and one reason only, and she was not going to lose sight of that fact. No matter what. Or the theatre's last hope would be dashed for good.

She had to stick to her plan. She would promote the theatre and do her absolute utmost to persuade Gio that investing in a sponsorship would give his company added profile in the British marketplace. If all else failed she'd remind him that he had offered her financial help. But under no circumstances would she let their history—or her hormones—sway her from her goal. No matter what the provocation—or the temptation.

'Good Lord, is that you, Issy Helligan? Haven't you grown up!'

Issy beamed a smile at the short, balding man sitting in the mini-cab cubicle. 'Frank, you're still here!' she said, delighted to see a familiar face.

'That I am,' the elderly man said bashfully, as his bald patch went a mottled red. 'How's your mother these days? Still living in Cornwall?'

'That's right, she loves it there,' Issy replied, grateful for the distraction.

'Awful shame about the Duke's passing last summer,' Frank continued, his smile dying. 'Son's back you know. Doing up the Hall. Although he never saw fit to come to the funeral. 'Spect your mother told you that?'

Edie hadn't, because her mother knew better than to talk to her about Gio after that fateful summer.

But the news that Gio hadn't bothered to attend his own father's funeral didn't surprise Issy. He and his father had always had a miserably dysfunctional relationship, evidenced by the heated arguments and chilly silences she and her mother had witnessed during the summers Gio spent at the Hall.

She'd once romanticised Gio's troubled teenage years, casting him as a misunderstood bad boy, torn between two parents who hated each other's guts and used their only child as a battering ram. She'd stopped romanticising Gio's behaviour a decade ago. And she had no desire to remember that surly, unhappy boy now.

It might make her underestimate the man he had become.

'Actually, I don't suppose you know whether Gio's at the Hall today? I came to pay him a visit.'

According to the articles she'd read, Gio lived in Italy, but his office in Florence had told her he was in England. So she'd taken a chance he might be at the Hall.

'Oh, aye—yes, he's here,' said Frank, making Issy's pulse skitter. 'Came in yesterday evening by helicopter, no less—or so Milly at the post office says. I took the council planners over to the Hall for a meeting an hour ago.'

'Could I get a lift too?' she said quickly, before she lost her nerve.

Frank grinned and grabbed his car keys. 'That's what I'm here for.'

He bolted the booth and directed her to the battered taxi-cab parked out front.

'I'll put your journey out on the house, for old times' sake,' he said cheerfully as he opened the door.

Issy tensed as she settled in the back seat.

No way was she going to think about old times. Especially her old times with Gio.

She snapped the seat belt on, determined to wipe every last one of those memories from her consciousness.

But as the car accelerated away from the kerb, and the familiar hedgerows and grass verges sped past on the twenty-minute drive to the Hall, the old times came flooding back regardless.

CHAPTER THREE

Ten Years Earlier

'I CAN'T believe you're really going to do it tonight. What if your mum finds out?'

'Shh, Melly,' Issy hissed as she craned her neck to check on the younger girls sitting at the front of the school bus. 'Keep your voice down.'

As upper sixth-formers, they had the coveted back seat all to themselves, but she didn't want anyone overhearing the conversation. Especially as she didn't even want to be *having* this conversation.

When she'd told her best friend about her secret plan to loose her virginity to Giovanni Hamilton two years before, it had been thrilling and exciting. A forbidden topic they could discuss for hours on the long, boring bus ride home every day. And it had had about as much chance of actually happening as Melanie's equally thrilling and exciting and endlessly discussed plan to lose her virginity to Gary Barlow from *Take That*.

Gio had been completely unattainable back then. When she'd been fifteen and he'd been nineteen the four years between them had seemed like an eternity.

But it hadn't always been that way.

When Issy and her mother had first come to live at the Hall, and Gio had appeared that first summer, the two of them had become fast friends and partners in crime. To a nine-year-old tomboy who was used to spending hours on her own in the Hall's grounds, Gio had been a godsend. A moody, intense thirteen-year-old boy with brown eyes so beautiful they'd made her heart skip, a fascinating command of swear words in both English and Italian, and a quick, creative mind with a talent for thinking up forbidden adventures, Gio had been more captivating than a character from one of Issy's adventure books.

Best of all, Gio had needed her as much as she'd needed him. Issy had seen the sadness in his eyes when his father shouted at him—which seemed to be all the time—and it had made her stomach hurt. But she'd discovered that if she chatted to him, if she made him laugh, she could take the sad look away.

At fifteen, though, when she'd first formulated her plan to lose her virginity to him, her childhood friendship with Gio had slipped into awkward adolescent yearning.

She'd been gawky and spotty, with a figure her mum had insisted on calling 'womanly' but Issy thought was just plain fat, while Gio had been tall, tanned and gorgeous. A modern-day Heathcliff, with the looks of a Roman god and a wildness about him that drew every female within a twenty-mile radius like a magnet.

At nineteen, Gio already had a formidable reputation with women. And one night that summer Issy had seen the evidence for herself.

Creeping down to get a glass of water, she'd heard

moaning coming from the darkened dining room. Getting as close as she could without being spotted, she had watched, transfixed, as Gio's lean, fully-clothed body towered over a mostly naked woman lying on her back on the Duke's oak table. It had taken Issy a moment to recognise the writhing female as Maya Carrington, a thirty-something divorcée who had arrived for the Duke's weekend house party that afternoon.

Issy hadn't been able to look away as Gio's long, tanned fingers unclipped the front hook of Maya's black lace push-up bra, then moulded her full breasts. Issy had blushed to the roots of her hair at the socialite's soft sobs as Gio traced a line with his tongue over her prominent nipples, then nipped at them with his teeth as his hand disappeared between Maya's thighs.

Issy had dashed back to bed, her glass of water sloshing all over the stairs with her palm pressed against her pyjama bottoms to ease the brutal ache between her legs as her ragged breathing made her heart race.

She'd dreamt about Gio doing the same thing to her that night and for many nights afterwards, always waking up soaked in sweat, her breasts heavy and tender to the touch, her nipples rigid and that same cruel ache between her legs.

But Gio had never stopped treating her like a child. During that last visit two years ago, when he'd paid so much attention to Maya, he'd barely even spoken to her.

Then, the day before, something magical had happened.

He'd appeared at the school gates on his motorbike, looking surly and tense, and told her the school bus had been cancelled and her mother had asked him to give her a lift home. She hadn't seen Gio in two long years, and the feel of his muscled back pressing into her budding breasts had sent her senses into a blur of rioting hormones. She'd spent today reliving the experience in minute detail for her starstruck classmates, but in reality she'd had to make most of it up, because she'd been so excited she could barely remember a thing.

And then this morning she'd caught him looking at her while he was having breakfast with her and her mother, and just for a second she'd seen the same awareness in those turbulent brown eyes that she had always had in her heart.

She didn't have a schoolgirl crush on Gio. She loved him. Deeply and completely. And not just because of his exotic male beauty and the fact that all the other girls fancied him too. But because she knew things about him that no one else knew. Unfortunately, her attempts to flirt with him that morning had been ignored.

It was past time to take matters into her own hands.

What if Gio didn't come back again for another two years? She'd be an old woman of nineteen by then, and he might have got married or something. Tonight she would make him notice her. She would go to his room and get him to do what he'd been doing to Maya Carrington two years ago. Except this time it would be a thousand times more special, because she loved him and Maya hadn't.

But the last thing she'd wanted to do was discuss her plans with Melanie. It made Issy feel sneaky and juvenile and dishonest. As if she was tricking Gio. When she really wasn't. She should never have mentioned the motorcycle ride. Because Melly had latched on to the information, put two and two together and unfortunately made four. And now she wouldn't let the topic drop.

'What will your mum say?' Melanie asked in a stage whisper.

'Nothing. She's not going to find out,' she whispered back, pushing aside the little spurt of guilt.

Up till now she'd told her mother everything. Because it had been just the two of them for so long Edie had been a confidante and a friend, as well as her mum. But when Issy had tried to bring up the subject of Gio as casually as possible after breakfast her mother had been surprisingly stern with her.

'Don't hassle him. He has more than enough to deal with,' Edie had said cryptically while she pounded dough. 'I saw you flirting with him. And, while I understand the lure of someone as dashing and dangerous as Gio Hamilton, I don't want to see you get hurt when he turns you down.'

The comment had made Issy feel as if she were ten years old again—sheltered and patronised and excluded from all the conversations that mattered—and still trailing after Gio like a lovesick puppy dog.

What did Gio have to deal with? Why wouldn't anyone tell her? And what made her mum so sure he would turn her down? She wanted to help him. To be *there* for him. And she wanted to know what it felt like to be kissed by a man who knew how, instead of the awkward boys she'd kissed before.

But everyone treated her as if she was too young and didn't know her own mind. When she wasn't. And she did.

She'd wanted to tell her mum that, but had decided not to. Edie had looked so troubled when they'd both heard

the shouting match between Gio and his father the night
before, coming through the air vent from the library.

'Do you have protection?' Melanie continued, still
talking in the stupid stage whisper.

'Yes.' She'd bought the condoms months ago, just in
case Gio visited this summer, and had gone all the way
to Middleton to get them, so Mrs Green the pharmacist
in Hamilton's Cross wouldn't tell her mum.

'Aren't you worried that it'll hurt? Jenny Merrin said
it hurt like mad when she did it with Johnny Baxter, and
I bet Gio's…' Melanie paused for effect. 'You know…is
twice the size. Look how tall he is.'

'No, of course not,' she said, starting to get annoyed.

Yes, it would probably hurt a bit, she knew that, but
she wasn't a coward. And if you loved someone you
didn't worry about how big their 'you know what' was.
She'd read in *Cosmo* only last week that size didn't matter.

The bus took the turning into the Hall's drive and she
breathed a sigh of relief. She wanted to get home. There
was so much to do before dinnertime. She needed to
have a bath and wash her hair, wax her legs, do her nails,
try on the three different outfits she had shortlisted for
tonight one last time. This was going to be the most important night of her life, and she wanted to look the part.
To prove to Gio she wasn't a babyish tomboy any more,
or a gawky, overweight teenager.

She felt the now constant ache between her legs and
the tight ball of emotion in her throat and knew she was
doing the right thing.

As the bus driver braked, she leapt up. But Melanie
grabbed her wrist.

'I'm so jealous of you,' Melanie said, her eyes

shining with sincerity. 'He's so dishy. I hope it doesn't hurt too much.'

'It won't,' Issy said.

Gio wouldn't hurt her—not intentionally—of that much she was certain.

So much had changed in the last few years, but not that. Before she'd fallen in love with him he'd been like a big brother to her. Teasing her and letting her follow him around. Listening to her talk about the father she barely remembered and telling her she shouldn't care if she didn't have a dad. That fathers were a pain any way. Things had been difficult, tense between her and Gio since she'd grown up—partly because they weren't little kids anymore, but mostly because he'd become so distant.

His relationship with his father had got so bad he hardly ever came to visit the Hall any more, and when she did see him now his brooding intensity had become like a shield, demanding that everyone—even her—keep out.

But tonight she would be able to get him back again. That moody, magnetic boy would be her friend again, but more than that he'd be her lover, and he'd know he could tell her anything. And everything would be wonderful.

Issy crept through the darkness. Feeling her way past the kitchen garden wall, she pushed the gate into the orchard. And eased out the breath she'd been holding when the hinge barely creaked. She sucked in air scented with ripe apples and the faint tinge of tobacco.

Kicking off her shoes, she stepped off the path onto the dewy grass. It would ruin the effect slightly, but she didn't want to trip over a root in her heels. After waiting for nearly three hours for Gio to come home she was nervous enough already, falling on her face would not be the way to go.

She pressed the flat of her hand to her stomach and felt the butterfly flutter of panic and excitement. Squinting into the shadows, she saw the red glow of a cigarette tip and her heart punched her ribcage. He'd always come to the orchard before whenever he argued with his father. She'd known he would be here.

'Gio?' she called softly, tiptoeing towards the silent shape hidden beneath a tree burdened with summer fruit.

The red glow disappeared as he stamped the cigarette out.

'What do you want?' He sounded edgy, dismissive. She ignored the tightening in her chest. He was upset. He didn't mean to be cruel.

She didn't know what his father and he had been shouting about this time, but she knew it had been bad—worse than the night before.

'Is everything all right? I heard you and the Duke—'

'Great,' he interrupted. 'Everything's great. Now, go away.'

As she stepped beneath the canopy of leaves her eyes adjusted to the lack of light and she could make out his features. The chiselled cheekbones shadowed with stubble, the dark brows, the strong chin and jawline. He stood with his back propped against the tree trunk, his arms crossed and his head bent. The pose might have been casual but for the tension that crackled in the air around him.

'No, I won't go away,' she said, surprised by the forcefulness in her voice. 'Everything's not great.'

His head lifted and the hairs on her nape prickled.

She could feel his eyes on her, even though she couldn't make out his expression, could smell his distinctive male scent, that heady mix of soap and musk.

'I mean it, Iss,' he said, the low tone brittle. 'Go away. I'm not in the mood.'

She stepped closer, feeling as if she were encroaching on a wild animal. 'I'm not going anywhere,' she said, her voice trembling but determined. 'What did he say, Gio? Why are you so upset?'

She placed a palm on his cheek, and he jerked back.

'Don't touch me.' The words were rough, but beneath it she could hear panic.

'Why not? I want to touch you.'

'Yeah?' The snarl was wild, uncontrolled. But before she could register the shock he grabbed a fistful of the silk at her waist and hauled her against him.

Her breath gushed out, adrenaline coursing through her body as he held her hips. She could feel every inch of him. The thick ridge of something rubbed against the juncture of her thighs, and she squirmed instinctively.

He swore. Then his mouth crushed hers. The faint taste of tobacco made all the more intoxicating by heat and demand.

He cradled her head, held her steady as his tongue plunged. She gasped, her fingers fisting in the soft cotton of his T-shirt as she clung on. She opened her mouth wider, surrendered to a rush of arousal so new, so thrilling, it made her head spin.

He lurched back, held her at arm's length. 'What the hell are you doing?'

'Kissing you back,' she said, confused by the accusatory tone.

Why had he stopped? When it had felt so good?

'Well, don't,' he said, his voice sharp. His fingers released her and he crossed his arms back over his chest.

'Why not?' she cried. She wanted him to carry on kissing her, to keep kissing her forever.

'Issy, go away.' The anger sounded almost weary now. 'You don't know what you're doing. I'm not some kid you can practise your kissing technique on. And I don't take little girls to bed.'

'I'm not a little girl. I'm a woman, with a woman's desires,' she added, hoping the line she'd read in one of her romance novels didn't sound too cheesy.

'Yeah, right.' Her confidence deflated at the doubtful tone. 'How old *are* you?'

'I'm nearly eighteen,' she said with bravado. Or rather she would be in six months' time. 'And I do know what I'm doing.' Or at least she was trying her best to know. Surely he could teach her the rest?

The silence seemed to spread out between them, the only noise the pummelling of her own heartbeat and the hushed sound of their breathing.

He reached out and traced his thumb down her cheek. 'For God's sake, Issy, don't tempt me,' he murmured. 'Not unless you're sure.'

'I am sure. I have been for a long time,' she replied. He needed her. She hadn't imagined it. The thought was so thrilling she locked her knees to stay upright.

He cradled her cheek. She leant into his palm.

'I want you, Gio,' she whispered, covering his hand with hers. 'Don't you want me?'

It was the hardest question she'd ever had to ask. If he said no now she would be devastated. She caught her breath and held it.

He pushed his fingers into her hair, rubbed his thumb against the strands. 'Yeah, I want you, Isadora. Too damn much.'

Her breath released in a rush as he pulled her close and his lips slanted across hers. The kiss was sensual, seeking this time, his tongue tracing the contours of her mouth with a tenderness and care that had her shuddering.

He leaned back. 'Are you sure you know what you're doing?' he said, searching her face, his hands framing her cheeks. 'I don't want to hurt you.'

'You won't hurt me. You couldn't.'

Dropping his hands, he linked his fingers through hers. 'Let's take this inside.'

Nervous anticipation made her stumble as he led her through the moonlit gardens and the gloomy shadows of the house's back staircase, his strides long and assured and full of purpose. She took the stairs two at a time, the first tremors of doubt making her legs shake. When he shoved open the door to his room on the second floor her heart beat so hard she was convinced he would hear it too.

He reached to switch on the light and she grasped his wrist.

'Could you leave the light off?' she blurted. She let go of his arm, desperate to disguise the quiver in her voice.

'Why?' he asked.

She scoured her mind for a viable excuse. If he knew how inexperienced she was he might stop, and she couldn't bear that. 'It's...it's more romantic,' she said.

He seemed to study her in the darkness for an eternity before he crossed the room and opened the drapes, letting the moonlight flood in.

'Issy, I don't do permanent,' he said as he came back to her. He brushed a kiss on her forehead. 'You know that, right?'

She nodded, not trusting herself to speak. That would change, she was sure of it, once he had the proof of how much she loved him. She draped her arms over his shoulders, calling on every ounce of her fledgling skills as an actress. She'd told him she wasn't a little girl. It was time to stop behaving like one.

'Yes, I know.' Driving her fingers into the short hair at his nape, she took a deep breath of his scent, revelled in the feel of him as he pressed her back against the door, captured her waist in hot palms.

'Good,' he muttered, as his teeth bit into her earlobe.

She shuddered, letting the delicious shiver race down her spine as his lips feasted on the pulse-point in her neck. The hot, vicious ache at her core throbbed in time with her deafening heartbeat. She reminded herself to breathe as he drew the zipper on her dress down, tugged her arms free. The shimmering silk puddled at her feet. She clung to his neck, the heady thrill making her dizzy as he bent and lifted her easily into his arms.

This was really happening at last. After years of fantasising, her dreams were coming true.

Silvery light gilded his chest as he cast off his T-shirt. He unfastened his belt and she looked away, suddenly overwhelmed. He looked so powerful, so strong, so completely male. The mattress dipped as he joined her on the bed. His hand settled on her midriff, drew her towards him. She felt the heat of his big body, the thick outline prodding her thigh.

His face looked hard, intent in the shadows, as his deft fingers freed her breasts from the confining lace of her bra.

'You're beautiful, Issy' he said, his voice low and strained as one rough fingertip traced over her nipple. 'I want to look at you properly. Let's turn on the light.'

She shook her head, mute with longing and panic. 'Please—I like it dark,' she said, hoping she sounded as if she knew what she was talking about.

'Okay,' he said. 'But next time we do it my way.' Her heart soared at the mention of *next time*, and then he bent his head and captured the pebble-hard nipple in his teeth.

A sob escaped as sensation raw and hot arrowed down to her core. She arched up, bucked under him as he suckled. Damp heat gushed between her thighs.

Her hands fisted in the sheets as she tried to cling to sanity. Tried to stop herself from shattering into a billion pieces.

'Open your legs for me, *bella*.' The urgent whisper penetrated, and her knees relaxed to let his palm cup her core.

Strong fingers probed, stroked, caressed, touching and then retreating. She cried out, begged, until he stayed right at the centre of ecstasy. The wave rose with shocking speed, and then slammed into her with the force and fury of a tsunami.

She struggled to find focus, to claw her way back to consciousness as hot hands held her hips. He loomed above her in the darkness. 'Dammit, Issy, I can't wait. Is that okay?'

She couldn't register his meaning, but nodded as he

fumbled with something in the darkness. Then she felt it—huge, unyielding but soft as velvet, spearing through her swollen flesh. A heavy thrust brought sharp, rending pain. She strained beneath him, a choking sob lodged in her throat.

He stopped, tried to draw out. 'Issy, what the—?'

'Please, don't stop.' She gasped the plea, gripping shoulders tight with bunched muscle. 'It doesn't hurt.' And it didn't. Not any more. The overwhelming pressure, the stretched feeling, had become a pulsing ache, clamouring for release.

He swore, but pressed back in slowly, carefully. Her hands slipped on slick skin, hard sinew, her jagged breathing matching the relentless thrusts. She heard his harsh grunts, her own sobs of release as the tsunami built to another bold crescendo, threatening so much more than before. Her scream of release echoed in her head as the final wave crashed, exploding through her as she hurtled over the top.

'For God's sake, Issy. You were a bloody virgin.'

Her eyelids fluttered open—and the bedside light snapped on, blinding her.

'I know.' She threw her arm up to cover her eyes, registering his temper. What had she done?

Tremors racked her body as afterglow turned neatly to aftershock.

'Shh. Calm down.' The hammer-beats of his heart thudded against her ear as he settled her head on his chest, gathered her close. 'I'm sorry, Iss. Stop shaking.' He brushed the locks from her brow. 'Are you okay? Did I hurt you?'

She opened her eyes. The soft light illuminated his features clearly. Love swept through her, more intense, more real than ever before as she saw the worry, the concern.

A smile spread as euphoria leaped in her chest. 'Yes, I'm okay.' She snuggled into his embrace and sighed. Despite the soreness between her legs, she'd never felt more complete, more wonderful in her life. 'I never dreamed it could be that amazing.'

He shifted back. Holding her chin, he lifted her face. 'Wait a minute. I asked you.' His eyes narrowed. 'Why didn't you tell me the truth?'

'I don't...I don't understand,' she stammered, chilling as he took his arm from around her and sat up.

Whipping back the sheet, he turned his back to her and stood up. As he paced across the room, the sight of his naked body had the heat between her thighs sizzling back to life. But then she noticed the sharp, irritated movements as he yanked on his jeans, pulled on the T-shirt.

'Is something wrong?' she asked, her pulse stuttering. She clasped the sheet to her chest. This wasn't right. This wasn't how it was supposed to be. This was the moment when they were supposed to declare their undying love for each other.

He twisted round, sent her a look that had colour rising in her cheeks.

'I asked you if you were a virgin.' The harsh tone made her flinch. 'Why did you lie?'

'I...' Had he asked? She gave her head a quick shake. 'I don't...I didn't mean to lie.'

'Sure you did.' He flung the words over his shoulder as he grabbed a bag from the closet, swept the few personal items on top of the dresser into it. He ripped open the top drawer, scooped out his clothes, shoved them in too. The tense movements radiated controlled anger.

Tears stung her eyes, swelled in her throat. 'Please, Gio, I don't understand. What are you doing?'

'I'm leaving. What does it look like?' He slashed the zipper closed.

Facing her at last, he slung the holdall over his shoulder. 'I'm sorry if I hurt you. I should have stopped once I realised what was going on. But I couldn't. And that's on me. But whatever game you were playing, it's over now.'

'It's not a game.' She clung to the sheet, kneeled on the mattress, desperate to hold on to her dream. This was a silly misunderstanding. He loved her. He needed her. She needed him. Hadn't they proved that together?

'I love you Gio. I've always loved you. I always will. We were meant to be together.'

He went completely still, and then his eyebrow rose in cynical enquiry. 'Are you nuts? Grow up, for heaven's sake.'

The cruel words made her shrink inside herself. She sank back, her body quaking as she watched him stamp on his boots and walk to the door.

He couldn't be leaving. Not now, not like this, not after everything they'd just done.

'Don't go, Gio. You have to stay.'

He turned, his hand on the door handle. She braced herself for another shot. But instead of anger she saw regret.

'There's nothing for me here.' His voice sounded

hollow, but the bitterness in the words still made the agonising pain a thousands times worse. 'There never was.'

A single jerking sob caught in her throat and the tears streamed down her cheeks.

'Don't cry, Issy. Believe me, it's not worth it. When you figure that out, you'll thank me for this.'

CHAPTER FOUR

The Present

Issy released her fingers to ease their death grip on the handle of her briefcase.

How could every damn detail of that night still be so vivid?

Not just the anguish and the pain, but the euphoria and the hope too—even the intense pleasure of their lovemaking. How many times had she played it over in her head in the months and years that had followed? Hundreds? Thousands?

Way too many times, that was for sure.

She forced herself to ignore the pressure in her chest at the thought of Gio's parting words that night. They couldn't hurt her. Not any more. All her tears had dried up a long time ago.

Gio had been right about one thing. She should thank him. He'd taught her an important lesson. Never open your heart to someone until you're positive they're the prince and not the frog. And don't be fooled by fancy packaging.

'Nearly there,' Frank called cheerfully from the front

seat. 'Wait till you see what the lad's done with the place. Amazing, it is. Must have cost a fortune by my reckoning.'

Issy drew a deep breath, eased it out through her teeth. No more ancient history. She had enough of a mountain to climb just concentrating on the here and now.

She glanced out of the window. Only to have her fingers tighten on the briefcase again.

Amazing wasn't the word. More like awe-inspiring, Issy thought as she stepped out of the cab onto the newly pebbled driveway and gaped at the magnificent Georgian frontage of her former home. Gio hadn't just restored the Hall, he'd improved upon it. The place looked magnificent. The bright sand-blasted stone gleamed in the sunshine. The columns at the front of the house had always looked forbidding to her as a child, but a terrace had been added which gave the house a welcoming Mediterranean feel.

Having failed to persuade Frank to take a fare for the journey, she bade him goodbye.

As the cab pulled away, she gazed up at the Hall. Why did Gio's transformation of the place make her feel even more daunted?

She adjusted the strap of her briefcase and slung it over her shoulder.

Don't be silly. Remember, this isn't about you, or Gio, or the Hall. It's about the theatre—and shutting the fat lady up long enough to see out another season. Absolutely no more trips down memory lane allowed. The past is dead, and it needs to stay that way.

'Hey, can I help you?'

She glanced round to see a young man strolling towards her. Her fingers locked on the strap.

Curtain up.

'Hi, my name's Isadora Helligan.' She thrust out her hand as he approached. 'I'm here to see Giovanni Hamilton.'

Stopping in front of her, he ran his fingers through his sandy-blond hair and sent her a quizzical smile. 'Hi, Jack Bradshaw.' He took her hand and gave it a hearty shake. 'I'm Gio's PA.' He put his hand back in his pocket. 'I'm sorry, I keep Gio's diary, but…' He paused, looking a little perplexed. 'Do you have an appointment?'

Not quite.

'Yes,' she lied smoothly. 'Gio made it himself a week ago. He must have forgotten to tell you.'

If Gio was going to kick her out, he would have to do it personally.

'No problem,' Jack replied. 'It won't be the first time. Creative geniuses rarely pay attention to the little details.' He extended his arm towards the Hall. 'He's finishing up with the planners on the pool terrace. Why don't you come through?'

As Jack led the way, Issy found herself too busy gazing at all the changes Gio had made to get any more nervous thinking about what she had to do.

How had he managed to get so much light into the interior of the building? And how come the place looked so spacious and open whereas before it had always seemed poky and austere?

The nerves kicked back in, though, as she stepped out onto the pool terrace and saw Gio. Tall and gorgeous and effortlessly commanding in grey linen trousers and an open-necked shirt, he stood on the other side of the empty pool, chatting with a couple of men in ill-fitting suits who were several inches shorter than him. Almost as if he sensed her standing there, staring at him, he turned his head. She could have sworn she felt the heat of his gaze as it raked over her figure.

Her stomach tensed as an answering heat bloomed in her cheeks.

She watched as he shook hands with the two men and then walked towards her over the newly mown grass. And was immediately thrown back in time to all the times she'd watched him in the past.

She'd always adored the way Gio moved, with that relaxed, languid, confident stride, as if he was completely comfortable in his own skin. He'd always been the sort of man to turn heads, even as a teenager, but age had added an air of dominance to that dangerous sex appeal. Unfortunately, the full package was even more devastating now. Tanned Mediterranean skin, the muscular, broad-shouldered physique and slim hips, that sharply handsome face and his rich chestnut-brown hair which had once been long enough to tie in a ponytail— to annoy his father she suspected—but was now cut short and fell in careless waves across his brow.

Was it any surprise she'd idolised him once—and mistaken him for the prince? Thank God she didn't idolise him any more. Unfortunately, the assertion didn't seem to be doing a thing for the heat cascading through her as he took his own sweet time strolling towards her.

Her heartbeat spiked, her nerve endings tingled and adrenaline pumped through her veins. She fidgeted with the bag's strap, trying to bring her breathing back under control.

Good grief, what on earth was happening to her? Had the extreme stress of the last few months turned her into a nymphomaniac?

Her knees wobbled ever so slightly as he drew level, a sensual, knowing smile tilting his lips.

'This is a surprise, Isadora,' he said, pronouncing her full name with the tiniest hint of Italy. 'You're looking a lot more...' His gaze flicked down her frame. Her knees wobbled some more. 'Sophisticated today.'

'Hello, Gio,' she said, being as businesslike as she could with her nipples thrusting against the front of her blouse like bullets.

Trust Gio to remind her of their last meeting. No way was he going to make this easy for her. But then she hadn't expected easy.

'I'm sorry to arrive unannounced,' she said, looking as meek as she could possibly manage. 'But I have something important I wanted to discuss with you.'

His gaze drifted to her chest. 'Really?'

She crossed her arms over her chest to cover her inappropriate reaction. Why hadn't she worn a padded bra? 'Yes, really,' she said, a little too curtly. 'Do you mind if we discuss it in private?'

If he was going to humiliate her, she'd rather not have an audience. Several of his employees were already staring at them from the other side of the pool.

'There are workmen all over the house,' he said calmly, but the challenge in his eyes was unmistakable as they fixed on her face. 'The only place we'll be able to have any privacy is in my bedroom.'

What? No way.

Her mind lurched back as the memories she'd been busy suppressing shot her blood pressure straight into the danger zone. But then she noticed the cynical curve of his lips and knew it wasn't a genuine invitation. He expected her to decline. Because he thought she couldn't handle the past, couldn't handle him.

Think again, Buster.

'That'd be great,' she said, even though her throat was now drier than the Gobi Desert. 'If you're sure you don't mind?' she added with a hint of defiance.

'Not at all,' he replied, not sounding as surprised as she'd hoped. He lifted his arm. 'I believe you know the way,' he said, every inch the amenable, impersonal host.

Blast him.

They climbed the back staircase without a word. His silent, indomitable presence starting to rattle her. How could he be so relaxed, so unmoved?

She cut the thought off. Of course he could be. What had happened in his bedroom all those years ago had never meant a thing to him. She pushed the residual flicker of hurt away, clinging to being businesslike and efficient. If he could be, so could she.

But even as the rallying cry sounded in her head he opened his bedroom door, and she had to brace herself against the painful memories. She caught his scent, that dizzying combination of soap and man, more potent this time without the masking hint of tobacco, as he held the door for her to walk in ahead of him.

Colour flooded up her neck as she stepped into the room where he had once stolen her innocence. And destroyed her dreams.

The walls were painted utilitarian white now, the bed a brand-new teak frame draped with pale blue linen, but the memories were all still there, as vivid and disturbing as yesterday. She could see herself kneeling on the bed, the sheet clutched to her chest, her heart shattering.

'So what exactly is it that's so important?'

She whirled round to see him leaning against the door, his arms folded over his chest, his expression indifferent. She held the briefcase in front of her, tried to control the rush of emotions. He was goading her deliberately. She had no idea why, but she wasn't going to let it mean anything.

'You offered me money. A week ago.'

His brows arrowed up. Seemed she'd surprised him at last.

'I wanted to know if the offer's still open,' she added.

'You came here to ask me for money?'

She heard the brittle edge and took a perverse pleasure in it. Good to know she could rattle him too.

'That's correct.'

'Well, now,' he said, pushing away from the door and strolling towards her. 'So what happened to the woman who has principles and wouldn't dare lower herself to take anything from me?'

He stopped in front of her, standing so close she could feel the heat of his body.

'It *was* you who said that? Wasn't it?'

'I apologise for that.' She lifted her chin to meet his gaze, refusing to take a step back. She knew perfectly well he was trying to intimidate her. She should never have said those stupid things, but he had provoked her. 'But I didn't think you cared what I thought,' she finished, knowing perfectly well her comments hadn't bothered him in the slightest.

He ran a finger down her cheek and she stiffened, shocking desire coiling in her gut at the unexpected touch.

'You'd be surprised what I care about,' he murmured.

She stepped back. Forced into retreat after all. How was he still able to fan the flames so easily?

'I should go,' she said hastily, her courage suddenly deserting her.

What on earth had possessed her to come here? He would never give her the money. All she'd done was humiliate herself for no reason.

But as she tried to step around him and make a dash for the door he grasped her upper arm.

'So it wasn't *that* important?' he said, a challenging glint in his eyes.

Spurred on by desperation and an unreasonable panic, her temper snapped. She yanked her arm out of his grasp. This wasn't a game. Not to her anyway. 'It *was* important. Not that you'd ever understand.'

She'd always been willing to fight for what she believed in. He'd never once done that. Because he'd never believed in anything.

He laughed, the sound harsh. 'Why don't you show me, then?' Holding both her arms, he hauled her closer. 'If you want the money so much, what do I get in return?'

'What do you want?' She hurled the words at him, angry, upset, and—God help her—desperately turned on.

His fingers flexed on her arms. 'You know what I want.' His jaw tightened. 'And you want it too. Except you always had to sugar-coat it with all that nonsense about love.'

The barb hit home, but did nothing to quell the flames licking at her core.

'Sex?' She huffed out a contemptuous laugh. Not easy when she was about to spontaneously combust. 'Is that all?' She pressed closer, rubbed provocatively against the thick ridge in his trousers. Past caring about pride, or maturity, or scruples, as temper and desire raged out of control.

He thought she was still the fanciful naïve virgin who expected love and commitment. Well, she wasn't, and she could prove it.

'If that's all you want, why don't you take it?' she goaded, revelling in the rush of power as his eyes darkened. 'You don't have to worry. I won't sugar-coat it a second time.'

His lips crushed hers. He tasted of fury and frustration and demand, his fingers caressing her scalp as he invaded her mouth. She clutched his shoulders and kissed him back, all thoughts of revenge, of vindication, incinerated by the firestorm of need.

He broke away first, only to swing her up in his arms. She fell back on the bed, feeling as if she were careering over Niagara Falls in a barrel—terrified and exhilarated, her body battered by its own sensual overload. He struggled to get the dress over her head, the sibilant hiss of rending fabric drowned out by their laboured breathing. She grasped his shirt, popping buttons, reached for the firm silky flesh beneath as he grappled with her bra, exposing her breasts.

He pushed her back on the pillows, kneeled over her. Unlike that first night, when she'd hidden herself from his sight, she basked in the intoxicating rush of desire as her nipples swelled and hardened under his assessing gaze.

He cupped the heavy orbs, rubbed his thumb over the engorged peaks.

'Dammit, you're even more beautiful than I remember.'

The stunned words touched her somewhere deep inside, but the fanciful emotion was lost as he bent forward and captured a nipple with his teeth. A staggered moan escaped as fire blazed down to her core. Grasping his cheeks, she pushed into his mouth. The rasp of stubble against her soft palms as primal as the crude heat burning at her centre.

She watched spellbound and desperate as he scrambled out of his own clothes. Kicking off his loafers, he wrestled out of the torn shirt, and dropped trousers and briefs in a crumpled heap to the floor.

Where once she'd been afraid to look at him, this time she devoured the dark male beauty of his body. Tanned skin, muscled shoulders, a lean ridged abdomen and powerful flanks all vied for her attention. But then her gaze fixed on the long, thick erection, and the tantalising bead of moisture at its tip. Her breath clogged in her lungs as he climbed onto the bed, caging her in.

Reaching, she closed her fingers around the hard, pulsing flesh. Vicious desire coiled as the magnificent erection leapt in response.

He pulled out of her grasp, deft fingers probing beneath the lace of her panties and finding the slick furnace at her core. Sensation assaulted her as he toyed with the hard nub. She sobbed, hurtling towards that brutal edge, but he withdrew.

Her eyes flew open, her senses straining. 'Don't stop!' she cried.

He laughed, the sound raw, and dragged off the thin swatch of lace, casting it over his shoulder. Leaning forward, he whispered against her ear. 'I'm going to be deep inside you when you come.'

She wanted to make a pithy comeback, but she could barely think let alone speak. All thoughts of caution, of consequences, were lost in the frantic hammer of her heartbeat as he grabbed a foil package from the bedside dresser and rolled on a condom.

He stroked her thighs, held her hips wide. Staring into her eyes, he gripped her bottom and pressed within. She gasped, quivered, stretched unbearably as he eased in up to the hilt.

He was a big man, and the fullness was as overwhelming and shocking now as it had been a decade ago. But this time she didn't panic. She held on, angling her hips as the pleasure intensified, battering her senses as he paused, allowing her to adjust to the brutal penetration.

She tensed, panting, her skin glowing with sweat as he began to move. She tried to hold back, to make it last, her body buffeted by rolling waves of ecstasy, but the rhythmic thrusts drove her towards orgasm at breakneck speed.

'Stay with me, *bella*,' he grunted, the molten chocolate of his eyes locking hot on her face.

But the tight coil exploded in a blast of raw, delirious sensation.

She screamed out her fulfilment as he shouted his own release, and collapsed with her into oblivion.

'I've never come that fast in my life.'

Issy stiffened at the muffled words next to her ear, the hazy afterglow shattering.

He was still buried deep inside her. Still firm, still semi-erect. His large frame anchoring her to the mattress.

She shoved his shoulder, tried to lower her legs—next to impossible with her thighs clasped tight around his hips. 'Let me up. I need to leave.' Now.

He lifted himself off her, and she stifled the groan as her swollen flesh released him with difficulty.

'What's wrong?' he murmured.

Was he joking?

They'd just had sex! Make that wild monkey sex. And they didn't even like each other. She closed her legs, curled away from him, the aching tenderness between her thighs a shameful reminder of the way they'd just ravaged each other.

It wasn't just wrong, it was insane. Forget ten years ago. This now classified as the biggest, most humiliating mistake of her life.

'Absolutely nothing,' she said caustically, the scent of sex suffocating her as she scooted over to the corner of the bed.

She sat up, ready to make a swift getaway, but one strong arm banded round her waist and dragged her back against a solid male chest.

Panic constricted around her throat. 'I really have to leave.'

'Settle down. Why are you in such a rush? You haven't got what you came for yet.'

'I…' She stuttered to a halt, his words slicing through the panic and cutting straight to the shame. 'I didn't…' She stopped, cleared her throat. The conversation they'd had before ripping each other's clothes off replaying in her mind at top volume.

She cringed. She hadn't meant to tell him she'd have sex with him for money, but somehow the desire, the need, the resentment had got all tangled up. And she had. Sort of.

Wild monkey sex had been bad enough, but adding in the money took things to a whole new level of sordid. 'The money wasn't the reason I…' She paused. Tried again to explain the unexplainable. 'I don't expect you to pay…'

His arm tightened. 'I know that, Issy. After what almost happened at the club, sex was inevitable.' He gave a rough chuckle. 'And, frankly, I'm insulted. I don't pay women for sex. Even you.'

She blinked. Furious at the sting of tears. 'Good, I'm glad you understand that,' she said, trying to regain a little dignity while she was stark naked and blushing like a beetroot.

She struggled. He held firm.

'Will you let go?' she demanded.

'What's the big hurry?' he said, his reasonableness starting to irritate her. 'Now we've got the sex out of the way, why shouldn't we talk about the money?'

Because I'd rather die on the spot.

She swung round, astonished at his blasé attitude. Was it really that easy for him to dismiss what they had done? Chalk it up to inevitability and forget about it?

She'd never had sex just to scratch an itch. Not until now anyway. She felt dreadful about it. Didn't he feel even a little bit ashamed about their behaviour?

Apparently not, from the easygoing look on his face.

She gripped the sheet in her fist. 'Yes, well, now we've got the sex out of the way…' How could he reduce everything to the lowest common denominator like that? 'I don't want to discuss anything else.' Because she, at least, had scruples. 'I need to get dressed. I'm getting a chill.'

Which was a blatant lie. She was the opposite of cold. The sun was blazing through the windows, and she could feel something that was still remarkably hard pressing against her bottom.

His hands stroked her tummy through the thin linen sheet, sending a shiver through her that had nothing to do with being chilled either.

'You can get dressed on one condition.' His breath whispered past her ear. 'That you don't run off.'

She nodded, so aroused again she would agree to tap dance naked to get out of his arms. Having to endure a conversation with him was by far the safer option, she decided as she dashed out of the bed.

To her consternation, he made no effort to get dressed himself, but simply relaxed back against the pillows, folded one arm behind his head and watched her. Ignoring him, she raced round the room in a crouch, with one arm banded across her breasts and the other covering what she could of her sex. Unfortunately she soon discovered that left her one crucial hand short to pick her bra and panties off the floor.

'Issy, what exactly are you doing?' Gio's amused voice rumbled from the bed.

She glanced round to find him staring at her, a puzzled smile on his face. 'I'm trying to maintain a little modesty. If that's okay with you,' she snapped.

Something he conspicuously lacked, she thought resentfully. With the sheet slung low on his hips, barely covering the distinctive bulge beneath, he looked as if he were auditioning for a banner ad in *Playgirl*.

'Isn't it a little late for that?' he said casually.

The blush burned as she concentrated on stepping into her knickers and fastening her bra behind her back one-handed.

She glared at him, having finally completed the tricky manoeuvres. 'Yes, I suppose it is. Thank you so much for pointing that out.'

Why did men always have to state the bloody obvious?

She turned away as he chuckled. Scouting around for her dress, she spotted it peeking out from under the bed. She whipped it off the floor and climbed into it, trying not to notice the torn seam caused by his eagerness to get the dress off her.

She then spent several agonising seconds trying to fasten the zip, with her arm twisted behind her back like a circus contortionist.

'Want some help with that?' His deep voice rumbled with amusement.

She huffed and gave in. The sooner she got dressed, the sooner she could get out of here.

She perched on the edge of the bed and presented her back to him. But instead of fastening the zip he swept the heavy curtain of hair over her shoulder and ran the pad of his thumb down the length of her neck.

'That's not helping,' she said, squeezing her thighs together as awareness ricocheted down her spine.

He chuckled as he tugged up the zip. He rested a warm palm on her bare shoulder. 'So how much money do you need?'

The softly asked question had a blast of guilt and despair drowning out her embarrassment.

The theatre!

What was she going to do now? Gio had been her last hope. Admittedly it hadn't been much of a hope, but she couldn't even ask him for the sponsorship now—it would make her look like a total tart, and anyway he wouldn't give it to her. Why should he?

'None,' she said, her mind reeling. How could she have been so reckless and irresponsible? 'Really, it'll be fine,' she murmured, her bottom lip quivering alarmingly

Don't you dare fall to pieces. Not yet.

She'd have to find another way. Somehow.

But as she went to stand he held her wrist. 'Why do I get the feeling you're lying?'

She looked down at the long, tanned fingers encircling her wrist. And suddenly felt like a puppy who had been given a good solid kick in the ribs.

'I'm not lying,' she said, alarmed by the quake in her voice. 'Everything's fine.'

He gripped her chin, forced her eyes to his. 'Issy, if you say everything's fine again I'm going to get seriously annoyed.' He pressed his thumb to her lip. 'I was there when you broke your wrist. Remember? You were twelve, and in a lot of pain, and yet you refused to shed a single tear. You look a lot closer to tears now. So there has to be a reason.'

She dipped her eyes to her lap, disturbed by the admiration in his voice—and the memory he'd evoked.

She hadn't cried that day, but she hadn't been particularly brave. The pain had seemed minimal once the sixteen-year-old Gio had discovered her in the grounds. He'd carried her all the way back to the Hall in his arms, the experience fuelling her fantasies for months and making her forget about her sore wrist as soon as he'd plucked her off the ground.

She brushed at her eyes with the heel of her hand. Gio's brusque tenderness that day was not something she needed to be thinking about right now.

'Maybe things aren't completely fine,' she said carefully. 'But I'll figure something out.'

He lifted a knee and slung his arm over it—edging that flipping sheet further south.

'That had better not mean more strip-a-grams,' he said.

'It *wasn't* a strip-a-gram,' she said, not appreciating the dictatorial tone. 'It was a singing telegram. There's a difference.'

'Uh-huh.' He didn't sound convinced. 'What's the money for? Are you in financial trouble?'

'Not me,' she murmured, her indignation forgotten. Strip-a-grams could well be the next step. 'It's the Crown and Feathers. The theatre pub I work for. I'm the general manager. I have been for the last four years. And we're about to be shut down by the bank.'

She stared at her hands, the enormity of the situation overwhelming her.

'All the people who work there and everyone in the local community who's helped us make the place a success will be devastated.' She blew out an unsteady breath, the truth hitting her hard in the solar plexus. 'And it's all my fault.'

She'd made a mess of everything. The fat lady was singing her heart out and, barring a miracle, there would be no shutting her up now.

* * *

Gio stared at Issy's pale shoulders rigid with tension, and at her slender hands clasped so tight in her lap she was probably about to dislocate a finger.

And wanted to punch his fist through a wall.

Why couldn't she have wanted the money for herself?

Of course she didn't. Issy didn't work that way. She'd always had too much integrity for her own good.

Now he didn't just feel responsible, he felt the unfamiliar prickle of guilt.

He shouldn't have goaded her. Made the money an issue.

But he hadn't been able to stop himself. The minute he'd spotted her waiting by the empty pool the desire he'd been trying and failing to handle for well over a week had surged back to life like a wild beast.

And he'd instantly resented it. And her.

She'd told him she detested him. Why did he still want her so much?

Suggesting she come up to his bedroom had been a ploy to humiliate her. He'd been sure she would refuse. But she hadn't. And her forthright acceptance had made him feel like a jerk.

Then she'd asked him for money. And resentment had turned to anger.

He'd seen the unconscious flare of desire in her eyes and decided to exploit it. She wasn't here for his money, and he could prove it.

The sex had been incredible. Better even than the first time. Explosive. Exhilarating. A force of nature neither of them could control.

And she'd enjoyed it as much as he had. So he'd been well and truly vindicated.

But her financial problems had ruined the nice buzz of triumph and spectacular sex, stabbing at his conscience in a way he didn't like.

'Exactly how much of a hole is your theatre in?' he asked.

'The interest on our loan is thirty thousand. And we've got less than two weeks to raise it.'

Her damp lashes made her turquoise eyes look even bigger than usual. And his conscience took another hit.

'Is that all?' he prompted.

She shook her head, looked back at her lap. 'We'd need over a hundred to be safe for the rest of the year.' She gave a jerky shrug, as if a huge weight were balanced on her shoulders. 'We've been trying to find sponsors for months now,' she continued. 'The two grants we got last year have been withdrawn. The pub revenue was hit by the smoking ban, and…' She trailed off, sighed. 'It was a stupid idea to come to you. Why should you care about some bankrupt theatre?' She brushed a single tear away. 'But I was desperate.'

He covered her clasped hands with one of his, surprised by the urge to comfort. 'Issy, stop crying.' He'd always hated to see her cry. 'The money's yours. All of it. It's not a problem.'

Her head lifted and she stared at him as if he'd just sprouted an extra head. 'Don't be silly. You can't do that. Why would you?'

He shrugged. 'Why wouldn't I? It's a good cause.' But even as he said it he knew that wasn't the reason he wanted to give her the money.

He'd never really forgiven himself for the way he'd stormed out on her all those years ago.

He didn't regret the decision to walk away. Issy had been young, romantic and impossibly sweet. She'd had a crush on him for years and didn't have a clue what he was really like. But he'd been much harder on her than he needed to be.

He'd accused her of keeping her virginity a secret. But he'd realised in hindsight that had been a stupid mis-understanding. She'd been too innocent to know they were talking at cross-purposes. But at the time he'd felt trapped and wary—and furious with himself for not withdrawing the instant he knew he was her first—and he'd taken it out on her.

Then she'd told him she loved him, and for one fleeting second he'd actually wanted it to be true—making him realise how much he had let his argument with the Duke get to him—and he'd taken that out on her too.

He wasn't about to explain himself now. Or ever. It was too late to apologise. But giving her the money would be a good way to make amends.

But as he looked into those luminous blue eyes the blood pounded back into his groin. And he realised he had a bigger problem to handle than any lingering sense of guilt.

Why hadn't the mind-blowing orgasm been enough?

'But you can't give me a hundred grand.' She pulled her hand out of his. 'That's a lot of money.'

'Do you want to save your theatre or not?' he replied impatiently. He wanted the money out of the way, so he could deal with the more pressing problem of how to re-establish control over his libido.

'Yes—yes, I do. But…' She trailed off.

'Then why are you trying to talk me out of this?'

'Because it's a hundred thousand pounds!'

'Issy, I spent close to that on my last car. It's not that much money. Not to me.'

Her eyebrows rose. 'I didn't know architecture was that lucrative.'

'It is when you do it right,' he said. And had to stifle the foolish desire to say a lot more.

He'd qualified two years early, beaten off a series of more experienced applicants to win a huge design competition, and then worked his backside off. And in the last three years it had paid off.

The Florence practice had won kudos around the world. He'd opened another office in Paris. Won a slew of prestigious architectural awards. And best of all he didn't have to bother entering competitions any more. The clients came to him. He was proud of how he'd managed to tame the destructiveness that had ruled his teenage years and turn his life around.

But he resisted the urge to launch into a list of his accomplishments. He didn't boast about his achievements. He didn't need anyone's approval. So why should he need Issy's?

'If it makes you feel better,' he began, 'I've been thinking of opening an office in London for a while.' Which wasn't exactly the truth. 'The Florence practice donates over a million euros to worthy causes every year. It's great PR and it keeps Luca, my tax accountant, happy.' Which *was* the truth. 'Sponsoring your theatre makes good business sense.'

She pressed her hands to her mouth, her eyes widening to saucer size. 'Oh. My. Lord. You're serious!' she shrieked, the decibel level muffled by her hands.

'You're actually going to give us the money.' She grasped his hand in both of hers. 'Thank you. Thank you. Thank you. You have no idea how much this means to me. And all the people who work at the Crown and Feathers.'

But he had a feeling he *did* know. And it made him feel uncomfortable. His reasons weren't exactly altruistic. And they were getting less altruistic by the second.

'I wish I knew how to thank you,' she said.

He almost told her it wasn't her thanks he wanted. But stopped himself because he'd just figured out what it was he did want.

He wanted Issy Helligan out of his system.

The girl and now the woman had been a fire in his blood for well over ten years. Why not admit it? He didn't fixate on women, but somehow he'd got fixated on her.

He'd tried walking away. He'd tried denial. And neither had worked.

Sorting out her financial troubles would finally put the guilt and responsibility from their past behind them. So why not take the next step? He had to return to Florence this afternoon, and he wanted Issy with him. So he could burn the fire out once and for all. Forget about her for good.

'There's only one snag,' he said, the white lie tripping off his tongue without a single regret.

No need to tell Issy about his plans yet.

She had a tendency to overreact, she was totally unpredictable, and she had a terrible track record for complicating sex with emotion. Better to get her to Florence first, and then deal with any fall-out.

'Oh, no—what?' she said, her face crumpling comically.

'You'll have to come to Florence with me. This afternoon.'

'To Florence?' She looked even more astonished than she had by the offer of money. But when he saw the flash of interest in her eyes he had a tough time keeping the smile of triumph off his face.

She needed this as much as he did. The only difference was she hadn't figured it out yet.

Issy tried to ignore the bubble of excitement under her breastbone. She had to get a grip on this thing... whatever it was. Now.

Maybe she could justify giving in to her hormones once, in the circumstances. She'd been stressed to the max in the last few months, hadn't dated in over a year, and Gio had always been able to short-circuit her common sense and make her yearn for things that weren't right for her. But she was *not* about to do the wild thing with him again. No matter what her body might want.

Gio was now officially the answer to the theatre's prayers. Which would make sex with him even more indefensible than it was already.

'Why?' she asked, hoping he wasn't about to suggest what she thought he was about to suggest.

'You need the money by next week, right?'

She nodded, still unable to believe that the theatre's problems could be solved so easily. And so completely.

'There's a ton of paperwork to sign, plus you may have to give a presentation to the board before I can release the money. It makes sense for you to come over. It shouldn't take more than a couple of days. The snag is, I'm leaving this afternoon. The helicopter's due here

at two to take me to London City Airport, and then I'm
taking the company jet back to Florence.'

'Oh, I see,' she murmured, disconcerted by the way
the bubble had deflated at his businesslike tone. 'I'll ring
my assistant Maxi. She can pack me a bag and meet us
at City Airport. Don't worry. It's not a problem.'

This was good news. Fantastic news, in fact. Gio had
committed to sorting out the theatre's financial situation.
And she could think of worse things than spending a few
days in Florence—especially after the hideous stress of
the last few months. She had earned a break. And they
could spare some of the theatre's money on a guesthouse
now they were going to have plenty. She might even find
time for some sightseeing.

'Arranging leave will be fine,' she said, managing to
be businesslike and efficient at last. 'The sooner we can
make it official the better.'

She and Gio probably wouldn't see that much of
each other, she thought, dismissing the prickle of disappointment. 'Is it okay if I have a shower?' she asked,
keeping her tone polite and impersonal.

'Go ahead and use the *en suite*,' he said, just as im-
personally. 'I'll take the bathroom down the hall.'

But as she stepped into the bathroom she caught a
glimpse of Gio's naked behind as he walked to his
dresser, and realised her pheromones weren't being
nearly as businesslike and efficient as the rest of her.

Gio grinned as the door to the *en suite* bathroom clicked
closed. The offer to scrub her back had been close to irresistible. But he wasn't twenty-one any more—and he
didn't plan to rush into anything he couldn't control. He

would have to make sure Issy understood exactly what their little trip to Florence meant, and what it didn't, before he made his next move.

And once they'd got that settled he planned to indulge himself.

He pulled jeans and a T-shirt out of the dresser, listened to the gush of water from the shower and imagined Issy's lush, naked body slick with soapsuds.

After ten years, and two bouts of mind-blowing sex, he was finally going to get the chance to seduce Issy Helligan without anything between them. No guilt, no responsibility, no hurt feelings and preferably no clothes.

And he intended to savour every single second.

CHAPTER FIVE

'THAT guy's your Duke?' Maxi whispered loudly, as she passed Issy her battered wheel-around suitcase. Her eyes remained glued to Gio's retreating back as he disappeared into the sea of passengers at the airport's security checkpoint. 'How could you have kept *him* a secret all this time? I mean, look at that backside.'

'Max, close your mouth. You look like a guppy,' Issy said testily. After the strain of the last few hours she was feeling more than a little out of sorts—and she didn't want to deal with Maxi's regression into a fourteen-year-old schoolgirl.

Frankly, she was having enough trouble dealing with her own vivid fantasies about Gio. They'd done the wild thing. Once. And that had been quite enough. For both of them. So why couldn't she stop thinking about doing it again? Especially given that Gio had made it crystal-clear he wasn't in the market for a repeat performance.

After a twenty-minute shower she'd arrived downstairs, to find Gio in a meeting with the landscape architects and Jack Bradshaw assigned as her chaperon.

Jack had graciously invited her to share a buffet of

delicious antipasti dishes with the group of young architects and engineers working on the Hall project. But her stomach had tied itself in tight little knots as she'd fielded a barrage of questions from Gio's team about their shared childhood at the Hall. Did they all know about her private appointment in his bedroom earlier? If only he could put in an appearance so she didn't have to deal with their avid curiosity all on her own.

But Gio hadn't appeared. Thankfully Jack had whisked her off on a tour of the Hall after lunch, so she hadn't had too much time to examine why she felt so disappointed.

It hadn't stopped the strange and inexplicable feelings that had sprung to the surface as she and Jack had strolled through her childhood home and he'd pointed out all Gio's improvements. She hadn't needed Jack's running commentary. She'd seen for herself the remarkable changes he'd made. And the tight little knots of disappointment and embarrassment had quickly turned to giant knots of confusion as she marvelled at the brilliance and artistry of Gio's redesign.

The forbidding, cramped and suffocating rooms had been turned into light, airy spaces by knocking down partition walls and reinstating windows that had been boarded up. Old carpets had been ripped out to reveal beautiful inlaid mosaic flooring, a new staircase had been constructed using traditional carpentry to open up the second floor, and the grimly unappealing below stairs kitchen had been turned into a state-of-the art catering space any master chef would have been proud of by digging out the basement and adding yet more light with a domed atrium.

Gio had brought the Hall back from the dead. But, more than that, he'd given it a new lease of life. And she couldn't help wondering why he would have gone to all this trouble.

He'd left the Hall all those years ago, and to her knowledge had never come back. Not once bothering to contact his father or even attend the Duke's funeral. She'd always thought he hated this place, so why had he restored it so sensitively? Had he wanted to prove something?

And why couldn't she shake the odd feeling of pride in his achievements? What Gio had done to his father's house had nothing whatsoever to do with her.

The helicopter ride to London had gone smoothly enough; the noise in the cabin making it impossible for them to speak without shouting. Gio had worked on his laptop and she hadn't disturbed him, even though a million and one questions about the Hall and what he'd done to it had kept popping into her head.

This was a business trip. And she had to keep it that way. Asking Gio questions about his motivations for restoring the Hall felt too personal.

Unfortunately, every time his thigh had brushed against the silk of her dress, or his elbow had bumped hers on the armrest, business was the last thing on her mind. And by the time they'd arrived at City Airport and been whisked into the terminal building, Issy's hormones had been cartwheeling like Olympic gymnasts.

She'd only had a moment to introduce Gio to Maxi, and watch her friend gush all over him, before he'd excused himself again, explaining that he had a few calls to make and would meet her on the plane.

The ludicrous thing was, she was starting to get a

bit of a complex about how eager he seemed to ignore her. Which was totally idiotic. She didn't need his attention. Or want it. It would only encourage her cartwheeling hormones.

Maxi's excited chatter wasn't helping. Reminding her of all the giggly conversations she'd once had about Gio in her teens.

'How do you know him?' Maxi asked, still gushing like his number one fan. 'It's obvious there's a connection between you. Is that why he offered to fund the theatre?' Maxi turned wide eyes on her. 'You're having a fling, aren't you?'

Colour flushed into Issy's cheeks. 'We are not,' she said, pretty sure one bout of wild monkey sex didn't count. 'We grew up together. He's an old friend.'

Maxi's eyes narrowed. 'Then why are you going to Florence with him? And why are you blushing?'

'I'm not blushing,' she lied, cursing her pale skin. 'And I have to go to Florence to sign the sponsorship papers. It's just a formality. I told you that.'

'Iss, don't get me wrong,' Maxi said, putting on her sincere face and grating on Issy's nerves even more. 'I think it's fab that he's taking you to Florence. You absolutely deserve a break. Especially with someone as tasty as that. You don't have to pretend with me. We're mates.' She nudged Issy's shoulder. 'And I'll give Dave and the troops the official story, I promise.' She smiled. 'So, how long have you two been an item?'

Good grief.

Issy yanked up the handle on her suitcase. 'It's not an official story. It's the truth.'

'Oh, come on,' Maxi scoffed. 'Let's examine the

evidence here,' she said in her no-nonsense voice. The one Issy usually appreciated. 'First off: no one needs to travel anywhere to sign a few papers these days, because it can all be done by e-mail.' She began to count off points on her fingers. 'Second: it's obvious you've had a shower in the last few hours, because your hair has started to frizz at the ends.'

Issy touched her hair self-consciously, remembering how observant Maxi was.

'And then there's the rip in the back of your dress to account for.'

Far *too* observant.

'And, last but by no means least,' Maxi continued, 'there's the way he looked at you just now.'

'What way?'

'Like he wanted to devour you in one quick bite.'

Okay, that was an observation too far. Gio had gone out of his way to avoid her for the last two hours. She ought to know. She had the inferiority complex to prove it.

'No, he didn't.'

'Yes, he did.' Maxi's quick grin had Issy blinking. 'I saw him. Those dreamy brown eyes went all sexy and intense, and he stared at you so long even I started to get excited. And I'm just an innocent bystander. If you aren't already having a hot, passionate fling with that guy, you should be.'

'But that's…' She sputtered to a stop, embarrassingly excited herself now. 'That's not possible.'

'Why not?'

'Because…' Her mind went totally blank as her hormones cartwheeled off a cliff.

'Miss Helligan? Mr Hamilton has asked me to escort you through Security.'

Issy turned to find a man in a flight attendant's uniform hovering at her elbow.

'Right. Fine.'

Please, God, don't let him have heard any of that.

She gave Maxi a quick hug. 'I've got my mobile if you need to call. But I'll check in tonight when I know where I'm staying. Give Dave and the troops the good news. And see if you can't locate the—'

'Issy, stop organising and go. Everything's under control.' Maxi squeezed her extra hard. 'Be sure to give His Grace my extra special thanks,' she whispered wiggling her eyebrows suggestively. 'And please feel free to do anything I wouldn't do.'

Issy shot her a hard stare, but couldn't think of a thing to say that would sound remotely convincing. It seemed she had some serious thinking to do—because her trip to Florence had just got a great deal more dangerous.

'This way, Miss Helligan. Mr Hamilton is waiting for you on the plane.'

Issy tried to take stock of the situation as the flight attendant led her past the endless queue snaking towards the security checkpoint.

'But what about passport control and security?' she asked, trailing behind him.

Did none of the usual headaches of air travel apply to a man with Gio's lifestyle?

But as she followed her battered suitcase through the door the attendant held open, and watched it being whisked through an X-ray machine by her own personal security official, it occurred to her that Gio's wealth and success were the least of her worries.

Mounting the metal steps of a sleek silver jet with the GH Partnership logo emblazoned on its tail, she tried to think rationally.

She'd planned to be in complete control here. But she wasn't. This was supposed to be a business trip. Plain and simple. Nothing more. Nothing less. But what if it wasn't?

Gio stepped out of the pilot's cabin as she boarded the plane—and she felt a traitorous thrill shoot through her. He looked relaxed and in control as he leaned against the metal portal, folded his arms over his chest and let his eyes wander over her figure. His casual attire of jeans and a faded T-shirt were at odds with the jet's luxury leather seats and thick pile carpeting, but they reminded her of the reckless, rebellious boy.

But he wasn't that boy any more. He was a man. A wildly successful, dangerously sexy man she'd agreed to go to Florence with. His gaze drifted back to her face. Make that a wildly successful, dangerously sexy man with a very predatory gleam in his eye.

How could she not have spotted that earlier?

'Hello, Isadora,' he said, his voice a husky murmur. 'Ready for lift-off?'

Her nipples puckered into bullet points, her toes curled in her pumps—and she wondered if he was talking in euphemisms just to annoy her.

Ignoring the flush working its way up her neck, she decided to wrestle back some control. He'd bulldozed her into this. It was about time she found out exactly what was going on.

'Is there really any paperwork to sign in Florence?'

He rubbed his jaw. 'Now, why would you ask that?'

he said as the predatory gleam went laser-sharp. And she knew she'd been had.

'This has all been a set-up, hasn't it? But why…?' Her indignation cut off as the blood drained out of her face. 'The sponsorship? That wasn't a joke too, was it?'

'You can cut the drama queen act.' He chuckled, stepped towards her. 'I've already spoken to Luca and the money will be transferred tomorrow, once you give him your bank details.'

Her relief was short-lived as indignation surged back. 'So why am I going to Florence?'

He placed his hands on her hips, his eyes darker than the devil's. 'Why don't you take a wild guess?'

'I've got a better idea.' She braced her palms against his chest. 'Why don't you give me a straight answer?'

'All right, then,' he said, not remotely chastened. 'I plan to spend a few days ravaging you senseless.'

'Ravaging…' Her jaw went slack as fire spiked her cheeks and roasted her sex. 'Are you insane?'

The smug smile got bigger. 'Stop pretending to be outraged. Once wasn't enough. And you know it.'

A sharp reprimand rose up in her throat, but got choked off when his fingers sank into her hair and his lips covered hers in a hungry, demanding kiss.

She pushed him away, clinging onto the last edge of sanity. 'I'm not doing this. It's…' *What?* 'A very bad idea.'

'Why?'

'It just is.' If he gave her a moment she could probably come up with a thousand reasons. Just because she couldn't think of any right this second…

His hands caressed her scalp, making it hard for her

to think straight. 'Issy, the past's over,' he murmured. 'But if you're still hung up on—'

'Of course I'm not,' she cut in. 'This has nothing to do with our past.' She pulled out of his arms. 'And everything to do with your unbelievable arrogance. How dare you trick me into coming to Florence? When exactly were you going to tell me about your plans to ravage me senseless?'

His lips quirked some more. 'I'm telling you now.'

'Well, that's not good enough. What if I want to say no?'

He drew a thumb down her cheek, his eyes black with arousal. 'And do you?'

Even as the denial formed in her mind, it was muted by the long, liquid pull low in her belly. 'No...I mean, yes,' she said, scrambling to keep a firm grip on her indignation.

His palm settled on her nape. 'Let's finish what we started.' His thumb stroked her throat, stoking the fire at her core. 'Then we can both move on.'

Could it really be that simple? Was this thing between them just left-over sexual chemistry?

But even as she tried to make sense of her feelings he tugged her towards him and took her mouth in another mind-numbing kiss.

Her fingers curled into the cotton of his T-shirt, but this time she couldn't find the will to push him away. The pent-up hunger of only a few hours ago burst free as her tongue tangled with his.

He drew back first, the slow smile melting the last of her resistance. 'No ties. No strings. Just some great sex and then we go our separate ways. It's your choice. If you can't handle it, we part now. I'm not interested in anything serious.'

'I'm perfectly well aware of your commitment problems,' she countered.

Not only did she have personal experience, but when she'd been Googling him yesterday she'd found numerous paparazzi shots of him with supermodels and starlets and society princesses on his arm. And not one photo of him with the same woman twice. The man's track record when it came to relationships sucked. Any fool could see that.

'As long as that's understood,' he said easily, clearly not insulted in the least, 'I don't see a problem.' The sensual smile made the heat pound harder. 'Florence is spectacular at this time of year, and I have a villa in the hills where we can satisfy all our prurient sexual fantasies. And, believe me, after ten years I've stored up quite a few.' He threaded his fingers into her hair, pushed the heavy curls away from her face. 'We had fun together when we were kids, Issy. We could have more fun now.'

Issy swallowed, the rough feel of his palm on her cheek making the promise of pleasure all but irresistible. 'And the theatre's sponsorship will be okay either way?' she clarified, desperate not to get swept away on a sea of lust too soon.

He gave his head a small shake. 'I already told you—'

'Okay. Yes,' she interrupted, placing her hands on his shoulders. 'I accept.'

Gio was dangerous. Yes. But danger could be thrilling as well as frightening. And right now the thrill was winning. Big-time. She felt like Alice, tumbling head first into Wonderland. Exhilarated, excited, and totally terrified.

His arms banded around her waist. 'Good.'

Issy had bounced up on her toes, eager to seal their devil's bargain, when she heard a gruff chuckle from behind them.

'You'll have to save that for later, Hamilton,' said an unfamiliar voice.

She jerked round, spotting a stout, older man in a pilot's uniform.

'Our slot's in ten minutes,' the man said, sending her an indulgent smile. 'I'm sorry, miss, but we need to do the final equipment check.'

Gio swore softly, touched his forehead to hers, then stepped to one side. 'Issy, this is James Braithwaite,' he said, keeping his arm round her waist. 'Co-pilot and all-round killjoy.'

Issy shook the man's hand before her foggy brain registered the information. 'Did you say co-pilot?'

'That's right,' Gio said nonchalantly, giving her a quick kiss on the nose and letting her go. 'You'd better get strapped in.'

'Wait a minute.' Issy held his arm, her fingers trembling. 'You're not flying this thing yourself?'

The sleek jet suddenly morphed into a metallic death trap. Images flashed through her mind of Gio as a teenager after he'd totalled his father's vintage Bentley, or Gio on his motorbike with her clinging on the back, shooting around blind bends at twenty miles above the speed limit.

Okay, maybe she could risk a quick fling with Gio, to finish what they'd started this afternoon, but she wasn't about to risk her life letting him fly her anywhere. The boy had always had a need for too much speed and far too little caution. On the evidence so far, she wasn't convinced the man was any less reckless.

Gio grinned at her horrified expression. 'Oh, ye of little faith,' he murmured. 'I happen to be a qualified pilot, Isadora. With a good solid one hundred hours of flying time under my belt.' His smile widened as he stroked her cheek, weakening her resolve, not to mention her thigh muscles. 'Trust me. You're perfectly safe in my hands.'

As she strapped herself into her seat and watched him duck into the pilot's cabin, Issy knew she'd be mad to trust Gio Hamilton with anything.

But forewarned was forearmed. And, given how well aware she was of Gio's shortcomings, she was more than capable of keeping herself safe this time.

After a smooth take-off, and an even smoother touch down in Pisa two hours later, Issy had to concede Gio could be trusted to pilot an aircraft without plummeting her to earth. But when he ushered her just as smoothly into an open-topped Ferrari at the airport, then sped her through miles of glorious sun-drenched Italian countryside, her pulse continued to thump like a sledgehammer and she knew she shouldn't trust him with anything else.

The noise of the wind and the rush of the heart-stopping scenery meant they couldn't talk during the drive. Which gave Issy more than enough time to think.

Was what she had agreed to do demeaning? After all, what self-respecting smart, capable career woman agreed to be ravaged senseless?

But after examining their arrangement Issy came to

the conclusion she didn't have a choice. Because Gio was right. She needed to get over the dirty trick her hormones had been playing on her for years.

She'd had a measly two proper boyfriends since Gio had introduced her to the joys of sex. And both relationships had ended with a whimper rather than a bang. At the time she'd told herself it was because she wasn't ready, because the timing hadn't been right, because the two guys she'd dated hadn't been right for her. But now she knew the truth.

That special spark, that frisson of sexual energy that had exploded in her face today had always been missing. Sex wasn't the *most* important thing in a relationship. She knew that. But it wasn't unimportant either. She'd compared Johnny and Sam to Gio in bed without even knowing it, and found them wanting. Maybe it was some sort of natural selection, a mating instinct thing— after all Gio was the ultimate alpha male in the sack— or maybe it was just that Gio had been her first. But whatever the problem was it needed to be dealt with.

Because if she didn't deal with it she might never be able to form a long-term committed relationship with anyone, ever. The sort of relationship she'd spent her girlhood dreaming about. The sort of relationship her parents had shared before her father's early death. The sort of relationship she'd almost given up hope of ever being able to find for herself.

This wasn't about letting Gio ravage her senseless— it was about releasing her from the sexual hold he had always had over her, ever since that first night, and allowing her to forget about him so she would be free to find the *real* one true love of her life.

Convinced she'd satisfied all her concerns about the trip, Issy couldn't understand why her pulse refused to settle down during the drive. In fact it was still working overtime when Gio steered the Ferrari off a narrow cobbled road in the hills around the city and onto a tree-lined drive.

The scent of lemon trees perfumed the air as he braked in front of a picture-perfect Florentine villa constructed of dusky pink terracotta stone. A grand fountain with two naked water nymphs entwined at its centre tinkled quietly in the circular forecourt.

Issy gawped as Gio leapt effortlessly out of the low-slung car.

She wasn't a stranger to wealth and privilege, for goodness' sake. She'd spent the formative years of her life living below stairs in a stately home. So why had her pulse just skipped into overdrive?

He opened the car door. As she stepped onto the pebbled drive she had to remind herself to breathe.

The carved oak entrance door swung open as they approached. A middle-aged woman with a homely face and a pretty smile bowed her head and introduced herself in Italian as Carlotta. Gio introduced Issy in turn, and then had a conversation with the housekeeper before she excused herself.

Hearing Gio speak Italian had Issy's heartbeat kicking up another notch.

How strange. Even though he spoke English with barely a hint of an accent, Issy knew he was fluent in Italian. But there was something about hearing the language flow so fluidly, watching him use his hands for emphasis, that made him seem very sophisticated and

European—as far removed from the surly boy she remembered as it was possible to get.

She tried to shake off her uneasiness and calm her frantic heartbeat, but as Gio led her through a series of increasingly beautiful rooms the unsettled feeling only got worse.

The house's furnishings were few, but suited the open Mediterranean layout and looked hand-crafted and expensive. The minimalist luxury should have made the place seem exclusive and unapproachable, but it didn't. As they walked into a wide, open-plan living area, the brightly coloured rugs, the lush, leafy potted plants and the stacks of dog-eared architectural magazines on the coffee table gave its elegance a lived-in feel, making the house seem unpretentious and inviting.

Gio held open a glass door at the end of the room and beckoned her forward.

Issy stepped on to a balcony which looked across the valley past a steeply terraced garden. At the bottom of the hill in the distance the sluggish Arno River wound its way through Florence, the city laid out below them like a carpet of wonders. She could make out the Ponte Vecchio to her right, probably heaving with tourists in the sweltering afternoon heat, and appreciated the citrus-perfumed breeze even more. Walking to the low stone wall that edged the terrace, she spotted a large pool in the lawned garden one level below, its crystal blue waters sparkling in the sunshine.

'Goodness,' she whispered, as her heartbeat pounded in her ears.

Who would have expected the wild, reckless boy

whom she had assumed would never settle anywhere to make himself a home almost too beautiful to be real?

'So what do you think?' he asked.

She turned to find him standing behind her, studying her, his hands tucked into the back pockets of his jeans. She thought she saw a muscle in his jaw tense. As if he were anxious about what she might say.

Don't be an idiot.

He didn't care what she thought. That had to be a trick of the light. He knew how amazing this place was. And she knew perfectly well she was only one in a very long line of women he'd invited here.

Don't you dare start analysing every little nuance of his behaviour, you ninny. Reading things into it that aren't there.

She cleared her throat. 'I think you have incredible taste.' She stared out at the breathtaking view. 'And calling this place a villa doesn't do it justice. I think paradise would be more appropriate.'

'It'll do for now,' he said casually.

His palms settled on her waist. Tugging her back against his chest, he nuzzled the sensitive skin below her ear. 'Although, given what I'm thinking right now, paradise lost would be the best choice.'

She gasped out a laugh, finding it hard to breathe as brutal realisation hit her. Being in Gio's home would involve an intimacy she hadn't bargained on during all her careful justifications.

'Why don't we go check out the master bedroom?' he said, the humour doing nothing to mask his intentions. He folded his arms around her waist, making her breasts feel heavy and tender as he drew her into a hard hug. 'I'd love to know what you think of the…' He paused provocatively, nipping her earlobe. 'View…'

She pictured the view the last time they'd been naked together. And the hot, heavy weight in her belly pulsed. Panic spiked at the vicious throb of desire.

I'm not ready for this. Not yet.

She whipped round to face him, breaking his hold. 'Could we go sightseeing?' she said, trying not to wince at the high-pitched note in her voice.

She couldn't dive back into bed with him. Not straight away. Sex was one thing, intimacy another, and she couldn't afford to confuse the two.

His brows rose up his forehead. 'You want to go sightseeing? Seriously?'

'Yes, please. I adore sightseeing,' she said, keeping her voice as firm as possible to disguise the lie. She could feel his arousal against her hip and eased back a step. 'I've never been to Florence. I'm dying to see as much of it as I can. Could we eat in the city tonight?' A couple of hours to establish some distance. That was all she needed. She was sure of it. 'I've never been to Italy before,' she rattled on, pretending not to notice the frown on his face. 'And I've heard Florence has some of the best *trattorias* in Italy.'

What the…?

Gio knew a delaying tactic when he heard one. And Issy's sudden transformation into super-tourist definitely qualified. He spotted the rigid peaks of her breasts beneath her dress, the staggered rise and fall of her breathing—and almost howled with frustration.

Hadn't they settled all this on the plane?

He was ready to get to the main event now. More than ready. In fact, if he hadn't been co-piloting the plane he would have got to it sooner, giving in to the temptation to initiate her into the Mile-High Club.

Thrusting his hands into his pockets, he kept his face carefully blank. Her cheeks were a bright rosy pink but he could see the alarm on her face.

He should have guessed things wouldn't be that straightforward, because nothing ever was with Issy. She'd been jumpy ever since they'd walked into the house. He'd enjoyed her nerves at first. Keeping Issy off-kilter was a good way to handle her. And it hadn't done his ego any harm to see how impressed she was with his home.

But when she'd turned round, her eyes wide with surprise, he'd had the strangest sensation she could see right through him. And for the first time in his life he'd wanted to ask a woman what she was thinking.

Not that he intended to do it. For one thing, straight answers were not Issy's forte. And for another, he had a golden rule against asking women personal questions. Once you opened that floodgate it was impossible to slam it shut again.

He'd already broken one golden rule by inviting her into his home. He generally avoided getting into any kind of routine with the women he dated.

'Sure. No problem.' He forced his shoulders to relax.

If Issy wanted to play hard to get for an evening, why not let her? He could slow the pace for a few hours. If he had to.

'I know a place not far from the Piazza della Repubblica. Their *bistecca fiorentina*'s like a religion.'

And Latini had the sort of low-key, unpretentious atmosphere that should relax her while still being classy enough to impress her.

He would ply her with a couple of glasses of their Chianti Classico, comfort-feed her the Florentine speciality and indulge in a spot of light conversation. Maybe he'd even show her a few of the sights. Keep things easy. He could do that. For an evening.

'Are you sure?' she said, sounding surprised but looking so relieved he smiled.

'Yeah. It'll be fun,' he said, forcing down his frustration. He could wait a while longer to get her naked. He wasn't *that* desperate.

Then a thought struck him, and he realised he could make it more fun than he'd figured. He smiled some more. 'We can take the Vespa. My mechanic Mario gave it an overhaul recently, so it's running fairly well for once.'

'A scooter?' She had the same shocked look he'd seen on the plane. 'You ride a scooter? That sounds a bit incongruous for a duke.'

'Now, Isadora.' He brushed a thumb across her cheekbone. 'I hope you're not saying I'm a snob?' he teased as her cheeks pinkened prettily. 'No Florentine with a brain takes a car into the city. A scooter is the only way to go.'

And, like all natives, he drove his Vespa at breakneck speed. Which meant she'd have to glue herself to him to stop from falling off.

His grin got bigger as his gaze flicked down her outfit. 'If you've got some jeans, you might want to put them on. The staff will have put your suitcase in the master bedroom.' Placing his hands on her shoulders, he directed her towards a wrought-iron staircase at the end of the terrace. 'Take those stairs and the door's at the end of the balcony. I'll get the Vespa out of the garage and meet you out front.'

By the time they got back here, he'd have her naked soon enough.

Mounting the stairs to the upper balcony, Issy watched Gio stroll across the terrace, those damn denims hugging his gorgeous butt like a second skin.

She dragged her gaze away and took a moment to admire the almost as phenomenal view of Florence at dusk. In the enormous bedroom suite she slipped into jeans and a simple white wraparound blouse, and stared at the king-size mahogany bed dominating the room. The reckless thrill cascading through her body at the thought of what the nights and days ahead would hold had the hot, heavy feeling turning to aching need.

She huffed out a breath.

Okay, abstinence had never been an option. Not where Gio was concerned. He was too irresistible. And trying to distract him from the inevitable would only end up frustrating them both.

But that did not mean he got to have everything his own way. He'd railroaded her into boarding that plane, then exploited the hunger between them to get exactly what he wanted. Mindless sex with no strings attached.

Well, fine, she didn't want any strings either. But it wasn't as easy for her to simply dismiss their past. And she wasn't quite as adept at separating sex from intimacy, the way he was. And the reason why was simple. She'd never had sex with a stranger before. Or not intentionally. But she could see now that was exactly what Gio was. Now.

Finding a lavish *en suite* bathroom, she spent a few extra minutes brushing out her hair, washing her face and reapplying her make-up. And struggling to slow the rapid ticks of her heartbeat.

She'd once believed she knew Gio and understood him. And from there it had been one short step into love.

After that first night she'd always thought the reasons why she'd been so foolish were simple. She'd been young and immature and in desperate need of male approval. She'd lost her father at an early age, and it had left an aching hole in the centre of her life that couldn't be filled. Until Gio had appeared, a sad, surly but magnetic boy, who had seemed to need her as much as she needed him.

But now she could see there had been another, less obvious reason why she'd fallen in love with a figment of her own imagination.

Even when they were children there had been an air of mystery about Gio. He'd always been so guarded and cautious about any kind of personal information.

She had talked endlessly about her hopes and dreams, about her mum, about her schoolfriends, even about the shows she liked to watch on TV. Gio had listened to her chatter, but had said virtually nothing about his own life, his own hopes and dreams in return. She'd never even had an inkling he was interested in design. No wonder she had been so surprised about his success as an architect.

And then there had been the wall of silence surrounding the ten months of the year he spent in Rome, with his mother.

As a teenager, Issy had been totally in awe of Claudia Lorenzo—like every other girl her age. A flamboyant and stunningly beautiful bit-part actress, who had fought her way out of the Milan slums, Gio's mother had reinvented herself as a fashion icon, gracing the pages of *Vogue* and *Vanity Fair* while on a merry-go-round of affairs and marriages with rich, powerful men. Not all that surprisingly, Issy had quizzed Gio mercilessly about 'La Lorenzo' in her early teens.

But Gio had always refused to talk about his mother. So Issy had eventually stopped asking, conjuring up all sorts of romantic reasons why he should keep his life in Rome a secret.

Issy squared her shoulders and ran unsteady palms down the stiff new denim of her jeans. Why not use this week to dispel that air of mystery. To finally satisfy her curiosity about Gio? She'd always wanted to know why Gio kept so many secrets and why he seemed so determined never to have a permanent relationship. Once she had her answer, his power to fascinate her, to tantalise her, would be gone for good.

Gio was unlikely to co-operate, of course—being as guarded now as he had ever been—and it would be hard not to get sidetracked while indulging in all the physical pleasures and revelling in the sights, sounds and tastes of the beautiful Tuscan capital.

But luckily for her she was a master at multi-tasking, and she never backed down from a challenge. Skills she'd perfected while running the theatre and handling everything from actors' egos to imminent bankruptcy. Why not put those skills to good use?

So she could enjoy everything the next few days

had to offer. Get over her addiction to Gio's superstar abilities in bed. And finally get complete closure on all the mistakes of her past.

CHAPTER SIX

'So why are you so petrified of commitment?'

Gio choked on the expensive Chianti he'd been sipping, so surprised by Issy's probing question he had to grab his napkin to catch the spray. He put the glass down on the restaurant's white linen tablecloth, next to the remains of the mammoth T-bone steak they'd shared. 'Issy, I've just eaten about a half pound of rare beef. What are you trying to do? Give me indigestion?' he said, only half joking.

Where had that come from?

Everything had been going surprisingly well till now. Their sightseeing trip had been less of a chore than he'd expected. Issy had always been sexy as hell, but he'd forgotten how refreshing, funny and forthright she was too.

Perhaps because she was still a little jumpy, she'd hardly stopped talking since they'd left the villa, but rather than annoying him the mostly one-sided conversation had brought back fond memories from their childhood. For a boy who had been taught as soon as he could speak that it was better to keep his mouth shut, listening to Issy talk had made him feel blissfully normal. Having her chatter wash over him again tonight had reminded him how much he'd once enjoyed just listening to her speak.

The only time she'd been silent was when he'd whipped his classic Vespa through the streets of Florence with her clinging on like a limpet. Which had brought back another more visceral memory of that first wild ride aboard his motorbike.

After that he'd needed a distraction. Her warm breasts pressing against his back had not done a great deal for his self-control. So he'd had the inspired idea of taking her on a private tour of the Uffizi while he cooled off. But as they'd walked hand in hand through the darkened Vasari gallery and she'd peppered him with questions, a strange thing had happened. He'd watched Issy's face light up when she took in the Renaissance splendour of Boticelli's *Primavera*, heard her in-drawn breath at the ethereal beauty of Titian's *Venus*, and he'd really started to enjoy himself.

He'd taken a few dates here before, but none of them had been as awestruck and excited by the beauty of the art as Issy.

When they'd got to Latini for a late dinner, Issy had devoured the rich, succulent Tuscan speciality with the same fervour. But, as he'd watched her lick the rich gravy from her full bottom lip, enjoyment and nostalgia had turned sharply to anticipation.

As much as he'd enjoyed Issy's company over the last few hours, her avid appreciation of the art and her entertaining abilities as a conversationalist, he didn't want to talk any more. And especially not about his least favourite subject.

But before he could think of a subtle way to change the subject, she started up again.

'You're always so adamant you don't do permanent. You don't do the long-haul,' she said, looking him straight in the eye. 'Don't you think that's a bit peculiar? Especially for a man of your age?'

'I'm only thirty-one,' he said, annoyed. It wasn't as if he were about to pick up his pension.

'I know, but isn't that when most men are thinking of settling down? Having kids?'

That did it. Forget subtle—he wasn't having this conversation. No way. 'Why do you care? Unless you're angling for a proposal?' he said, a bit too forcefully.

Instead of looking hurt or offended, she laughed. 'Stop being so conceited. A man with your commitment problems is hardly the catch of the century.'

'That's good to know,' he grumbled, not as pleased as he would have expected by the off-hand remark.

Propping her elbow on the table, she leaned into her palm and gazed at him. 'I'm just really curious. What happened to make you so dead set against having a proper relationship?'

'I *have* proper relationships,' he said, not sure why he was defending himself. 'What do you call this?'

She giggled, her deep blue eyes sparkling mischievously in the candlelight. 'An *improper* relationship.'

'Very funny,' he said wryly as blood pounded into his groin.

Signalling the waiter, he asked for the bill in Italian. As the man left, laden with their empty plates, Gio topped up their wine glasses. 'Let's go back to the villa for dessert,' he said. Time to stop debating this nonsense and start debating which part of her he planned to feast on first. 'And discuss *how* improper.'

Seeing the heat and the determination on his face, Issy struggled to keep the simmering passion at bay that she was sure he'd been stoking all evening.

Every time his fingers cupped her elbow, every time his palm settled on the small of her back, every time his breath brushed across her earlobe as he whispered some amusing story or anecdote in her ear, or his chocolate gaze raked over her figure, her arousal had kicked up another notch. And she was sure he knew it.

But she wasn't going to be distracted that easily. Not yet anyway.

'What's the matter, Gio. Don't you *know* why you can't maintain a relationship?'

He drummed his fingers on the table, the rhythmic taps doing nothing to diminish the intensity in those melted chocolate eyes. 'It's not that I can't,' he replied. 'It's that I don't want to.' He leaned forward, placed his elbows on the table, a confident smile curving his lips. 'Why would I bother if it will never work?'

'What makes you think that?' she asked, stunned by the note of bitterness.

'People get together because of animal attraction,' he said, adding a cynical tilt to his smile. 'But that doesn't last. Eventually they hate each other, even if they pretend not to.' He took her wrist off the table, skimmed his thumb across the pulse-point. 'It's human nature. Relationships are about sex. You can dress it up with hearts and flowers if you want. But I choose not to.'

Issy sucked in a breath, shocked by the conviction in his voice and a little hurt by the brittle, condescending tone.

The evening so far had been magical. So magical she had been lulled into a false sense of companionship to go with the heady sexual thrill.

From the moment Gio's vintage scooter had careered down the steep cobbled hill into the city, his rock-hard abs tensing beneath her fingertips and the wind catching her hair, the sexual thrill had shot into her bloodstream like a drug. She was in Florence with a devastatingly handsome man who knew how to play her erogenous zones like a virtuoso. Why not ride the high?

But as the evening wore on it wasn't just the promise of physical pleasure that excited her.

Their first stop had been the world-famous Uffizi art gallery, where an eager young architectural student who worked as a night-guard and obviously idolised Gio had ushered them into a veritable cave of wonders of Italian art treasures.

Gio had taken courses in art history as part of his degree, and hadn't seemed to mind answering her endless questions. He'd regaled her with fascinating stories about the paintings on display, and talked about his love of art and architecture with a knowledge and passion so unlike the reticence she remembered about him as a boy it had captivated her.

When they'd stepped out of the gallery, darkness had fallen, the cloaking spell of evening giving the city a new and enchanting vibrancy. The tourists had all but disappeared, no doubt retiring to their hotels after a day spent sightseeing in the merciless August heat, and the locals had reclaimed their streets. Crowds of young, stylish Florentines, posing and gesticulating, spilled out of bars and cafés into cramped alleyways and grand *piazzas*, illuminated by neon and lamplight. As she'd clung on to Gio and watched Florence and its inhabitants whip past, Issy had been assailed by a powerful sense of belonging. Tonight, with Gio beside her, it didn't seem to matter that she didn't speak a word of Italian and couldn't have looked less Mediterranean if she tried. She knew it was a fanciful notion, conjured by the city's enchanting allure, but it had brought with it a buzz of anticipation to complement the desire coursing through her veins.

What if she and Gio could become friends again, as well as lovers, during their weekend of debauchery?

The meal had been equally glorious. The small but packed *trattoria* wore its centuries-old history on its smoke-stained walls and in the sensational tastes and textures of its signature dish. Gio was clearly a regular. The head waiter had clapped him on the back and led them to the only table which wasn't communal as soon as they'd arrived.

Issy suspected Gio had entertained hundreds of other women here before, but she refused to care. This was a few days out of time for both of them. A chance not just to indulge in the intense physical attraction between them, but maybe also to renew the precious childhood companionship they'd once shared before misunderstandings and maturity—and one night of misguided sex—had destroyed it.

But how could they do that if Gio insisted on shutting her out and treating her as if her view on love and relationships was beneath contempt?

Maybe she'd been young and foolish at seventeen, and she'd certainly made an enormous mistake picking Gio as her Mr Right, but she intended to carry on looking—and she resented him implying that made her an imbecile.

She tugged her hand out of his. 'That's all very interesting, Gio. But what about love? What about when you find the person you want to spend the rest of your life with?'

'You don't still believe that's going to happen, do you?' he said with an incredulous laugh.

'Yes, I do. It happens all the time. It was exactly like that for my parents,' she said with passion, her temper mounting. 'They adored each other. My mum still talks about my dad, and he's been dead for twenty-one years.'

'If you say so,' he said, sounding sceptical. 'But that would make *your* parents the exception, not the rule.'

She heard the tinge of regret, not quite drowned out by his condescension, and her temper died. 'What makes you think your parents aren't the exception?'

He stiffened at the quiet comment, and she knew she'd hit on the truth. Gio's cynicism, his bitterness, had nothing to do with his opinion of her but with the terrible example his own parents had set.

Although the Hamiltons had divorced three years before she and her mum had come to live at the Hall, lurid stories about the split had fed the rumour mill in Hamilton's Cross for years afterwards.

Two impossibly beautiful and volatile people, Claudia Lorenzo, the flamboyant Italian socialite, and Charles Hamilton, the playboy Duke of Connaught, had indulged in years of vicious infighting and public spats, before Claudia had finally stormed out for good, taking their nine-year-old son back to Italy with her. The brutal custody battle that followed had made headlines in both the local and national press. Although Issy had never understood why the Duke had fought so hard for his son when he'd treated Gio so harshly during his court-ordered summer visits.

As a teenager, Issy had found the concept of Gio as a tug-of-love orphan both fabulously dramatic and wonderfully tragic, like something straight out of *Wuthering Heights*, but she could see now it must have been a living hell for him as a child. And could easily have warped his view of relationships ever since.

'Your parents were selfish, self-absorbed people,' she said. 'Who didn't care about love or each other.' *Or you*, she thought. 'But you shouldn't let that make you give up on finding a loving relationship for the rest of your life.'

Gio groaned, dumping his napkin on the table. 'Will you give it a rest? You don't know what you're talking about.'

It wasn't quite the reaction she'd been hoping for, but she wasn't going to give up that easily.

'I know enough,' she countered. 'My mother and I heard how your father shouted at you and belittled you. And I saw for myself how much it upset you,' she persevered, despite the rigid expression on his face. 'On that last night, when I found you in the orchard, you'd just had a massive row with him. You looked so upset. So...' She trailed off as he turned away, a muscle in his jaw twitching. And she realised something she should have figured out years before.

'*That's* why you needed me that night. *That's* why we made love,' she said softly, her heart punching her throat. 'Because of something he said to you.'

His head swung back, his eyes flashing hot, and she knew she'd touched a nerve.

Whatever his father had said that night had made him reach out to someone, anyone, to ease the pain. And, thanks to circumstance, that someone had been her.

The revelation shouldn't really matter now. But it did. She'd believed for ten years that their first night had been a terrible mistake, brought about by her immature romantic fantasies. But what if he really *had* needed her—just not in the way she'd thought?

'We didn't make love,' he said flatly. 'We had sex.'

She didn't even flinch at the crude words. 'What did he say?' she asked, her heart melting at the anguished frown on his face.

'Who the hell cares what he said? That was a million years ago.'

It wasn't a million years ago, but even if it had been it was obvious it still hurt.

'Dammit, you're not going to let this go, are you?'

She shook her head. 'No, I'm not.'

'Fine.' He dumped his napkin on the table. 'He told me I wasn't his son. That Claudia had screwed a dozen other men during their marriage. That I was some other man's bastard.'

Shock reverberated through her body at the ugly words. 'But you must have been devastated,' she murmured. How could the Duke have harboured that nasty little seed in his head all through Gio's childhood? And then told his son? 'But what about the custody battle. Why would he…?'

'He needed an heir.' Gio shrugged. 'And he enjoyed dragging Claudia through the courts, I suspect.'

The words were delivered in a gruff, deliberately contemptuous monotone. But underneath it she could hear a plea that he couldn't quite disguise, of the little boy who had been so easily hurt by the two people who should have cherished him the most.

'Gio, I'm so sorry.' She covered his hand where it lay on the table, and squeezed.

'Why should you be sorry?' he said, pulling his hand out from under hers. 'It didn't matter to me. In fact, it was a relief. I'd always wondered why I could never please the man.'

He was lying. It *had* mattered. He'd brooded for days every time the Duke had reprimanded him as a teenager. She'd seen the hurt and confusion he'd tried so hard to hide behind surly indifference. And she'd seen how unhappy, how volatile he'd been that night.

And still mattered now.

No wonder he found it so hard to believe that love existed. That relationships could last.

His eyes narrowed sharply. 'Bloody hell,' he said. 'Stop that right now.' Standing up he threw a fistful of euro notes on the table.

'Stop what?' she gasped as his fingers locked on her wrist and he hoisted her out of her chair.

'Stop psychoanalysing me.' He shot the clipped words over his shoulder as he walked out of the restaurant, tugging her behind him.

'I'm *not* psychoanalysing you,' she panted, trying to keep up with his long strides. 'I'm just trying to understand why…'

'There's nothing to understand.' He stopped on the street outside, his voice stiff with frustration. 'I wanted you and you wanted me. There wasn't anything significant about that night except you were a virgin. And if I'd figured that out sooner, believe me, I wouldn't have touched you no matter how tempted I was.'

The fervent denial made her emotion swell to impossible proportions. Why did he find it so hard even now to admit he'd needed someone? Even fleetingly?

'All right,' she said placatingly. 'But I still find it moving that—'

'Well, don't.' He cut her off as he marched down the street again. 'Because it's not.' They reached the scooter. 'That night was about animal passion.' Lifting the spare helmet off the handlebars, he thrust it at her. 'Climb aboard, because I've got some more animal passion for you.'

Great. She wasn't feeling that moved any more. 'Stop ordering me about.' She shoved the helmet on her head. Damn, he'd made her pout—and she hated to be a cliché. 'How about if I said I didn't *want* your animal passion?'

'You'd be lying,' he said with infuriating certainty as he mounted the scooter and jammed the key into the ignition. 'Now get on. You've got exactly ten seconds.' He stamped his foot on the start pedal. 'Or we're going to be doing it against the back wall of Latini instead of in the privacy of my bedroom. Your choice.'

'I will *not* get on your scooter!' she shouted, as colour flooded her cheeks at the sensual threat—and her traitorous nipples pebbled beneath the thin silk of her blouse.

'Ten…'

'How dare you talk to me like that?' she cried, flustered now, as well as outraged.

'Nine…'

He's kidding. He has to be.

'Eight…'

'I am not your personal floozy!'

One dark brow arched. 'Seven…'

Her knickers got moist.

'Six…'

'And, frankly, you've got an awfully high—'

'Five…'

'—opinion of your powers of seduction,' she tried to scoff, but rushed the words.

'Four…' He slung his arm across the handlebars of the scooter, looking relaxed but ready—like a tiger waiting to pounce. 'Three…'

'As if you could get me to *do it* with you in a public place,' she hedged desperately, her voice rising. Time was running out.

'Two…' He stood up on the scooter, looming over her.

She slapped her hands on her hips. 'Now, listen here—'

'One.'

Oh, hell.

She scrambled onto the seat behind him and grabbed two fistfuls of his T-shirt.

'All right. All right.' She yanked. 'You win. For now,' she said, sighing with relief as he sank back with a triumphant chuckle.

'I'm so not finished talking about this, though,' she continued, fighting a rearguard action as he revved the engine and she wrapped her arms around his waist. 'You arrogant, oversexed…'

The protest was lost in the roar of the Vespa's engine as it careered away from the kerb.

Issy clung on, her mind spinning, her tender breasts vibrating against the muscled sinews of his back.

As they sped over the Ponte Vecchio she caught sight of a couple embracing in the shadows of the ancient bridge. And agonising desire flooded between her thighs.

She held on for dear life. What were the chances she was going to be in any fit state to conduct a conversation, let alone an argument, once they got back to the villa?

Not a lot, actually.

After the fifteen-minute journey up the hill, Gio clasped her hand in his and walked through the darkened house. He didn't utter a word. And neither did she. Too preoccupied by the thought of the animal passion they had already sampled to remember why she'd objected to sampling some more.

Within seconds of slamming his bedroom door, he had her naked.

As he flung off his own clothing she stood shaking, mesmerised by the hard, masculine beauty of his body gilded in the moonlight. Then her eyes snagged on the powerful erection jutting out as he sheathed himself.

And the animal passion that had smouldered all evening leapt into flame.

'No more delaying tactics.' He lifted her easily in his arms. 'There's nothing to understand.' Gripping her thighs, he hooked her legs around his waist. 'All we need is this.'

'Why can't we do both?' she asked, as her back

thudded against the door. But she knew she was fighting a losing battle as the head of his erection probed at the folds of her sex.

His eyes met hers in the half-light. 'Later, Isadora.' He planted a possessive kiss on her lips. 'We're busy.' And impaled her in one powerful thrust.

She sobbed at the fullness of the penetration.

Okay, later works, she thought vaguely, as he sank in to the hilt.

A long time later, her body aching from an overdose of physical activity and sexual pleasure, they finally collapsed onto his huge *bateau* bed.

'Do you think we'll ever get to slow and easy?' she mumbled, curling against his side and pillowing her head on his shoulder, so tired she would happily beg for oblivion.

She heard his chuckle, felt the soft rumble in his chest before his arm drew her close and his hand caressed her bottom. 'That would be next time. Now, go to sleep.'

Her eyes fluttered closed as his lips brushed her hair, and she heard him take a deep breath before releasing it.

'Issy. What the hell am I going to do with you?' he murmured.

Despite the fuzziness of exhaustion, she heard the confusion in his voice and felt her heart stutter in response.

Become my friend again.

She nestled deeper into his embrace as the warm, languid afterglow of sensational sex pulled her into a dreamy sleep.

CHAPTER SEVEN

'WAKE UP, Sleeping Beauty, you need to get out of the sun before you end up with third degree burns.'

Issy shaded her eyes to see Gio standing by her sun-lounger, looking tall and delicious in chinos and an open-necked shirt.

'You're back already?' She stretched lazily, ignoring the persistent flutter beneath her breastbone at the sight of him. He'd left for a meeting in town after breakfast, and she'd taken a swim in the pool. It was a surprise to see him back so soon.

He crouched down on his haunches until they were eye to eye. 'I've been gone for over two hours.' He rested his arm across his knee and touched her nose. 'And you're looking a little pink.'

'What's the time?' she asked groggily, determined not to read too much into how her spirits lifted at his look of concern.

Despite Gio's assertions that all they had was animal passion, they had drifted into friendship again as easily as breathing. After only a few days the companionship they shared had become as exciting as their sexual relationship.

If the first day's sightseeing had been magical, yesterday's had been even more so. They'd brushed shoulders with businessmen and market traders alike in a *trattoria* at the Mercado Centrale, while Gio had chuckled at her pathetic attempts to order in Italian. He'd taken her to see the stunning golden mosaics in the Romanesque basilica of San Miniato al Monte, then cuddled with her under the stars as they watched *La Dolce Vita* in flickering black and white on the ten-foot open-air screen in a nearby park.

In the last twenty-four hours she'd seen a man emerge who was cultured and charismatic, had a decidedly mischievous sense of humour, and was passionate about his work and the beautiful city he lived in.

Maybe they hadn't talked about their past or anything else too personal again—something she knew was deliberate on Gio's part—but she hadn't pushed. Taking the sweet, steady glide into friendship and getting an enchanting glimpse of what that unhappy boy had made of his life had been enough. Frankly, friendship didn't get much better than this. Why ruin the mood?

Gio glanced at his watch. 'It's after one,' he replied. 'And about the hottest time of the day.'

'Oh.' She'd been asleep for over an hour. And would probably be a bit sore tomorrow as a result. Thank goodness she'd slathered factor fifty sunscreen on before she'd dozed off.

She gave a jaw-breaking yawn and sighed. 'I don't know why you're looking at me like that. This is all your fault.'

'How?'

'You're the one who hasn't let me sleep since I got here,' she teased, although it wasn't far from the truth.

This was a friendship with some exceptional benefits, she thought, as her pulse spiked at the sight of his trousers stretching across muscled thighs.

They'd done hard and fast, slow and easy, and everything in between. Gio's powers of recovery had proved to be Herculean, and she'd never been more satisfied, more sated—or more exhausted—in her life. When she'd woken up snuggled in his arms that morning, inhaling the familiar musk of his scent had sent shockwaves through her oversensitised flesh, but her hunger had been as insistent as ever when his morning erection had brushed her bottom.

Okay, so she'd felt a strange dragging sensation when he'd left her to shower alone this morning because he had an important meeting. But she hadn't let it bother her. The let-down feeling was to be expected. They were having a fabulous time, but it would be over soon. The ennui was probably just to do with endorphins, or something.

'Exactly how long have you been out here?' he asked. 'Did you even put on any cream?'

Her grin widened. 'Yes, boss.'

'It's not funny,' he said, all serious and intense. 'You've got very fair skin. Sunburn's no joke.'

'Spoken by a man who's probably never had it.' She ran her fingernail over one tanned bicep, enjoying the way the muscle bunched. 'Honestly, Gio. You sound like my mum.'

'Oh, yeah?' His eyebrow lifted, the frown replaced by a slow smile.

'Yes, yeah,' she said, desire curling anew in her belly. 'Just for that…'

She shrieked as he thrust one hand under her knees and the other behind her back.

'What are you doing?' she said, gripping his neck as he straightened with her wriggling in his arms.

'Helping you cool off.'

She started to wriggle in earnest when she saw his direction. 'No. No way. I've already had a swim today.' And the water would feel freezing after she'd been lying in the sun.

Ignoring her protests and her struggles, he hefted her towards the pool. 'Yes, but I haven't,' he said, and stepped off the edge fully clothed.

'So, is that sunburn or are you still blushing?' Gio asked, a teasing smile lurking on his lips.

'I don't know what you're talking about.'

He sat at the terrace table, his wavy hair furrowed into slick rows, damp wisps of chest hair visible through the open lapels of his robe.

'I had no idea you could move that fast.' He poured a glass of lemonade from a pitcher on the table and passed it to her. 'I think you may have set a land-speed record.'

She took a swallow of the icy drink to calm the giddy beat of her pulse. 'It's not remotely funny,' she said dryly, trying to control her flush. 'Your housekeeper will think I'm a tart.'

If she doesn't already.

They'd been about to ravage each other during their impromptu dip when Carlotta had interrupted them to announce that lunch had been set out on the terrace. Issy had scurried off to the bedroom wrapped in a towel and dying of embarrassment. Gio's laughter had echoed behind her. She still hadn't quite managed to get over her mortification.

'No, she won't,' he said lazily, slicing into the veal *parmigiana* on his plate. 'She's Italian. They don't get as hung up on social niceties as you Brits.'

'You Brits? Aren't you half-British?'

He grinned. 'When it comes to social niceties, I'd say I'm more Italian.'

'So would I,' she said emphatically.

He chuckled.

Issy smiled back. But as she crossed her legs and smoothed her robe over her knees the heat continued to burn in her cheeks.

How could she not have noticed Carlotta beside the pool?

And how could she have got carried away like that, knowing there was a houseful of servants who could interrupt them at any minute? Gio had turned her from nun to nymphomaniac in the space of a few days—and it was starting to concern her.

Shouldn't the passion have begun to fade a little by now?

Gio lifted her hand off the table and linked his fingers with hers. 'In deference to your British sensibilities, I suggest we retire to the privacy of the bedroom after lunch.'

The familiar thrill shot through her as he pressed his lips to her knuckles. Concerning her even more. Why couldn't she say no to him? Ever?

Carlotta stepped onto the terrace, holding a small silver tray, and Issy tugged her hand free.

Gio took a large envelope off the tray and thanked the housekeeper. Issy sent Carlotta what she hoped was a friendly smile and the woman smiled back, apparently unperturbed by what she'd almost interrupted in the pool.

As Issy watched the housekeeper leave, she wondered how many more of Gio's sexual escapades Carlotta had witnessed. The instant prickle of jealousy made her frown. This was temporary—with no strings attached. Gio's other women didn't matter to her in the least.

'Dammit.'

At the whispered curse, she turned to see Gio dump a large magnolia card into the wastepaper bin and throw the torn envelope on top.

'What was that? It's not bad news, is it?'

'No, it's nothing,' he said as he picked up his knife and fork.

The movement made his robe gape open. Issy pulled her gaze away from the sprinkle of dark hair that arrowed down his abdomen.

It wasn't nothing. That much was obvious from the tense, annoyed expression on his face.

Brushing off the torn envelope, she lifted the card out of the bin. The fancy gold lettering was in Italian, but she could make out today's date.

Why had he reacted so violently to something that looked so innocuous?

'Who is Carlo Nico Lorenzo?' she asked, reading out the name printed in the centre of the card.

He glanced up, his eyes stormy. 'I threw that away for a reason. It's rubbish.'

'Is he a relative of yours?' she asked, pretending she hadn't heard the rude comment as curiosity consumed her. 'Did your mother have brothers and sisters?' She trailed off, waiting for him to fill in the blanks.

'Carlo is the baby they're baptising,' he said curtly, then leaned forward and plucked the invitation out of her hand. 'He's the grandson of Claudia's oldest brother. Who's also called Carlo.' He dumped the card onto the table, face down. 'Now, can we finish our lunch?'

'You mean he's your uncle's grandson?' she prompted. Why had he never mentioned his Italian family before? She'd had no idea he had relatives in Italy.

'I guess.' He bent his head to concentrate on his food. The tactic so deliberate, her curiosity only increased.

Picking up the invitation, she scanned the contents again, then flipped it over. 'What does this say?' She pointed to the spidery handwriting scrawled across the back.

He chewed, swallowed, his eyes narrowing. 'You know, Issy, sometimes your persistence can be very annoying.'

She waited calmly for a proper answer.

He huffed, snatched the card and read aloud. 'It says: "We miss you, Giovanni. You are family. Please come this time."' He flicked the card back into the bin. 'Which is insane, because I hardly know the man—or his family.'

'This time? How many times have they invited you to a family event?' It went without saying that he'd never attended any—had probably never even bothered to RSVP.

'I don't know. Hundreds.' He blew out a frustrated breath. 'There's a lot of them. Claudia had five older brothers, and they all had tons of kids. There's an event every other week.'

'Where do they live?' Maybe they lived on the other side of Italy? Maybe that was why he had never bothered to visit them?

'About an hour's drive,' he said. 'The family owns an olive farm near San Giminiano. Most of them still live around there, I guess.' He sent her a bored look. 'So, do you want to tell me why you're so interested?'

A spurt of temper rose up.

Her own family had only consisted of her and her mother. She'd always dreamed of having more. Of having brothers and sisters, cousins and aunts and uncles. She knew perfectly well Gio was an only child too—and from what he'd already told her she knew he'd been a lot more alone than she had as a child. So why hadn't he embraced the chance to get to know his own family?

'For goodness' sake, Gio,' she said, riding the temper. 'Why haven't you been to see them? They're your *family*.'

'I don't have a family. I don't even know them,' he continued. 'They disowned Claudia before I was even born. Cut her out of their lives.'

'Is that why you dislike them?' she asked, confused now, and a little appalled by his indifference. 'Because they treated your mother badly?'

'Of course not!' He sounded annoyed now—annoyed and something else she couldn't quite define. 'I expect she made their lives a misery. I can testify to the fact that she was a nightmare to live with, so I don't blame them for kicking her out.'

She heard the contempt in his voice. So that was why he never talked about his mother.

'Are you upset that they never got to know you as a boy, then?' Issy asked carefully, still trying to understand his hostility towards the rest of his family. *Why* was he so determined to have nothing to do with them?

He pushed his plate away and reached for the pitcher of lemonade. 'Issy, in case you haven't realised yet—'

he poured himself a glass, gulped some down '—this conversation doesn't interest me.'

'Well, it interests *me*,' she said, determined not to back down—not this time. 'I think you *do* blame them. But you shouldn't. It doesn't—'

'I don't blame them.' He shoved his chair back, walked to the balcony rail. 'Why should they care about me? I'm nothing to them.'

Her temper died as she heard the defensiveness in his tone, saw his knuckles whiten where they gripped the terrace rail.

'That's clearly not true,' she said, feeling desperately sad for him. 'Or why would they have invited you to this christening?' She watched his shoulders tense, but he didn't say anything. 'There must be a reason why they didn't try to get to know you as a child. Maybe they—'

'They did try,' he interrupted her. 'I met Carlo. Once. He came to our apartment in Rome.' He paused, his voice barely audible above the breeze. 'Claudia wasn't there. She'd been out all night at some party, and I was in the place alone.'

'How old were you?' she asked gently. She'd tried not to think of him as a boy too much since their first night in Florence. Had tried not to make the mistake of reading too much into his parents' behaviour and its effect on him. But now she wanted to know. How bad had it been?

'Ten,' he said, as if it weren't particularly significant.

She bit down on her lip, tried not to let the thought of that neglected boy get to her.

But then another shattering thought occurred to her, and she felt tears sting the back of her throat.

As long as she had known Gio he had always called his parents Claudia and the Duke. Even as a boy he had never referred to them as Mum or Dad. And now Issy knew why. Because in all the ways that counted they had never been his mother and father. Just people who had battled over him and then rejected him.

'What happened?' She asked. 'With Carlo?'

Gio shrugged, the movement stiff. 'Not a lot. He asked to see Claudia. We waited together for her to come home. He told me who he was, asked me about myself. How old was I? What did I like doing? My Italian wasn't great then, and his questions confused me.'

He sounded so puzzled, even now, and her heart ached. No wonder Gio had no faith in relationships, in family. He'd never been part of one. Not one where people cared for you and about you and were interested in what you did and said.

'She came home eventually,' he said, derision edging his voice. 'Coked up to the eyeballs as usual. They had a massive row, she called the police, and he had to leave. He never came back. But the invitations started to come a few months later. Always addressed to me. She threw them away—wouldn't let me open them. After her death I replied to a few, giving excuses why I couldn't come, but they didn't get the hint so now I throw them away.'

'I think you should go.' Taking the card back out of the bin, she crossed the balcony, placed a hand on his back. 'I think you should go to this christening. See your family. See Carlo again.' Suddenly it seemed vitally important.

He turned round, stared down at the card she held but didn't take it.

'Issy, for God's sake.' He cupped her cheek in his

palm, his eyes shadowed. 'Haven't you heard a word I've said? I don't want to go. I don't belong there,' he murmured.

She rested her hand on his heart, felt the rapid beats. 'Yes, you do. You don't have to be scared of them, you know.'

'I'm not scared. Don't be idiotic.'

But she could hear defensiveness behind the irritation.

He was scared. He was scared to let them get too close. To trust them. To trust anyone.

Her heart clutched as he looked away.

Every child deserved to be loved unconditionally, supported in whatever they chose to do. She thought of the way her own mother had loved and supported her in every mad decision she'd ever made in her life. Edie had always been there. Praising her as if she'd been Sarah Bernhardt when she'd played a tomato in her first school play. Providing a shoulder to cry on when she'd bawled her eyes out over Gio. Even nagging her into admitting that her lifelong dream of becoming an actress needed some serious tweaking after she'd begun her job at the Crown and Feathers and discovered that she preferred bossing people about to angsting about her motivation.

For all his apparent confidence and charisma, Gio had never had any of that as a child. He'd been entirely alone—criticised and rejected by his father, or neglected and ignored by his mother. Even though he'd made a staggering success of his life, he'd survived emotionally by closing himself off and convincing himself he didn't need love.

He'd persuaded himself it wasn't important, that it didn't matter to him, when obviously it did.

Gio had needed a friend as a boy, and he still needed one now. To show him there was another way.

'They can make your life so much richer, Gio. Can't you see that?'

He gave a harsh laugh. 'You've still got a romantic streak a mile wide, haven't you?' He leaned back against the rail, his stance deliberately casual. 'I'm not interested in meeting Claudia's family. I've got nothing to offer them. And they've got nothing to offer me.'

She stared at him, saw stubborn refusal, but she knew it wasn't true. He had so much to give. And he could get so much back in return.

'There's only one thing I need.' He took the invitation from her. 'And it's got nothing to do with this.' He flicked the card onto the table behind her.

He grasped her waist, tugged her close, then slanted his lips across hers.

She curled her fingers into his hair and kissed him back, not caring that he was trying to make a point. Not caring any more what the point was. Because she could taste his desperation right alongside his desire.

He bracketed her waist, boosted her into his arms. 'Wrap your legs around me.'

She did as he commanded, feathering kisses over his brow, his chin, his cheeks, as he strode through the French doors into the master bedroom.

He took her mouth again as he lay beside her, his hard, beautiful body covering hers. The kiss was so deep and dangerous and full of purpose she wanted to scream.

They wrestled their robes off together.

He delved into the curls at her core with clever, insistent fingers.

'I love the way you're always wet for me,' he murmured as she bucked beneath him, cried out, the twist and bite of arousal so vicious it stunned her.

She peaked in a rush of savage sensation. Before she had a chance to draw a steady breath he gripped her hips and settled between her thighs.

She grasped his shoulders, opened for him as he plunged.

The fullness of the strokes had her building to a crescendo again with staggering speed, the harsh grunts of his breathing matching her broken sobs. But instead of cresting this time she cruised the brutal orgasm for an eternity, shooting up and then clawing back until she felt trapped in a vortex of pleasure too intense to survive.

Straining, desperate, she crashed over into the abyss at last, and heard his roar of fulfilment as he crashed and burned behind her.

Issy combed the damp curls at his nape with shaking fingers, her body still quivering from the aftermath of the titanic orgasm.

Had that been sex? She felt as if she'd just survived an earthquake.

He lifted his head. But he didn't speak. He looked as stunned as she felt. Easing out of her, he flopped down by her side.

Then cursed. 'I didn't wear a condom. Is that going to be a problem?'

The flat words took a moment to penetrate her fuzzy brain. 'Sorry. What?'

'No condom.' He cleared his throat. 'I forgot.' He propped himself up on his elbow, leaned over her. 'When's your next period?'

'I…' She tried to grasp the meaning, the rigid tone.

'You're not in the middle of your cycle, are you?'

'No. No, I'm not. I'm due soon.' She did a quick mental calculation. 'Tomorrow, I think.'

He lay back on the bed. 'Thank God.' The relief in his voice made her cheeks burn.

'What about emergency contraception?' she whispered, her mind trying to cling to practicalities. 'Is there somewhere near here we could get it?' The thought of taking the morning-after pill, something she'd never had to do before, made her stomach clench.

'You'd probably need a prescription,' he said, so matter-of-factly it made her heart pound.

'Oh.' She sat up, disorientated. 'It doesn't matter. It'll probably be fine,' she said, the words catching in her throat. 'I can get it from a pharmacy in the UK— perhaps I should arrange a flight just in case.' They hadn't talked about when she would leave. Why hadn't they talked about it? It suddenly seemed vitally important. 'I'll look into that now.' She swung her feet off the bed, struggling for calm as she pulled on her robe.

He caught her arm as she tried to stand. 'You're being irrational. There's no need to book a flight.' He paused. 'I'll get the jet to take you.' He caressed the inside of her elbow with his thumb. 'But let's wait till tomorrow.'

The quiet comment brought with it a rush of excitement that made no sense at all.

This was silly. She should leave—sooner rather than later after their little accident—so why was she so pleased with the casual offer?

'But we only agreed to a couple of days.' She should go. Why didn't she want to?

He brushed her hair behind her ear. 'We did something stupid, that's all. You said yourself it probably won't lead to anything.' He tucked his index finger under her chin.

She tried to rein in her galloping heartbeat. His eyes were full of an intensity she'd never seen before.

'Don't worry. We'll sort it out if we need do.' His deep, steady voice was reassuring, the stroke of his hand on her hair making her heart-rate slow to a canter.

Why did it feel as if everything had spun off its axis and nothing made any sense any more?

He took her shoulders, held her at arm's length to look into her eyes. 'Let's not think about it today. Tomorrow is soon enough. Go and get dressed. Wear something fancy. We'll go somewhere special.' He brushed a kiss across her brow, making her smile despite her confusion. 'It'll take our minds off it.'

'Do you really think—'

'We can go anywhere you want,' he interrupted her. 'Your choice.'

'Okay,' she said, more pleased than she probably should be at the thought that she didn't have to go today.

She hurried into the bathroom, shut the door and leaned back against it, letting the excited little hammer-beats of her pulse drown out the doubts. Everything was fine. More than fine. They'd made a silly mistake, but it didn't have to mean anything.

She'd always found it hard to hold back as a teenager, to weigh and judge and interpret other people's feelings properly. It was the reason she'd fallen so easily for Gio, and she'd worked long and hard in the decade since at keeping her emotions in check and never letting them get the better of her again. But maybe she'd held on too hard, turned herself into someone she really wasn't.

It didn't have to be a bad thing that she had such strong feelings for Gio. They had a shared history, and now she'd spent time with him, and understood the extent of his parents' neglect and what it had done to him, it made sense that she would feel their friendship more keenly.

She twisted the gold-plated taps on the large designer tub.

She'd come here to get over her past mistakes, but surely the best way to do that was to heal the part of herself she'd lost that night. She didn't have to be frightened of her feelings for Gio any more.

When their fling was over they would go their separate ways, having reclaimed the good things from their childhood and left behind the bad.

As the water gushed out, and she sprinkled bath salts, another thought occurred to her and she smiled.

Gio had said she could pick their destination for this afternoon. And she knew exactly where she wanted to go. She wasn't the only one who needed to heal.

But as Issy slipped into the steamy, scented water, and let the lavender bubbles massage her tired muscles, she couldn't quite shake the suspicion she had failed to grasp something vitally important.

* * *

What the hell had he done?

Gio lay on the bed, his arm folded under his head, as he stared at the fan on the ceiling.

He'd taken her without a condom. He turned his head to stare at the bathroom and heard the reassuring hum of running water.

Except he wasn't feeling all that reassured.

Had he totally lost his mind?

He never, ever forgot to wear condoms. Partly for personal safety reasons, but mostly because he had absolutely no desire to father a child. Even if the woman said she was on the pill. No matter how hot he got, or how desperate he was to make love, he always used protection.

But Issy got him hotter and more desperate than any woman he'd ever met—and for the first time ever the thought of contraception hadn't entered his head.

She'd made him feel raw and vulnerable with all that nonsense about getting to know Claudia's family, until he'd been desperate to shut her up. But the minute he'd tasted her, the minute he'd touched her, the usual longing had welled up inside him and all he'd been able to think about was burying himself inside her. Before he knew what was happening he'd been glorying in the exquisite clasp of her body and shooting his seed deep into her womb without a thought to the consequences.

It hadn't been a mistake, or an oversight. It had been sheer madness.

Getting off the bed, he shrugged into his robe, then scraped his fingers through his hair.

How the hell had this happened? He felt more out of control than ever now.

What if she actually got pregnant? He knew Issy. She

would never consider an abortion. But he didn't want a child. He knew what it was like to be an afterthought, an inconvenience, a mistake.

And why had he asked her to stay? By rights he should have been breaking the speed limit to race her to the airport even now, and then piloting the plane back to England to make sure she got whatever she needed to ensure there was no chance of a baby.

Temporary insanity had to be the answer. He slumped into a chair by the terrace table and frowned at the remnants of their aborted lunch. Although he wasn't sure how temporary it was any more.

The woman was driving him nuts. In the last few days he'd become addicted to everything about her.

The fresh, sweet scent of her hair when he woke up beside her in the morning, the sound of her voice as she chatted away about everything and nothing, even the stubborn tilt of her chin and the compassion in those deep blue eyes when she had tried to insist he go to that stupid Christening.

He'd become so enthralled he'd gone to the office this morning just to prove he could. But the plan had backfired—because he hadn't been able to stay away. And then he'd found her on the sun-lounger, her skin pink from too much sun, and he hadn't been able to keep his hands off her.

They'd nearly made a spectacle of themselves in front of Carlotta. And, while he'd found Issy's outraged dignity amusing at the time, it didn't seem all that funny any more.

But the worst moment had come when she'd announced she was going to book a flight home. He'd actually felt his stomach tighten with dread. And it had taken a major effort not to let the panic show.

He never got worked up about women. But he'd got worked up about her.

He walked towards the guest suite, steadfastly resisting the urge to join Issy in the master bath. He needed to take a break, because ravaging Issy senseless wasn't turning out to be the cure-all he'd been hoping for.

He frowned as he entered the bathroom of the guest suite.

Maybe that was the problem. He wasn't used to sharing his home with the women he dated, having unlimited sex on tap. As soon as the novelty wore off he'd be able to let Issy go with no trouble at all. And everything would be back to normal. Getting her out of his system was just taking longer than originally planned.

He reached for the shower control. A trip into town might be just what he needed.

He never would have believed it, but maybe you really could have too much of a good thing.

'You want to go *where*?' Gio's fingers clenched on the Ferrari's steering wheel as all his positive feelings about their afternoon out crashed and burned.

'I have the address right here.'

He watched, stunned into silence, as Issy pulled the christening invitation out of her handbag and reeled off the address.

'You were right,' she chirped. 'It is in San Giminiano. And I've got my posh frock on, just like you suggested. So we're all set.' She smiled, looking deceptively sweet as she pressed the button on the dash to bring up the car's inbuilt navigation system. 'Shall I programme the GPS?'

He shoved the panel back into the dash. 'We've already had this conversation. We're not going,' he said firmly, prepared to argue the point if she decided to sulk.

But instead of the expected pout she simply stared at him. 'You said I could choose. I choose to go to your cousin's christening.'

There was that stubborn little chin again. And it wasn't enchanting him any more.

'He's *not* my cousin.' Why couldn't she get that through her head? 'He's nothing to me. None of them are.'

'If that's the case, why are you so frightened of paying them a visit?'

'I'm *not* frightened.' She'd accused him of that before, and it was starting to annoy him.

'Then prove it,' she said softly.

He opened his mouth to tell her to go to hell. He wasn't ten any more, and he didn't take dares. But then he saw the sympathy, the understanding in her eyes, and the words wouldn't come.

He cursed under his breath. 'Okay, we'll go to the christening.' He flipped up the GPS. 'But you're going to be bored out of your brain. I guarantee it.'

As he stabbed in the co-ordinates, she leaned across the console and kissed his cheek.

'No, I won't be. And neither will you.' Her fingers touched his thigh, stroked reassuringly. 'It's going to be an experience you'll never forget.'

I know, he thought grimly, as he gunned the engine.

CHAPTER EIGHT

'*GIOVANNI, mio ragazzo. Benvenuto alla famiglia.*'

Issy blinked away tears, hearing the gruff affection in the elderly man's voice as he threw his arms wide to greet his long-lost nephew.

Stiff and hesitant in the designer suit he'd worn for a different occasion entirely, Gio leant down and accepted the kisses Carlo Lorenzo placed on his cheeks. The old man chuckled, then clasped Gio's hand with gnarled fingers, talking all the time. Issy hadn't a clue what was being said, but she could guess from the confusion on Gio's face and his short, monosyllabic answers that Carlo was as overjoyed to see him as the rest of his family.

She huffed out a breath, so relieved she had to reach into her purse and find a tissue.

As the Ferrari had swung round the twisting mountain roads to the Lorenzo farm, she'd begun to doubt her decision to make Gio come to the christening.

What if she'd been wrong to suggest he come? What if the family didn't welcome him as she expected?

With each mile that passed Gio had become more tense and withdrawn, answering her questions in curt sentences and handling the car with none of his usual skill. It was the first time she'd ever seen him nervous, and his reaction had forced her into admitting an unpleasant truth.

What had made her think she had the right to meddle in his life? He'd never shown any interest in meddling in hers. They'd been in an intimate relationship for a grand total of three days. An intimate relationship that would be over very soon. Yes, they were friends, but that was all they were. Did that really give her the right to make assumptions about what he needed in his life?

Now, as Carlo continued to chat away to Gio, she let her pleasure at the wonderful way Gio's family had greeted him push the doubts away. This could have gone so horribly wrong. But it hadn't—which counted for a lot.

'You are Giovanni's *ragazza*, yes?'

Issy glanced round to see a petite, pretty and heavily pregnant young woman dressed in a colourful summer dress smiling at her.

Issy stuffed the tissue back into her bag and held out her hand. 'I'm Issy Helligan,' she said quickly, not quite sure how to reply to the question.

Didn't *ragazza* mean girlfriend? Was she Gio's girlfriend? Not really. Not in any permanent sense.

'I'm a friend of Gio's,' she said, feeling oddly dispirited. 'I'm so sorry, but I don't speak much Italian.'

'It is good I speak excellent English, then,' the woman said, her brown eyes—which were the exact shade of Gio's—alight with mischief. 'Or we would not be able to gossip about my long-lost cousin. My name is —after La Loren.' She wrinkled her nose. 'Sadly, I only got her name and not her body.'

Issy laughed, liking Sophia instantly. 'When is your baby due?' she asked.

Sophia looked down at her bump, her eyes glowing as she stroked it. 'In two weeks. But my husband Aldo says it will be sooner. Our two boys were early, and he will not let me forget it.'

'That's sweet,' she said unable to deny the whisper of envy.

Hearing the love and contentment in Sophia's voice made Issy want to reach for her tissue again. This woman looked younger than her, and she already had two children and another on the way—and a man who loved her.

What on earth have I been doing with my life?

'Come.' Sophia deftly linked her arm with Issy's. 'I have been told to fetch you by my sisters, my aunts and all my girl cousins.' She drew her away from Gio, who looked shell-shocked and a little hunted as Carlo introduced him to more relatives he had never met.

'They all want to know about you and Giovanni,' Sophia added, dropping her voice to a conspiratorial whisper. 'He is like the prodigal son, no? You are very beautiful.' She gave Issy an appreciative once-over. 'And we are very nosy.'

'Oh, Gio and I aren't really…' Issy hesitated. 'We're not exactly…' She paused again. She didn't want to mislead Sophia, but how did she describe what she and Gio were, exactly? 'There isn't that much to gossip about,' she said lamely, glancing over her shoulder. 'And I feel like a traitor leaving Gio alone. I'm the one who suggested he come today.'

Gio glared at her as he was kissed and hugged by a group of older men she assumed were his other uncles.

'Giovanni is a big boy,' Sophia said, patting Issy's arm and tugging her towards a huge trestle table on the farm's flagstone terrace, laden with an array of mouth-watering dishes. 'And he will not be alone.'

A large group of women and girls, ranging in age from twelve to ninety, clustered around the table, watching Issy with undisguised curiosity—making her feel like even more of a fraud.

'My father has been waiting for over twenty years to see *il ragazzo perduto* again,' Sophia added. 'He will be showing him off for hours. But when the dancing starts we will get him back for you.'

Dancing? Issy smiled at the thought. Funny to think she'd never danced with Gio before.

She allowed Sophia to lead her away, ignoring the panicked plea in Gio's eyes. It would do him good to be fêted by his family. That was exactly why they were here. So that he could reconnect with what really mattered in life. And it wouldn't do her any harm to stay out of his way. To absorb the wonder of this large, happy and loving family—and reconnect with her own priorities in life.

'What does *il ragazzo perduto* mean?' she asked absently.

Sophia sent her a warm smile. 'Carlo calls Giovanni "the lost boy". He has worried about him ever since he went to Rome years ago and met him. Carlo said without the family he had no one to love him, to care for him.' Sophia's smile turned knowing. 'But, seeing the way you look at him, I don't think he's lost any more.'

Issy's pulse jumped at the softly spoken words.

Pardon me?

* * *

'Let's dance, Isadora.'

Issy's head turned at the deep, commanding voice as strong fingers gripped her elbow. 'Oh, hi, Gio.' Her lips tilted up in an instant smile.

He looked confused, harassed and exhausted.

'So you finally escaped from your uncle?' she said brightly.

'Don't you dare laugh.' He skewered her with a quelling look. 'The man has been talking my ear off for two solid hours. And he's introduced me to more people in one afternoon than I've met in my entire life. All of whom he insists I'm related to.'

He treated Sophia and the other women to a quick greeting in Italian, but before any of them could reply, he clamped his hand round Issy's arm and directed her towards the wooden dance floor that had been constructed in the middle of the olive grove.

Dusk was falling, but fairy lights had been hung from the heavily burdened olive trees, casting a magical glow on the couples already slow-dancing in the twilight.

'I've had my cheek pinched by not one but two grannies,' he continued, his voice pained as they stepped onto the uneven boards and he swung her into his arms. 'I've been made to recite my life story about twenty times.' He wrapped his arm round her waist and pulled her flush against his lean, hard body. 'I've been force-fed my Aunt Donatella's *fusilli ortolana* and my second cousin Elisabetta's rabbit *cacciatore*.' He twirled her round in time to the slow, seductive beat of the music before holding her close in his arms. 'And come within a hair's breadth of getting peed on by the guest of honour.'

Issy stifled a laugh as her heart kicked in her chest.

Beneath the confusion and the fatigue she could see the creases around his eyes crinkling and hear the amusement in his voice.

The day had been a success. He looked tired, but happy.

She rested her cheek on his chest, gripped his hand. There had been no need to panic. All the questions she'd been fielding from Sophia and her family had unsettled her, but coming to the christening had been an unqualified success.

'I'm shattered,' he said, leaning down to whisper in her ear, his hands flattening on the bare skin of her back. 'And the only thing that's kept me going is the thought of all the ways I'm going to make you pay for this later tonight.'

Issy pulled away to lay a palm on his cheek. 'Poor Gio. It's tough being loved, isn't it?'

He stopped in the middle of the dance floor. 'What did you say?' His face was masked by the lights behind him, but she could hear his wariness, his sharpness.

'I said it's tough being loved,' she said, wishing she hadn't seen him tense. The emotional stability she'd been working so hard on in the last few hours started to wobble again.

'They don't love me. They're just good people doing what they consider to be their duty.'

They did love him. How could he not see it?

She wanted to argue the point, but knew from the rigid line of his jaw he would refuse to believe it. The ripple of disappointment had her shivering, despite the sultry evening air.

'My father wants me to translate for him.' Sophia stood beside Carlo as the old man clasped Issy's hands.

'Because Giovanni has told him your Italian is not so good. Yet.'

'Oh, has he now?' Issy joked, although her emotions felt perilously close to the surface.

Sophia smiled back as Carlo began to speak in a sober, steady voice, before lifting Issy's hand to his lips and giving it a chivalrous kiss.

Sophia translated. 'My father says that his heart is full with gratitude to you for making Giovanni come today, after being lost to his family for so many years. He says that you are a beautiful woman both inside and out and he hopes that Giovanni can see this too.'

Issy felt herself blush, dismayed by the old man's words.

Carlo turned to Gio and took his hand. Issy felt Gio tense beside her as his uncle spoke. He dipped his head, spots of colour rising on his cheeks beneath his tan as Carlo patted his cheek, his voice rough with pride.

Tears pricked the back of Issy's eyes as Sophia translated.

'My father says that the Lorenzo family is very proud of Giovanni.' Even Sophia's voice sounded more sober than Issy had ever heard it before. 'For all he has made of his life, despite a mother who did not know how to be a mother. Carlo says that Giovanni has made strong, important and beautiful buildings that will stand for a long time.' Sophia swallowed, her voice as thick with emotion as Issy felt. 'But he must not forget that the only thing that lasts forever is a man's family.' Sophia gave a half-laugh as Carlo finished his speech. 'And that Giovanni is getting older and shouldn't waste any more time getting started.'

Issy laughed too, at the old man's audacity and the

roguish sparkle in his eyes. As Gio replied in Italian Issy noticed the measured tone, devoid of his usual cynicism, and felt her heart lift. He wasn't completely blind to what these people had to offer, whatever he might think.

As they said their goodbyes to everyone, Issy's hand strayed automatically to her belly.

What if their mistake ended in a pregnancy?

To her surprise, the question didn't bring the panic she might have expected. But she forced the thought away anyway. A pregnancy was highly unlikely. And today had been quite emotional enough already.

The last to say her goodbyes was Sophia, who gave Issy a final hug as Gio climbed into the Ferrari.

'You must both come to the next *battesimo*, as it will be for my baby,' she whispered, before standing back and winking at Issy. 'And if Giovanni does as he is told, maybe the one after that will be yours.'

Issy waved furiously as Gio reversed the car down the farm track, sniffing back tears and trying not to take Sophia's little joke to heart.

What she and Gio had was fleeting. That had always been understood.

But as the whole family shouted salutations at them, and a group of children raced after the car, a few tears slipped over her lids. This was what it felt like to belong, to be part of something bigger than yourself—and she'd never realised how much she wanted it until now.

'That wasn't so bad,' Gio said, resting his palm on Issy's knee as he turned the car onto the main road.

Issy sank into the leather seat and watched the dark shapes of San Giminiano's fortress walls disappear into the night as Gio accelerated. Leaning her head against the door, she rested her palm on her belly, the emotion of the day overwhelming her.

'Will you go back again?' she asked.

He said nothing for several seconds. 'I doubt it.'

Despite the murmured reply, a tiny smile touched the corners of Issy's mouth. Was it wishful thinking, or did he sound less sure of himself than usual?

Easing up the handbrake, Gio stared at the woman fast asleep beside him in the car. She'd been incredible today. So beautiful, so captivating and so important to his peace of mind. He'd needed her there in a way he never would have anticipated.

All through the afternoon and evening, whenever the impact of being introduced to his family had become too much, his gaze had instinctively searched her out. As soon as he'd spotted her—chatting to Sophia and the other women, or playing games with some of the younger children, or charming his elderly uncles with her faltering Italian—and their eyes connected, his heartbeat had levelled out and the strangling feeling of panic and confusion had started to ease.

At one point she'd been cradling baby Carlo in her arms. He'd marvelled at how she could look so relaxed and happy, as if she were a part of this family, even though these people were strangers and she didn't even speak their language. When his uncle had whispered in his ear, 'She will make an excellent mother for your children, Giovanni. She is a natural.'

The old man was hopelessly traditional and senti-mental. It hadn't taken Gio long to realise that. But the foolish words had still made Gio's heartbeat pound, just as it was doing now.

He continued to stare at her in the moonlight—her rich red hair framing that pale heart-shaped face and her hand lying curled over her belly. A picture of her lush body heavily pregnant with his baby formed in his mind. He imagined her full breasts swollen with milk, the nipples large and distended, and her belly round and ripe, ready to give birth. Desire surged to life so fast he had to grit his teeth.

Okay, this was more than temporary insanity. This was becoming an obsession. An obsession he was beginning to fear he had no control over whatsoever.

Adjusting his trousers, he waited in the darkness until he'd finally calmed down enough to scoop Issy up and carry her to their bedroom without causing himself an injury. She barely stirred. But as he undressed her and tucked her into bed the visions of her body ripe with his child refused to go away.

It wasn't the desire that bothered him, though, as he climbed into bed beside her. Their livewire sexual attraction had always been as natural as breathing. It stood to reason a pregnant Issy would turn him on too.

What disturbed him much more was the irrational need and the bone-deep longing that went right along with the lust.

Sweat trickled down his back as the fear he'd been holding onto with an iron grip all day kicked him in the gut.

Issy squinted at the pre-dawn light filtering through the terrace doors, then moaned softly as cramping pain gripped her abdomen. Gio's warm hand stirred against her hip as she listened to the low murmur of his breathing, and tears caught in her throat. The familiar pain could mean only one thing. She was about to start her period.

She bit down hard on her bottom lip, lifting his hand and laying it down behind her. She didn't want to wake him up and have him see her in this state. Slipping out of bed, she made a beeline for the bathroom.

After taking care of the practicalities, she donned one of Gio's bathrobes and sat on the toilet seat, feeling utterly dejected. Which was ridiculous.

The fact that there was no baby was good news.

She'd have to be an idiot to want to get pregnant under these circumstances. She wasn't ready for motherhood yet. And Gio certainly wasn't ready to be a father. Yesterday's trip had proved that beyond a shadow of a doubt. The man was deeply suspicious of love and families and relationships in general. And even though that may have started to change, it would take a lot more than an afternoon spent with his extended family to repair the damage his parents had done.

But, despite all the calm common-sense justifications running through Issy's mind, she felt as if a boulder were pressing against her chest, making it hard for her to breathe.

She got off the toilet seat and reached for some tissues, swiped at her cheeks to catch the errant tears. She blew her nose, brushed her fingers through her hair and stared blankly into the mirror, but the boulder refused to budge.

As she stared at her reflection she thought of Gio the evening before, his cheeks flushed a dull red while his uncle bade him farewell.

Tenderness and longing and hope surged up. And the boulder cut off her air supply.

'Oh, God!'

She collapsed onto the toilet seat, her fist clutching the tissue, her knees trembling and every last ounce of blood seeping from her face.

'I can't have,' she whispered. 'It's only been a few days.'

But she sank her head into her hands and groaned. Because there was no getting away from it. She'd let her emotions loose and now look what had happened? She'd only gone and fallen hopelessly in love with Giovanni Hamilton. Again.

She wanted to deny it. But suddenly all those wayward emotions made complete sense.

Her Pollyanna-like obsession to get Gio to embrace his family. Her blissful happiness at their renewed friendship. Her relentless attempts to understand the traumas of Gio's childhood and then help him fix them. Even her bizarre anguish at the discovery that she wasn't pregnant.

Her fabulous holiday fling had never been about sex, or friendship, or putting the mistakes of her youth behind her. That had been a smokescreen generated by lust and denial.

She groaned louder.

Fabulous. She may well have just made the biggest mistake of her life. Twice.

It took Issy a good ten minutes to get off the toilet seat. But in that time she'd managed to get one crucial thing into perspective.

Falling in love with Gio again didn't have to be a disaster.

The man she'd come to know wasn't the surly, unhappy boy she'd once fallen for. He was more settled, more content and much more mature now. And so was she.

She hadn't imagined the connection between them in the last few days. The power and passion of their love-making. The intensity of their friendship. Or the aston-ished pride on Gio's face when his uncle Carlo had welcomed him into the bosom of his family.

All of which meant Gio wasn't necessarily a lost cause.

But she also knew that the spectre of that boy was still there. And, given all the casual cruelty that boy had suffered, it wasn't going to be easy for the man to let his guard down and accept that she loved him. Especially not in the space of three days!

After splashing her eyes with cold water, Issy prac-tised a look of delighted relief in the bathroom mirror for when she informed Gio of her unpregnant state.

She mustn't give Gio any clues about how she felt. Not until she'd worked out a strategy. She needed to be calm and measured and responsible this time. The way she *hadn't* been at seventeen. Which meant taking the time to gauge Gio's feelings before she blurted out her own.

Putting her hand on the doorknob, she took a steady-ing breath—and decided not to dwell on the fact that her strategies so far hadn't exactly been a massive success.

Stepping out of the bathroom, she closed the door behind her, grateful for the darkness.

'What's going on? You okay?'

The deep, sleep-roughened voice made her jump.

'Yes. I'm absolutely fine,' she said, forcing what she hoped was a bright smile onto her face.

'You sure?' He paused to rub his eyes. 'You've been in there forever.'

Propped up on the pillows, the sheet draped over his hips, Gio looked so gorgeous she felt the boulder press on her chest again. She made herself cross the room.

'Actually, I'm better than fine. I've got some good news.' She shrugged off the bathrobe and slipped under the sheet. 'I've started my period.'

He frowned, and something flickered in his eyes, but the light was too dim to make it out. 'So you're not pregnant?' he said dully, as his hand settled on her hip, rubbed.

She snuggled into his arms, pressing her back against his chest.

'What a relief, right?' she said, swallowing down the words that wanted to burst out.

Don't say anything, you ninny. It's far too soon.

'Which means there's no need for any emergency contraceptives,' she continued. 'Here or at home. Thank goodness,' she babbled on, the mention of home making the boulder grow. He'd asked her to stay another night. Did that mean he would expect her to leave today?

He said nothing for a long time. His hand absently circling her hip. The only sound was the deafening hum of the air conditioner.

Would he say something? Give her a sign that he'd like her to stay a little longer? She needed more time.

Eventually he moved. Warm palms settled over her belly and stroked gently, easing the ache from the dull cramps.

'That's good,' he said at last, the murmured words devoid of emotion.

Issy placed her hands over his and breathed in his scent. 'Yes, isn't it?' she said, trying to ignore the now enormous boulder.

He hadn't asked her to stay. But he hadn't asked her to leave either. That had to be a good sign. Didn't it?

'*Buongiorno, signorina.*'

Issy blinked at Carlotta's greeting as she pushed herself up in bed, gripping the sheet to cover her nakedness. She pushed her hair out of her eyes and watched the older woman place a tray on the terrace table, put out a plate of pastries, a pot of coffee and one cup.

She felt achy and tired, as if she hadn't slept at all. Probably because she hadn't. All the questions she didn't have answers for had made her emotions veer from euphoria to devastation during the pre-dawn hours as she'd tried to sleep.

'*Scusami, Carlotta. Dové Signor Hamilton?*' she asked, doing her best to pronounce the question correctly.

The housekeeper smiled and replied in Italian, speaking far too fast for Issy to catch more than a few words. Then Carlotta took a folded note out of her apron pocket, passed it to Issy, bobbed a quick curtsy and left.

Issy waited until the door had closed, a feeling of dread settling over her, before glancing at the clock on the mantelpiece. It wasn't even nine o'clock yet. Where could Gio have gone?

She opened the note, her hands trembling. But as she read it her breath gushed out in a shaky puff.

Sorry, Issy.

Had business at the office. You'll have to survive without me today.

Back around dinnertime. Ask Carlotta if you need anything.

Ciao, Gio

A lone tear trickled down her cheek as the hope she'd been clinging to dissolved.

How could he have gone to the office without waiting for her to wake up? She sniffed heavily. Well, she wouldn't have to worry about blurting out her feelings, seeing as he wasn't even here.

It was only after she'd read it three more times that the full import of the curt dismissive note dawned on her.

What had Gio really been hoping for when he'd left this morning? The veiled message in the cursory note seemed obvious all of a sudden. When he returned home tonight, he hoped to discover the sticky business of ending their affair had been dealt with in his absence. He hadn't said anything about her leaving last night because he'd hadn't felt he needed to. It had always been understood that she would go once her period started.

The agony threatened to swamp her as she choked down breakfast and got dressed, but she refused to let any tears fall. There would be time enough for that when she got home.

After breakfast, Issy packed her bag and arranged a flight home via the computer terminal in Gio's study. She rang Maxi and told her she would be at the theatre tomorrow, ready to get back to work. The conversation fortified her. She needed to return to her own life. To start grounding herself in reality again. But as she disconnected the call and keyed in the number Carlotta had given her to book a cab to the airport, her fighting spirit finally put in an appearance.

Her fingers paused on the buttons.

Why was she making this so easy for Gio? Why was she letting him call all the shots, even now?

By keeping quiet about her feelings earlier, by trying to be mature and sensible and take things slowly she'd played right into his hands.

She'd been prepared to give Gio everything—not just her body, but her heart and her soul too. And even if he didn't want them, or the family and the life they could build together, didn't she at least owe it to herself to tell him how she felt?

After getting an address for Gio's office out of Carlotta, Issy booked a cab to take her to the airport. But when the cab arrived twenty minutes later she handed the driver the piece of notepaper with the Florence address scribbled on it, explaining in her faltering Italian that she needed to make a quick stop first.

She had four hours before her flight. More than enough time to see Gio one last time and let him know exactly what he was chucking away.

CHAPTER NINE

EXHAUSTED, but determined, Issy walked into the domed reception area of the stunning glass and steel building on the banks of the Arno.

She'd figured out exactly what she was going to say to Gio and exactly how she was going to say it during the drive into the city. She would be calm, poised and articulate, and would keep a tight grip on her emotions. Under no circumstances would she dissolve into a gibbering wreck as she had at seventeen and let Gio see her utterly destroyed.

Because she wasn't. She'd matured over the last ten years—enough to know that she had to accept the things she couldn't change. However much it hurt. Because she couldn't afford to spend another ten years pining over a man who had nothing to offer her.

'*Mi scusi, parle inglese, signor?*' she asked the perfectly groomed young man at the reception desk, praying he did speak English.

'Yes, signorina. What can I do for you?' he replied in heavily accented English.

'I would like to see Giovanni Hamilton.'

'Do you have an appointment?'

'No, I'm…' She stuttered to a halt, the heat spreading up her neck. 'I'm a friend of his.'

The young man didn't show by a single flicker of his eyelashes what he thought of that statement, but the heat still hit Issy's cheeks as her hard-fought-for composure faltered. How many other women had come to his offices like this? Looking for something he wasn't going to give them?

'I need to see him if at all possible,' she soldiered on. 'It's extremely important.'

To me, at least.

She wasn't sure if the receptionist believed her or simply took pity on her, but he sent her a sympathetic smile as he reached for the phone on his desk. 'I will contact his office manager. What is your name?'

'Isadora Helligan.'

After conducting a brief conversation in Italian, the receptionist hung up the phone.

'His office manager says he is at a site meeting, but if you would like to go up to the top floor she will contact him.'

The stylish young men and women working on state-of-the-art computers and at large drawing easels stopped to watch as Issy walked through the huge open-plan office on the sixth floor—and her composure began to unravel completely.

What was she doing here? Was this another of her hare-brained ideas that was destined to end up kicking her in the teeth? And how the hell was she going to stop herself dissolving into tears with a boulder the size of Mount Everest already lodged in her throat?

Given her tenuous emotional state, she was extremely grateful when Gio's calm, matronly officer manager, who also spoke English, ushered her into Gio's office and informed her that Signor Hamilton had interrupted his meeting at the site office and would be with her in about ten minutes.

Well, at least he wasn't avoiding her.

Unfortunately Gio's office, which took up one whole corner of the floor, was made completely of glass. As she sat down on the green leather sofa adjacent to his desk, and stared out of the floor-to-ceiling window at the Florence cityscape, she could feel the eyes of all his employees burning into the back of her neck.

After suffering from goldfish-in-a-bowl syndrome for an endless five minutes, she paced to the window and stared out at the Florence skyline, the enormity of the task ahead hitting her all over again.

Did she really want to do this? If Gio dismissed her feelings, the way he had done ten years ago, how much harder would it be to pick up the pieces of her shattered heart?

'Issy, this is a nice surprise. Why don't I take you to lunch?'

She lifted her head and saw Gio standing in the office doorway, his shirtsleeves rolled up and his suit trousers creased and flecked with mud. He looked rumpled and ridiculously pleased to see her. His impossibly handsome face relaxed into a sexy, inviting smile.

Mount Everest turned into the Himalayas.

How could she love him so much and not know whether he was even capable of loving her in return?

'I don't have time for lunch,' she said, glad when her

voice hardly faltered. 'I dropped by to tell you I'm catching a flight home this evening.'

The smile disappeared, to be replaced by a sharp frown. He closed the door and walked towards her. 'What the hell for?'

Tell him now. Tell him why.

She tried to find the words, but the dark fury in his eyes shocked her into silence.

'You're not getting a flight home tonight…or to-morrow.' He grasped her arm, hauled her against him. 'You're staying at the villa even if I have to tie you to the bloody bed.'

'You can't do that.' She was so astonished the words came out on a gasp.

'Don't bet on it. This isn't over. And until I decide it is you're not going anywhere. So you'll have to call your people and let them know.'

'My…? What?' she stammered, her mouth drop-ping open.

'*Dio!*' He let go of her arm and stalked past her, a stream of what she assumed were swear-words in Italian coming out of his mouth.

Flinging the door open, he shouted something at a colleague. It was only then that she noticed every one in the office beyond was standing up at their desks and gawking at them. Some were whispering to each other, others were gaping in open curiosity. They'd all heard every word. And, knowing her luck, they probably all spoke perfect English.

But as she stood there being stared at, while Gio's office manager made an announcement to the staff, she simply didn't have it in her to blush. So she and Gio had made a spectacle of themselves? So what? Frankly, she was past embarrassment and past caring what anyone else thought.

She was too busy trying to figure out Gio's temper tantrum.

Clearly he hadn't intended his note to be a thinly veiled invitation for her to go before he got home, as she had suspected.

The news should have pleased her. But it didn't.

Why was he so angry with her? And what right did he have to order her about like that? Had she really been that much of a push-over that he thought he could treat her like his personal possession? This didn't feel like good news. Had they ever really been friends? Or had that been an illusion too?

She waited by the desk, folding her arms across her midriff to stop the tremors racking her body as she watched Gio's employees troop off towards the lifts. Most of them glanced over their shoulders as they left, to get one last juicy look at the crazy lady.

Five long minutes later they were entirely alone, the whole floor having been evacuated.

He propped his butt on the desk, braced his hands on the edge. 'Now, I want to know what's going on.' The stiff tone suggested he was making an effort to keep hold of his temper. 'Why do you want to go home?'

The question had the Himalayas rising up in her throat to choke her. But she couldn't tell him she loved him now. Not until she knew whether she had ever meant more than all the others.

'Why do you want me to stay?'

* * *

I want you to love me.

The plea formed in Gio's mind and he recoiled.

He couldn't say that. Now now. Not ever. He didn't want her love. He didn't want anyone's love.

After lying awake for hours this morning, listening to her sleep, he'd forced himself to leave the house in a desperate attempt to put the whole fiasco out of his head.

Unfortunately burying himself in work hadn't had the effect he'd hoped. Instead of forgetting about her, he'd missed her even more than yesterday. To the point where, when his manager had called to say she'd arrived to see him, he'd broken off an important site meeting to rush back and take her to lunch.

And then she'd told him she was leaving and he'd lost it completely.

He was behaving like a lovesick fool. Which was preposterous. He wasn't in love. He couldn't let himself be in love.

'What do I want?' he replied. 'I want what I've always wanted.' He sank his fingers into her hair, drew her mouth close to his, vindicated by the flash of arousal in her eyes.

Her lips parted instinctively, but as he plundered she dragged her mouth away, staggered back.

'That's not good enough,' she said, the deep blue eyes turbulent with emotion. 'Not any more. I can't stay just for the sex.'

'Why not? It's what we do best,' he said, unable to prevent the bitter edge in his voice.

She'd tricked him into this—just as she'd tricked him into going to that christening yesterday. And now he was paying the price.

She flinched as if he'd struck her. 'Because I want more than that.'

'There isn't any more.'

'Yes, there is. I love you.'

He heard the words, and felt panic strangle him as the great gaping wounds he'd kept closed for so long were ripped open. 'Don't worry, you'll get over it.'

'I don't want to get over it,' Issy stated, the sharp, searing pain at his dismissal ramming into her body like a blow. It had taken every last ounce of her courage to say the words. Only to have them thrown back at her with barely a moment's hesitation.

How could he be so callous? This was worse than the last time—much worse.

'Doesn't it matter to you at all how I feel?' she whispered.

'I told you right from the start I'm not looking for…that.' He couldn't even bring himself to say the word. 'You chose to misinterpret that. Not me.'

She felt numb. Anaesthetised against the pain by shock and disbelief. How could she have been so wrong about him? How could she have been so wrong about everything?

She crossed her arms over her chest, forced her mind to engage. 'I see,' she said dully, her voice on autopilot. 'So this is all my own fault? Is that what you're saying?'

Suddenly it seemed vitally important that she understand. Why had she made so many mistakes where he was concerned?

'Issy, for God's sake.' He stepped close, tried to take

her hand, but she pulled back. 'I never meant to hurt you. I *told* you what I wanted—'

'Why does it always have to be about what *you* want?' she interrupted, allowing resentment through to quell the vicious pain. But as she looked at his handsome face, tense with annoyance, she suddenly understood what it was he had always lacked. And the reality of how he'd played her—of how she'd *let him* play her—became clear.

'I never realised what a coward you are,' she said softly.

He stiffened as if she had slapped him. 'What the hell does that mean?'

She scrubbed the tears off her cheeks with an impatient fist. 'You say all you want is sex, that relationships don't matter to you, because you're too scared to want more.'

'That's insane!' he shouted. But his angry words couldn't hurt her any more.

He'd never wanted what she had to offer—and that was something she would have to learn to live with. But he hadn't needed to be so cruel.

They *had* been friends. She hadn't imagined that. And maybe one day they could have had more—but he'd thrown it away because he didn't have the guts to try. And she knew why.

'Your parents hurt you, Gio. They treated you like a commodity and never gave you the love you deserved. You survived. But you'll never be truly free until you stop letting what they did rule your life.'

'This has nothing to do with them,' he snapped, with the same closed-off expression on his face she had seen so many times before. He still didn't get it—but, worse than that, she knew now he never would.

'Doesn't it?' she said wearily as she walked past him towards the door.

'Come back here, dammit.'

She didn't turn at the shouted words. Didn't have the strength to argue. What would be the point when she could never win?

'I'm not going to come chasing after you, Issy, if that's what all this is supposed to achieve.'

She carried on walking, her heart breaking all over again at the defiant tone.

She had never been the enemy. Why couldn't he see that?

CHAPTER TEN

'DO YOU think our new sponsor will want his company's name on the cover page?'

Issy's fingers paused on the computer keyboard at Maxi's enquiry. 'Sorry? What?' she asked, even though she'd heard every word.

'I'm putting the finishing touches to the new programmes. Shouldn't we add your Duke's company name to it?'

'Yes, I suppose so,' she replied, as the all-too-familiar vice tightened across her torso. 'That's a great idea,' she added, with an enthusiasm she didn't feel.

She'd left Florence over two weeks ago. And she couldn't even talk about the sponsorship without falling apart.

When was she going to get over this?

She didn't want to think about it any more, go on replaying every little nuance of Gio's behaviour during the hours she had spent in his house. Apart from the fact that it was exhausting her, it wasn't going to change a thing.

She'd thought she'd made a major breakthrough a week ago, when she'd come to the conclusion that she hadn't been crazy enough to fall in love after only three short days. She knew now she'd never stopped loving him. In all the years they'd been apart her love had lurked in some small corner of her heart, just waiting to be rediscovered.

But now she knew how hopeless it was, shouldn't she be able to move on?

To start rebuilding her life?

Gio would have moved on the minute she'd walked out the door. And, however sad that made her, she should be grateful. At least his indifference meant his company hadn't pulled the theatre's sponsorship.

She'd allowed herself to get so wrapped up in Gio she'd completely forgotten about the theatre. Which had added a nice thick layer of guilt to the heartache and recriminations in the weeks since her return.

Taking a professional attitude now was essential. And if she had to deal with Gio in the future, as a result of his donation, it would be a small penance to pay. The theatre was now her number one priority.

'Why don't you give the Florence office a call and see what they say?' she said to Maxi, not quite ready to take the next step.

'Are you sure you don't want to ring them?' Maxi asked, a quick grin tugging at her lips. 'They might put you through to the Dishy Duke.'

'No, that's okay,' she said tightly. 'I'm busy doing Jake's bio.' She turned back to her keyboard.

She hadn't told Maxi what had happened in Florence, despite a lot of probing, and she didn't intend to. Talking about it would only make it harder to forget.

She continued to type, glad when the hammer thumps of the keys shut out Maxi's call to Florence. But

as she tapped in the final piece of biographical information from Jake's scribbled notes she couldn't miss the
sound of Maxi putting the phone back in its cradle.

'Everything go okay?' Issy asked, as casually as she
could.

'Better than okay,' Maxi said excitedly. 'Thank God
I happened to call them. The e-mail must have got lost.'

'What e-mail?' Issy asked, a strange sinking feeling
tugging at the pit of her stomach.

'The e-mail informing us about his visit.' Maxi
glanced at her watch. 'His plane touched down over an
hour ago, according to his PA. He could be here in less
than an hour.' Springing up, Maxi began stacking the
files on her desk. 'We should get this place cleared up.
I expect he'll want to come up here and check out the
office before he catches the afternoon show.'

The sinking feeling turned to full-on nausea. All her
erogenous zones melted and a vicious chill rippled
down her spine.

'Who are you talking about?' Issy asked, but her
voice seemed to be coming from a million miles away.
All her carefully constructed walls were tumbling down,
to expose the still battered heart beneath.

'The Dishy Duke,' Maxi said confidently. 'Who else?'

'When did you say she'd be back?' Gio lifted the ale
glass to his lips, but the lukewarm beer did nothing to
ease the dryness in his throat as he glanced round the
mostly empty pub.

He noticed the autographed photos on the wall, the
yellowing playbills under glass. Issy had talked about
this place often during their time together in Florence.

But had he ever really listened, or even bothered to ask her about it? While her assistant had showed him round this afternoon, and he'd been introduced to all the people who worked here and clearly adored Issy, he'd come to realise how much work she'd put into the place and how much it meant to her—and yet he'd been too self-absorbed, too wrapped up in his own fears to notice.

He'd been a selfish bastard about that, as well as about everything else. How could he even begin to make amends?

Issy's assistant sent him a puzzled look, probably because he'd asked her the same damn question approximately fifty times since he'd arrived at the tiny theatre pub two hours ago.

'I'm really not sure. Would you like me to try her mobile again?' she replied, polite enough not to mention that she'd given him the same answer ten minutes ago.

He put his glass down on the counter.

How the hell had Issy got word of his arrival? He'd been careful not to tell anyone but his PA of his plans, just in case she did a vanishing act.

He stared at the girl, who was looking at him with a helpful smile on her face. He couldn't wait any longer. Which meant he'd have to throw himself on this girl's mercy.

It made him feel foolish, but any humiliation was likely to be minor compared to what he would face when he finally got Issy alone again.

Don't go there.

He forced the panic back. That was exactly what had got him into this mess in the first place.

'I need to ask you a favour,' he said, hoping he didn't

sound as desperate as he felt. If she said no, he'd have to find out where Issy lived, which could cost him another night. Now he'd finally built up the courage to do this thing, he needed to get on with it.

The girl's eyebrows lifted. 'Of course, Your Grace.'

'Call me Gio,' he said, straining for the easy charm which had once come so effortlessly. 'I didn't come here to see the theatre. I came to see Issy.'

The girl didn't say anything, her eyes widening.

'We had a disagreement in Florence.' Which was probably the understatement of the millennium. 'I think she's avoiding me.'

'Oh?' the girl said. 'What's the favour?'

'Call her and tell her I've left. I can wait in your office until she gets back, and then say what I need to say.' Although he didn't have a clue what that was yet.

The girl stared at him.

The murmured conversation of the pub-goers got louder, more raucous, and the musty smell of old wood and stale beer more cloying as he waited for the girl's answer.

How had he managed to screw things up so badly?

Ever since he'd returned home from the office that day he'd known he'd made a terrible mistake. But he had refused to admit it.

Anger had come first. Just as it had all those years before. He'd spent a week furious with Issy. How *dared* she delve into his psyche and tell him what he'd made of his life wasn't enough? He'd thrown himself back into work. Determined to prove it was all he needed.

But as the days had dragged into a week the anger had faded, leaving a crushing, unavoidable loneliness in its wake. She'd been at the house for only a few short days—how could he miss her so much?

He'd tried to persuade himself the yearning was purely sexual. And the mammoth erections he woke up with every single morning seemed like pretty good proof. But even he had to accept, as the days had crawled past and the yearning had only got worse, that this was more than just sex.

Whenever he had breakfast he imagined her smiling at him across the terrace table, and felt the loss. Whenever he woke up in the night he reached for her instinctively, but she was never there. He couldn't even visit any of the galleries and churches he loved, because without her there he couldn't see the beauty any more. But what he missed most was the simple pleasure of listening to her talk. The silence had become acute, like a suffocating cell that followed him about, just as it had during his childhood, before he'd met her.

He'd been sitting in his office that morning when he'd finally acknowledged the truth. The only way to remedy the problem was to get Issy back.

He didn't kid himself it would be easy. But he had to try.

He studied her assistant, trying to hold on to his patience. What was taking the girl so long?

Finally she pulled her mobile out of her pocket, began keying in a number. As she lifted it to her ear she sent him an astute look. The helpful smile had vanished.

'Just so you know, I don't care if you are a duke. Or if you're the theatre's angel. If you hurt her, I'll have to kill you.'

He nodded, knowing the reckless threat wasn't the worst that could happen.

'Is Maxi still here?' Issy shouted above the pub crowd to Gerard, one of the barmen.

'Think she's backstage,' he replied, pulling a pint of Guinness. 'Dave had a wardrobe emergency with one of the trolls. I can send Magda to get her.'

'No, that's okay.' She was being ridiculous. Maxi had told her over an hour ago that Gio had left. She needed to stop being such a wuss.

Dipping behind the bar, she sent Gerard a quick wave and started up the narrow staircase to the office. It was after seven, and she still had all the ticket sales from the matinee and evening shows to put on the computer and bank. Staying away all afternoon meant she was going to be here till gone midnight, finishing up, but she didn't care as she pushed open the door. Maybe she'd be able to face Gio again one day, but why pile on the agony before she was ready?

'Hello, Isadora.'

She whipped round at the husky words, her heart ramming full-pelt into her ribcage.

He sat at her desk, looking exactly like the man who had haunted her dreams. One leg was slung over his knee, his hand gripping his ankle, and his hair was combed back from his brow.

She turned back to the door. Staccato footsteps stamped on the wooden floor as her frantic fingers slipped on the knob. She dragged the door open but a large hand slapped against the wood above her head and slammed it closed.

His big body surrounded her as she continued to struggle pointlessly with the handle. She breathed in the spicy scent of his aftershave and her panic increased to fever pitch. The ripple of sensation tightening her nipples and making her sex ache.

'Don't run away, Issy. We need to talk.'

Hot breath feathered her earlobe. They had been in the same position all those weeks ago at the club. Her response to his nearness had been just as immediate, just as devastating then. But why couldn't her body be immune to him even now?

'I don't want to talk,' she said, her voice shaking with delayed reaction. 'Leave me alone.' Her knees buckled.

His arm banded around her midriff, held her upright. 'Are you okay?'

She shook her head. His prominent arousal evident even through their clothes. She tried to pry his arm loose. She couldn't afford to fall under his sensual spell again.

'If you've come here to have sex, I'm not interested,' she said, the melting sensation at her core making her a liar.

'Ignore it,' he said as he let her go, stepped back. 'I came to talk, Issy. Nothing else. I don't have any control over my body's reaction to you.'

She forced herself to face him. 'Once you've said what you have to say, do you promise to leave?'

Regret flickered in his eyes, and his jaw tensed, but he nodded. 'If that's what you want.'

She edged away from the door, moved to stand behind her desk, needing the barrier between them. 'Go on, then,' she prompted.

He said nothing for what seemed like an eternity. The only sound was the muffled noise from the pub downstairs.

'I want you back.'

The irony struck her first. A few short weeks ago she would have given anything to hear him say that. But then anger seeped in. How pathetic. To think she would have settled for so little. 'What do you expect me to say to that?'

He ducked his head, sank his hands into his pockets. When he lifted his head she saw something she hadn't expected. 'I want you to say you'll give me another chance.'

It almost made her weaken. The plea in his voice, the look of raw need darkening the chocolate brown. But she knew she couldn't give in—not after everything he'd put her through.

'I can't.' She pressed her lips together, swallowed the ball of misery back down. 'I've already given you too many chances. I've loved you ever since we were kids. I don't want to love you any more.'

He stepped forward, braced his hands against the desk. 'That's not true,' he countered. 'You didn't love me when you were a girl. That was infatuation.'

'No, it wasn't,' she cried, temper strengthening her voice. How could he ask her for another chance and still belittle her feelings?

'You fooled yourself into believing it, Issy. Because you were young. And sweet.' He turned away.

She shook her head. 'That's not true. I was immature. I know in many ways I was still a child. But I did love you. Because when I met you again the feelings were all still there.'

He swung back. 'No, they weren't. You detested me,' he said. 'You said so yourself.'

Despite the off-hand remark she could see the anguish in his eyes, and she realised the rash words had hurt him.

She'd assumed he couldn't be hurt, that she had never meant that much to him. But what if she had misjudged the strength of his feelings all along? In the same way as she'd misjudged her own.

'Why did you push me away?' she asked, tentative hope flickering to life. 'Why didn't you believe me when I said I loved you?'

He gave a deep sigh. 'You're going to make me say it, aren't you?'

She heard the turmoil, the resignation in his voice, and hope blossomed. 'Yes, I am.'

His eyes met hers. 'Because I'm not the man you think I am.'

'And what man is that?' she asked simply.

He dipped his head, the gesture weary. 'One that deserves you.' His voice broke on the words and she realised that finally, after all these years, all the heartache and confusion, the barriers were at last crumbling away.

'Gio, you idiot,' she murmured. 'What makes you think you don't deserve me?'

'I spent my whole childhood trying to make them care about me. And they never did. I knew there had to be a reason. Then you came along and filled up all those empty spaces. And I never even had to ask.'

'But you kept shutting me out.' He'd done the same thing when they were children, as soon as she'd got too close. 'Why would you do that?'

'Because I was petrified,' he murmured. 'I didn't

want to need you and then have you figure out you'd made a mistake.'

Stepping out from the desk, she wrapped her arms round his waist, laid her head on his chest. And the last of the chill burned away as his hands settled on her shoulders.

'You were right, Issy. I've let what they did control my life. I'm not doing that any more.' His lips brushed her hair. 'Give me another chance. I know you probably don't love me any more, but…'

'Gio, be quiet.' She squeezed him and then looked up. Resting her hand on his cheek, she felt the rough stubble and saw the tired smudges under his eyes she hadn't noticed before. 'Love doesn't work like that. I couldn't stop loving you even when I wanted to. And believe me, I gave it a really good try.'

The realisation that now she wouldn't have to brought with it a surge of euphoria.

'I'll give you another chance,' she said, knowing all her hopes and dreams were written on her face, 'as long as you promise not to shut me out ever again.'

'You've got your promise,' he said, kissing her. But then he pulled back, framed her face, his eyes shadowed. 'Wait a minute—don't you want me to say I love you back?'

She almost laughed at the look of bewilderment on his face. 'When you're able to do that, that will be lovely.' And she knew he would be able to one day— once he'd become completely secure in the knowledge that she meant everything she said. 'And my romantic heart will cherish the moment. But in the end they're just words, Gio. What really matters is how you feel. And whether you want to be with me and make a commitment that matters.'

Ten years ago she would have demanded he say the words. But she wasn't going to pressure him into it now. He'd come such a long way already.

'That's really noble of you, Issy,' he said, the amusement in his eyes puzzling her. 'But it may surprise you to know I'm not that much of a coward. Not any more.'

'I know,' she replied, not sure where this was leading. To her surprise, he took a step back and got down on one knee. 'What are you doing?'

'Be quiet and let me do this properly.'

'But I told you, it's not necessary.'

'I know what you told me,' he said, his lips quirking as he squeezed her hands tight. 'And you probably even believe it at the moment. Because you're sweet and generous and you never think anything through before you open your mouth.'

'Gee, thanks,' she said, pretty sure that wasn't a compliment.

'Stop pouting and let me say what I've got to say,' he said, his voice sobering. 'Maybe you don't need to hear the words, but I sure as hell need to say them. I owe you this, Issy—for what I said to you ten years ago, and for the things I said a fortnight ago.' He cleared his throat, took a deep breath. 'So here goes.' His eyes fixed on her face as excitement geysered up her chest and made her knees tremble.

'*Ti amo*, Isadora Helligan. I love your sassy wit, the smell of your hair, the feel of your body next to mine when I wake up in the morning. I love that you are always ready to fight for what you think is right and you never back down. I love your passion for life and your spontaneity, and I especially love that drama queen tendency that makes you so damn easy to tease.'

'Hey!' she said, grinning like a fool.

'But most of all, Issy,' he continued, chuckling at her mock outrage, 'I love your courage and your tenacity and your ability to always see the best in people, and that because of all those qualities you gave me all the chances I needed till I finally got it right.'

She flung her arms around his shoulders, almost toppling him over. 'I love you, Gio. So much I'm not even going to make you pay for that drama queen comment.'

He laughed, standing up with her arms still wrapped around his neck. Holding onto her waist, he lifted her easily off the ground, then kissed her with the passion and purpose she adored.

Setting her down at last, he held her face in his hand, brushed a thumb over the tears of joy rolling down her cheeks. 'Don't cry, Issy. This is where the fun starts.'

She smiled up at him, her body quivering with need as his hand stroked under her T-shirt.

'Is that a promise, Hamilton?' she said, lifting a co-quettish eyebrow.

'Pay attention, Helligan,' He hugged her close, his lips hovering above hers. 'That's not a promise, it's a guarantee.'

And then he proved it—in the most delicious way possible.

EPILOGUE

'I MAY have to hate you.' Sophia smiled cheekily as she settled beside Issy on one of the comfortable upholstered chairs that had been set out among the olives groves. 'How did you get your figure back so quickly?'

Issy smiled, weary but blissfully happy. It had been a very long day—she and Gio had been woken up at three that morning by their baby son—but she wouldn't have missed a moment of it. 'Are you joking?' she scoffed. 'Haven't you noticed? My boobs are the size of two small hot-air balloons!'

Sophia laughed. 'Hasn't anyone ever told you? Here in Italy, big is beautiful.'

Colour rose to Issy's cheeks as she spotted Gio making his way towards them across the makeshift dance floor. The loose languid gait she adored made even more beguiling by the tiny baby perched on his shoulder.

'Aha!' Sophia said. 'Someone *has* told you, I think.'

Issy didn't even attempt to hide the blush as her smile spread.

'Someone may have mentioned it,' she replied demurely, enjoying Sophia's delighted giggle as she watched her husband being stopped and kissed by an elderly woman whose name she couldn't remember. There had to be at least a hundred people gathered at the Lorenzo farm to celebrate their son's birth—and even with her greatly improved skill in Italian she was struggling to keep all the names and faces and family connections straight.

As she observed Gio, he took the baby off his shoulder to show him off to the cooing lady, and Issy's grin grew. All the anxiety and confusion of their first visit a year ago had gone. Gio had been relaxed and completely comfortable today—and she suspected it was mostly their son's doing.

One more thing to thank little Marco Lorenzo Hamilton for, whose unexpected arrival had deepened and strengthened their relationship in ways she could never have imagined.

To think she'd agonised for weeks about how to break the news to Gio when she'd fallen pregnant ten months before. Their relationship then had seemed so precious, and yet so vulnerable.

Neither of them had spoken about children since that first early pregnancy scare, and, as much as Issy might have fantasised about having Gio's baby, the abstract romantic dream had swiftly turned into a downward spiral of doubt and panic when that little pink plus sign had appeared in the window of the home pregnancy test.

How would Gio respond to the prospect of becoming a father? How could she ask him to make more changes in his life when he'd already made so many? And how would they both cope with adding yet more pressure to an already difficult domestic situation?

For, once the romance of that mutual declaration of love had worn off, they'd soon discovered that living together was a logistical nightmare. They both had homes they loved and careers they were passionate about in two different cities, hundreds of miles apart.

To solve the problem Gio had insisted on buying a penthouse apartment in Islington, and flying between the two cities three or four times a week. But the long hours Issy put in at the theatre and the nights Gio was forced to spend in Italy meant that even with the exhausting commute they had hardly any quality time together.

Which was how she had managed to get pregnant in the first place, Issy thought wryly, her face flushing as she recalled the many frantic and shockingly explosive encounters they'd snatched together, often in the most preposterous places. She still hadn't quite worked out how she was going to tell her son, if he ever asked, that he had been conceived on the stage of the Crown and Feathers's Theatre Pub late one night after Gio had flown back unexpectedly from Florence and caught her as she locked up.

In the end she would have waited a lot longer to tell Gio about the pregnancy than just a couple of weeks. She'd still been trying to second-guess his reaction and formulate a viable strategy when morning sickness had struck with a vengeance, exactly a month into her pregnancy.

Gio had patted her back while she retched. Made her nibble some dry toast and sip peppermint tea and then insisted she sit down. He had something to tell her. To her total shock he'd announced that they were getting married. That he'd planned to wait until she told him about the baby, but that he couldn't wait any longer. And that he knew the reason she hadn't told him was because she thought he would make a terrible father, but it was way too damn late to worry about that now.

Issy had promptly burst into tears, feeling miserably guilty and totally ecstatic and extremely hormonal—all at the same time. When she'd finally got over her crying jag she'd accepted his proposal, apologised for being such a ninny, and told him she'd never doubted his abilities as a father.

She'd seen he didn't believe her, and it had crucified her, but in the months that had followed the agonising guilt had faded as their relationship changed and developed in new and exciting ways.

Their marriage had been immediate, at Gio's insistence, and necessarily low-key, but still impossibly romantic to Issy's mind. They'd said their vows together one wintry afternoon at Islington Town Hall, with only Issy's mum, Edie, in attendance and had been thrown a surprise reception party by Maxi and the gang at the Crown and Feathers. The baby's first ultrasound scan the day before had only added to the magic of the evening's festivities. Issy had watched, dizzy with happiness, every time Gio whipped out the scan photo—which had looked to her very much like a picture of a large prawn—and showed it to anyone who stood still long enough.

No longer prepared to commute, Gio had announced two days after the wedding that he was relocating his architectural practice to London. The announcement had caused their first major row as husband and wife—because Issy had refused point-blank to let Gio do such an idiotic thing, explaining that *she* was giving up her job at the theatre instead and moving to Florence.

Gio had huffed and puffed, then cajoled and shouted, and eventually sulked for over a week. But Issy had got her way in the end—and enjoyed every minute of his irritation and anger and exasperation.

Gio had been prepared to give up everything for her, and, even though she hadn't been consciously aware of her doubts, when he'd blithely informed her he was moving to London those last nagging doubts about his commitment to their life together had disappeared.

Once he'd informed her of his plans in that matter-of-fact way, and the more strenuously he'd tried to convince her it was the right thing to do, the more Issy had known it wasn't. Her body was ripening more each day with their child, the weight of his ring on her finger made her feel content and secure, and she could see the enthusiasm and excitement on his face when he kissed her growing bump each morning and wished their baby *buongiorno*.

The time was right to give up one dream and concentrate on another.

The ease with which she'd handed over control of the theatre to Maxi and supervised the move to Florence had confirmed her decision. And then to top it all had been that heady rush of love when the Ferrari had pulled up outside her new home and Gio had insisted on carrying her over the threshold—even though she knew she weighed more than a small semi-detached house.

They had begun an ever more exciting phase of their lives as they'd spent those last two months together waiting for the baby's arrival. And she hadn't had a single regret about what she'd left behind.

Not that she had left it entirely behind. She'd kept in touch with Maxi and the gang, and she'd even found some voluntary work at a small children's theatre in the Oltarno before she'd got too huge to move.

But she was more than happy to put her career on hold for now, and enjoy the fruits of her labour. Watching Gio blossom into a warm, loving and ludicrously proud papa had been the sweet, gooey icing on a very large cake. The last of the barriers had dropped away, the last of his insecurities had disappeared. He hadn't just given his whole heart to her and their son, but also to his huge extended family. And being there to witness his transformation had been so intoxicating Issy could feel tears stinging her eyes even now as she observed him chatting easily with the old woman he'd never met before today—as comfortable and relaxed in her company as if he'd known her for years.

She sighed, contentment settling over her like a warm blanket. They both had a place to belong and a future so bright with exciting challenges it was hard not to want to rush to the next one.

As Gio approached, having bade goodbye to his latest friend, Sophia bounced up and kissed him on both cheeks.

'So, how is the proud father holding up?' she asked.

'I'm exhausted.' He sent his cousin a quelling look. 'Next time you and your father and my wife concoct one of these "little get-togethers" my son and I are going to demand full disclosure of the numbers involved.'

Sophia gave an impish giggle. 'Stop pretending you haven't enjoyed showing off your *bambino*,' she said, brushing her hand down the baby's downy black curls. 'I've never seen a man's chest puff up so much.'

The *bambino* in question gave a tired little cry and began to wriggle in Gio's arms. Feeling the instinctive dragging sensation in her breasts, Issy knew what the problem was. She reached for her son. 'How's he holding up to being adored?'

Gio lifted the baby off his shoulder, and kissed his son's cheek before passing him over.

'He's been a superstar. He didn't even grumble when Uncle Carlo lectured him about the intricacies of olive oil production and the importance of carrying on the family tradition.'

Both women laughed.

'Don't panic, Gio,' Sophia said. 'My father has been giving that speech to every baby born in the last forty years. So far only Carmine's son Donato has fallen for it.'

Issy settled back into the chair and eased her breast out of the nursing bra. The baby latched on to the nipple like an Exocet missile and began sucking voraciously.

Sophia patted the baby's head. 'I should find my own *bambino*, before Aldo comes looking for me.' She leaned down to kiss Issy's cheek, then gave Gio a hard hug. 'If I don't catch you later, we'll see you next month for Gabriella's first Holy Communion, yes?'

Gio nodded. 'Wouldn't miss it for the world,' he said, and meant it as he watched his cousin leave. Who would have thought that one day he'd actually be looking forward to these insane gatherings?

He sat beside his wife and child, the feeling of pleasure and contentment and pride that had been building all day making his throat burn. Slinging his arm over the back of Issy's chair, he played with the ends of her hair. Staring at his young son feasting on her lush breast in the gathering twilight he wondered, not for the first time in the last year, how the hell he had ever got so lucky.

'Slow down, fella,' he murmured as the baby's cheeks flexed frantically. 'Anyone would think you hadn't been fed in months.'

'Your uncle Carmine calls it the Italian appetite for life,' Issy said, her throaty giggle sending heat arrowing down to Gio's groin.

He shifted in his seat to ease the pressure, and brushed the curtain of hair behind her ear so he could see her face. 'That sounds like the sort of daft thing Carmine would say. What he means is, our son's greedy.'

Issy turned, her lips curving, and his heart thumped his chest wall. 'Apparently it's a Lorenzo family trait, though, so that's okay,' she said, laughing.

Unable to resist a moment longer, Gio cupped her cheek and touched his lips to hers.

He hadn't meant to be too demanding, hadn't meant to take the kiss any deeper, but when she shuddered and her lips parted his tongue swept into her mouth of its own accord. His hand gripped her head as their mouths fused. He feasted on her, the hunger clawing at his gut like a wild thing.

The little wiggle against his chest and the grumpy little wail had him springing back, so ashamed of himself he felt physically sick.

'Issy, I'm sorry. I don't know what the hell got into me.'

Seeing the look of horror on Gio's face, Issy didn't know whether to laugh, or cry, or scream with frustration. It had been six weeks now since their son's birth. And that brief moment had been their first proper kiss!

'Why are you apologising?' she said, deciding to go

with exasperation as she noticed the large bulge in his loose-fitting suit trousers.

She'd been ready and eager to resume their sex life for weeks now. And she'd seen Gio's almost constant state of arousal recently, so she knew he had to be as frustrated as she was. Still, she'd waited patiently for him to tell her what the problem was. But he hadn't. And her patience had finally run out.

'I want to make love again,' she said, annoyance sharpening her voice. 'And I'm getting a bit tired of you pulling back every time we get intimate.'

His eyebrows rose, and then he frowned. 'I'm being considerate,' he said tightly. 'You've just given birth.'

'I gave birth six weeks ago,' she shot back. 'And I was lucky enough not to need any stitches, so I'm completely healed.'

He paled beneath his tan and winced.

Lifting the now dozing Marco off her breast, Issy readjusted her clothing and placed the baby on her shoulder. She kept her eyes fixed on Gio.

'What exactly is the problem?' she said, her voice rising. 'Are you squeamish about having sex with me because I've had a child? Because if that's the—'

'For God's sake, Issy,' he interrupted, his tone rising to match hers. 'You know perfectly well that's not true. I've been sporting erections Superman would have been proud of in the last month.'

He looked so embarrassed, sounded so frustrated, her bubble of amusement burst out without warning.

'What's so funny?' he asked, his frown deepening.

'Gio,' she said, placing her hand on his cheek as she

tried to stifle the giggles, 'what on earth are you waiting for then?'

His lips quirked. 'Good question.'

Putting his hand on her nape, he rested his forehead on hers, blew out a frustrated breath. 'As much as I love my family, let's sneak out. I'm liable to explode if we have to say goodbye to all these people. And I don't fancy walking around with an erection the size of the Leaning Tower of Pisa while I'm doing it.'

Issy had trouble keeping her mirth under control as they crept furtively through the olive trees to their car. As Gio strapped the sleeping baby into his seat, swearing softly in Italian in his haste, Issy felt desire curl low in her belly and a thrilling surge of heat make her head spin.

Issy rested her palm on her husband's thigh, slid it up seductively as the low-slung car jolted down the rough farm track,

'There's no need to hurry, Gio,' she said, smiling cheekily as his harsh handsome face turned towards her in the shadowy light. 'We've got the rest of our lives.'

He gripped her hand and drew it deliberately off his thigh. 'I know,' he murmured, kissing the tips of her fingers. 'And as soon as we get home I plan to make the most of every single second.'

The cheeky smile turned serene as a rush of love overwhelmed her.

'Well, good.' She sighed. 'That makes two of us, then.'

HOW TO WIN THE DATING WAR

BY
AIMEE CARSON

The summer she turned eleven, **Aimee Carson** left the children's section of the library and entered an aisle full of Mills & Boon® novels. She promptly pulled out a book, sat on the floor, and read the entire story. It has been a love affair that has lasted for over thirty years.

Despite a fantastic job working part time as a physician in the Alaskan Bush (think *Northern Exposure* and *ER*, minus the beautiful mountains and George Clooney), she also enjoys being at home in the gorgeous Black Hills of South Dakota, riding her dirt bike with her three wonderful kids and beyond patient husband. But, whether at home or at work, every morning is spent creating the stories she loves so much. Her motto? Life is too short to do anything less than what you absolutely love. She counts herself lucky to have two jobs she adores, and incredibly blessed to be a part of Mills & Boon's family of talented authors.

To my editor, Flo Nicoll.
Thanks for all your hard work and dedication.

And to Dan.
Without you none of this would be possible.

CHAPTER ONE

Maneuvering tools while lying on his back wasn't easy with the relentless stabbing in his chest, and when the wrench slipped, Cutter's hand plowed into the drive shaft. Pain smashed, and the underside of his '71 Barracuda was lit with stars.

"Damn." The muttered word was lost in the rock music wailing in his garage.

Blood dripped from his knuckles onto his T-shirt. He shifted to the right, and his ribs screamed in protest, eliciting a groan of agony as he pulled a rag from the pocket of his jeans, wrapping it around his hand. His chest still sent crippling signals, but—on the good side—the sting in his fingers now took precedence over the two-month-old, lingering ache in his left arm.

Because Cutter Thompson, former number-one driver in the American Stock Car Auto Racing circuit, never did anything half-assed. Even screwing up. He'd ended his career in style, flipping his car and sliding across the finish line on his roof before crashing into a wall.

Pain he was used to. And even if crawling beneath the belly of the 'Cuda went against the doctor's orders, Cutter was going to complete this project even if it killed him.

The music cut off, Bruce Springsteen's voice dying mid-verse, and a pair of high-heeled sandals tapped their way across the concrete toward the 'Cuda. Cinnamon-colored toenails. Nice ankles. Slender, shapely calves. Too bad the rest was blocked by the bottom of the car. The fine-looking legs were most likely encased in a skirt. From this angle, if he rolled his creeper forward, he'd get an eyeful.

And you could tell a lot about a woman by the underwear she wore.

With a delicate squat, knees together, the owner of the legs leaned low until her face appeared beneath the car. Dark, exotic eyes. Glossy, chestnut-colored hair.

"Hello, Mr. Thompson." Her voice was smooth. Warm. Like heated honey. Her smile genuinely bright. The kind of enthusiasm that should be illegal. "Welcome back to Miami."

Welcome home, Thompson. Like a career-ending injury at thirty was a blessing.

Cutter stared at the lady. "You interrupted Springsteen."

Her smile didn't budge. "I'm Jessica Wilson." She paused. "Did you get my messages?"

Jessica Wilson. The crazy lady who wouldn't take no for an answer. "All five of them," he said dryly. He turned his attention back to his work, his tone dismissive, his words designed to send her away for good. "I'm not interested in a publicity stunt," he said firmly. He wasn't interested in publicity, period.

He used to like it. Hell, he'd *lived* for it. And his fans had been fiercely loyal, following him around the circuit and supporting him unconditionally. Sticking with him through thick and thin. The kinds of things parents usually did.

Except for his.

And now what was he supposed to say to the press? Awesome wreck, huh? And how about that stellar suspension the officials had slapped on him? 'Course, that was before anyone knew his split-second decision had cost him more than separated ribs, a fractured arm and a humdinger of a concussion. It had cost him a career.

Pain of a different sort pierced the base of his skull, and regret hollowed out his stomach. Cutter gripped the wrench, awkwardly wrestling with the bolt again. He'd had to go and ruin his dominant hand, too.

Slowly he became aware the lady was still here, as if waiting for him to change his mind. Some people were too persistent for their own good. He tried again. "I'm busy."

"How long have you been working on the car?"

He frowned, thrown by the change in topic. "Fourteen years."

"So fifteen more minutes of a delay won't be too inconvenient?"

Amused, he rolled his head to stare at her. He was trying to be rude and get rid of Little Ms. Sunshine. Why was she still being so friendly? Her eyes were wide. Luminous. The color of melted chocolate. Cutter lowered the wrench warily. "Inconvenient enough."

"As I explained in my messages, the Brice Foundation wants you for their annual charity auction," she went on, obviously undaunted by his attitude. "We need a fifth celebrity to round out our list."

"Five celebrities gullible enough to participate will be hard to find."

She ignored his comment and went on. "I think your participation would generate a lot of excitement, especially as a native Miamian and a national hero."

Cutter's gut clenched. "You've got the wrong guy."

No heroes here. Not anymore. That had ended with his self-destructing, split-second decision on the track. But if she was looking for a night of sex, the fulfillment of a few fantasies, then he was the man for her. Doubtful she was. And right now he wasn't interested in involvement of *any* kind, in bed or out. "My answer is still no."

She stared at him with those big, Bambi, don't-shoot-me eyes. It had to be an uncomfortable position, balancing on the balls of her feet with her chest against her thighs, her head hanging low enough to look under the bottom of the car. But her voice remained patient. "Will you please just hear me out?"

Damn, she wasn't going to go away.

With a frustrated groan, Cutter rubbed a hand down his face. He needed peace. He needed The Boss blaring on the stereo, drowning out the turmoil in his head. And he needed to get the 'Cuda up and running. But he wouldn't get any closer to accomplishing these if the lady didn't leave. Though, much longer in that position and she'd pass out from a lack of blood flow to her brain. At least then he could haul her out of his garage.

But no matter how much he wanted her to go away, he couldn't let a person continue to hold this discussion while impersonating a contortionist. Even if his chest hadn't recovered from the effort it had taken to climb beneath the car in the first place, even if moving would bring more pain, he had to convince her to leave from a standing position.

With a forced sigh and a grunt of agony, he gripped the chassis of the 'Cuda and pulled the creeper on out from beneath the car, wheels squeaking as he went. He rolled off, his ribs screeching louder in protest, and he sucked in a breath… and got hit with her delicate scent. Sweet, yet sensual, infused with a hint of spice. A lot like her voice.

When he finally managed to straighten up, he got a view of her willowy body wrapped in a cool sundress the color of the sky in springtime. Silk clung to her hips and thighs.

Her shoulder-length dark hair framed a delicate face that housed beautiful brown eyes. Classy. Feminine. A girly girl through and through. The visual was almost worth the excruciating pain that now pounded his ribs.

Almost.

She sent him another smile and nodded toward his car.

"Fourteen years is a long time. It looks like it still needs a lot of work."

Cutter's eyebrows pulled together. Sweet or not, no one was allowed to dis his 'Cuda. "Engine's almost fixed." Mostly because when the doctor had delivered the bad news, Cutter had dragged the vehicle out of storage and given himself until the end of the month to get it done. Better than dwelling on his messed-up life. "Be ready for a test run any day now."

She peered in the window. "But there's only a backseat."

"I kissed my first girlfriend there. Happens to be my favorite spot. Just a few more technicalities to take care of."

"Hmmm," she murmured. Stepping back, she glanced at the concrete blocks the car was perched on. "Are tires considered a technicality, too?"

He quirked an eyebrow, amused by her dry tone. "I'll get to it. I've been busy." Busy racing. Ruining a career.

A scowl threatened. Couldn't a man retreat to his garage for a little one-on-one time with his car without a cheerful, pushy woman tracking him down? Maybe if he looked busy she'd go away now.

He rounded the car to where the hood was propped open and twisted off the oil cap. With the clap of heels, she appeared beside him. Ignoring her proximity, and after pulling out the dipstick, he used the rag wrapped around his mashed knuckles to check the level.

She peered around his right shoulder. "Plenty of oil," she said, sounding amused. "Though I doubt you'd lose much since the car doesn't run."

Busted. Not *too* girly a girly girl. "Can't be too careful."

"Words to live by, Mr. Thompson."

"Precisely." Though not exactly his motto until recently. With a self-chastising grunt, he shoved the oil stick back with more force than necessary. "No publicity stunts for me."

"It's for a good cause."

"Always is."

"You haven't even heard the details."

"Don't need to." Refusing to look at her, he screwed the oil cap on. "I'm not doing it."

She placed her hands on the car frame and leaned close, her evocative scent enveloping him. "The Brice Foundation does the kind of work you and your sponsors have always supported in the past. I know if you hear the details, you'll agree."

The optimistic little lady sounded so sure of herself. Cutter straightened and placed his hands on the frame beside hers, finally meeting her face-to-face. Her olive skin tone suggested a distant Mediterranean ancestor somewhere. Even features. High cheekbones. Full mouth, but not too lush. Nice. "I don't have sponsors anymore." He raised an eyebrow to bring his point home. "And you don't know anything about me."

"You started in the ASCAR truck series at seventeen. Two years later you were dubbed someone to watch by *Top Speed* magazine." Her wide, deep-brown eyes held his. "You burst into the stock car series and blazed your way to the top. You're known for your cutting words and for being fearless on the track, earning you the nickname the Wildcard. You've held the number-one rank for the past six years—" a brief hesitation before she went on "—until your accident two months ago when you intentionally bumped your biggest rival, Chester Coon."

Acid churning in his gut, Cutter suppressed the urge to look away. He'd pay for that moment for the rest of his life. He relived it every night in his sleep. The roaring engines. The smell of rubber. And then he spies Chester to his left. Cutter grips his steering wheel...and then he wakes with a jerk, drenched in sweat, heart pounding.

And feeling every one of his injuries as if they were fresh.

But the actual moment of bumping Chester—and fortunately, the crash itself—were a blank. Retrograde amnesia the doctor had called it. A gift bestowed upon him by his concussion.

Or perhaps it was a curse.

His fingers clenched the car frame harder. "The officials should have suspended Chester for the Charlotte incident last year. Damn rookie put everyone at risk when he drove. And then he nearly got another driver killed."

"There was a lot of hard driving the day of your wreck. Everyone knew Chester had it coming."

Surprised, he cocked his head. Jessica Wilson clearly knew the unwritten rules of the track. A familiar niggle of doubt resurfaced. "You're not one of those fanatics who likes to stalk their favorite driver, are you?" After her five messages that was exactly what he'd assumed, though she didn't seem crazy in person. But it could be she was crazy *and* smart enough to hide it. He'd met a few of those along the way. "If so, your charity ruse is imaginative. Though it's hard to beat the fan who snuck past security at the track, picked the lock on my RV and climbed into my bed naked."

The spirited sparkle in her eyes was captivating. "I hope you tossed him out."

Despite his mood, a rusty bark of a chuckle escaped his throat, knifing his still-smarting ribs. He was beginning to like the pushy little do-gooder, overly optimistic or not. "I tossed *her* out." He leaned close, his senses swimming in her scent. "I would have definitely thought twice about getting rid of you."

"I'm a fan, Mr. Thompson," she said evenly. "Not a fanatic." She hiked a brow, loaded with meaning. "And I'm not a groupie."

He dropped his eyes to her mouth. "Too bad. I'd love to have you wrap yourself in nothing but a bow and mail yourself to me in a crate."

She looked at him suspiciously. "You're making that one up."

"Nope." He tipped his head. "The story has been passed around the track for years. Could be just an urban legend though."

She leaned closer, narrowing her eyes, and his unfamiliar urge to grin was strong. Her voice dropped an octave. "And you are legendary for supporting organizations that work with disadvantaged kids."

The do-gooder was back. "And here I thought you leaned closer just to flirt with me."

Her bottomless brown eyes were unwavering. "I never use flirting as a tool."

"Too bad." But he liked her close, so he stayed put. "And I told you, no way will I—"

"These kids need support from role models like you."

Role models.

The words slammed with all the force of his career-ending crash, killing his urge to grin. Outside of setting a spectacular example of how to destroy the single good thing in your life, what did he have to offer the public now? His one claim to fame was gone. He was just a washed-up driver who'd taken a risky move and gone down in a blaze of shame.

Other than an amused glint in his sea-green eyes, Jessica had yet to see Cutter smile. She watched the glint of humor die as the masculine planes of his face hardened.

"Look, lady." Cutter ruffled an impatient hand over closely cropped, light-brown hair. "You have me confused with some-one who cares. My sponsors paid me millions. They told me which charities to support. The only person I support is me."

Jessica's smile faded at the egocentric words.

Cutter turned and walked past shelves of car parts and tools, heading in the direction of a utility sink in the corner. "And right now I have a car to fix," he added with a tone of finality.

Disenchantment settled deep in Jessica's chest. So he didn't care. So he'd only thought of his bank account. And maybe his moving words of support in the past were speeches written by a paid writer. This wasn't about her disappointment that an idol of hers wasn't the hero she'd thought. This was about the Brice Foundation Steve had started. And she'd promised him she'd get Cutter Thompson on board. Because she owed Steve.

How many ex-husbands helped their former wife get a business up and running?

Her online dating service had given her a sense of purpose at a time when her life was falling apart. And finding The One for others, in some small way, compensated for her personal failure.

And though she'd vowed long ago that melancholy wasn't allowed, the garage smelled of gasoline and motor oil, stirring poignant memories. Toward the last months of their marriage, Steve had withdrawn, spending more and more time tinkering with his boat. Maybe twenty was a little young for marriage, but Jessica had been confident they could work through anything. She'd been wrong. And Steve had begun to insist he couldn't give her what she needed.

In the end, Jessica had agreed.

But, between her father and her ex, she was used to men and their masculine domains. And Cutter Thompson was man in its rawest form. Long, powerful legs encased in worn jeans. Well-muscled arms. The wide expanse of back beneath his gray T-shirt was a veritable billboard sign for male power. He was a media favorite for his rugged charm, so the blunt honesty wasn't new. But the slight hunch as he walked certainly was. Why was his gait uneven?

Curiosity trounced her good sense. "If it was your arm you fractured in the crash, why are you limping?"

"I'm not. I'm splinting. The torn cartilage between my ribs still hurts like a mother."

At the sink, he turned on the tap, and—without a hiss or a grimace—stuck the mashed knuckles of his right hand under the water. His left arm reached for the soap, and he dropped it twice before a stab of sympathy hit her.

Selfish or not, no one deserved permanent nerve damage from a broken arm.

"Let me," she said as she moved beside him.

His eyes lit with faint humor. "Promise you'll be gentle?"

Ignoring him, Jessica picked up the soap and reached for his bleeding hand. It was large, calloused, and a disturbing sensation curled in her stomach, permeating lower. Neither of them spoke, increasing the crackle of tension. The sound of running water cut the silence as her fingers gingerly cleaned the wounds, finally finishing her task.

The glint in his eyes was bright. "Sure you didn't miss a spot?"

"Quite sure." She calmly dried his hand with a paper towel. "The weakness in your left hand is worse than your publicist let on." Once finished, she looked up at him. "I can see why you decided to retire."

The glint died as an unidentifiable flicker of emotion crossed his expression, but his gaze remained steady, his tone droll. "A man can't drive two hundred miles per hour packed bumper to bumper with an unreliable grip. Keeping a firm grasp on the steering wheel is important."

She looked for some sign of sadness, but there was none. "I'm sorry."

"Happens." He shrugged, a nonchalant look on his face. "I can't complain. I made enough money that I never need to work again."

They stared at each other for three breaths, Jessica fighting the urge to beat a hasty retreat. He'd made his millions. Racing had served its purpose. She knew he was planning to reject her request again, but Steve was counting on her. Despite Cutter's casual air, instinct told her to let the reminder of his injuries—the loss of his money-making career—fade before bringing out her best shot at persuasion…her pièce de résistance.

Her mind scrambled for something to say, and her gaze dropped to the marks on his shirt. "You should wash out the blood before it stains."

"Because it clashes with the motor oil?"

Boy, he had a comeback for everything. "No," she said dryly. "Because blood stains are so last season."

The light in his eyes returned with a vengeance. "Blood is always in style," he said. "And rising from a horizontal position about did me in. I'm just now able to breathe again without wanting to die. If I attempt to pull this shirt over my head, I'll pass out from the pain." He finally flashed the rarely dispensed yet utterly wicked suggestion of a smile. The one that sent his female fans into a frenzy. "So how about you pull it off for me?"

She lifted her eyes heavenward before meeting his gaze. "Mr. Thompson, I spent half my childhood following my father around his manufacturing plant full of men. I'm not susceptible to your brand of testosterone."

And one dream-crushing divorce later, she considered herself fully vaccinated, immune and impenetrable to anyone who couldn't totally commit. She needed someone who was willing to work hard to keep the romance alive.

Egocentric bad boys, no matter how gorgeously virile, had never made it to her list of acceptable dates. While all her friends were swooning over the rebel-de-jour, Jessica had remained untouched. Even as a teen, she'd avoided risky relationships that were destined for failure. She supposed she had her parents' divorce to thank for that.

But she refused to slosh about in dismal misery. Making a plan—being proactive—was the only way to avoid the mistakes of the past. Both her parents'…and her own.

"I don't know, my brand of testosterone is pretty potent,"

Cutter said. "And seduction could go a long way in convincing me to participate."

"Believe me." Her smile was tight. "I have no intention of seducing you."

Cutter almost managed a grin again. "After six painful career accidents, this is the first time I've ever felt like crying."

"Don't shed any tears on my account, Mr. Thompson." Rallying her courage, she crossed to her oversize purse by the stereo, pulled out a folder, and returned to Cutter. She would not be sidetracked. "I'm just here to recruit you." Jessica extracted a photo of an eight-year-old boy with a sweet smile. Without preamble, she continued. "Terrell's father died of cancer. He attends the Big Brothers' program the Brice Foundation supports."

The almost-smile died on his face, and the pause stretched as a wary look crept up his face. "And what does that have to do with me?"

"It's easier to say no to a nameless, faceless child. And I want you to know who you'll be letting down when you refuse to participate." She pulled out a second photo of a freckle-faced kid. One way or another, she was going to get him to agree to the charity event. "Mark is an eleven-year-old foster child attending a program that helps young people learn to find their place in a new home." She paused theatrically, hoping to draw attention to her next statement. "Older kids are harder to place."

"Orphans." Cutter frowned. "You're bringing out bloody *orphans?*"

His response left her feeling hopeful, so Jessica pulled out a third photo—a scowling teen. Dark hair reached his shoulders. Baggy pants hung low on his hips, red boxers visible above the waistband. The belligerent look in his eyes was sharp. If sweet smiles and freckled faces weren't enough, an adolescent with a defensive attitude would be harder to refuse. Not a smidgen of Cutter's history had been overlooked in her quest to get him to agree.

She was on a mission, and Jessica Wilson was famous for following through.

"Emmanuel dropped out of high school," Jessica said. "The Brice Foundation hooked him up with a mentor who took him to see you race." She made sure her face went soft, her eyes wide.

Cutter's frown grew bigger. "Are you trying to work up some tears?"

She blinked hard, hoping she could. "He was getting into trouble street racing." When the tears wouldn't come, she opted to drop her voice a notch. "Just like you."

His frown turned into an outright scowl. "Damn, you're good. And you did your research, too. But the mushy voice is a bit much. I'd respond better to seduction."

Jessica ignored him and went on. "Now he's attending night school to get his diploma." When his face didn't budge, she dropped her pièce de résistance. "He's decided he wants to be a race-car driver…just like you."

Cutter heaved a scornful sigh, and the exaggerated breath brought a wince to his face. He propped a hand on his hip, as if seeking a more comfortable position. "If it will get you to leave so my ribs can commune with an ice pack and some ibuprofen, you can put me down on the list of gullible five."

Mission accomplished. With a flash of relief, Jessica sent him a brilliant smile. "Thank you," she said. "I'll get the packet of information so we can go over—"

"Sunshine." He winced again, shifting his hand higher on his hip, clearly in pain. "We'll have to put off the rest of this discussion until tomorrow. But don't worry…" A hint of amusement returned to his eyes. "I'll leave the offer to remove my shirt on the table, just for you."

CHAPTER TWO

"HELL no," Cutter said.

"But we've already released the press announcement," Jessica said.

The rising sense of panic expanded as she watched Cutter cross his modern living room. And though the room was adorned with leather furniture, glass-and-chrome accents, it was the plate-glass window overlooking a palm-tree-lined Biscayne Bay that took masculine posh to outright lavish.

If he backed out now, it would be a publicity nightmare. "It was announced on the local six o'clock news last night," Jessica went on.

She'd been full of hope when she'd arrived back at his home this evening to discuss the fundraiser. Cutter was clearly feeling better than he had yesterday, no longer splinting as he walked. All she'd had to do was explain the plans for the fundraiser, get him signed on to the social-networking site hosting the event, and then her duty to Steve would be complete. Which meant her dealings with Cutter Thompson would be through.

Wouldn't that have been nice?

Cutter turned to face her, the waterway and its line of luxury-boat-filled docks beyond the window. "You should have waited to announce my participation until *after* you explained how this little publicity stunt was set up."

"We're short on time. We start next week. And I don't understand your problem with it."

His face was set. "I thought it would be the same auction they do every year. Men show up and strut their stuff. Women bid. The Brice Foundation makes money for homeless children, and I get to sit at the benefit dinner with the victorious socialite who doesn't have a clue—or cares—what poor kid her outrageous bid is helping." He crossed his arms, stretching the shirt against hard muscles. "I had no idea I'd have to *interact* with the women competing to win a date with me."

"But that's the beauty of the setup." Jessica rose from the leather couch, unable to restrain the smile of enthusiasm despite his misgivings. She'd worked long and hard to create something that wasn't the usual superficial masculine beauty show. "It's not as demeaning as auctioning off a celebrity like a slab of high-priced meat."

He sent her a level look. "I find nothing degrading about women trying to outbid each other all in the name of scoring a dinner with me."

Her smile faded a bit. "Maybe *you* don't. But I wanted something a little more meaningful. Watching intelligent men prance across a stage in an effort to increase the bidding is an undignified way to raise money."

"You forgot my favorite part: the screaming women." Cutter sent her the first hint of a grin for the evening. "You have to know how to work the crowd. Bring them to the edge of their seats. The key to raking in the dough is to wait until just the right moment to take off your shirt."

His chest was impressive covered in fabric; no doubt he'd made millions for various fundraisers over the years.

Jessica focused on the task at hand. "The board wanted something fresh and new, not the same old thing they've done the past ten years." She crossed thick carpet to stand beside him. "Except for your attendance at the benefit dinner, all the interaction is done online. You engage in a little flirty debate with the ladies competing for you. It's supposed to be an entertaining battle of the sexes over what comprises the perfect date." Her smile grew. That was her favorite part. Since her marital misstep, the study of relationships had become a passion. "For a nominal fee, the public can cast their vote for the 'most compatible.' So the people decide your companion to the benefit dinner, not the socialite with the most money to bid."

It had taken her weeks of brainstorming to finally land on a plan she was proud of, and she waited for some sign of his approval.

"So the masses decide which contestant—a lady I've never met nor will ever see again—I'm most 'compatible' with?" It was obvious from the air quotes with his fingers that he found her plan ridiculous. "Who the hell came up with this Trolling for a Celebrity idea?"

Jessica frowned. "It was my suggestion. And it's supposed to be all in fun, so I'd prefer you use the term *flirting* to *trolling.*"

"What the hell do you think flirting is?"

"It's engaging in meaningful dialogue that shows you find a person interesting."

He stared at her. "Maybe if you're twelve. For adults, it's all about sex."

She barely kept the criticism from her voice. "No it's not." She bit the inside of her lip, and inhaled, forcing herself to go on calmly. "There is plenty of data to support the notion that successful people are those who market themselves in a positive manner. Building strong relationships is the key to success, no matter what your goal, be it business, friendship or love. And *flirting,*" she continued with emphasis, "establishing that rapport between two people, proves that the most important aspect of a romantic relationship is effective communication."

Cutter's brows had climbed so high Jessica thought his

eyelids would stretch clear over his forehead. "Who has been feeding you all this bullshit?"

"It isn't bullshit."

"Sunshine, you are up to your black, sooty little eyelashes in it." The amused look in his eyes almost constituted a smile. "You are so Pollyanna-ish you could light the world with the sunbeams that glow from beneath your skirt." His voice turned matter-of-fact. "The attraction between a man and a woman is built on spark, pure and simple. And you can't *communicate* your way around the lack of it."

She'd had plenty of experience with a man who lacked the ability to engage in earnest dialogue. The spark starved without it, and though she'd done everything in her power to prevent the death of her marriage, a small part of her—the part that had *failed*—could never be made right.

Gloom weighed down her heart, and she folded her arms across her chest to ease the load.

Think positive, Jessica. We learn from our mistakes and move on. Don't let Mr. Cynical bring you down.

"Sparks are sustained by emotional and intellectual attraction," she said. "And both are much more important than the physical one."

His eyebrows pulled together in doubt. "What's that have to do with an online flirting fiesta between virtual strangers?"

Jessica inhaled slowly and quietly blew out a breath, regaining control. She'd gotten off track. Convincing him of her views wasn't important. All she needed was for him to follow through on his initial agreement. If he backed out now, the fundraiser would fail before it even started. Hundreds of fans would be disappointed. And then Steve would kill her, because signing Cutter on had been her idea. Steve had thought the retired driver was a risky proposition, but Jessica had always been impressed with Cutter's magnetic, if a little unconventional, charm on TV.

Apparently he was really good at faking it when money was involved.

Lovely to be finding that out *now.*

"Forget that I think the basic concept is flawed," Cutter said, interrupting her thoughts. "We still have several problems. First, I don't know a thing about social networking."

Feeling encouraged, she said, "I can teach you."

"Second, I don't have time for all this online interaction stuff."

"You can do it anywhere, even while standing in line at the grocery store. It takes five seconds to text a question to the contestants. Maybe ten to respond to their answer."

"I don't text."

Stunned, Jessica stared at him. "How does anyone inhabiting the twenty-first century not text?"

He headed for a bar made of dark mahogany and glossy black marble along the far wall. "Sunshine, I do all my interacting with women live and in the flesh." He lifted a bottle of chardonnay from the rack, removed the cork and set the wine on the counter, meeting her gaze. "If I want to ask her out, I speak to her in person. If I'm going to be late for a date, I call her on the phone." He pulled a beer from the refrigerator, twisted off the cap with a hissing pop, and shot her a skeptical look. "I do not spend 24/7 with a cellular attached to my hand so that I can inform my friends via Twitter that I'm leaving for the store to buy a six pack of beer." He flipped the cap with his fingers, and it hit the garbage can with a ping.

She bit back a smile. "That's good, because I doubt anyone is interested in those kinds of details." She wasn't sure whether she was making headway with him. After a pause, she pulled down a wineglass from the hanging rack over the marble counter and poured herself some chardonnay. She sat at the bar and sent him a measured look. "Cutter, I'm not asking you to provide the public with a banal running commentary on every detail of your life."

Beer in hand, Cutter rounded the counter and climbed onto the stool beside her, planting his elbows on the bar. "So my search for just the right toilet paper isn't relevant."

Jessica couldn't help herself. She smiled. "No."

He swiveled in his seat to face her. "What about those annoying little emoticons?" A faint frown appeared. "Smiley faces aren't my style."

"I've noticed. And the double smiley faces are definitely out. Though there is one for a devilish grin that would work really well for you."

"I could do a devilish grin." He demonstrated one on his face.

She subdued the laugh that threatened to surface. "LOLs and exclamation points aren't a requirement either."

"What about using all caps?"

"Caps are for amateurs."

He leaned forward a touch. "What if I have something important to do? Like turning a woman's head with my sparkling wit and personality? Wouldn't I want to capitalize the word *beautiful* when I compliment her on her looks?"

The intensity in his eyes made it clear he was talking about her. A low burn started, but she ignored it. "Forget the looks. You'd win more points complimenting her on her sense of humor. And a sophisticated texter doesn't need the caps button." She tipped her head. "He leaves a woman weak in the knees with just the right words."

The hint of a smile appeared on his face. "A real man leaves a woman weak in the knees with just the right *look*."

Absolutely. Which was why it was a good thing she was sitting down. Because he was sending out some potent, powerful vibes. She was almost tempted to be charmed. She took a fortifying sip of crisp, dry wine, eyeing him warily over her glass.

"I'll agree to go through with this if you lend me a hand in the beginning," he said.

"What do you mean?"

"We get together and you share my texting responsibilities."

She coughed on her wine, the words sputtering out in a squeak. "You want me to flirt with other women for you?"

"Just help me out until I get going."

"Absolutely not." She turned to face him in her seat. "You have to do your own flirting."

"Why? I'm not marrying any of them. I'm not even agreeing to date them. All I'm promising is one lousy dinner in the name of a good cause."

"Because it's…because it's…" as her mouth grappled to catch up with her brain, Jessica's mind scrambled for the right word. *Sacrilegious* sounded melodramatic. *Rude* he clearly wouldn't care about. At a loss, she set her glass down with a clink. "Because it's unromantic, not to mention unethical. You cannot outsource your flirting."

He tipped his head in disbelief. "Jessica, we're not talking about destroying our local economy."

"You're the Wildcard," she said levelly. "Women elude security and pick locks to climb into your bed. I'm sure you're more than qualified to handle a little internet flirting with several women at the same time."

Unimpressed by her attempts at flattery, Cutter said, "I've never had to flirt with a woman online in my life." He gave a small shrug. "It's either have some help to get me started or I won't do it."

Jessica propped her elbows on the counter and covered her eyes with her palms. Cutter Thompson was frustrating and cynical. But she'd promised Steve.

She *owed* Steve.

He might not have been the love of her life as she'd once hoped, but he'd helped her find her passion. The great gift of career satisfaction. She loved her work. It defined her. And, despite their divorce, Steve had been a big part of that discovery. And his advice during her fledgling business years had been invaluable.

She wouldn't be the success she was today with his support.

"Fine." She dropped her hands to the counter and turned her head to meet Cutter's gaze. "But here are the rules. Once you get the hang of it, I'm done. And no one can know I'm helping you. They have to believe that everything comes from you or the whole thing crumbles in a heap of shame. Maintaining the integrity of the event is my top priority."

The expression on his face promised nothing. "I want to have my 'Cuda done by the end of the month. That's my priority."

With a sense of victory and relief, Cutter pulled open the glass door and entered the small but elegant reception room of Perfect Pair Inc., pulling off his baseball cap and sunglasses. It had taken twenty minutes to shake the reporter trailing him since he'd left his house. A full week of media hype about the fundraiser had the worst of Miami's parasitic paparazzi on a renewed quest to hunt Cutter Thompson down. He'd left North Carolina and moved back to Miami to avoid this kind of scrutiny.

Of course, his sudden aversion to interviews only made the press hungrier for tidbits of his activities, but he was determined to keep the facts about his memory loss private. Bad enough he'd regained consciousness in the ambulance in the worst agony of his life; no need for the world to rehash every gritty detail. He refused to tap dance his way around another grilling over what was next for Cutter Thompson. And he sure as hell wouldn't field one more question about his reason for illegally bumping Chester Coon.

Hell, when—*if*—he ever figured out the answers, he'd take out a flippin' full-page ad in the *Times* and let everyone know.

Until then, every member of the press was persona non grata in Cutter's book.

Even though he'd managed to lose the newshound tailing him, the encounter had left him with a foul mood he couldn't shake. He'd been having a good day in the garage. The pain was tolerable, and the new camshaft went in like a dream.

But then he'd had to take a trip across town with a blood-sucker on his trail. And he owed his ramped-up publicity appeal to do-gooder Jessica Wilson—the lady who'd toppled his plans for seclusion with a barrage of sympathy-invoking photos.

Weak. He was well and truly weak.

His only option now was to get in and out as quickly as possible. Complete the first round of chatting with his contestants and get back to the peace of his garage. He needed to crawl back under the 'Cuda. Solving problems there was simple. Things connected and made sense. Broken parts could be easily repaired or replaced.

Unlike his life.

With a frown, he scanned his surroundings. The small reception room off to the left was decorated like a cozy living area, complete with a collection of leather couches arranged in a circle, the walls lined with pictures of smiling couples mocking his black mood. Some looked candid, some were professionally done, and others were wedding photos of happy brides and grooms.

He grimaced at the marital bliss propaganda being displayed on the wall.

Jessica appeared in the hallway, her lovely long legs bare beneath a gray skirt that ended in a dainty ruffle. A gauzy pink blouse clung to gentle curves. She was an intriguing mix of sophisticated class, professionalism and soft femininity. But she believed in true love and things like 'effective communication.'

"Thanks for coming here," Jessica said. "I have to meet someone for dinner at eight, so I'm pressed for time."

Yet, here she was, championing her cause. Helping him do his part. He was still trying to figure that one out. "Why is this fundraiser so important to you? Was your childhood so awful you feel obligated to fix it for others?"

Her expression was one of restraint, with a hint of annoyance. "No. My childhood consisted of two parents who loved and nurtured me. I'm a longtime supporter of the work the Brice Foundation does, and my ex-husband is chairman of the board. I promised him I'd recruit you for the benefit dinner."

His eyebrows lifted. That she was divorced came as a surprise. That she was still on speaking terms with her ex was a shock. "Seems strange to hear the words *help* and *ex-husband* in the same sentence."

"This is the twenty-first century, Mr. Thompson," she said as she started down a hallway.

He followed beside her. "So you keep telling me."

"Our marriage failed," she said. "But our friendship didn't. And I owe him."

Owe?

Growing up in his world meant divorced parents who talked about each other with animosity and refused to speak to one another. Which had left a five-year-old Cutter carrying messages between them…because they couldn't get along for the two minutes it took to discuss his visitations. By all reports, his parents had been head-over-heels in love until his mom had got knocked up with Cutter and they'd had to tie the knot. According to his mother, for the entire four years of her marriage, bliss had been a distant memory.

Who needed that kind of misery?

He hiked an eyebrow dryly. "What's with the sense of obligation toward your ex? Did you treat him like crap during your marriage?"

She shot him a cutting look. "I owe him because he helped me start my online dating service after our divorce."

Cutter came to a halt and watched her continue down the hall. "So your *ex-husband* helped you start a business finding love for other people?" It was hard enough comprehending how a woman so thoroughly indoctrinated in the happily-ever-after club could have joined the till-divorce-do-us-part league. But the irony of her profession was comical. "Shouldn't a failed marriage disqualify you from the job?"

She stopped and turned to face him, a frown on her face, her voice firm. "A divorce doesn't disqualify you from any-thing."

He moved closer to her, puzzlement pulling his eyebrows higher. "Ruining your own life wasn't good enough, you feel the need to make others miserable, too?"

She actually bit her lower lip. Cutter was sure it was to cut off a sharp retort, and he was amazed she managed to sound so civil. "When two people are compatible, marriage isn't miserable." She turned into an office clearly decorated for a woman, done in soft mauves and creams. "And despite my divorce, I still believe in romantic relationships."

Cutter followed her inside, letting out an amused scoff. "I'm not divorced, and even I know they're a crock."

She rounded her leather-topped desk adorned with a vase of cheerful yellow lilies and took a seat at her computer, eyeing him warily. Her tone held more than a trace of concern. "Mr. Thompson," she said. "Let's try not to bring up your jaded views while discussing your ideal date online." It seemed she'd concluded he was a hopeless cause.

Hell yeah. Count him up as one who had seen the light a long time ago.

"My views aren't jaded," he said. "They're realistic." And the sooner the two of them got started, the sooner he could be done with this fake flirt fest. "Okay. How do we start?"

"With a question for the contestants. Something to get the conversation going."

"About dating, right?" He crossed to stop behind her chair and frowned at the waiting computer, feeling foolish for getting involved. Cutter hoped the sullen teenage Emmanuel wound up a friggin' Supreme Court Justice. Nothing less would justify caving in to this absurd unreality show. "How about asking their favorite date destination?"

Jessica folded her arms across her chest. "You need something more open-ended. All someone has to say is the beach or a restaurant and the conversation dies."

"At least I'd be done for the evening. And you'd have time for a pre-dinner drink."

Jessica looked up at him with a determined pair of brown Bambi eyes that said she'd miss the dinner before she'd do less than her best.

Her ex must be one hell of a guy.

With a resigned sigh, Cutter sat on her desk. "Okay, what if I ask them about their worst dating experiences?"

"Same problem. Those require individual responses and you're looking for an interactive debate." A small grimace filled her face. "Not to mention it's a negative way to start."

He stared at her. "You mean, not only do I have to have this debate, I have to be *upbeat* about it?" He didn't know how, not since he was a kid when his dad had left for good and his mother had blamed Cutter.

Not a lot to be upbeat about there.

"Number-one rule of first dates," Jessica said with a soothing smile, but he had the feeling she was faking it. Somehow, that made it all the more intriguing. "No one likes a whiner."

He wasn't sure why, but he found her amusing. "I thought it was don't eat anything with garlic and wear comfortable clothes."

For a brief moment, she almost looked horrified. "Your

clothes should make a *statement*. They are a reflection of you."

"True," he said matter-of-factly. "You can tell a lot about a woman by the underwear she wears."

With a sigh, she raised an eyebrow dryly, her tone carefully patient. "By the time you get to her underwear, you should know quite a bit about her already."

He shook his head. "You go for pastel colors. Lace. No thongs. Nothing see-through. Practical, yet pretty. And not too racy."

A hint of color appeared on her cheeks, but her tone was defiant. "Have you thought of a question for your contestants yet?"

Cutter rubbed his jaw, enjoying her flushed face. "I take it favorite lingerie choices are out?"

Her answer was a slight narrowing of her eyes and an expression of forbearance that was downright adorable, and Cutter realized his foul mood was long gone. Damn, when had he started enjoying himself? And how could someone so ridiculously optimistic about relationships pull him out of his funk with her militant views on dating? He pulled his gaze from her caramel eyes and tried to concentrate on the task at hand, staring at the blank screen.

Cupid's longest-running gag was torturing mankind with the opposites-attract rule.

The thought inspired him. "How about—*What creates a spark between two people?*"

He knew he'd succeeded when the light in her eyes flickered brighter. And the admiration on her face was worth waiting for. "Perfect," she said, her bone-melting smile of approval skewering his insides.

Jessica turned to the computer and typed. A few moments later, she looked up, her dark, exotic gaze on him. "Love Potion Number Nine's reply: *chemistry.* What do you want to say in response?"

Caught in her spell, and captivated by her sooty lashes, he had no idea. "What happened to love potions number one through eight?"

"You can't mock her user name."

"Is that first-date rule number two?"

"No," she said dryly. "It's just assumed under the one about negative whiners."

His lips twitched, itching to grin, but he persevered. "You sure have a lot of dating rules." He forced his gaze from chocolate eyes to the monitor. "Ask her to define chemistry."

As Jessica entered his question, another contestant's answer popped onto the screen, and Cutter leaned forward to read it. "Calamity Jane says spark is defined by sexual attraction."

That was a no-brainer. He looked down at Jessica again, her sweetly spiced scent tantalizing him while her smoky eyes eroded his need for distance. Not only was she beautiful, she was feisty without getting too defensive. Sensual, and confident in her sexuality without being desperate.

Used to be, getting in the zone could only be achieved by high speeds. That feeling of intense focus, a heightened awareness and being both mentally and physically in tune with his body. Now, one look from the beautiful Jessica Wilson and he was in the zone.

And how could he be so attracted to an optimistic, self-styled guru on relationships?

Because he was definitely in tune with his body. Maybe *too* in tune.

Blood pumped through his veins, disturbing in its intensity. "I'd say Calamity is on to something," he murmured. "No discussion necessary. I'll just agree with her."

Her eyelids flared in panic. "You can't."

"Why not?"

"First of all, if you agree then there's no give and take. No debate is boring. Second of all, spark isn't defined simply by sexual attraction. The physical is just a small part. Chemistry is a connection based on shared interests."

Amused, Cutter hiked a brow. "Unless we're talking about a shared interest in each other's bodies, that's not what Calamity Jane said."

The pink mouth went flat. "Calamity is wrong."

As Cutter looked down at her, the urge to smile was now almost overwhelming. "Now who's being negative?" From this angle, he noticed her blouse gapped at the neckline, and the curves of her breasts were cupped in a lacy bra.

He was right, except it was light purple, not pink. Lavender and lace.

Ms. Sunshine was wearing a cliché.

Delight spread through him. He'd changed his mind. Suffering the disruption of his day, enduring the bloodsucking journalist's chase, both were worth her company.

"Back to Calamity," Jessica said. "Why don't we start with this for a response—*Sexual attraction is important*." She looked up at him. "What should we add?" Her beautiful gaze looked thoughtful.

A pair of eyes that could make a guy willingly trade his man cave for an evening in a mauve-colored, foo-foo office peddling romance online.

He sent her a faint grin. "How about…*I also like a woman who challenges me*."

Her smile was like healing salve on a burn. "That's better."

Yes…it was. Cutter's grin grew more defined. "Oh, and tell her I also have a thing for lavender-and-lace underwear."

CHAPTER THREE

Disaster.

The fundraiser for the Brice Foundation was going to be a monstrous disaster, and it was all her fault.

Stopping for a red light, Jessica glanced at her watch. She only had ten minutes to get to her dinner date. The past hour had been long, frustrating and infinitely illuminating, and she was amazed she hadn't pulled out every hair on her head.

And, as if Cutter's attitude alone wasn't enough, he'd looked down her shirt. Like an impulsive twelve-year-old riding a testosterone high he couldn't control. Granted, from his angle on her desk it would have been hard to prevent. But still, mentioning what he saw was less than gallant.

The word *gallant* had no business existing in the same universe as Cutter Thompson.

In the beginning, she'd been less than thrilled to continue her involvement with Cutter during his Battle of the Sexes participation. Now it seemed it was a blessing in disguise.

Because Cutter Thompson in a stock car was sure to get a woman's heart racing.

Cutter Thompson in a TV interview was truly electric.

But Cutter Thompson flirting online was a catastrophe.

Every time a contestant responded, his automatic response would have alienated half the participants and a good portion of Miami as well. He didn't appreciate that a cocky response—where the words weren't tempered with a handsome face, green eyes that sparkled with humor and a teasing tone—could have disastrous effects.

In retrospect, maybe she should have realized the pitfalls of asking ASCAR's former number-one driver to participate. When she'd offered to do this stunt for Steve it was to help make it a success, not steep it in shame. And Steve had been right. She should have gone for the local cello player who had won the North American Academy of Musicians' competition last year. So he'd been a little soft and a bit too sweet. No one would have noticed online.

Now she was stuck with the Wildcard, Master of the Cutting Comment.

And how many years had he been honing that ability to whip out a blithe insult with stunning clarity, just skirting the edges of amusing charm?

Jessica turned her car into a parking space at the restaurant, cut off the engine, and sat, tapping her fingernails on the steering wheel. The Battle of the Sexes was a month long, and she didn't want to hover over the man and deflect his every inappropriate remark for the entire competition. Which meant Mr. Cutter Thompson needed a lesson or two in how to behave online. He was way beyond help in his personal, face-to-face interactions, but if she could just get him through the publicity stunt, the rest didn't matter. After she was done with him, he could insult the Pope if he wanted.

Tomorrow when they met for round two, she was going to review online etiquette and the rules of acceptable behavior. Surely the man was trainable.

If he wasn't, she'd have to spend the next month glued to his side, fending off furtive peeks at her underwear. And the thought of that was far from appealing.

"Nice job, Jess," Steve said, his voice muffled. One hand on the steering wheel, Jessica adjusted the earpiece of her cell phone, and Steve's words were clearer when he went on. "Last night's Cutter Thompson debut was pure gold. Is he a prima donna to work with?"

Prima donna? Her fingers clenched the wheel. More like a cross between a prima donna and a raging hormonal teen. And he wielded a masculinity that would make him millions if it were bottled and sold. Actually, it had—Jessica had enjoyed the perverse pleasure of eating her breakfast this morning while staring at Cutter in his racing uniform, arms crossed, his trademark suggestion of a grin plastered on her cereal box. And for the love of God, why couldn't he just *smile?* It was as if he knew his hint at a grin was more powerful than the beaming smile of a Hollywood leading man.

"He was a little difficult. But I was ready for him," she said, feeling guilty for lying. How could anyone ever be ready for the likes of Cutter?

"No one is ever more prepared than you," Steve said. "And speaking of, how did your dinner go last night?"

Jessica made a face as she turned the car into Cutter's neighborhood. "He was certainly nothing like his online dating profile."

"There are a lot of weirdos out there." Steve's voice grew concerned. "You're steering clear of the stalkers, right?"

Jessica smiled. "No stalkers yet."

"Good. But if you need me to hire a hitman to break some knees, just let me know."

"A true sign of a good friend."

Steve paused before he went on. "I just want to see you happy, Jess."

Jessica gripped the wheel harder, and signed off, disconnecting her cellular.

She *was* happy. And one day she'd find someone to share that happiness with. Because he was out there. She could feel it. The perfect man for her. It was like she told her customers at Perfect Pairs…

"You have to be open to love to find it. And you have to be willing to work hard, before *and* after you do."

Steve was a great guy; he just hadn't been the right guy. And all the hard work in the world couldn't overcome a mismatched choice. The blues threatened to color her mood, and she swatted them back.

For now, it didn't matter anyway. Her life, full with running her business, had taken on a bursting-at-the-seams quality since she'd dragged Cutter into the fundraiser. For a little while, dating would have to take a backseat.

And she'd learned a lot from her mistakes; next time she was positive she'd get it right. Then again, as a child she'd been positive her parents were happy, too, and look how wrong she'd been about that. She ignored the dull ache in her heart, the pain an unwelcome guest she'd learned to live with.

She pulled into the driveway of Cutter's modern three-story home, hidden from the street by a jungle of thick, woody banyan trees and patches of bamboo. A yard as wild as the owner itself. The garage constituted the entire first level, and on the door was a note: *Come Around Back.*

After rounding the house, Jessica passed a sparkling blue pool and headed down the grassy, palm-tree-studded backyard that ended at Biscayne Bay. A powerful-looking speedboat was parked at the dock, and Cutter was on deck, coiling a rope with easy, confident movements.

She crossed to the end of the dock. His brown hair had streaks of gold that glinted in the sunshine. In khaki shorts and a knit shirt, he made casual cool.

"You look like you're feeling better," she said.

"I'm waiting on a part for the 'Cuda, so I spent the day tuning up the boat. I figured we could take a test run and woo my contestants at the same time." His sea-green eyes roamed down her peach princess-styled dress to her two-inch sandals. "But you look overdressed."

"Much like blood, silk is always in style."

A twinkle appeared in his eyes as he held out his hand. "Then climb aboard."

As he helped her onto the boat, the skin-on-skin touch was more disturbing than she'd prepared for. Perhaps she simply needed to acclimate to the sight of bare, muscular legs. "Nice boat," she said, carefully removing her fingers from his.

"With a four-hundred-and-thirty-horsepower engine, she's one of the fastest crafts in the neighborhood."

Jessica settled onto the leather bench that stretched across the stern, resting her arms along the back. This was one element of Cutter Thompson she was equipped to deal with. "That's because your neighborhood is full of wimpy vessels."

From the bucket seat in front of her, hand on the key in the ignition, Cutter turned to shoot her a look. "Are you saying my equipment is small?"

She smiled and crossed her legs. He was defending his boat the way he'd defended his car. He was such a *guy*. "I'm telling you your equipment is *slow*."

"Sunshine—" he hooked his arm on the back of his chair "—nothing about me is slow." He lifted his brows. "Including my boat."

"I've driven faster."

His face exuded skepticism. "What boat would that be?"

"A Mach III Sidewinder."

He stared at her, the chiseled, masculine planes of his face lit by the sun. Finally, he let out a reverent whistle. "Damn. Those top out at a hundred and seventy miles per hour."

"I know. My father builds them." And after her parents' divorce, she'd spent hours with her father at his plant, her life divided evenly between two worlds. One ultra-feminine, the other pure male.

"I suppose my plan to impress you with speed won't work," he said.

"I'm afraid not."

Suddenly, his mouth held the potential for a smile, but even skirting the edge of possibility he managed to leave her breathless. "Guess I'll have to come up with something better." His look brimmed with cocky promise.

Stunned, Jessica realized her heart was thumping in her ribs. Cutter's mesmerizing gaze released hers when he turned to start the boat and eased them out into the channel, where she finally inhaled a breath of salty, fresh air. The sun was warm, and, without his focus on her, she was able to relax. But since when was she even fleetingly susceptible to Neanderthals?

She pushed the thought aside as they cruised past exclusive homes with tropical landscapes, private boats aligned in a parade of wealth, under bridges, and finally through downtown. Columns of condominiums and skyscrapers dwarfed them, stainless-steel-and-glass giants gleaming in the sun.

After finding a safe spot with a view of the city, Cutter cut the engine and tossed out the anchor, taking a seat beside her. He propped his legs up on the edge of the boat, the extension of hard muscle seemingly going on forever.

Yes, it had to be the naked limbs that were getting under her skin.

But she was here to complete her task, not gawk at powerful legs dusted with dark hair. Jessica sat up a little higher and forced her gaze to his face. But the square-cut jaw, green eyes and brown hair with touches of gold were striking in a wholly masculine way. Not exactly the visual relief she needed. Jessica cleared her throat, reining in her reaction. "We need to discuss social-networking etiquette."

The grimace on his beautiful face was absolute. "I'd rather you pull out my fingernails."

She went on, ignoring his lack of enthusiasm. "You need

to remember that your words minus the facial expression and the inflection in your tone are open to interpretation." Holding his gaze, she used her tone to emphasize her point. "You think you're being charming and witty, and the recipient thinks you're being insulting."

"Most of the time I am."

She stared at him and realized he was telling the truth. Why would someone go out of their way to be disagreeable? "Well...that won't work for us."

"I don't know how to be a suck-up."

She held back the lift of her brow at the understatement. "Just be aware of the subtle nuances in your words and how they can be interpreted."

"Nuances?" he said, as if the word had a foreign taste.

"And remember," she said, continuing her usual spiel on online interactions, pleased he was at least pretending to listen—even if her every statement was followed by a sarcastic comment. "People are interested in those who are interested in *them*. A little self-deprecating humor is good, as it's humanizing, but not too much or you'll appear to lack self-confidence." Of course, this piece of advice hardly applied to Cutter Thompson. But she was offering up her full speech, because this man needed all the help he could get.

His brows drew together in doubt. "Maybe I should have agreed to establish peace in the Middle East instead," Cutter said. "Might have been easier." He settled deeper into the bench. "But I did manage to come up with today's question for my contestants—*If I invited you to a costume party, which superhero pair would you want to go as and why?*"

Jessica smiled. Impressive progress. Mr. Thompson appeared to be trainable. Maybe after today's session he could carry this off on his own. "I like it. It has humor, a flirtatious quality and requires more than a one-word answer." Feeling encouraged, Jessica pulled her phone from her purse. "I'll send it out now."

"No need." Cutter retrieved his cellular from his shorts and went to work, his thumbs clumsily pushing the buttons.

She blinked. "I thought you didn't text."

"I spent the day practicing." He met her gaze. "Gave my old pit crew buddies a blow-by-blow account on the tune-up of my boat."

Jessica's mouth twitched in a smile, trying to picture a bunch of men, hands smeared with grease, phones beeping in their back pockets. "And what did they think?"

"That I'd gone off my rocker." By his tone and the look on his face, she could tell he agreed with their assessment.

"It's a quick way to send out a message," she said. "It's also perfect for when I don't have time for one of my mother's lengthy conversations." She sent him a dry smile. "You might find it useful with your family."

The lines of skepticism vanished from his face and Cutter looked to the city. Staring across the glistening urban landscape, he went on in an even tone. "I don't have a family."

Jessica's heart did a double take. "Where are your parents?"

"My dad took off when I was a kid and my mom died five years ago."

His tone was matter-of-fact, and held no trace of emotion.

"I'm sorry," she said quietly.

"Don't be." His tone was easy, and the small twist of his lips didn't betray a hint of lingering sadness. "The Thompson mantra is when life sucks, deal with it."

Which had served him well, no doubt. She studied his profile thoughtfully, wondering how old he'd been when he'd adopted the attitude.

When he turned to look at her, he must have caught the question in her eyes. "Sunshine," he said with a light scoff as he sent her an amused look. "I don't have any feelings to share and I don't do Dr. Phil. If you're looking for a man with a feminine side…" He leaned in, bringing his hot, sea-green eyes and bold gaze so close that her breath momentarily froze in her throat. "You're looking at the wrong guy."

She was looking all right. Despite the rising rate of her heart, and now her breathing, she resisted the need to break eye contact. As she stared at Cutter, her brain frantically broadcast a warning about their incompatibility. Unfortunately, her body wasn't picking up the signal.

Because when it came to men, she preferred charm. And she insisted on polite. Or—for the love of God—at least *agreeable*.

None of which described Cutter Thompson. But when his gaze dropped to her mouth, as if contemplating kissing her, the rate of her breathing dropped to zero.

He'd take what he wanted with no apologies. No slow, sensual lead-ups. No rose petals on silk sheets. And she was unfamiliar with the rebel breed. Steve had been her first lover, and what had started out gentle had grown into comfortable fun. The sex, at least, had been good. And she'd entered into two intimate relationships since her divorce. Satisfying, both, but not the kind that lit the world and left scorch marks on the ground.

And not one of the men wore the raw edges that defined Cutter.

Water lapped the boat as they stared at each other until his phone beeped. Cutter glanced at the small screen, breaking the spell, and Jessica quietly sucked in air, relieved with the fresh supply of oxygen again.

"Calamity Jane says she wants to go as Batman and Batgirl because I'd look good in tights." Cutter shot her a lazy, brash look. "Guess I'll have to explain that real men would choose the sexy, villainous Catwoman over the friends-with-predictably-boring-benefits Batgirl every time."

Jessica didn't bother stifling her groan. So much for progress.

Lovely, his self-centered ways went beyond money, they

applied to women, too. She shouldn't have been surprised, but his flippant attitude towards relationships went against every value she held dear.

His smoldering glance...the bold stare... No doubt he delivered that look to every woman he found attractive. Cutter Thompson was the worst of the worst, a man with the emotional depth of a flatworm and a derisive attitude toward romance. He didn't believe in The One, more like The Many. He was everything she *didn't* want, wrapped up in a package that was oh-so-much worse. And if the rate of her thumping heart was any indication, her body's reaction was about more than naked, muscular legs.

Which meant she wasn't quite as immune to the egocentric bad boy as she'd thought.

An hour later Cutter watched Jessica maneuver the boat towards home. She'd taken over the helm so he could continue his instant messaging, and he was impressed with her ability to handle the craft and intercept his inappropriate comments at the same time. The more appalled her look, the more he'd enjoyed himself. And although peace and quiet had been his only goal since the day he'd announced his retirement, Jessica Wilson had fast and furiously become a major exception to the rule.

He should find Emmanuel, the teenager with the bad-ass photographic attitude, and thank him personally.

She was too easy to tease. "I think I have the hang of this online flirting thing," he said. "I don't need your help anymore."

Jessica stared at him, wide-eyed, and with more than a trace of fear.

A small grin slipped past before he could stop it. He hadn't smiled this much since he'd first won Nationals. "What?" he said with as much innocence as a thirty-year-old washed-up race-car driver could muster. "You don't trust me?"

She skillfully maneuvered alongside his dock and cut the engine. "I absolutely trust you to alienate Susie Q Public."

After hopping out, he secured the boat, and then hiked a brow at Jessica. "Women know better than to look for Prince Charming in me." He liked how she managed to maintain her femininity while commenting on the oil level in his car or parking a boat with finesse. "That's why they find me so attractive. It's a primal propagation-of-the-species thing." Cutter leaned in, took Jessica's hand and helped her onto the dock beside him. Her ethereally lovely face and mysterious scent entwined around his senses. "Deep down they know that nice guys finish last." He'd learned that the same way he'd learned everything else. The hard way. And early on.

"Nice guys do *not* finish last." Her doe-eyed brown gaze held his. "And if you don't mind, I'll hang around and moderate the Cutter Thompson mouth until this nightmare of a flirting debacle is over."

He almost grinned again. Much more of this and he'd lose his reputation. "Don't mind at all."

Jessica looked as if it wouldn't matter if he did. Cutter was still contemplating smiling in amusement when she continued. "Don't forget the cocktail party at the Miami Aquarium on Saturday. Steve invited reporters to the mixer so the media will have access to our Battle of the Sexes celebrities. It should help increase our press coverage."

Media, reporters and press coverage—hell no.

The idea left a nasty taste in his mouth, and his jaw muscles hardened, all thoughts of smiling gone. "I have no intention of attending a party with journalists." Fun time was over. Time to get back to the 'Cuda. He'd find something else to work on until the new carburetor arrived.

Cutter headed toward the house, and Jessica fell into step beside him. "It's not a press conference," she said. "Just a couple of reporters from a few of the major papers will be in attendance."

Sure, the same journalists who had been staking out his house since he'd returned to Miami. Cutter was better at losing them now, but no way was he gonna *choose* to be in the same room with the press.

"I have no interest in interviews," he said. "The last thing I want is a hotshot reporter grilling me about my dating methods and writing an exposé on my social life." He knew damn well that wasn't what they'd ask. They'd use the Battle of the Sexes publicity stunt as an excuse to get close and then badger him hard about the accident.

A tumultuous riot of tension and nerves broke out in his body.

Jessica slowly came to a stop and stared at him, looking baffled. "You never seemed to worry about the media's opinion before."

He halted on the walkway. "That was when dealing with them went with the job description."

When the questions had been easy to answer and the banter had been full of fun and camaraderie. Lately all the banter had been replaced by hard-core grilling about his wreck, his *reason* for the rash move that ended his career. And he was no closer to knowing the answer now than he had been two months ago.

He might never remember the moment he'd screwed up his life.

His gut roiled, and his gaze locked with hers. "No cocktail party. No schmoozing with the press." He frowned and continued up the walk, heading for his garage. "And no changing my mind."

The next morning Jessica ate her breakfast, flipping through the morning paper as Cutter's picture stared at her from her cereal box. She had yet to figure out how the man could have such an effect on her.

Handsome, yes.

Virile, most definitely.

But what did it matter when he was the antithesis of everything she was looking for?

In the five years since her divorce, she'd been on a lot of first dates, had been subjected to every possible combination of good looks and charm imaginable. She'd even gone to dinner with a model who regularly appeared in *GQ* magazine. He was drop-dead gorgeous and sweet, but the chemistry during the evening was flat. They had nothing in common. When he asked her out for a second date, she'd politely turned him down.

She'd thought she was impervious to the sexual appeal of an unsuitable guy, yet the powerful pull of Cutter Thompson was proving greater than the sum total of her experiences.

With a sigh, Jessica flipped to the society section of the morning newspaper and spied the front-page photo, a bolt of shock zipping along her nerves. Her spoonful of granola hovered in the air as she scanned the picture of her and Cutter. They were sitting side by side in the boat, Cutter texting on his cellular, and Jessica leaning in to look at his message. But the headline was the worst part—Is Local Racing Hero Turned Recluse Now Dating?

Shock turned to horror as she read the accompanying blurb, mostly about Cutter's refusal to appear in public since retiring. And whoever had snapped the photo had done their homework, accurately identifying her. They'd even mentioned her motto at Perfect Pair: Fostering honest dialogue in finding The One. Multiple questions regarding their relationship were raised in the paragraph, suggesting she and Cutter were hot and heavy into an affair.

Panic spread and, without a second thought, she grabbed her purse and headed out the door.

Twenty minutes later Jessica stepped out of her car and onto Cutter's driveway. The garage door was open, and rock music blared. After she passed through the entrance, she switched off the music and headed toward the old muscle car and the pair of tennis shoes protruding from beneath.

Balancing on the balls of her feet, she squatted and leaned forward, staring up past long legs, a flat abdomen, to arms that jutted into the underbelly of the vehicle. "Cutter, we have a problem."

He kept right on tinkering. "I'm gonna start thinking you don't like my taste in music."

Jessica summoned her patience and tried again. "Cutter, our picture was in the paper."

His hand continued torquing the wrench. "So?"

With an exasperated sigh, Jessica reached down and pulled on Cutter's feet, rolling him from beneath the vehicle in a smooth motion.

Flat on his back, Cutter stared up at her, the wrench still clutched in his hand. After a brief pause, Cutter said, "I gather it wasn't a flattering photograph."

"It shows the two of us texting together."

A doubtful frown appeared. "And again I say…*so?*"

Jessica covered her eyes with her palm and counted, but only made it to seven. "Cutter," she said as calmly as she could, dropping her hand. "This doesn't look good for our contest. What if someone guesses I'm helping you? And even if they don't come to that conclusion, if you *were* seriously dating me as the paper suggested, then you shouldn't be flirting with other women online."

Her words triggered a skeptical lift of his brow. "Not all of us hold ourselves to the same restrictions."

Lips pressed flat, she ignored the temptation to comment on his unromantic morals and went on. "Okay, forget that you're a lost cause. But you agreed to the rules, remember? Like the one that stated you would keep your relationships private until the contest was over. Image is important. And how will it look to my customers if I'm dating a man who is flirting with other women? Or worse, if I'm *helping* him flirt with other women." Panic filled her chest, and her palms grew damp. "My business is built on the belief that you can find a soul mate through honest communication."

"Sunshine, too much honest communication will kill your matchmaking attempts." A still-skeptical eyebrow eased higher, though his tone grew thoughtful. "And I never could understand how the word *soul* got linked to the enjoyable act of *mating*."

"Cutter." Her voice was sharp. "This isn't about your hopelessly warped views."

He blew out a sigh and lowered his wrench. "Okay. Help me sit up so I can have this torturous conversation without the physical pain as well."

Jessica grasped his hand and helped him into a sitting position. His fingers were warm, the calluses rough against her palm, and the blaze sweeping through her body was heating her from the inside out. She braced her feet and provided support as he rose.

All six foot three of his muscular frame towered over her, and he stood way too close for reasonable heart rates. The telltale suggestion of a grin returned. "I must be healing. That didn't hurt at all."

Yes it had. And it still did, because his musky scent was tempting. Jessica frowned, annoyed by her pounding heart. "Too bad." Because if he dropped dead right now all her problems would be solved.

His lips twitched. Well, he might think the situation was funny, but this year's Battle of the Sexes was her creation. And her business meant the world to her. Bringing people companionship, finding The One for others is what sustained her hope that, someday, she would find the guy for her. "The public cannot think we are dating. Not when it could put the contest and my business at stake. Perception *is* reality."

"The public doesn't give a rat's ass what you do in private. And for all anyone knows, we're just good friends who went out for a boat ride while following some movie star on Twitter."

Frustrated by his teasing tone, Jessica closed her eyes and inhaled and exhaled—twice. "I know you think my job is ridiculous." She lifted her lids. "I *know* you think true love is a crock. But this is what I do." The rising panic made her voice tight. "This is who I am. And if I ruin my reputation, it could have serious repercussions for my business."

A frown appeared as he blew out a breath. "I don't want you to ruin your business either," he said. He ruffled a hand through his hair, a look of resignation on his face. "You have a wall full of grateful customers. And I respect that."

"Thank you." She blinked back the budding tears of frustrated relief, stunned by his words. "But that still doesn't solve my problem."

His face thoughtful, Cutter crossed to the car and leaned his back against the door, folding his arms across his chest. The distance was nice, but his biceps bulged beneath his T-shirt and, for a brief second, Jessica lost her train of thought.

"What did it say?" he asked

Blinking, Jessica tried to focus. "What did what say?"

"The paper."

"It mentioned your reclusive status, who I was, my business, and then it questioned our relationship."

He studied her thoughtfully for a moment, rubbing the back of his neck. "Damn," he muttered, and her anxiety winched higher as he went on. He dropped his arm to his side. "I know what to do."

Jessica suppressed the urge to grab his shirt and shake him to spill the goods. The look on his face spoke volumes. Whatever his plan, he wasn't happy about it.

"You go to the Aquarium with a date and I'll go alone," he said, his voice grim. "An evening with the two of us at the same party—but clearly not as a couple—will support the theory that we're just friends."

Jessica held his gaze as the full implication of his words washed over her. He was offering to go to the party. Attending a function that included the media. One he had adamantly refused to participate in before.

Cutter Thompson wasn't the completely selfish bastard she'd thought.

Gratitude flooded, overriding her good sense, and she launched herself forward, throwing her arms around his chest for a hug. She landed against a wall of warm steel that smelled of musk and man, momentarily paralyzing everything but her pulse, every particle in her body aware of Cutter at a primal, cellular level.

Cutter's voice was strained, as if in pain. "No need to get mushy. It's not like I asked you to marry me."

Jessica released a small laugh; intense relief over her business, mixed with an armful of potent male, was making her uncharacteristically giddy. "Quit being an idiot, Cutter. I appreciate what you're doing for me." She dropped her arms and stepped back, ordering her heart to ease its pace. Though her body still pulsed, her gaze never wavered. "And I would never say yes to a proposal from you."

His expression mixed a grimace with amusement. "No need to worry, Sunshine." The rare but devilish almost-grin returned. "I'd never ask."

CHAPTER FOUR

THE sprawling lobby of the Miami Aquarium was dotted with twinkling lights, huge tanks of colorful, exotic fish, and people in elegant finery. Phillip Carr, CEO of Carr Investments, looked as if he'd been born into this world wearing an expensive tuxedo. He had blond hair, blue eyes and a smile so smooth it warranted its own flavor of ice cream. But as far as Cutter was concerned, the man was too polished. Too refined.

And much too comfortable with his hand on Jessica's back.

Whatever the guy's game, he'd been the perfect date for her, making sure the two of them had hit every cluster of chattering guests, working the crowd with the dedication of a campaigning politician in November. And finally, he'd stopped at Cutter's little band of social renegades, folding Cutter into a knot.

Because, from a distance, Jessica was a knockout—but up close, she was devastating. A red halter-top dress hugged her breasts and narrowed at her waist before flaring gently to the floor. With her hair piled on top of her head, wispy tendrils brushing her graceful neck, her creamy shoulders were exposed in a display that had Cutter's libido beating a drum that made concentration difficult.

She was one-hundred-percent ultra-refined *class*.

Just like the man whose hand clung to the small of her back like an accessory. And suffering through a twenty-minute rundown about Phillip Carr's business was about nineteen minutes and fifty-five seconds more than Cutter could stand.

Phillip was the kind of man any parent would proudly call their son, would go out of their way to claim—despite the fact the man was a pompous jackass. He monopolized the conversation with tales about himself and looked down on everyone in a way that was beyond patronizing. The man sought society's adoration, and no doubt society shoveled it back at him in spades, despite the obvious lack of sincerity beneath the man's intent.

Because the people loved charm, no matter how blatantly false.

And they approved of manners, no matter how bogus the intent beneath the etiquette.

Cutter didn't play those games anymore. He'd bent over backwards to behave as a kid, but it hadn't worked out for him then, and he sure as hell wasn't going to start again now. Suffering in silence was the best he could do. Unfortunately, there was little to celebrate when Phillip finally steered the topic of conversation away from himself.

"There's a new art exhibit at the gallery this week," the man said.

Jessica's face lit up, the sight punching Cutter in the gut. "I've heard," she said.

Phillip Carr aimed his too-slick smile at Cutter. "Have you seen the display of Picasso's work?"

Since the man was gazing directly at him, silence was no longer an option. And somehow, Cutter knew he was being intentionally singled out. "Nope," Cutter said. "I hate his stuff."

Apparently *hate* was too strong a word, because Jessica's gaze cut to Cutter, her eyes widening in a what-are-you-doing? look. The remainder of the group's chatter died, and Philip Carr's face oozed a tolerance that was annoying. Cutter was apparently a simpleton to be pitied because he didn't appreciate the subtle 'nuances' of fine art.

"His work from the later years can be difficult for some people to grasp," Phillip said.

Cutter took the condescending slap in the face without a flinch, calmly taking a sip of his beer before answering, his gaze leveled at the man. "What's there to grasp about a lady with a nose that protrudes from her cheek?"

A tight smile appeared on Phillip's face. "It's an artistic style referred to as cubism."

"Don't care what you call it," Cutter said with a nonchalant shrug, pausing before he went on. "It's still ugly," he said easily.

By now Phillip Carr's smile was huge, but still nowhere near his eyes, and the visual daggers Jessica was hurtling at Cutter were whistling close by. Pissing contests weren't Cutter's usual style, but Phillip's preening-peacock attitude, not to mention his constant possessive touch on Jessica, were grating.

"Picasso was gifted," Phillip said.

"Picasso was anatomically challenged," Cutter returned.

Jessica cleared her throat and, this time, the knife she hurled could have parted Cutter's hair.

"Yes, well..." Flustered at first, Phillip then sent Cutter a condescending look that elevated annoying to hellaciously irritating. "Driving fast around a circular track is hardly a challenge."

The ignorant description of his sport, and the man's agitated look, brought a smile to Cutter's lips as he took another sip of his beer, eyes on Mr. Tuxedo. "Racing can be difficult for some people to grasp."

Jessica chucked an optical barb that hit Cutter smack in the forehead, but he'd had more than he wanted of the conversation. And he wasn't going to stand here and listen to the two of them discuss their opinion of art.

"If we're done with our little artistic critique session," Cutter said, "I'm going to check out the selection at the buffet."

Frustrated, Jessica watched Cutter head towards a table of appetizers set up between a huge tank of puffer fish and an aquarium with floating Portuguese man-of-war. When Phillip began discussing his business yet *again,* Jessica knew it would be a while before he let up. One eye on Cutter, she murmured an excuse to the group and wove her way through the guests, picked up a plate, and went to stand across from him in the buffet line.

Not wishing to attract attention, she kept her voice low. "What was that all about?"

Looking unconcerned, Cutter continued to study the display of food. "I believe I was discussing Picasso with your date while you were giving a running commentary via your visual claws."

"I was *trying* to get you to play nice."

"I don't do nice."

An exasperated breath escaped her lips. "Can't you at least pretend?"

His gaze lifted, spearing her and halting her movements. "Sunshine, whatever you get from me is guaranteed to be one-hundred-percent genuine."

"Insults and all?"

"Insults and all." His lips twisted in suppressed amusement. "It appears you have a problem with my every conversation today."

Jessica tilted her head with false patience at his mention of the day's Battle of the Sexes debate. "I wasn't about to let you encourage Calamity to share her stories of her sexual exploits at work."

The light of humor in his eyes grew bigger. "I like Calamity."

"Of course you do," she muttered. "She has sex on the brain."

"An admirable quality in a woman."

Lips pressed in a line, Jessica kept her eyes on her task as she began to spoon strawberries onto her plate. Why did she let this man's suggestive comments fluster her? "Just because Calamity Jane said she'd pass on a date with the CEO in favor of the firefighter because he'd know how to 'put out her fire'…" Jessica couldn't prevent the roll of her eyes "…does *not* mean she was the instant winner of tonight's debate."

Serving spoon in hand, Cutter paused to look at her. "Love Potion certainly wasn't the winner," he said dryly. "Claiming she'd prefer the CEO because she likes her men both physically *and* mentally commanding was an insult to firefighters everywhere. It also shows her to be an intellectual snob." The humor returned to his eyes. "I'd much prefer hearing about Calamity's escapades."

Her fingers gripped her plate. "Not acceptable."

Cutter stopped in the middle of reaching for a canapé, lifting his gaze to hers. "Why not?"

She shot him a heated look and leaned in, keeping her voice low. "Because she'll only be too happy to tell you about every one of them."

One corner of his lips almost curled into a grin. "You got a problem with that?"

"Yes," Jessica said. After scanning the surrounding guests and finding none of them interested in the two of them, she rounded the table and came to a stop beside Carter. "I have a very big problem with that," she whispered.

And in a weird way she felt oddly left out of every conversation. She was a modern, successful woman. She knew how to flirt. And she was in touch with her sexual self. So why did the banter between Cutter and Calamity intimidate her so?

Cutter leaned uncomfortably close. "What do you have against a few little stories?"

The heat that infused her face was sure to fry the cold shrimp appetizer, and she struggled to maintain her cool. Deep down, she had the awful suspicion that Calamity's details would throw Jessica's entire sex life into sharp relief—sedate, quiet…

And *boring*.

She pushed the annoying thought aside.

Jessica gripped her plate harder. "Sexual relationships are not for public consumption. They should be kept private." She went on, grappling for the right words. "Sharing the details belittles the intimacy between two people and…" Her voice died as she saw the look on his face. "Why are you smiling?"

He hardly *ever* smiled. Hinted at one, yes. Skirted the edges, absolutely.

But full engagement was rare.

And the one he was sending her now sent her body into a sensual tizzy. "Because my bullshit-o-meter is shooting off the charts again," he said.

The surge of overheated blood to her face went nuclear, and she forced her gaze back to the buffet table with no idea what she was spooning onto her plate. "It is *not* bullshit."

"Sunshine," he said as he stepped closer. His voice was low, rumbling with intent. "I don't know who forgot to send you the memo, but sex does not have to be a mystical meeting of two souls. Sometimes it's just a physical release between two people who have the hots for each other." He hiked a brow and the look of desire in his eyes melted her on the spot, fusing her to the floor. "And there is nothing wrong with that."

While her body fought to unwind the tangle of her seared nerves, he turned and headed for another table of food across the way.

Dignity scrambling for a foothold, she scraped her poise up off the floor and crossed to stand beside Cutter. "Maybe for those of you who haven't evolved beyond a lower species of animal," she whispered fiercely.

Cutter's low rumble of laughter sounded rough from disuse, the delight in his eyes obvious. And the full implication of its meaning hit her squarely between the eyes.

Stunned, she said, "You're doing this on purpose, aren't you?"

"Doing what?" The innocent look on his face was clearly false.

"You *are*." She stared at him, perturbed she'd walked solidly into his trap. "You're shoveling out your chauvinistic twaddle just to get me going."

He pressed his lips together, as if suppressing a grin. "Jessica Wilson on her relationship soapbox is a sight to behold." With that, Cutter strolled in the direction of the dessert display.

Heart still thumping from her passionate speech, she blinked and pulled herself together, watching him examine his options for a sugar injection. Finally, she strode across to stand beside him at the display of chocolaty decadence.

"Sunshine…" he said. His hand paused above a plate as he lifted his eyes to hers. "If you keep following me around, people are gonna think you've got a crush on me."

She bit back a fiery retort and sucked in a breath. "And if I strangle you next to a platter of chocolate truffles, the we're-just-friends theory will be impossible to pull off." Cutter ignored her and went back to filling his plate, and Jessica continued, her voice flat. "Exactly how many of our previous conversations were real and how many were for my benefit only?"

"Not saying," Cutter said. "Women like men who are mysterious." He shot her a look brimming with amusement. "Enigmatic." He stepped closer and leaned in. The proximity of his smoldering green eyes sent her nerves skyrocketing. "Men who know how to put out a woman's fire."

Her body felt as if it was being roasted over an open spit, but she stood her ground. "Some of us are more than walking shells of sexual urges, Mr. Thompson." She managed to keep her tone smooth and confident, but her knees were knocking. So she'd never had a wild fling. So her experiences were with men who treated a woman with care. That did *not* mean she was missing out. "We have higher goals in life than simple physical relief. Like romance. Meaningful, *intelligent* conversation." She sent him a wide-eyed innocent look. "Speaking of which…if you'll excuse me, I'm going to find my date now."

His blood pumping from the stimulating exchange, Cutter watched Jessica glide gracefully away, her slender figure elegant as she tossed him a falsely sweet smile over a delectable shoulder.

Jessica Wilson was so sure her emotions were stronger than her physical needs. That basic concepts such as lust and desire couldn't pollute her lofty goals of spiritual connection and happily ever after. She smiled brightly at Phillip as he handed her a dainty flute of champagne, and then her eyes cut in Cutter's direction, a self-satisfied smirk on her face.

Little Miss Sunshine was certainly pleased with herself. Poise bordering on a sanctimonious smugness that tickled Cutter no end. The Battle of the Sexes had just gotten interesting, smashing his off-limits vow towards women until he figured out his life.

Because sometimes exceptions had to be made. Sometimes challenges were meant to be met. And explored.

Namely, Jessica Wilson.

Cutter's gut revved in anticipation, like the shift of lights at a starting line, going from red to yellow to outright, *hell-yeah* green.

The petite blonde in the beaded cocktail dress looked confident in her answer. "Love Potion Number Nine was right.

Most women choose men who provide intellectual stimulation as well as strength," she said, looking around their female gathering. The lobby was crowded, and Cutter was standing one group over, but Jessica knew he was listening in. The blonde sent everyone a smile. "What good are muscles if a man lacks intelligence?"

Jessica caught Cutter's eye and lifted a brow in triumph, and his gaze glimmered with amusement.

Not wanting to be surrounded by five women who were giving a detailed analysis of every online debate since the beginning of the competition, Phillip had left to corral a potential client in the corner. From her experience during their first date, Jessica knew Phillip wouldn't resurface any time soon.

The tall, black-haired lady sent the blonde a supercilious smile. "Susan, I've been married and divorced multiple times. Believe me," she said dryly. "A woman can overlook plenty if her man knows how to put out her fire."

With murmurs of agreement from the cluster of females, all in support of Calamity Jane's answer, Jessica's smile froze. As she struggled for a diplomatically worded comment, she saw Cutter thread through the guests in her direction. He looked intent on joining their debate. She opened her mouth to speak, hoping to cut off any comment he might make, but as he passed by behind her…his fingers grazed her backside, bombarding her body with wicked messages.

Hair standing on end, heart frantically pumping molten lead through her veins, she turned to watch Cutter disappear through a doorway. It took a full thirty seconds for her to recover from the sensual flyby. Or at least long enough for a single rational thought:

Just who did he think he was?

Ticked beyond belief, body on fire, she murmured an excuse to the ladies and followed in his path. When she crossed the threshold into the empty corridor, Cutter appeared to take her arm, eliciting a resurgence of the delicious signals.

"You groped me," Jessica hissed, annoyed at her instant reaction to the skin-on-skin contact. Her voice went ultra-high frequency. "In *public*."

"Yep." Cutter ignored her distress as he steered her down the deserted hallway, away from the crowd. "'Cause I knew you'd track me down."

"Groping is unacceptable." Her feet dragged, slowing their progress. "And I had something to add to the group's conversation."

"Hence my actions," he said, guiding her along. "I was saving you from wasting your time. Obviously those women haven't evolved as high up the evolutionary ladder as you. Probably stuck somewhere between spider monkey and chimpanzee."

Her feet finally stopped protesting his movements, her anger easing as she remembered the black-haired lady's comment. "Her priorities are warped."

The look of mild disgust on his face was amusing. "You people are taking this contest way too seriously," he said. "And maybe her experience has taught her the importance of sex in maintaining a marriage."

The light was dim as they headed down the passageway, but she shot Cutter a sharp look anyway. "Or perhaps her warped priorities led to the demise of all her marriages."

Cutter didn't reply, just pulled her into a vast room at the end of the corridor, and Jessica halted in surprise, the last of her anger fading away. Too bad he was still holding her arm.

"You brought me to the shark tank?" she said.

"It's deserted, so it's a safe place for a conversation. Besides," he lifted a brow, "it seemed fitting after your encounter with the professional divorcée." He released her and stopped at the massive glass wall to watch the creatures glide ominously through the water. Cutter turned and leaned a shoulder against the tank. "Speaking of relationship demises, where is this wonderful ex of yours?"

Disturbed by Cutter's focus on her, Jessica stepped up to the aquarium and kept her eyes on a nurse shark as it slowly passed by, the sinuous undulations mesmerizing. "He got called away on business so he couldn't make it."

"And where is Phillip?"

The tone in his voice left no doubt about Cutter's feelings toward the man. For some reason, Jessica felt the need to defend him. "Phillip is brilliant, charming and a sophisticated conversationalist. And yes," she went on at the look Cutter shot her, "he is a little fixated on his business." She cleared her throat. "Right now he's talking to a potential client."

Cutter sent her a questioning glance. "Does this happen to you regularly?"

She studied him, bewildered. His presence made it difficult to concentrate, but it was the expression on his face that finally lifted the confusion.

"Ahhh," she said, with a small smile. Silly man thought he had her all worked out. "I get it." Amused, she tucked her hands behind the small of her back and leaned against the glass, palms against the tank. "You think my attitude towards sex stems from disappointment in my relationships. That I've been withering away like a piece of neglected fruit on a vine."

"Well, there's sex." He lifted an eyebrow suggestively. "And then there's *sex*."

The promise in his voice, and the memory of his touch, set her body throbbing again, but she simply rolled her eyes. "Thanks for clearing that up."

Cutter reached out and touched a single finger to her arm, sending a shock wave of shivers up Jessica's back. The dim light couldn't disguise the heated look in his green eyes. And there was no amusement on his face, just determination and conviction.

He ran his finger from her elbow to her shoulder, leaving a sizzling trail in its wake. "I can clear it up right now."

Her body launched into a sensual tizzy, her breathing forced. "I'm here with a date."

A date of convenience only, and Phillip knew that. But still…

"So having sex with one guy while out with another is a no-no, huh?"

Her heart was tapping so vehemently, the vibration shook her from the inside out. But appearing confident was paramount. And she *was* confident.

"Of course it is," she said. But the intent in Cutter's eyes— and the potential hanging between them—tinted her words with desperation. "And great sex does not take the place of common interests." Lovely, now she was beginning to sound like a ridiculous prude, but everything about the man left her rattled. He stepped closer, enveloping her senses, and her body wound impossibly tighter. Determined to throw him off, she lifted her chin, hoping her voice was calm. "Or scintillating conversation."

Ignoring her lecture, Cutter slowly leaned his head forward, and her nose filled with his musky scent. Sweat dotted the nape of her neck. She closed her eyes, waiting. Anticipating. But instead of kissing her, as she'd expected, he gave her shoulder a small nip.

Desire flooded her every cell, and her palms grew damp against the glass.

The gesture was not meant to be soothing. Or to gently seduce. It held the promise of fantasies her dreams had hinted at but never fully explored. The kind that slipped away when you woke, leaving you wanting, but unsure of exactly *what*.

Lips against her shoulder, he said nonchalantly, "What kind of conversation?"

She swallowed hard, her throat constricted. "Books." He moved to nibble at her ear, and goose bumps pricked, leaving her hair on end again. She bit her lip to prevent a groan from escaping, trying to focus on the cool glass against her hot, slick palms.

What was wrong with her? Where was her backbone? She should push him back. But she couldn't. She should walk away.

But she didn't want to.

Because deep down she wanted to know what those dreams had contained. Intuitively, she knew Cutter could show her.

His mouth moved down her neck, nipping gently, coiling her nerves, searing her skin as he went. "Any other topics allowed?" He pulled her hips against his hard thighs, and her knees went wobbly.

Her mind swimming in the heat of desire, she whispered, "Movies." One of his hands moved higher up her rib cage, and her voice broke a bit. "Good wine, music and current events," she finished desperately, proud she could speak coherently.

He lifted his head to stare at her, his thigh between her legs, and his hand cupping a breast. "Do you want me to do this?" He flicked his thumb across a tip. Her tenuous grip on sanity shattered like crystal on marble, and her nipples went taut, pleasure sluicing down her spine. "Or do you want me to discuss the historical significance of Picasso?"

Staring up at him, she heard her answer come out as an unintelligible mumble. And, as if the babbling words were a signal, his mouth landed on hers. The kiss absolutely lacked gentle finesse. Brimmed with power. Basic. Unapologetic.

Just like the man.

It lit a fire deep within, more decadent than she'd ever known, and kindled her response in return. Jessica reached up and gripped Cutter's shirt, clutching him as her lips met his turn for turn. Hands, large and scalding her through her silk, cupped her backside, and he arched her hips firmly against him, his hard thigh rubbing against her center.

At the shocking skitter of pleasure, a small cry escaped

her, and after several strokes, Cutter pulled his mouth from hers and said, "Maybe you'd rather discuss the merits of imported over domestic wines?"

Her comeback strangled in the back of her throat, desperate for another kiss.

He nibbled on her bottom lip, teasing her as he went on. "Debate the meaning behind the latest foreign film?"

"Oh, for the love of God," she ground out in frustration. "Give it a rest." And like a heat seeker, her mouth sought his.

The kiss went from wild ride to raw need. No hiding behind convention. No subtle hints as to what he wanted. Cutter's grip on her backside grew tight, pulling her hips firmer against his leg, increasing the contact, and twisting her stomach into tight knots of desire. Seconds slipped into minutes as Jessica drowned in the feel of hard lips and harder thigh, a visceral riot of sensation.

Desire wrapped her securely within its grasp, demanding satisfaction. Demanding release. Overwhelmed, she felt tears of pleasure burn the backs of her lids and choke her throat with need. Abandoning her lips, Cutter dropped his mouth to her shoulder again, this time nipping a touch harder, throwing her further into the inferno, and the sharp stab mirrored the ache in her body…and sent her toppling over the edge.

A psychedelic burst of color erupted behind her lids, and her muscles knotted tightly as the pleasure rippled along her body.

Cutter's touch grew gentle as Jessica slowly descended to terra firma. She gradually became aware of the cold glass of the shark tank at her back, Cutter's mouth at her neck, his warm breath on her skin. Her legs felt shaky, and she was definitely feeble in the knees.

Feeble…what an apt description.

After all her stupid, prudish attempts to keep him at arm's length, it only took a single nip to get her to drop her ideals faster than she could scroll past an unsuitable online match.

Cutter straightened up, but Jessica kept her eyes closed and somehow found her voice. "I do not want to see one ounce of smug satisfaction on your face."

His voice managed to convey the emotion anyway. "Agreed." Jessica opened her eyes and met his gaze as he went on. "I'll just say I told you so and leave it at that."

That was because the brash look in his eyes was all he needed.

Jessica, still wobbly and too shell-shocked to engage in further conversation, allowed Cutter to take her arm as he led her back up the empty hallway. As they neared the lobby, she finally managed to move under her own strength.

With a sinful expression on his face, he gazed down at her. "You look like you could use a drink," he said. She'd never seen him so animated before. "Why don't you hunt your sparkling conversationalist of a date down, and I'll tell the waiter to bring you more champagne."

She narrowed her eyes at him and repressed the utterly unfamiliar and completely undignified urge to stick out her tongue. They passed into the lobby, and, after tossing her his signature almost-grin, Cutter turned in the direction of the bar.

From seemingly nowhere a reporter from the *Miami Insider* materialized in front of him, and an irritated expression, mixed with resigned acceptance, crawled up Cutter's face.

"Good to see you again, Mr. Thompson," the reporter said. The bad toupee and snarky smile didn't look any better teamed with a tuxedo. "The sporting world was beginning to think you'd avoid the press forever."

Cutter's face closed down, all pretense of patience gone. "I've been working on a project."

Undaunted by Cutter's attitude, the journalist's smile grew bigger. "Just one question."

Cutter's green eyes went to granite, and Jessica held her breath as the reporter went on.

"Why did you bump Chester?" the reporter said.

Cutter frowned, his tone dismissive. "It doesn't matter. He won and I didn't."

Hoping that was the end of it, Jessica blew out her breath. But when Cutter tried to continue into the lobby, the reporter stepped in front of him, blocking his path.

"But Chester had been pushing the lines of fair play, and most of the drivers were calling for ASCAR to step in." The journalist shot Cutter a meaningful look. "There was a lot of bad blood building between you two." The reporter paused, but when Cutter refused to reply the man continued. "Some say it was your competitive nature going for the win. Some say you took one for the team to teach Chester the rules of the track." The pushy newsman cocked his head. "So why did you take the risk?"

A scowl now permeating his every pore, Cutter stepped around the man. "At this point, the reason is irrelevant."

The reporter watched Cutter get about ten feet away before calling after him, the words sinking Jessica's heart. "It is when it turns ASCAR's number-one driver into its biggest has-been."

CHAPTER FIVE

HAS-BEEN.

Washed up.

Springsteen's voice wailed in the garage. Hips pressed against the 'Cuda as he leaned forward under the yawning hood, Cutter wrestled with the bolt on the air filter. It didn't need changing as much as he needed something to keep him from pummeling the car in anger.

Used to be he would have taken out his feelings with a practice run around the track. It was zooming two hundred miles an hour in his car that had gotten him in the zone. Made him feel alive and eased all the black emotion.

But that wasn't an option anymore. Ever since he'd screwed up his life, he felt as if he'd been bound and gagged. And with the release valve of racing now gone, the pressure of negativity was building in his chest, making him downright surly.

Not that he'd ever done cheerful.

After he'd left the aquarium Saturday night, he'd spent Sunday beneath the car. His ribs still sent crippling reminders of the grueling twelve hours of overexertion. The two-hour exercise binge this morning hadn't helped either. By his tenth set of bench presses, his shirt was stuck to his damp skin, and his chest screamed in protest. In a way, the constant agony was a relief, keeping his thoughts from drifting back to the reporter's question. Still, Cutter knew it was going to be a major ibuprofen, ice-pack kinda day.

Struggling with the bolt, irritated at the filter's stubborn insistence to remain locked in place, Cutter tossed a cuss word at it, just for good measure.

Tally so far? 'Cuda one, Cutter zilch.

"Maybe you should try sweet-talking it," a voice called from behind him.

Jessica.

After a brief pause, he gripped the wrench tighter. "I don't do sweet," he said as he continued his tussle.

And he was in no mood to chat with the beautiful lady. The pain in his chest mirrored the chaos churning in his mind, and neither was leaving him in a sociably acceptable mood.

Or more accurately, his mood was even less social than usual.

"I'm not going away just because you're ignoring me," she said.

The sound of heels tapping was followed by the death of a guitar on the stereo, and the resulting silence vibrated in the air like a washing machine set on spin.

Her voice came from behind and was soft, yet stubborn. "Burying your head beneath that car is not going to fix your problems."

The lady didn't know the half of it, and Cutter just managed to suppress the scowl. "Didn't say it would."

"That's the problem," she said. "You're not saying anything at all."

Jessica leaned on the front of the car next to him, her spicy scent invading his senses, turning him on, revving him up. His emotions. His lust. Even the bitterness. But it was the memory of her beautiful face as she came that swamped him the most.

Cutter raked a frustrated hand through his hair. He didn't need a damn do-gooder coming around trying to do-good on him. What he needed right now was to be left alone. And if Miss Sensitivity couldn't pick up on that, he might as well go take that shower he *should* have taken after he pumped iron this morning. Might ease the pain knifing him in his ribs.

After straightening up, he tossed the wrench at the tool box, and it landed with a loud clatter. "Talking doesn't change a thing."

"You don't know that until you try."

He stared at her lovely face. The wide, expressive brown eyes looked at him with uncertainty—wariness mixed with a generous dollop of fear. No need to wonder *why*.

After the aquarium episode, she clearly didn't trust herself around him. The speed with which she'd come apart in his hands had been stunning. And if it had shocked the hell out of him, there was no guessing the size of the jolt she was recovering from.

The thought brought a large measure of satisfaction that almost chased away his foul mood, but the compassion in her face brought it all back. Her sundress exposed the creamy skin of her shoulders, and her long, leggy look ended in a pair of flat sandals. Feminine. A girly girl. A lady who loved to roll out a spotlight and shine it on every feeling. Analyze it from every angle.

"Sunshine," he said, his voice deceptively quiet as he stepped closer. Her lids flared briefly, as if unsure what he'd do next. Good, she should be nervous. "If you're smart, you'll scram." He shot her a look he *hoped* would end their conversation and headed towards the door. "I'm going to take a shower."

Absently gnawing on the inside of her cheek, Jessica watched Cutter disappear inside the house. Why was she even here? She should definitely go. But when the reporter had called him a has-been, the look on Cutter's face had stolen her breath. And it was that expression she kept seeing. That and the one of smug satisfaction after he'd brought her to her figurative knees…while she was out on a date with another man.

The memory rolled in her belly. Granted, the only reason Phillip had agreed to go to the affair was to push his business at the function. But still, her part in the incident left her slightly queasy. When Cutter requested help with his flirting responsibilities, she'd called him unromantic and unethical, but what did her actions make her?

She closed her eyes and pinched the bridge of her nose. Probably best not to answer that question. But just as divorce didn't preclude her belief in forever, one little indiscretion…

Jessica's mind drifted back to the monumentally sensual moment by the shark tank, a shiver coursing up her spine.

Okay, so *little* was a gross understatement. But one brief moment of weakness…

The excuse died, cut off by the memory of her clutching Cutter, desperate to bring his mouth back to hers, prolonging their contact and drawing it out, until she practically demanded he finish the job.

Okay, so it hadn't been brief either.

With a grimace, she racked her brain, searching for a better platitude.

Ah yes, the oldie but goodie: We learn from our mistakes and move on. That one worked nicely. Thank God for rationalization.

With a small breath, Jessica rubbed her forehead, staring at the closed door Cutter had disappeared through. Instinct told her to go, to leave him to his brooding. But the only reason he'd gone to the party, and had hence been waylaid by the reporter, was to help her with her publicity problem.

With a forced exhalation, she crossed the garage and went up the flight of stairs to the living area. Down the hall a door was open, and she heard a cabinet door close and water running. Her belly exchanged nausea for anxiety as she slowly approached the doorway and leaned against the frame.

The bathroom was done in gray marble dotted with gold fixtures. Glass blocks enclosed the shower, water spraying from the showerhead and steaming up the enclosure. Cutter stood at the double sink, hands on the hem of his T-shirt, as if about to take it off.

Their eyes collided in the mirror, locked, and—for a brief moment—the intimacy of their surroundings almost chased her away. The dark expression on his face hardly helped. But she persevered.

"Even Cro-Magnon man, limited though his vocabulary was, probably expressed a feeling or two when he was upset," she said.

He dropped his hands to his sides, and his gaze slid to the sink. "I'm not upset."

She slowly entered the room. "I'm not leaving until you talk to me."

"Why?"

"Maybe I feel responsible for dragging you to the function in the first place."

His gaze crashed into hers again. "Consider the shark tank payment in return."

A burning sensation hit her between the legs and in the face, all at the same time, though they had vastly different meanings. Ignoring his suggestion, she went on. "So what's bothering you?" Jessica studied him in the mirror. "The loss of a career, the injury…or is it the loss of the adoration of a tabloid journalist with a bad toupee?"

His scoff was one part disgust and two parts skeptical amusement. "I don't give a rat's ass about the press and their opinion." Cutter leaned forward and braced his arms against the counter. "And yeah, I'm ticked my racing career is over." There was a tiny lift to his eyebrows. "Not all of us can be optimists."

"Are you making fun of me?"

He looked at her dryly. "I'm stating facts."

True. It was all she knew how to be. After a period of mourning over her parents' divorce, she'd looked for the positive, grateful their split had been amicable. After grieving over the death of her marriage, with Steve's help she'd dusted herself off and redefined herself.

What other choice had she had?

She tipped her head curiously. "Why did you let the reporter's questions upset you?"

After a quick pivot, Cutter opened the shower door and cut off the water. He turned and leaned back against the glass blocks, hooking his thumbs through the belt loops of his jeans. His T-shirt clung to his every muscle, his ankles crossed. The stance was casual. Easy. His life might be in turmoil, but he was at home and sure of his physical presence. He was the epitome of masculine beauty.

But his eyes were directed somewhere beyond her, his gaze distant. And when he finally spoke, the words surprised her. "I have no memory of the wreck."

She stared at him, the last droplets of water dripping to the shower floor as she processed the news. But, given an option, who would choose to remember such a frightening ordeal? "That's probably a good thing."

"Is it?" he said, slowly shaking his head. He still refused to look her in the eyes. "One minute I was in the lead and the next I woke up in agony, my left hand weak." The muscles in his jaw tensed. "And I knew my racing days were over." It was clear from his tone that the realization had been worse than the physical pain. His expression was hard, though his voice was soft as he went on. "I made a decision that ended it all, and I can't even remember why."

She studied him for a moment. "It would be tough to lose a career."

"It was more than that." He swiped his hand through his hair, as if frustrated, and then crossed his arms, finally meeting her gaze. "Since I was a teen, I've never been a laid-back kind of guy. I don't go along to get along. I don't smile if I don't feel like it. And the track…" He gave a faint shrug, as if searching for the right words. "The track was the one place where I could be myself."

After a brief pause, she lifted an eyebrow wryly. "Disagreeable?"

Instantly, his lips twisted in a repressed smile. "More like I didn't have to pretend to be agreeable." The seconds ticked by as she turned his words over in her head. It was impossible to picture Cutter going out of his way to be pleasant. "Racing suited me," he said simply, and a shadow crossed his face. "And now it's gone."

Gone.

The short word was long in meaning, and it struck a chord in Jessica. This was something she could relate to. The end of her marriage wasn't quite the same, but there were definite similarities. Been there, felt that.

Jessica went to stand beside him, leaning a hip against the counter. "Cutter, I know what it's like to feel lost."

His voice sounded unconvinced. "You're comparing my injury to your divorce?"

She folded her arms in front of her chest. "I know you think marriage is a bunch of bunk, but it was the loss of *my* dream." His brows scrunched together with doubt. "And regardless of whether you agree with my choices, I still had to pick myself up and move on," she said. The sarcasm on his face eased a touch, and he took on a more thoughtful look, as if considering her words. Encouraged, she pressed on. "And you'll only find your way again by taking active steps. Which isn't possible if you're hiding from the world by burying yourself beneath your car."

"Right now all I have is the 'Cuda. When that's done, what do you suggest? I find another career? Racing is all I've ever known. It's all I've ever done. It's all I've ever *wanted* to do."

"You find something else you love, too."

"I don't love anything else."

"Then you find something you love almost as much. But if all you do is concentrate on what you've lost, you'll never be able to see what you have left. And Cutter," she said, taking a small step closer, "your negative attitude is blinding you from the possibilities."

He looked at her as if she was nothing short of crazy. "What possibilities?"

She brushed her hair from her face in exasperation. "I don't know," she said, dropping her hand to her side. "Only you can figure it out." She took another step forward, holding his gaze with hers, enunciating each word for emphasis. "But that won't happen until you *stop* feeling sorry for yourself."

Cutter stared down at her face for what felt like two eternities, and then some. Finally, his lips twitched again, losing a little of their edge. The hard set to his face softened with a hint of humor. And the light in his eyes was a definite improvement over the bitter skepticism. "No one likes a whiner, huh?" he said.

Amazed by the transformation, a smile slipped up her face before she could stop it. "No."

The cereal-box trademark suggestion of a grin infiltrated his face, sending electrical signals tingling along her nerves. When he took a small—but very meaningful—step in her direction, the tension in the air shifted, taking on definite sensual undertones.

After swallowing hard, she pushed away from the counter. "I'll leave you to your shower."

"Wait," he said, reaching into a drawer and pulling out scissors. "Right before you appeared to dispense a dose of that sassy sympathy of yours…" The light in his eyes grew bigger, as if still amused by her accusation of self-pity. He certainly didn't look offended. "I tried to take off my shirt and discovered how bad a number I did on my ribs during my workout. I can't lift my arms without experiencing all kinds of pain." He held out the scissors, the teasing expression back in full force. "Cut my shirt off for me?"

Heart tapping in her chest, she frowned at the obvious setup. She glanced at the ASCAR T-shirt covering his chest. "You'll ruin it."

"Sunshine, I've got a million of them." His brow crinkled in amusement. "What about a little compassion for a man in pain?"

Jessica narrowed her eyes. "You know," she said, swiping the scissors and pointing them at Cutter. "You deserve it for continuing to push yourself before you're fully healed." Eyes fixed on her task, she began to snip from the hem towards the neck, the stretchy cotton parting to display a flat stomach and nicely defined pectorals. The vision was more disturbing than she'd prepared for, than she could *ever* prepare for, her fingers growing clumsy as his chest was revealed. The mix of musky cologne tinged with motor oil was mesmerizing. She stepped back, the shirt now completely split, the sleeves clinging to his shoulders.

Nothing moved but his eyebrow. "I still can't shower."

The fun wasn't over yet. After heaving a large sigh, she said, "Turn around."

Cutter presented her with a back large enough to require a GPS to find her way from one side to the other. But it couldn't be nearly as disturbing as the front. She cut up the fabric, exposing a beautiful expanse of corded muscle, sinew and tanned skin. Who'd have guessed his back would be as impressive as his chest?

Stunned, Jessica gripped the scissors as Cutter turned around. Chest. Back. Gorgeous. Or breathtaking. Either view, Cutter Thompson was eye candy of the sweetest kind. Sure to rot every thought in even the most rational of brains.

And she *used* to excel at being rational.

He cleared his throat, startling her into taking action, and she jerked both sleeves down his arms.

Cutter grimaced with a small hiss. His pain had clearly been real. "Nice touch," he said through clenched teeth. "Your seduction efforts would have worked if it wasn't for the agony."

"I am *not* going to seduce you."

"No return favors, huh?"

Her cheeks burned with memory. It grew worse when Cutter, his hot green gaze fixed on hers, pulled the snap on his jeans, exposing a little more of his flat abdomen. Her heart started banging harder beneath her ribs, sending her messages, as if the rest of her body was too stupid to notice the danger.

His mouth hinted at a smile. "Sure I can't change your mind about that, too?"

Too. As in *also.* Just like he'd proven her wrong by the shark tank.

Without a word, Jessica turned and forced her feet down the hall, trying to ignore the sound of his jeans hitting the floor and the shower door opening. He was back there. Naked. And willing. Water streaming down his beautiful back and buff chest. And after the blatant invitation, all she had to do was strip off her clothes and follow him into the shower.

The mental image left her legs unsteady, and her footsteps faltered.

After rounding the railing, she descended the staircase, her steps growing firmer as she went. Her resolve strengthening with every stride.

She'd already tasted the dark desire he stirred. A bigger slice might choke her focus for sure. Touching him again was out of the question. He was too tempting, encouraging her to stray from the path she'd laid out the day she'd signed her divorce papers. Cutter made her question her vow to stick to her well-thought-out plan for finding a partner.

The *right* partner.

Jessica exited the front door and slipped into her car, gripping the steering wheel. Her heart still thumped shamelessly, and her body, hot, aroused and eagerly pleading its cause, was insisting she take Cutter up on his offer.

But logic was her ally.

Setting—and reaching—her goals was her specialty.

Unfortunately the fundraiser and keeping The Wildcard on a leash and wearing a muzzle had sidetracked her. Cutter Thompson wasn't the only man on the planet with sex appeal. It was time to start searching again. If she looked hard enough, she knew she could find a modern guy who not only wanted a relationship, but connected with her on both a physical *and* emotional level.

A man who knew how to play nice and be polite.

A man who believed in forever, like her.

The curvaceous redhead on the sidewalk clung to the muscle-bound blond as if he required an anchor to keep him grounded on earth. The two were smiling at each other, one set of perfect white teeth flashing, and another set answering the call. Frowning, Cutter watched the love-fest from his low-slung sports car parked in front of the office plaza that was home to Perfect Pair.

Jessica, as graceful and beautiful as ever, stood talking to the couple at the front door. Her tailored skirt ended above the knee, accentuating her long legs. Her cranberry-colored blouse made her olive complexion glow. The dark, glossy hair was partially pulled back, hanging in gentle waves to her shoulders, exposing the arch of her neck and framing her smiling face. The happy couple obviously brought her immense satisfaction.

Cutter studied her, captivated by her expression.

Her unyielding enthusiasm—her steadfast optimism about love, relationships and the potential for the future—

was intriguing. She could have taken her ex-husband for all she could get and spent the rest of her life pleasing herself. Shopping and doing lunch with friends. Bitterly complaining about her ex's faults, her crushed dreams and life's little cruelties.

Instead, she'd chosen to spend her days helping other divorced people find love. Now that he knew her better, it was hard to take her breakup cavalierly. And while he didn't buy into her belief of happily ever after, it was clear the woman had taken her lumps with dignity and turned her misfortune into something positive.

Unlike him...a man who'd been knocked on his ass by a catastrophe of his own making, unable to figure out how to get back up. And if he was completely honest, Jessica was right. He was still throwing himself a massive pity party.

And nobody likes a whiner.

The memory brought a faint smile to his lips. Maybe it was time to borrow a page from Jessica's book on self-improvement and pull his sorry self up by his bootstraps and start moving on.

Satisfied by the decision, when the couple on the sidewalk left, Cutter exited his car.

He knew the moment Jessica spied him, her body growing tense, a guarded look in her eyes. But her caution didn't prevent her usual gracious manners.

"Thanks for agreeing to stop by here," she said as he came closer. They entered the building, and she paused to lock the front door behind them. "I'm meeting someone for dinner on this side of town in about an hour."

He found her news...disturbing. Hit with her delicate scent, and a sharp twist of the ever-present desire, Cutter stepped closer. And had the satisfaction of seeing her eyes grow more uneasy in response.

Good. She still felt it, too. She might be eating dinner with another man, but there was no way she could deny their burning attraction. Several days after their encounter at the aquarium—and the snapping tension in his bathroom—his body's reaction was triggered just by her presence. Desire had become a living, chest-heaving entity.

And it was only a matter of time before Jessica Wilson gave in.

"A date, huh?" He struggled to maintain a serious face. "Firefighter or CEO?"

She shot him a dry look. "Neither," she said as she turned and headed down the hallway. "He's a pharmacist."

Cutter pursed his lips and fell into step beside her. "Unless he's packing Viagra, it'll be hard to put out those fires wielding nothing but a bottle of pills."

She kept her eyes straight ahead. "He's only thirty. I doubt Viagra is necessary."

"You never know," he said. "And are you sure he believes in forever?"

"He's already made the commitment once."

"I smell an oxymoron coming on."

She sent him a cutting, sideways glance. "He and his wife divorced two years ago."

"Am I the only one who sees the irony in this?" When she didn't meet his gaze, he went on, trying a different tactic. "He might still be stuck on his ex."

She halted in the doorway to her office and leaned her back against the doorjamb, arms folded, a familiar look of forbearance on her face. "Mike and I have a lot in common. We're both professionals who enjoy helping people. We have a shared interest in jazz music. And we're both looking for a long-term relationship." Jessica held his gaze, as if everything she'd said was aimed directly at him. "But the main reason I agreed to meet him is because we connected over an in-depth email discussion about divorce."

"That's romantic." He leaned against the opposite side of

the doorjamb. "What happened to the number-one rule of being positive?"

Was it his imagination or was she clenching her teeth?

"When two people click," she said evenly. "The rest is frosting. And romance is more than candied hearts, roses and candlelight."

"So comparing divorce settlements is the twenty-first-century thing now?" he said. She lifted her eyes toward the ceiling in that heaven-help-me way of hers he never grew tired of, and a grin threatened to overtake Cutter's face as he headed into her office. "I suppose we'd better get started. Wouldn't want to keep Mike and his bottle of Viagra waiting."

An hour later, Cutter leaned over the back of Jessica's chair and stared at her computer screen, the last response blinking on the monitor.

Complete honesty should always be a priority.

"Damn." Cutter frowned. "Thank God that's over. It was like trying to flirt with someone's straitlaced grandmother." His frown grew deeper. "I hope Too Hot to Handle doesn't get voted to be my date."

Jessica shot him an amused look. "She's not that bad."

"So if she asks me if I like her dress, and I hate it, she wants me to tell her the truth?"

"There is always a way to phrase things diplomatically."

"Sunshine," he said dryly. "There is no diplomacy in ugly." He rested one hip on her desk and hooked his thumbs through the belt loops of his jeans, looking down at her from his perch. Her scent was driving him crazy as he tried to identify the fragrance. "You seem to have hit it off with her. Maybe the two of you should attend the benefit dinner together. When Calamity Jane wins me as her prize, we could double date."

"I'll find my own date, thank you very much." Jessica

leaned back in her chair. "And Too Hot is only trailing Calamity by four percent. After our first airing went viral on the internet, people are now tuning in from all over the country, making this the number-one most anticipated pairing since the last episode of *The Bachelor*." Jessica's smile was radiant, her bottomless brown eyes bright with delight. It took every ounce of self-control he possessed to keep from pulling her into his arms, much less listen as she went on. "The Foundation has grossed one million dollars on the voting alone."

At the astronomical number, both his eyebrows lifted in surprise before settling into a position of doubt. "I'm not sure if I'm encouraged by the generous nature of our fellow countrymen or disturbed by their questionable tastes in entertainment."

Jessica chuckled. "Careful, Cutter. Your cynicism is showing again."

Enjoying the sound of her laugh, Cutter's lips twisted as he attempted to contain the grin. He failed miserably, and a moment of mutual amusement passed between them. When it was gone, it left the two of them staring at each other.

And the look was full of all those moments he'd wanted her, of her wanting *him*…and more.

The tense silence dragged until Jessica cleared her throat. With a glance at her watch, she pushed back her chair and stood. "If I don't leave now I'll be late."

Late for her dinner date.

Perched on her desk, he gazed at Jessica, studying her intently. Rich, dark hair. Wide exotic eyes. The gentle curves of her breast outlined in her blouse. The low thrum in his body, always present when he was around her, began to thrum harder. If it was time to stop hiding from the world beneath the 'Cuda, it was time to meet their attraction head-on as well. No more innuendo.

"Why don't you pass on meeting Mike and do what you *really* want," he said.

"Which is…?" She stared at him, as if afraid to hear the answer.

"Spend the night in my bed."

Fire spread up Jessica's neck and touched her cheeks, leaving her damp at the nape of her neck. There was no tease in his tone. His sea-green eyes were bright, hard and glittered with a frank desire that sapped the air from her lungs. And as Cutter stared at her, T-shirt hugging the muscles of his chest, his lovely biceps exposed—*God,* she loved those arms—she gripped the back of her chair, steadying her knees as another awkward silence stretched between them.

When she felt strong enough, she opened her desk drawer and pulled out her purse. "I don't have time for this."

Cutter's look of sardonic amusement was absolute and complete. "I love it," he said, crossing his arms across his chest. "You ladies are a piece of work. Honesty is only vital when it's convenient." She bit back the denial as he went on. "When I was in a crappy mood and wanted you to leave me alone, you chased me down and refused to leave until we talked about my *feelings*." He raised a brow at her, the cynicism rolling off him in waves. "But when sex is the subject, you scuttle away and avoid the truth like the plague."

"That's not true."

Okay, so it was. But she wasn't going to admit it.

"Bullshit," he said. "Even after the aquarium, you're still tiptoeing around the two of us."

It took her two tries to swallow against her tight throat. "I'm not tiptoeing."

And that wasn't a lie. She wasn't tiptoeing. She was in allout commando-crawling stealth mode. Trying to stay beneath the volley of sensual fire raging around her.

The knowing look he shot her left her heart throbbing in her throat. "What a crock," he said.

She didn't owe him anything. One ultra-hot, shark-infested moment in the dark—desire flared high in her body, but she ignored it—did not mean he had some sort of power over her. At least not any she was going to admit to. But she *did* have something to say.

"Okay, here is some honesty for you." She lifted her chin. "I want you to stop coming on to me."

"Why?" He leaned closer. His musky scent teased her, and his green eyes went dark as his voice turned husky. "Because you don't trust the spark between us?"

Yes.

"No. The right guy is more important than any spark," she said. She rubbed her temple, her mind spinning as the look on his face slayed her again. "And because it's making our work on this competition uncomfortable."

His brow crinkled in suppressed amusement. "I must have been gone the day they passed out the manual on when honesty is allowed and when it's not. Apparently it's all about your comfort levels."

Oh yes, indeed it was.

Heart pumping harder in her throat, Jessica forced herself to hold his gaze, twining her fingers through the strap of her purse. "If I don't leave now I'll be late." She didn't care that it was an obvious retreat. She needed time to regroup. "Where shall we meet for the next session tomorrow? Do you want to come by here? Or shall I swing by your place?"

Or perhaps they could engage in a video conference with Cutter on the next continent over. She stared at the handsome cut of his face and the athlete's well-honed body. Make that *two* continents over.

Antarctica should do.

Cutter studied her, as if considering his options for the meeting place. "Neither. I'm giving the 'Cuda a day off." His lips hinted at a smile. "Meet me at my boat at five."

CHAPTER SIX

"SUBTLETY really isn't your forte," Jessica called out to Cutter.

She watched him emerge from the water in swim trunks, bare-chested and dripping, the Atlantic extending forever behind him. Lining the shoreline were pockets of muted aquamarine and bright turquoise, while in the distance dwelled shades of deep indigo. Sunday Key, a tiny speck of an island, lay just south of South Beach, accessible only by boat. Close enough for cell phone service, but far from rogue reporters.

In shorts and a tank top, Jessica wrapped her arms around her knees and curled her toes into the warm sand. Not that she needed the extra heat.

Because the almost-grin on Cutter's face was more devastating than a tsunami.

Cutter dropped onto the towel beside her and reclined—extending his long, muscular legs peppered with dark hair—and closed his lids.

How could being wet make him look hotter?

His eyes remained closed. "You didn't like today's question?"

"You posted it when you went to unload our stuff from the boat, just so I wouldn't see it." Jessica stared down at him. The responses from the contestants had come in thick and fast, and they didn't bode well for her cause. "And it's a blatant attempt to use your contestants against me."

"I thought you'd be happy I was finally getting into the spirit of the competition."

"Which is more important, the spark or the man?" she said, repeating his posted question to the participants. She narrowed her eyes, frustrated his lids were closed and he was unaware of her glare. "Why don't you simply say I should toss out my priorities and indulge in a succession of meaningless sexual encounters?"

"That's your interpretation?"

Fortunately, his eyes were still shut, so he couldn't see the heat rushing to her cheeks.

Lovely. She'd probably just fallen into some devious trap he'd spent all night formulating. Doing her best to ignore a near-naked—and dripping-wet—Cutter was hard enough, but did he have to smell good, too? No cologne, just a hint of fresh soap, salt water and the vague scent of warm man that Cutter exuded. Maybe it was the smell of testosterone. Or pheromones. God knows he had plenty to spare. And how could she focus on the conversation with him exuding a masculine, lusty cloud that blocked every hope of a rational thought?

Despite everything, talking Cutter into participating in the publicity stunt had turned out better than she'd ever imagined. If she could just keep her physical responses under control, everything would be fine.

A breeze blew the fronds of a palm tree, shifting shadows across Cutter's face. "So how was the Viagra-totin' Mike?" One lid cracked open as he peered up at her. "Prince Charming material?"

The memory of last night swooped in on her, and defeat tried to rise like the undead. Jessica flopped back, stretching out beside him and staring up at the blue sky. Why did her every date seem destined for disaster lately? "More like the Prince of Darkness."

"The Ozzy Osbourne, bite-off-the-heads-of-bats kind?"

"No. A depressing the-end-of-the-world-is-near and I-can't-wait-for-it-to-happen kind."

"Not a happy guy, huh?"

She rolled onto her side and propped her head on her hand, looking across at him, his gaze now fully on hers. "Let's put it this way. He spent the whole evening talking about his ex-wife. And every time he veered off to rehash his breakup—yet again—he started crying." Jessica rubbed her brow with the tips of her fingers. She should have spotted the signs in their earlier emails. "And we're not talking silent sniffles. They were outright sobs that drew the attention of every table around us."

His lips twitched, yet no grin appeared. But there was a definite light in Cutter's sea-green eyes, and Jessica wondered what ocean depth the shade represented.

Certainly nothing deep.

The crinkle of his brow betrayed his amusement. "I could see that coming a mile away." He sent her an innocent look that was so blatantly *not* Cutter it was ridiculous. "At least he was in touch with his feelings."

She flashed him a you're-so-not-funny stab of her eyes. "In touch is good," she said dryly. "Enmeshed is bad."

"Apparently your method for picking your dates is flawed."

If there was one thing she was an expert on, it was dating. She lifted a brow. "I hardly think yours is better."

"You don't even know what it is."

"Sure I do. If you like what you see, you go for it."

As he lay on his towel looking up at her, his expression was patently amused, as if waiting for the punch line. Of course he'd see nothing wrong with his procedure. She, however, refused to be ruled by lust. She'd heard too many stories from her customers about that potentially ugly blunder. She'd made plenty of mistakes on her own, letting her self-centered libido run the show would be worse.

And signing one set of divorce papers was enough—never

again, thank you very much. The murky shadow of sadness peeked from behind her usual positive thoughts, and she shoved it back.

If she stuck to her plan, everything would be fine.

"*You* are reactive." Her tone left no doubt to her meaning. "However *I* am proactive. I don't accept dates with men unless I know we're both on the same page." His eyebrows crept higher, and she could sense his sarcasm coming. She brushed her hair from her cheek. "Ask any online dating service and they'll tell you finding your match is a numbers game. I choose from the database very carefully."

One corner of his lips curled. "Must get tiring kissing all those frogs."

After yesterday, it seemed important to retrace that line in the sand between them. Or, given her previous lapse in good judgment, maybe construct an impossible-to-scale wall. Jessica shook her head. "I don't engage in a physical relationship until *well* after I've established a firm emotional connection."

His look started out puzzled and then landed on disbelief. "You're kidding."

Something in his tone made her defensive. "No. And I don't initiate email conversations until I've ensured a man meets my profile."

After a brief pause—and more disbelief—he said, *"Seriously?"* Cutter rolled onto his side to mirror her position, elbow on his towel, head propped on his hand.

The proximity of those beautiful shoreline eyes was disturbing, and she buried her trembling fingers in the white sand between them, sifting some through her fingers.

His mouth tap-danced around a grin yet never engaged, but his eyes were clearly amused. "Profiling? Isn't that what the FBI uses to track down criminals?"

He certainly seemed entertained by her process. But since

her divorce, she'd honed it until it sparkled like a diamond in the sun.

When she refused to dignify his comment with a response, he finally went on. "So you mean to tell me your *every* relationship begins with the future in mind?" he said. "You never just kick up your heels and enjoy the moment?"

"Cutter…" Giving up on the glares, Jessica tried the feigning-patience route. "I'm not like you. I have emotions. Feelings. Sex is an intimacy that should start with caring. And I don't want to waste my life with men who are inappropriate."

"This is why you're still single. You're too picky."

She lifted her gaze skyward. "I'm *discerning.*" She sent him a pointed look. "It's also useful in weeding out the men who are only interested in one thing."

"Sunshine," he said softly. "They're all interested in that one thing."

Heat filled her belly and rubbed between her legs, steaming up her insides, fogging her brain and making it difficult to breathe. If relationships were built on animal attraction, Cutter would be the man for her. But they weren't. And he *wasn't.*

Because sex appeal didn't have staying power, nor was it willing to engage in an intimacy that was a foundation for lasting commitment.

And she would keep rephrasing that reality until her body understood the message.

Unfortunately, the look on his face was almost as mesmerizing as the well-defined muscles of his chest, and she was getting pulled deeper into his gaze. All her good intentions about the need for reality were getting lost in the heat coursing through her veins.

Cutter's phone beeped, breaking the spell, and he reached to pull his cellular from his pants pocket. As Jessica gave her body a stern lecture on the rules, Cutter scanned the screen before glancing up at her. "Too Hot says when two people share a bond, that's all the spark they need." Without a word of discussion, Cutter began to type in his reply.

A waft of concern filled her. "What are you typing?"

He kept his eyes on the screen. "Just my response."

Her anxiety expanded. "Which is?"

A faint lift of his lips appeared, his fingers moving across the keys. "Don't worry. I'm just giving her that honesty she values so highly."

Her frown was instantaneous. "Let me see." Jessica reached for the phone, but he held it just out of her reach. "Cutter." Her voice was sharp now as she wildly sought the phone high in the air. "What are you saying to her?"

The rare sighting of a grin so wide it split his face left her staring in awe, and the sexy rumble of his voice curled her toes. "Just that I hope the kind of bond she's talking about involves whips, chains and handcuffs."

A squeak of dismay escaped her throat. Eyes hurling daggers, Jessica lunged for the phone, and Cutter rolled onto his back with a gravelly chuckle, holding the cellular well out of her reach. His laugh died when she lost her balance and landed with an unladylike thump on his chest.

As she sprawled atop his torso, her heart lodged so high in her throat it blocked all hope for air. Cutter looked up at her, and Jessica's sensory input narrowed to his body beneath her hands, the thud of his heart beneath her palm. The crisp hair. Hard muscle. Hot skin.

The pause was torture. "You know what your problem is?" he said, staring up at her.

Outside of enjoying the cynical man's company?

Or craving his rare smile?

Or the mind-bending, soul-consuming lust that was pumping in her veins this very moment?

Her head swam, and her voice came out as a croak. "What's my problem?"

"You need a guy's perspective while profiling your potential dates."

Jessica gaped at Cutter as she pulsed with an energy that threatened to turn her very existence inside out. A total body inversion. She was fantasizing about the two of them having sex on the beach—and not the alcoholic-drink kind—and he was giving her dating advice?

The impassive face was paired with an amused glint in his eyes. "But this is your lucky day."

Lucky.

The carnal potential to the words didn't bear thinking about.

"How so?" she asked, afraid of his answer.

Another rarely dispensed grin broke on his face. "I've decided to help you choose your next date."

The next day, Cutter parked his car in the driveway of Jessica's quaint, Cape Cod–style home. Immaculately maintained, painted a bright yellow with white shutters, it sported a cozy front porch. The cheerfulness exuding from the house was the perfect reflection of its owner, and Cutter settled back in his seat, amused.

Yesterday, when Jessica had landed on his chest, it had required every scrap of willpower he possessed not to act on the need pounding his body. And it was pretty easy to make out that the feeling was mutual. The rich, hot-chocolaty eyes brimmed with lust. But it was the simultaneous horror in her expression that stopped his raging impulse to roll her over and take what he needed, to give her what he knew she desired.

Because she didn't want to want him.

Staring at the brightly painted, sunny house, Cutter was less than amused now. When he had sex, it was with women who wanted him as much as he did them—no, actually *more*. He'd never pursued a woman in his life. And he wasn't about to start now. The *last* time he'd chased somebody he'd been a seven-year-old kid in hot pursuit as his father had driven away for good. Cutter gripped the gearshift as the unwelcome memory resurfaced.

The day had started out perfect. With his dad's visits growing farther and farther apart, Cutter had been waiting for months to see him. The temperature was warm, the cotton candy was plentiful and the raceway was packed with fans. It was every boy's ultimate fantasy.

Until his father started buying him everything he'd asked for, and Cutter had known something was up. When the race was over, his dad pulled up in front of his mom's house…and finally dropped the bomb. He was moving out of town.

And Cutter had instinctively known he'd never see him again.

Of course, his dad had denied it. And no amount of begging, pleading or tears would change the man's mind. As he watched him drive away, Cutter panicked and took off, chasing the car down the street. And as the taillights disappeared around the corner, Cutter was too winded to keep going.

A car honked somewhere in Jessica's neighborhood, and Cutter's fingers tightened on the gearshift. Damn, he hated that memory. He hated his father for leaving, but he hated himself the most for begging him to stay.

He forced himself to ease his grip and stared at Jessica's door. He was certain they would eventually engage in a hot and heavy affair. But he sure as hell refused to push. He wanted her so ready for him that she hunted him down and demanded he take her. He wanted her actions to be deliberate. Well thought out.

Not an impulsive, spur-of-the-moment decision that would be easy to dismiss as a passing hormonal fluke.

He craved Jessica more than a caffeine addict craved a hit of double espresso at 4:00 a.m. And the spark between them was powerful. Any date she went on now was sure to feel washed-out in comparison to the boiling beaker of chemistry they shared.

So offering some helpful advice about who to meet next in her never-ending line of possible Mr. Rights was a safe course of action. The more time she spent with the soft, touchy-feely, let's-talk-about-our-feelings specimens she chose, the quicker she'd succumb to the sensual vortex pulling them closer.

Pleased with his plan, Cutter climbed out of his car just as a very sleek Italian sports car pulled up to the curb. A black-haired man in a dark suit stepped out, but Cutter ignored him until, a moment later, they were strolling beside each other up the walkway to Jessica's house.

Maybe he was too late to choose her next victim.

"Are you Jessica's date for the evening?" Cutter asked.

The man shot Cutter an assessing look. "I'm her ex." He stuck out a hand but kept on walking. "Steve Brice."

The ex-husband she owed. The one she went out on a limb for.

Nothing about Steve Brice screamed touchy-feely. Business, yes. Sophisticated, most definitely. But certainly not soft.

Cutter warily returned the shake. "Cutter Thompson."

"I recognized you from the paper." Long and lean, Steve cast him a guarded look. "Are you here to take Jess out?" he said, as if sniffing out Cutter's intent.

Why the look? Was he jealous of Jessica dating? Cutter wasn't here to sleep with her—not yet, anyway—and he could take the guy, but he didn't relish the idea of duking it out with Jessica's ex on her front lawn over a misconception.

They climbed, side by side, up the front steps. "I'm here to help her select the perfect next date," Cutter said.

"Yeah?" The laugh from Jessica's ex was neither expected nor malicious. More of a you-have-no-idea-what-you're-in-for kind of chuckle. Jessica opened the door, and Steve's voice dropped to an amused mutter. "Good luck with that."

* * *

Fifteen minutes later, a jazz song played softly in the background, Jessica's laptop rested on the coffee table and Cutter sat on her overstuffed couch, waiting in the living room. The soft colors—muted lavenders and greens—and the presence of enough wicker furniture to fill a Pottery Barn made Cutter feel like a diesel truck in a race with a pretty Mini Cooper.

"I opened a sauvignon blanc if you're interested." Jessica emerged from the kitchen with a bottle of wine and two wineglasses. "Chilled to a perfect fifty degrees."

Steve followed with two bottles of beer, one of them half-empty. "You struck me as more of a beer guy." He held out the full bottle. "I don't know the temperature, but it's cold."

Amused, Cutter gratefully accepted the man's offer. "Cold is good."

Up until now their interactions had been relatively guarded. And when the talk had turned to the new gym Steve's foundation had funded at the local Boys and Girls Club, Cutter had left them in the kitchen to finish their discussion about its grand opening party. Apparently, they were attending it together.

Steve nodded at the photograph of the thirty-year-old Hispanic man displayed on the laptop. "Did you choose the doctor or the lawyer?" He sat on the loveseat across from Cutter.

Jessica took the spot next to Cutter on the couch, and he ignored the instant sense of male satisfaction. "Lawyer," he said. Steve winced, and Cutter bit back the smile. "Environmental law," Cutter added, just to be clear. "He's been a champion for protecting the Everglades. Won the coveted Green Goals award just last year." His lips twitched. "So he's a do-gooder, too."

Steve gave a nod. "Good choice." The man's eyes danced merrily as he sipped his beer. "She does have a soft spot for the altruistic ones."

Like her ex—a man famous for his charitable work. Which

brought up a whole host of questions Cutter had been mulling over since yesterday. Jessica's take-no-prisoners attitude toward dating was impressive, and it led him to assume she was either an over-the-top organizational freak…or she'd been massively mucked about during her marriage.

After meeting Steve, Cutter's curiosity about their married life had grown a thousandfold. Just because the man seemed decent didn't mean he was husband material, but Steve obviously cared about Jessica and wanted to see her happy. So what had done their relationship in?

The thought was cut short when Steve gestured towards the computer. "I told her a long time ago I'd help find the right guy."

Jessica shot her ex a dry look. "There is something inherently wrong with husband number one choosing my dates."

Cutter eyed her over his beer. "Definitely not romantic."

"No." Jessica's gaze cut to him. "It isn't." She paused, and then her face grew curious. "And what do you have against the doctor, anyway?"

"His paragraph stated he'd worked in Angola, Afghanistan, India and Somalia," Cutter said.

She stared at him, as if waiting for more. When he didn't go on, she said, "So he likes to help people, too. What's wrong with that?"

Steve answered for him. "Difficulty focusing."

"Trouble with commitment," Cutter added.

"Probably has a girl in every port," Steve went on.

Jessica poured her wine, picked it up and shifted her gaze between the two men, eyeing them both warily. "Do I get to participate in this discussion at all?"

Despite the fact that Steve had responded too, her gaze settled on Cutter. Another intensely satisfying moment. These two might have been married, they might still be friends, but Jessica's full attention remained on Cutter.

As their gazes remained locked, the tension in the room

stepped up a notch, yesterday's conflict, today's goal—and the delicious potential always stirring between the two of them—all rolled into one. The room vibrated with an energy that should have left the walls shaking.

"You can participate in the final decision," Cutter said. "But if the Prince of Darkness is any indication, I think your track record speaks for itself." As an afterthought, Cutter threw a glance at Steve. "Present company being the exception, of course." After all, the man had saved him from being stuck with a glass of perfectly chilled sauvignon blanc.

Steve raised his beer in a silent salute of thanks, but Jessica kept her eyes on Cutter as she went on with a hint of defiance. "There is nothing wrong with my track record."

Cutter hiked a brow. "Not if you like weepy men."

"Or ones who live in their parents' garage," Steve added.

Amused, Cutter turned toward Steve. "I haven't heard about him."

Jessica's tone was firm. "And you're not going to either."

"He was a doozy," Steve said with a chuckle, which died when Jessica lobbed him a look.

Pink coloring her cheeks, Jessica sipped her wine and then rested the glass on her knee. But she kept her chin high, as if refusing to let her past forays into dating hell get her down. Cutter wondered how she sustained the energy for the constant optimism.

"I still don't understand your problem with the doctor," she said.

Her question had him shifting in his seat to face her as another unwanted memory stirred. He hadn't thought of his dad in years. But lately, long-buried, vague impressions were emerging with a frequency that was disturbing, leaving far-reaching ripples when they surfaced. Even before his old man had left and never looked back, he'd always been changing employers. And every time he'd told Cutter about his new job opportunity, his dad had seemed excited. But none of them had held his attention for long.

And his attention span for his son had lasted all of seven years. Nine if you included the phone calls Cutter received on his eighth and ninth birthdays.

After that, there was only silence.

Trying to ease the tightness in his chest, Cutter threw his arm along the back of the couch, but the twinge of pain refused to ease. "The doctor has been employed by three different agencies and worked in four different countries in less than two years," Cutter said to Jessica. "My take is he's too easily distracted by the shiny objects."

She tipped her head, clearly not following. "Shiny objects?"

Who knew if Jessica's coveted doctor filled the same bill as his father? Their actions—at least on paper—were similar. "No matter where he is," Cutter lifted a brow meaningfully, "or *who* he's with, the lure of possibility is more interesting than the reality in front of him."

He studied the very beautiful, very real woman sitting by his side.

Jessica lowered her brow doubtfully. "The grass is always greener on the other side of the fence?"

"Greener grass. Shiny objects." Cutter hiked a shoulder dismissively. "It all means the same thing."

She lifted her glass and then paused, gaze locked on his, the dark melted-chocolate eyes holding him captive over her wine. She didn't look convinced. Maybe she didn't *want* to be convinced. "You can't possibly know the reasons behind the doctor's actions."

"True." Cutter leaned forward, bringing his head a little closer to hers. "But Sunshine," he said, pleased as the pulse in her neck began to bound faster. "You're gonna have to let him through that grueling prescreening process of yours and actually *meet* the guy to find out."

Jessica's eyes smoldered, but Cutter wasn't sure if she was irritated by his mocking reference to her dating rules…or disturbed by his proximity. He had a feeling it was both. The moment grew longer, the air popping with electricity, until Steve cleared his throat. Cutter turned to face him, realizing he'd forgotten the guy was in the room.

Jessica's ex had a look of intense amusement on his face as he set his beer on the coffee table and stood. "I have a business dinner I need to get to, so I'll leave you two to it," he said. "Jess, don't forget the Boys and Girls Club dinner starts at seven on Saturday." Steve crossed the small space and leaned in to kiss her on the cheek. "Good luck with your plans tonight." And as he straightened up, the look he flashed Cutter was filled with awareness, as if he was onto Cutter's strategy. "You, too."

Steve's smile added a silent *'You're going to need it.'*

CHAPTER SEVEN

As they stood in front of Puerta Sagua restaurant, the scent of tomato and garlic Cuban *sofrito* permeating the night air, Kevin smiled at Jessica. His dimples reappeared for the hundredth time that night. "Would you like to have dinner again this Saturday?"

Jessica stared up at him. The man was perfect. Interesting. Funny. Polite and articulate. And the blond, blue-eyed good looks were certainly nice. She'd been on the receiving end of several jealous looks from their waitress. And yet, throughout dinner, Jessica had compared him to Cutter with every word that came from his mouth.

After all the time she'd spent with Cutter, frustrated by his attitude and the brash words that drove her crazy, she couldn't even get a rest while out on a date. In his absence, her mind had been supplying all the sarcastic observations he *would* have made if he'd been there. Kevin's mention of the art gallery had started it, and the next thing she knew she was filling in for Cutter in his absence—a Wildcard running commentary in her head.

Most distracting.

Frustrated, Jessica smiled tightly as she met Kevin's gaze. "I'll be busy this weekend." Busy figuring out how to get Cutter Thompson out from under her skin. And the desperate hope she'd be successful made her leave the door open for Kevin. "Maybe some other time?"

"I'm looking forward to it."

He leaned in, and Jessica held her breath in anticipation. This was what she'd been waiting for. The moment when all would be redeemed. But when he kissed her oh-so-lightly on the lips, she felt...

Nothing.

No sizzle. No spark.

Not even a weak hint of a faint flicker.

Annoyed with herself, she pulled back and said good-night—the irritation mounting as she watched him walk to his car at the curb, step inside and take off down the road. And the hope she'd want to see Kevin again took off in the backseat with him.

If a kiss couldn't raise her pulse even a notch above flat-line dead, what was the point?

Jessica heaved a sigh and headed for her car parked a little further up the street, ignoring the people streaming around her on the sidewalk.

Cutter had teased her for being too picky in her prescreen-ing process, but this had been the third man she'd met *face-to-face* this week. Each time the evening should have been enjoyable, but it wasn't. Every night she'd gone to bed, list-ing the favorable qualities of her date in her head, but had slipped into a sleep where her dreams were filled with Cutter. Spine-tingling, erotic dreams that left her shaking with need. Dark, dangerous dreams that left her dying to know how they ended. But she always woke way too soon, heart pounding, her body on fire and feeling unfulfilled.

Awake or asleep, it didn't matter—the man with the rare devilish grin and the cynical attitude was now constantly at her side. Either live and in the gorgeous flesh, or in her thoughts and dreams. At this rate, he would follow her to her grave.

Frowning, Jessica reached her car, unlocked it and slid into the driver's seat, pulling the door closed with a frustration-driven thunk.

It hadn't helped that Cutter had remained silent about her lack of enthusiasm after each date. Amazingly, there had been no sarcastic comments; he'd kept his opinion to himself and helped her choose her next prospect. And damn him, despite his cynicism, he'd chosen well.

In theory, each of the men Cutter had selected looked perfect. But, when presented with the reality, not one of them had clicked for her.

With a sigh, she sank back against her seat and watched the people stroll by on the sidewalk. Tourists and locals. Families and groups of friends out on the town. And then there were the couples…

And why was she enormously successful at helping others find love, but a miserable failure when it came to herself? It was the feedback from her work, the delighted clients who stopped by to thank her, that kept her going. And *hoping*. But lately she'd had moments of worry, times when a small part of her had wondered if Cutter was right about her divorce disqualifying her from her profession.

Lovely, now the man had her doubting her business skills.

But she had abundant proof that—at least professionally—she knew what she was doing. No, her biggest doubts were reserved for herself, because all her relationships had ended in failure. But unlike her female clients, those that had been treated poorly, Jessica couldn't even blame the *men*. Every one of her failed relationships had been with guys that other women dreamed about.

So what did that say about *her*?

Anxiety spread from her gut to her veins, circulating to every corner of her body. She'd held out for the good guys, invested herself and worked hard to keep the romance alive. Yet every single time it had ended, she was left questioning what had happened. Alone and wondering why. The whole it's-not-you-it's-me platitude was getting annoyingly old. It had started with Steve and continued since her divorce.

She had *zero* proof she could be successful at love, so... did that mean she was just destined to fail?

When she was alone, that soul-sucking fear was overwhelming. But now she was so massively attracted to a man who was the polar opposite of what she needed that she couldn't mount a speck of enthusiasm for anyone else. Her body was immersed in a fog of desire that clung to her whether Cutter was with her or not.

She closed her eyes and dropped her forehead to the steering wheel.

Think, Jessica. *Think*. Where is the woman famous for formulating logical plans and following through?

In an effort to cope with the sadness, the day her divorce was finalized she'd mapped out her goals for the future. She'd done it before. She could do it now.

So how did a woman purge a diabolically sexy man from her thoughts? Jessica nibbled on her lip, considering her options. Denying herself hadn't helped. Pretending the attraction didn't exist and trying to move on hadn't worked. And if her body's lack of response to the fabulous Kevin was any indication, she was in serious trouble. So maybe she needed to get Cutter out of her system? Scour away his influence over her by discovering what sex would be like with the bad boy with a bad attitude. End the mystery, once and for all.

The possibility set her heart pumping in a way full-frontal contact with Kevin never could. Maybe it was time to shut off her brain and heart and indulge the body. Just once. She'd never had a one-night stand in her life, had never even wanted one before. Yes, she'd have to deal with Cutter until the contest was over. But she was an intelligent, sophisticated woman. She could handle it.

More importantly, she *had* to handle it.

Because deep down she feared that if she didn't exorcise Cutter from her thoughts, she'd be stuck in this sensual limbo forever. Wanting him for the rest of her life.

Heart thumping like a wild thing, Jessica started her car and pulled out into the street, heading for Cutter's.

Kneeling on the floor of the 'Cuda, Cutter gave the bolt on the driver's seat one more wrench until, satisfied it was secure, he settled onto the passenger bench lining the back of the car, admiring his handiwork.

"Cutter?"

Jessica's voice toppled his thoughts, scattering them. "In here."

Her elbows rested on the door frame as her face appeared in the window. "Why are you sitting here without music?"

"Wasn't in the mood."

The small smile on her face didn't quite reach her eyes, and he wondered why. "Is Springsteen losing his charm?"

"Just preferred silence."

Actually, Cutter had been so busy lately he'd forgotten his need for loud music. He'd installed the carburetor, purchased new tires and today he'd mounted them—leaving his hand weak and his chest throbbing from the heavy lifting. The remainder of his time this week had been spent researching his idea for a new business venture. It was turning out to be more viable than he'd thought. Overall, Cutter was pleased with his progress towards taking back his life.

But not nearly as pleased as he was to see Jessica.

And therein lay the problem.

He studied her for a moment, wondering why she looked distracted. "Your date ended early." No surprise there. If he'd known how safe it was to shove her in the direction of other men, he might have come up with the plan earlier. When she didn't reply, he went on. "What was wrong with Kevin?"

His question brought a slight frown to her lips and she

stared at him a moment more, as if about to protest she'd found anything wrong at all. But she always did. Which, in some ways, he found extraordinarily amusing.

All those do-gooders and not one had captured her interest.

The three successful men had been well-rounded, charmingly funny in their emails and good-looking. One owned several hip hotels that were so cool they'd landed him on the cover of *Entrepreneur* magazine. Hell, Cutter would have dated the man himself—if he'd been oriented in that direction, of course. Which he wasn't.

Jessica opened the car and climbed in to sit beside him, pulling the door shut with a thump and tossing her purse on the seat. Her seductive scent closed in around him. Surprised by her actions, he swept his gaze down and took in the sight. Breasts outlined by her silk blouse, a skirt that ended midthigh, offering him an eyeful of bare skin. Yeah, he was definitely firmly oriented in the female direction.

Most notably *this* female.

But why did she look so disturbed?

She stared at the front seat, as though a great secret was embossed in the black leather. With a deep inhalation, she opened her mouth and then paused, biting her lower lip. When she blew out a breath, her words came out in a rush. "I've decided to engage in the first one-night stand of my life."

Comprehension hit him hard, and there was a collective groan of 'about damn time' in his every molecule. The pain in his ribs faded as desire, the living entity that had consumed him for days, throbbed to new heights. He wanted her more than he'd ever wanted a woman in his life.

But the depth of his desire was another snag he hadn't counted on.

And as her words *one-night stand* settled deeper, as if she was already prepared to move on before she'd even experienced what they could share, Cutter frowned—bothered by the limitation she'd set before they'd even started. She'd assumed it wouldn't be good enough to make her want more.

She was writing the whole thing off before the first taste.

Her silky blouse was a brilliant red that made her brown eyes brighter and her skin glow. She looked at him expectantly as his fierce need battled his growing impatience, both with her…and with himself for wanting her so much.

As the seconds ticked by without him responding, she lifted both eyebrows. "Aren't you going to say anything?"

He shifted in his seat to face her. "I'm thinking."

He was pondering how it felt to have this woman change her mind. But not by much. Clearly, he still wanted her more than she wanted him. And he hated being left holding the short end of the stick. Old resentments flared, and it was impossible to ignore that hard-earned childhood lesson.

Never invest yourself in someone who wasn't invested in you.

A furrow appeared between her brows, a faint frown on her lips. "Last week you were trying to convince me to skip out on my date and spend the night in your bed."

The need to needle was strong, and he feigned surprise. "So I'm the lucky recipient of your decision?"

She looked at him as if he were crazy. "Would I come here to tell you I was going against my usual good sense with someone *else?*"

He bit back a bitter laugh at her statement. The woman based her life's work on fostering honest dialogue. And she wasn't sparing his ego now. "Maybe I've decided I don't want to be your consolation prize while you look for something better."

Her frown grew deeper, as if refuting his statement. "It's not about a better man. It's about finding the right one for me."

He lifted a brow dryly. "I hate to break it to you, but your paint-by-numbers approach to selecting a guy won't work."

He considered it a moment more as a new thought washed over him. "Could be the whole reason you're attracted to me is because you consider me unattainable." And the idea wasn't comforting—to be wanted not because of who you were, but because of what you weren't.

"That is not why I find you attractive," she said.

Despite his doubts, the words brought a measure of male satisfaction. But watching her so obviously not wanting to want him was hell. He should teach her a lesson, tell her to go away and come back when she was *really* ready.

But it appeared he'd been damned as a kid and now he was damned as an adult.

Because, even though his ego had taken a hit, he wanted her to stay. Desire was winning the war inside, but he refused to roll over and make it easy for her. If she wanted him enough for *one* night—his gut burned at her limiting assumption— then he'd make her affirm her actions every step of the way.

"Why *do* you find me attractive?" Cutter finally responded.

Staring at Cutter, Jessica's mind scrambled for a response. She'd been asking herself the same question since their first ride on his boat—when she'd wondered what kissing him would be like. And after the soul-wrenching decision to chase him down, to go against every plan she'd laid out the horrible day her divorce was finalized, here he was looking unhappy with her decision.

He'd looked down her shirt during their first Battle of the Sexes session. He'd seduced her beside shark-infested waters and the moment had sizzled in her memories since. So where was *that* guy? The one who had unsnapped his jeans in his bathroom, lust in his eyes, and stepped closer, telling her to let him know when she changed her mind. Well, she finally had, and this was his response?

She bit her lower lip, swimming in a mix of desire and doubt. She'd assumed all she would have to do was tell him,

'Take me, I'm yours,' and he would. But nothing about this encounter was going as expected, leaving her unnerved.

Cutter threw his arm along the back of the seat. "Well?"

Her breaths came faster. "Well what?"

"Aren't you going to seduce me?"

The question knocked her hard, and the jolt to her nervous system probably guaranteed she wouldn't sleep for a month. Jessica gaped at his face. There was no tease in his expression. No subtle smirk that meant he was messing with her. His expression was serious as he waited…and comprehension arrived with a bang.

Oh. My. God. He was going to make *her* do all the work.

Asserting herself sexually within a comfortable, secure relationship was one thing, but in a casual encounter? The kind she'd never had before?

The frank gaze proved too much, and she dropped her attention to her suede skirt, drawing circles in the velvety nap. For the first time in her life she'd made a plan she wasn't sure she could carry out.

His voice was low. "Changing your mind?"

Her finger stalled on her skirt as she looked up. Arms crossed, Cutter was studying her. His musky scent, and the sight of all that masculine beauty, hard and unyielding, stretched her desire tight. And he looked as if he'd wait all night before he'd make the first move.

Her eyes dropped to the gorgeous biceps that fired her imagination with their perfection—powerful without being too bulky. His green eyes glittered with restrained desire, and the cropped brown hair looked as if he'd recently swiped a frustrated hand through it.

All the raw, edgy energy pulsing beneath his surface was evident in his face, driving the heat from her belly to her inner thighs. Time slowed, filled with the sound of their breathing and the smell of his musky soap. Cutter's gaze shifted to her mouth….

And the embers in her gut flared to beads-of-sweat-producing levels.

He'd kissed his first girlfriend in this backseat. Had they made love here as well? But the real question was—did Jessica have the guts to push him to make love to *her?*

Thighs trembling, the mental imagery consumed her and drove Jessica to ignore her doubts. She reached out to lay a palm on his chest, splaying her fingers over hard muscles. Absorbing his heat.

The ever-present glimmer in his eyes intensified. "Sunshine." The words rumbled beneath her hand. "Just be sure this isn't about your frustration that you can't find whatever the hell it is you're looking for."

"It's not."

He hesitated a moment. "And I don't want you turning to me out of sadness either."

She sensed a crack in his resolve. Hope—and the firm chest—made her bolder, and she sent him a faint, teasing smile. "What emotion am I allowed?"

Her thumping heart marked out the passage of time until a trace of return humor touched his face—shortening the leash on her fears and lengthening her need.

His gruff voice skittered up her spine. "Desire is always welcome."

The words tipped the scales heavily in favor of desire. Biting her lip, she considered her options. The delicious sight of denim-covered thighs and a visible erection simplified her decision. She wanted him close. Wiggling her hips, Jessica hiked up her skirt, threw her leg over his lap, and straddled him, her body softening at the feel of steely thighs. Amused by the surprise—and spark—in Cutter's eyes, she said, "That's good to know."

Cutter looked up at her with a laser-like gaze, arms still at his sides, forcing her to continue.

Every cell taut with tension, she tried again, placing both

hands on his chest. She smoothed her palms down his torso, relishing the ripples and longing to unzip his jeans. But right now her fingers were shaky from nerves. Perhaps teasing him would loosen his restraint. "This is your chance to prove to me that great sex is better than discussing common interests."

His eyes smoldered as her hands explored his flat abdomen, but his expression didn't budge. "Didn't I do that already?"

Jessica's limbs grew heavy with the memory, her body burning for his touch. "That was just an appetizer," she said softly, her gaze holding his. Hoping she could *will* him into taking action. "I want the full meal."

His eyes grew dark, going from close-to-the-shore sea green to over-her-head jade, and, desperate for a response, Jessica placed her mouth on his.

The kiss was vastly different from the one at the Aquarium. She'd initiated this one, and she continued to work on persuading the man to join in. A barely there pressure of soft lips against unconvinced firm ones, as if he still wanted more from her, but the feel, the taste and all his coiled energy drove her wild. And any lingering uncertainty began to drop by the wayside. After years of dedication to her well-laid-out plans, after all the worries that had plagued her since her divorce, right now she was sure of only one thing: There was no one she'd rather toss caution aside for than Cutter.

Her breath mingled with his as she teased and tasted her way from one corner of his mouth to the other, coaxing him to participate. His thighs were hard between hers, his chest a solid wall beneath her worshipping hands. And his mouth began to shift slightly, tasting her back. But he didn't touch her.

Dissatisfied with his lack of involvement, outside of his almost reluctant mouth, she ran her tongue along his lip, and Cutter inhaled sharply. With a muttered curse, he finally grasped her arms. But instead of pulling her closer, the way she wanted, he pushed her back several inches, his expression going from restrained desire to serious—and she nearly groaned in frustration.

"I still don't fit your profile, Jessica."

She stared at him, her head swirling with need. She knew what he meant. He didn't believe in happily ever after. He thought true love was a joke. He could make her laugh with a cynical comment, tease her—he'd even sleep with her…but he wouldn't give her a commitment.

Her heart thumped with desire even as her uneasiness grew. But Jessica was tired of holding her breath, waiting for the fascination she had for him to fade.

Most of all, she was tired of wanting this man and not having him.

"All I have to know is—" her finger traced the moisture left by her tongue on his lower lip "—how are you at undoing buttons?"

Eyes on hers, he held her arms as his thumbs stroked her skin, sending electrifying messages. "Slower than I used to be."

Jessica raised her hands to the front of her blouse. "Then I'll undo mine." She started at the top, slipping buttons through the holes. When her bra-enhanced cleavage came into view, Cutter's gaze dropped to her chest, and fire shot between her legs.

"I'll sleep with you." His words throbbed with energy, sapping the moisture from her mouth. "But I won't start boning up on my current events."

Encouraged, fingers still working on her shirt, she bared more skin. "How are you on foreign films?"

His voice grew tight. "I could probably fake a conversation about fine wine."

She finished the last button. "Are you up for Picasso yet?" She slipped her blouse to the floor, her satin bra the only barrier left.

This time his voice was husky, his eyes hungry, but the words were detached. "Picasso was the Paris Hilton of his time. Way overrated."

Jessica had to smile at the man with the blunt words, killer good-looks and well-cut physique. Despite his casual remark, the dark, restless potential surrounded him like an aura, boldly pushing her out of her comfort area. He was a lethally potent mix. Afraid her false courage would fail, she quickly unhooked her bra and dropped it to the floorboard.

"Jessica…" Complete capitulation looked close at hand as his gaze roved every inch of her bared breasts, scorching her skin.

Heart soaring from his look, she basked in the first full drop of what she hoped was the beginnings of enough water to save a woman dying of thirst.

And she was dying for *him*.

Too eager to linger, Jessica slid his shirt up his chest. And though Cutter raised his arms to help, with his back pressed against the seat, removing the fabric was difficult. The tantalizingly limited view of lean abdomen and muscular chest taunted her. Growing impatient, she tugged harder, trying to work the cotton higher.

Arms lifted, T-shirt caught around his shoulders, Cutter infuriated her with the amused light in his eyes. "You in a hurry?"

Her hands paused. "Yes," she said, unable to keep the irritation from her voice. The seduction wasn't going as fast as she'd hoped. "And you could be a little more helpful."

Almost smiling, Cutter leaned forward, finally giving Jessica room to jerk the fabric over his head.

"I should have planned for bigger quarters," she said.

"I figured you'd like the romantic tradition of a backseat."

She tossed his shirt aside, planting her hands on her hips. "Are you ever going to make love to me?"

Without a word, he pulled her close, his mouth landing on

hers with decisive force, giving her a heavenly taste of the hard lips she craved. Raw. Rough. And powerful. His hands kneaded her lower back, fueling her desire, and she melted against him, relieved he'd finally taken over.

His chest hair tickled the sensitized tips of her breasts, and Jessica moaned against his mouth, relishing the feel of the firm muscles she'd battled his shirt for. The moment lingered. Pleasure took a firmer hold. And grew stronger when Cutter's hands abandoned her back for her legs. As he pushed her skirt higher, his thumbs raked her inner thighs, searing her skin, creating an achy longing.

While his hot, wet mouth consumed hers, his thumb reached her underwear-covered clitoris and stroked once, eliciting a jolt of lightning, and Jessica bolted upright, her hands shooting to the ceiling of the car.

Cutter stared up at her, caressing her through the silk. Hands braced against the top of the 'Cuda, she closed her eyes as the agonizing pleasure wound her tighter, her undies growing damp.

His thumb taunted. Teased. Until she was so slick she feared she'd spontaneously combust before they actually had sex. "Cutter," Jessica groaned, lifting her lids to look at him. "I can't wait anymore."

His gazed burned into hers. "Then do something about it." Her stomach swerved lower and her breath caught. His voice rough, he continued. "This is your show."

Her show. Her choice. Her decision. And he was forcing her to confirm it over and over again. So much for Cutter making it easy. But his thumb continued to slay her bit by bit, and she was shaking with the need to be filled by this man.

Willing herself to focus despite the haze of pleasure, Jessica reached into her purse on the seat, pulling out one of the condoms she'd purchased on the way here. Her hands shook with barely contained impatience. And *desire*. Horribly conscious of her trembling fingers, she ripped the package open and the condom fell to Cutter's lap. Jessica stared mutely at the latex lying next to his denim-covered bulge.

A blatant visual of the reality of her decadent, self-indulgent decision.

After a heart-pounding pause, Cutter muttered, "Sunshine, condoms won't work that way."

Despite his measured response, she sensed his need, encouraging her to release his snap and the zipper, her knuckles grazing his hard erection. Cutter shuddered with a small groan, and the reaction was gratifying. Growing more confident, she stroked his shaft, marveling at the soft skin.

The impossibly hard length.

Her wet sex throbbing with urgency, Jessica sheathed him in latex and lifted her hips, aiming his erection between her legs. But as she pulled her panties to the side, Cutter made the final decision for her and arched up.

Plunging deep.

Jessica cried out in relief and dropped her head back, relishing the delicious stretch as, hands gripping her hips, he pulled back and filled her again. And again. Cutter's hard thrusts and languid pace were a blend of sweet ecstasy and delicious torment. Overwhelmed, she closed her eyes and braced her hands on the ceiling again, nails digging into the fabric from the pleasure, praying he'd end the torture soon.

Jaw clenched, Cutter fought to control his breathing, clasping Jessica firmly as he moved beneath her. Their hips rocked with a single intent, straining in unison, the rhythm slow, yet powerful. Purposeful. His need was strong, and though the temptation to take her fast was just as urgent, Cutter held back.

Used to be, patience wouldn't have been an option. But he'd learned the value of it recently. And if one night was all he'd get, he wanted to savor every moment. Bask in every sensation. For the first time in his life, he didn't want to come and go in a rush. And after twelve years of pushing himself to go faster, jockeying for every advantage, reveling in the thrill of barreling at high speeds towards the peak of the ultimate adrenaline rush—both on and off the track—the discovery of the pleasures in a more measured pace was a revelation.

The sight of her lovely body and their undulating hips was too much, and he cupped her breasts, urging her closer for a kiss, slanting his mouth across hers. Her hair framed his face, a silky curtain that smelled of apples and a spice he couldn't identify.

Her softness, sweet fragrance and the satiny feel of her skin contrasted sharply with his hard edges. Despite the contrast they blended well. He was used to being alone, and never had he felt so in sync with another human being. Of all the sexual experiences Cutter had enjoyed, the encounters had never been more than a simple exchange of satisfaction between two people. With Jessica, it was infinitely more, and in some ways that made him uneasy as hell.

Their breathing grew rough, ragged, and Jessica pulled her mouth from his, clutching his shoulders, her exotic eyes dark and desperate. Her whispers urged him on. But even this close to the climax, he was determined to wring every ounce of pleasure from the moment. Instead of increasing his pace, he shifted his hands to the small of her back, increasing the force and intensity of his thrusts. Arching higher. Deepening the contact. Slow, heavy, demanding strokes that pushed the edges of the pending orgasm until it built so high it towered with a frightening promise.

Jessica's nails bit into his shoulders. "Cutter—" Her voice choked on his name.

And he knew. With her shattered look, and her tremble of need, he knew. She felt the massive potential too, and intense satisfaction surged inside him. With every buck of his hips he drove them higher, reminding her that—*yes*—she desired him as much as he desired her.

With every hard thrust, he pushed the ecstasy further, making *sure* she'd never deny it.

Until, both their bodies damp with sweat, Jessica sobbed his name just before she tensed, letting out a shout as she came. The energy pulsed from her muscles to his, toppling his waiting orgasm, pleasure wracking his body.

CHAPTER EIGHT

Two days later the small reception room of Perfect Pairs was crowded, a dozen divorce-group attendees filling the leather couches. It was Jessica's largest turnout since she'd started hosting the meetings five years ago, but her face strained to maintain a smile. When the hour was finally up, instead of lingering over the goodbyes, she retreated into her office, grateful it was done.

Jessica slumped into the chair at her desk, kneading the tension in her temples—every muscle taut since she'd said an awkward goodbye and shot from Cutter's car like the hounds of Hades were hot on her heels.

She should have seen it coming. Until Cutter, all her sexual partners had been involved with her in a committed relationship, and stepping outside that safe domain had been harder than she'd imagined. So when the self-conscious morning after—or, in this case, the moment after—arrived, she'd panicked. Freaked, actually.

And she kept remembering the stunned 'what the hell' look on Cutter's face as she'd fumbled for her blouse before bolting from the car.

Embarrassment hit again. "Oh, God," she groaned, dropping her head to her hands.

She was a confident adult, why had she acted like an awkward fool? Logic and reason were supposed to be her specialties, so why couldn't she have maintained her cool?

Stupid questions, because she knew the answer. Everything about making love to Cutter had come as a surprise. From his initial reluctance to his attitude to the way he'd refused to be hurried. He was a former race-car driver, for God's sake.

So where had been his need for speed? Why hadn't he come and gone in a heated rush?

Deep down, that was what she'd expected when she'd hunted him down. A hard, fast hit of satisfaction. Get in. Get out. And then get *on* with her life.

Instead, he'd taken her with deliberate intent, the intensity overwhelming. Towards the last few deliciously agonizing moments, it was as if he'd sensed her sudden need to hurry it along, to end the torture of feeling so *much*. But he'd purposefully prolonged every little sliver of pleasure until she'd thought she'd die.

And then she had…experiencing the most mind-shattering orgasm of her life.

Memory moved through her, drowning her in desire, and Jessica closed her eyes. She'd never sobbed anyone's name during sex before. Or shouted it out for that matter.

But this time, she'd done both.

"Jessica," a familiar female voice called, and Jessica's heart settled lower in her chest.

Oh, lovely. Fate wasn't done with her tonight. It had shown up to twist the knife and finish her off. Nice.

With another forced smile, Jessica looked up at her office doorway. Susan—a regular support-group attendee after each of her four divorces—was a vivacious, fortysomething brunette who excelled at ending a marriage.

"I came to return this." Susan held out the book *Twelve Steps to Better Intimacy.* "Thanks for loaning it to me."

Jessica rose and rounded her desk, taking the self-help guide. "My pleasure." She slid the hardcover back into her packed bookcase, hoping the woman would sense she was in the midst of a crisis and leave.

But fate twisted the knife harder.

Susan paused, shifting on her feet. As if she had something important to say. "Marrying the men I had affairs with hasn't worked out well." Jessica froze. With a sheepish smile, Susan shrugged. "I guess following the sex wasn't the wisest decision." Jessica's decision to sleep with Cutter made maintaining the calm expression difficult, but she persevered as Susan went on. "But listening to you share your goals has really motivated me to make some changes."

"I didn't do anything," Jessica said. Oh, but she had. She'd glibly assumed she was stronger and smarter than Susan. But is that how people like her got started? One hot, intensity-filled moment at a time? Feeling like a fraud, she said, "I simply suggested a book when you asked for a recommendation."

Susan shook her head. "No, it's your levelheaded dedication to holding out for the right relationship that's inspired me." The irony was so heavy Jessica could barely withstand the weight as Susan continued. "I just wanted you to know I've decided to follow your example."

Jessica bit back the hysterical laughter, hating her new role as a hypocrite as Susan said good-bye. When she left, Jessica sank into her chair.

Where had that levelheaded Jessica gone? She'd been slowly disappearing since Cutter upended her life. Had she really thought sex with him would make things better? Her mind scrambled for a reassuring platitude…but nothing seemed appropriate.

Except maybe the one about hindsight and clarity of vision.

The second she'd returned from orbit and landed back in that car, she'd known Cutter had smashed her plans for exorcising him from her system.

Worse, he was more embedded in her mind than before. The memory of his body seared into hers. And why was the man she'd tossed out her rules for—the one so wholly un-suitable—why was *that* the guy who gave her the greatest pleasure?

For the love of God, he'd had her howling his *name*.

With a growing apprehension, her stomach writhed with nerves. One week and two Battle of the Sexes sessions left to go. And for the first time in her life, Jessica wondered if there was a plan that would save her.

The white paint on Cutter's home reflected the brilliant Florida sun, emphasizing the lines that formed the right angles of the contemporary architecture. Nothing soft. No rounded corners.

Just like the man himself.

After climbing the flight of steps to the second-floor en-tryway, Jessica glanced anxiously at the doorbell. How long could she stare at the intricate details of the etched glass around the door before he'd find her standing there like a silly coward?

She nervously fingered the strap of her casual halter dress. The bright colors were supposed to inspire confidence, but it wasn't working. When she caught herself staring at the door-bell again, she grunted in disgust and pushed the button.

You can do it, Jessica. Just get the contest done. You don't need a plan beyond that. And just try *to pretend—*

The door opened and Cutter came into view, knocking her pep talk from her head.

She had no idea what he was thinking, the hard planes of his face impassive as he leaned in the doorway, hands hooked on his hips. The snug jeans and black T-shirt left little to the imagination—except she had no need for one now. She had memories scorched so heavily on her brain they'd never be scrubbed away. The waves of brown hair were damp, as if he'd just showered, and he eyed her dryly. "You're back."

His statement, and the look in his green eyes, only served to remind her of how she'd left, and heat slid up her spine. "Of course I am." In an attempt to appear unflustered, she sent him a cool smile. "We have work to do."

"Oh, yeah," he said with a hint of sarcasm. "The Battle of the Sexes."

He stepped aside to let her pass. She felt his gaze on her as her high heels tapped against the hardwood leading to his modern living room. The expansive floor-to-ceiling windows displayed the sparkling Biscayne Bay as if it were a tropical mural painted on the wall. Sunlight streamed inside, glinting off the glass-and-chrome accents in the room. Jessica studied the contemporary furniture, trying to decide where to sit. The leather couch implied intimacy, and she couldn't stand around like a fool forever, so she targeted the mahogany bar in the corner.

Cutter's voice came from behind as he followed. "I thought you were here to finish my promised one-night stand."

Her body flooded with memory, fire pooling between her legs, and she almost tripped on the plush rug. She climbed onto a bar stool, resting her overheated palms on the cold marble as he rounded to the other side. When he braced his hands on the counter, his biceps grew more defined, and her body hummed the familiar tune of desire. She held her tongue as he gazed at her expectantly.

And Jessica fought to remain calm in the face of the world's most perfect male storm.

"Or was the 'Cuda all the night I'm allowed?" he finally went on.

Keen to hear Jessica's reply, Cutter raised an eyebrow wryly and waited. The tense look on her face would have been vaguely amusing if he wasn't so worked up himself.

When she spoke, there was no answer to his question. "May I have a drink?"

He pursed his lips and studied her. Silky brunette hair hung in waves to bare shoulders, and her dark eyes looked troubled. The halter top of her dress clung to the breasts that had haunted his dreams since the 'Cuda, and lust returned with a vengeance to his veins.

He could definitely use a drink.

"All I have is beer." He sent her a pointed look. "And I can't guarantee the temperature."

"Anything above freezing and below the boiling point will do."

Cutter turned toward the small refrigerator, grateful for a moment to cool down. In the two nights since he'd made love to Jessica, his sleep had been sketchy. Whatever parts weren't taken up with erotic dreams of the two of them had been spent reliving the lead-up to his accident. He'd woken repeatedly, heart pumping, body sweating, either from a wicked dream about Jessica or from anticipating his crash.

He was no closer to recovering those missing moments surrounding his wreck. And for the life of him, he couldn't figure out why she'd bolted from his car.

The memory of her taking off—and the old, familiar sensation of being left behind—curdled in his stomach like sour milk as he pulled two bottles of beer from the refrigerator, closing it with a thump.

He twisted off the lids, set her beer on the counter, and tried to pin down the escape artist with his gaze. "I'd love to know where on your long list of rules it states dashing off after sex is polite."

Or that coming back just for a lame publicity stunt was okay. Because when she'd given her reason for returning, he realized he'd been hoping she was here to see him. He gripped his cold bottle.

Man, was he a glutton for punishment.

She nervously feathered her fingers through her hair, the Bambi eyes wary, as if he'd just whipped out a gun. "Dashing off isn't on my list." Color touched her cheeks, making her complexion glow, and a small frown appeared. "Then again, neither is sex just for fun."

His eyebrows shot higher. "Fun?" Of all the things he'd felt while making love to Jessica, lighthearted fun wasn't one of them. "That's not the word I would use." Intense pleasure, yes. Immeasurable satisfaction, absolutely. Life-altering, spine-tingling orgasm, hell yeah.

And being left alone as he watched her take off didn't meet his criteria for fun either.

"I told you before, Cutter," she said. "I don't engage in meaningless sexual exploits."

Meaningless. He leaned closer, his gaze intent on her face, his stomach churning harder now. "Sunshine," he said. "Just because I don't believe in forever doesn't mean what we shared was trivial."

"I didn't say it was trivial."

"Sounds like you did to me."

"You're twisting my words."

He paused, realizing he was asking for more frustration… but he had to know. "Then what is your problem?"

Her lips pressed flat, and her creamy, delicious shoulders slumped a little. "I'm just…" She closed her eyes and rubbed her forehead. "Disappointed in myself."

The statement slammed into him. She wore a look of misery—a feeling he was sure she felt all the way from her sooty black lashes to her pretty, cinnamon-colored toes. And her demeanor made him feel like shit. Just one more layer of hell this lady was heaping upon him.

"Why?" he said.

Cutter waited to hear how he wasn't her usual choice. How a rebelliously bad-mannered, blue-jean-sportin' guy with a surly attitude wasn't on her wish list. Or how she'd always chosen dates like Kevin, successful men who spent their time being nice. Polite. And so charitable they made Cutter's teeth hurt.

"No sex without an emotional investment," she said. The look on her face grew more troubled. "I broke one of my most important rules."

Once again, Jessica's response surprised him, and the doubtful skepticism was hard to contain. "What is it with you and these rules?"

The pulse in her lovely neck bounded hard, as if fighting to break free. "Can we just get on with the competition?"

Cutter stared at her, considering his next move, stumped by her fixation with guidelines that guaranteed to suck all hope for spontaneity in life. The lady was clearly disturbed about their backseat rendezvous, but he was beginning to believe it was about more than *just* him.

And if she insisted on ignoring the issues and proceeding with the competition, so be it.

An idea formed in his head, and he reached into his pocket and pulled out his cellular. "Tell you what." His thumbs wrestled with the tiny keyboard, the weak one on the left and the non-dominant on his right clumsily performing their tasks, but he pushed the irritation aside. "Why don't we let our contestants chime in on the subject?"

Jessica's voice was two octaves higher than normal, with a healthy dose of concern. "What are you typing?"

Cutter finished his text and looked at her. "I asked if an emotional commitment was a requirement for a physical relationship, and why or why not."

She stared at him with such a mixed bag of emotion, Cutter wasn't sure if she was about to laugh, cry or run screaming from the room in frustration.

He knew exactly how she felt.

"Listen…" Cutter slid his phone into his pocket. "I haven't eaten dinner." He picked up the two untouched bottles of beer.

"Let's take our drinks to the kitchen and rummage up some food while we wait for our contestants to respond."

Damage control.

That's what she should be working on. How to fix Cutter's ridiculous post. How to straighten out her life after getting so thoroughly distracted. But even more pressing, how to convince her body to pay attention to all the worries swirling in her head.

Apparently her body refused to care.

Because, after twenty minutes in Cutter's kitchen of rich wood and pricey appliances of stainless steel, Jessica still had no idea how to exercise that damage control. Or had even pondered it, for that matter. But she *had* managed to repeatedly peek at Cutter from the corner of her eye to admire his form. He'd been silently cooking steaks on the indoor grill, infusing the air with the smell of sizzling beef, while she'd been at the granite countertop arranging a salad. But the paucity of fresh vegetables in Cutter's refrigerator was hindering her efforts. She headed for the fridge to make another sweep for something appropriate when she spied a pamphlet on the counter.

Jessica picked up the real-estate brochure with the picture of a sleek, metal warehouse in an upscale industrial park. Intrigued, she finally gathered the courage to break the silence.

She turned to face Cutter. "What is this?"

"It's the building I just bought."

Surprised, she stared at him, the brochure hanging from her fingertips. Property like that cost a hefty sum. Not exactly a purchase one made on a whim. Jessica's curiosity rose exponentially. "What are you going to do with it?"

He continued with his task at the grill. "I'm starting up my own business," he said, as if his statement was no big deal.

But it was. She'd seen the look on his face as he'd struggled to face what came next in his life. When he didn't go on, she said, "Do I at least get to hear what the business is?"

Cutter lifted the steaks onto a plate, set them aside and cut off the grill. "I contacted a buddy of mine who used to work as a mechanic on my team before he retired. Turns out he's bored stiff and ready for some fun." He shifted to face her, leaning a hip against the counter and crossing his arms. With the display of gorgeous muscle, Jessica almost forgot to listen. "I'm going to open a garage that specializes in modifying cars for amateur racers."

She tipped her head curiously. "What kind of modifications?"

"Those that improve the vehicles' performance and efficiency." For the first time since he'd started his story, a spark appeared in his eyes. "Which basically means Karl and I get to soup them up so they go faster."

His first hint of a grin reminded Jessica how devastatingly beautiful he was when he smiled—or came close to smiling, anyway—and she tried hard not to gape at him. She was enormously pleased he was moving on with his life, but she was also taken by his mood. She could sense his anticipation, his excitement about the new opportunity. And the only other time she'd seen those emotions in Cutter was when he'd made love to her.

Hot memories of them steaming up the 'Cuda's windows left Jessica struggling to breathe. She was saved from the treacherous thoughts when Cutter's cellular beeped.

He pulled the phone from his pocket, checking the message. "It's Calamity Jane."

Her heart felt as if it had been tossed an anvil to catch. "Oh, for the love of God," Jessica said. "Not her." When he opened his mouth to speak, she held up a hand. "Don't tell me." She dropped her arm to her side. "You just asked if an emotional commitment was a requirement for a physical relationship." Jessica briefly lifted her gaze heavenward. "Of *course* she said no."

"Technically," he said, his mouth twisting dryly. "Her reply is: *hell no*."

She narrowed her eyes at him. "Are you two in cahoots?"

His brow crinkled in curiosity. "What do you have against Calamity?"

The question hit too close to home, and she carefully set the brochure clutched in her hand onto the counter, buying some time. Because what was she supposed to say? That the woman made her feel dull? Uninspiring? Because her past sexual experiences, including her marriage, had fallen within the confines of a certain…respectability.

When she looked up, she was surprised to find Cutter now standing two feet away. Jessica's heart rate responded accordingly. His intent expression wasn't reassuring either. There would be no escaping this conversation.

When she didn't answer his question, he tried another. "Why did you take off the other night?" he said.

She'd hoped he'd let the matter slide without further discussion, but that dream died with his words. She should have known he would demand honesty.

"Cutter," she said, leaning her back against the refrigerator. "All my relationships have been with men who have made me feel…" She struggled to find the appropriate word. "Safe," she finally finished. It was the truth, and she had no one to blame except herself, because she'd always chosen her relationships for that very reason. But not this time. She frowned, nibbling on her lip and remembering her cries in the 'Cuda. "But you make me feel…"

When her voice died out a second time, Cutter leaned closer, the proximity doing nothing to ease her heart rate. "Sunshine," he said, his voice low, "what do I make you feel?"

She fought to hold his heated gaze. "Like I don't know what to expect next. I *hate* that feeling."

And exploring the spaces outside her usual safe zone—or more like running around it with scissors in her hand—was too open-ended for comfort.

"I built a whole career out of pushing boundaries," he said. "There is nothing wrong with setting your worries aside and going with your gut."

"Yes," she said adamantly. "There is." His eyes were fixed on her, and he smelled of the musky soap that had filled the 'Cuda when they'd made love. The memory weakened her resolve, and she shifted her gaze to his chin, trying to breathe. To *think*.

Flustered, Jessica pushed her hair from her forehead, deciding the truth was the only way to go. "I still remember every detail of the day my divorce was finalized." Cutter's body stilled, his face guarded, yet she could tell he was listening carefully. Good. "The lawyer's office was on the top floor of a downtown Miami skyscraper. The sun was shining. The sky was blue. And the view of the Atlantic was beautiful. *Everything* was beautiful, yet I had this horrible, awful feeling of failure. And I was sitting there, amongst all that beauty, thinking…how did this happen?" She fisted her hand, the desolation washing over her again. "I invested fifteen months and worked hard to keep my marriage going. And then it was gone."

"What happened?"

Her gaze drifted to the window overlooking the bay, wishing she knew for certain. Frustrated that she *didn't*. "I think I simply chose poorly, because I needed more from Steve than he had to give, and marriage required more than he wanted to devote to it." She shrugged. "I don't know," she went on, her voice soft. "Maybe we were just too young. Maybe we wanted different things." She returned her gaze to Cutter's. "But in the end, the reason doesn't matter because there was nothing I could do about it."

Just like when her parents had split, and her family—her

life as she'd known it—had been over. She rubbed her brow, as if to erase the memory of the entire fabric of her existence changing, and being powerless to stop it. The terrible feeling of *helplessness*.

She blinked and looked up at him. "So I vowed I'd be more careful in the future. That I wouldn't set myself up for failure again."

And maintaining a measure of control in a relationship was paramount.

"There's a fine line between being cautious and living with restrictive rules that suck the enjoyment from life." He closed a bit of the gap between them. "I think you need to stop analyzing your every move and let go and live a little."

The expression in his eyes set her blood simmering. And it was the cool stainless steel of the refrigerator door at her back that kept her from collapsing.

The beep of a message came again, and Cutter glanced at the phone in his hand. When he looked up, there was a definite light in his eyes as he held up the screen. "Too Hot to Handle's reply."

Requirement is too restrictive a word. Sometimes rules are meant to be broken.

And as Cutter continued to hold her gaze, the look heavy with everything they'd shared and the achy potential for more, Jessica's body burned.

"Cutter," she said, trying to sound confident, her resolve slowly slipping away. "Blindly following your libido isn't a good idea. I've heard the stories." It sounded weak, but she didn't care. "I lead divorce-support groups where people discuss where they went wrong."

His tone left no doubt what he thought of her extracurricular activity. "You volunteer to listen to other people bitch and moan?"

She sent him an overly patient look. "Having a safe place to vent your emotions is healthy."

"Yeah," he said dryly. "But that doesn't mean you have to be the one to listen to it. That's what unsuspecting strangers are for." Cutter's frank gaze scanned her face. "Jessica, you need to relax. Quit being so…" He lifted a hand and traced her collarbone with a finger, sending delicious messages along her nerves. "Focused."

She was focused all right. On his scent. On the seductive feel of his finger. After fifteen months of marriage and two sexual relationships, it wasn't fair that one touch from Cutter lit her up like the neon lights of South Beach at night.

"Or do I have to send you out on another date to get you back in my arms again?" he said.

The sensation of his skin on hers clouded her brain, producing goose bumps and sizzling heat, and understanding rose slowly. Until it toppled over her, and she pressed her back harder against the refrigerator, her voice a squeak. "You were manipulating me?"

"'Course not," he said. His finger explored the sensitive hollow above her collarbone. "I just encouraged you to compare your options." And every one of those men had left her wanting.

More specifically, wanting more of Cutter.

"So what's it going to be?" he said. Cutter's hand paused on the tie at the back of her neck—the one that held up her bodice—and Jessica's heart almost slowed to a stop. "Safety and security?" His green eyes grew dark. "Or a little bit more of the unknown?"

CHAPTER NINE

Despite her need for comfortable control, the ache inside Jessica demanded she explore more of the unknown with Cutter. It was either that or therapy—perhaps in a detox facility specializing in brainwashing. Or maybe memory-erasing.

Heart revitalized and now thumping boldly, she stared at him, knowing she was losing the battle. But he'd made her work for him in the car, and then she'd bolted like a coward.

Pride demanded she play this round with more cool.

"Our first time was in a backseat," she said. "And now you're offering me either a countertop or a kitchen table." Not that she'd ever experienced either, but that was irrelevant. She lifted her chin. "My decision would be easier if I was presented with something more original."

Without a word he took hold of her shoulders and turned her around, placing her palms against the refrigerator, like a cop about to frisk her. Her heart rate skyrocketed. Hands covering hers, his hard thighs, chest—and harder erection—pressed against Jessica, enveloping her in steely muscle. Stunned by the wicked sensation, she forgot to breathe.

"Refrigerators are far from standard." His voice went husky at her ear. "But what turns *you* on?"

Paralyzed by an uncontrollable desire for a bad boy, she couldn't reply. And how did one play it cool while oxygen-deficient? Dizzy, she inhaled sharply. "I…"

It was a pathetic effort.

"Come on, Sunshine. For once, apply that honest dialogue to your sex life." His low, rough voice was electrifying. "What does Jessica Wilson fantasize about?"

Her body throbbed. Since they'd made love, her dark dreams had grown more vivid. Detailed. And decadent, leaving her defenseless in their wake. Cutter's form, plastered to her back, triggered her answer. But handing over that much power was impossible. "Nothing."

"Liar." And with that, he tugged on her tie and pushed her dress and panties to the floor. Her thoughts were still spinning from the sudden turn of events when Cutter shifted her two steps to the right, replanting her hands against the freezer side of the fridge. "Stay here."

And then he moved away.

Dumbfounded, Jessica blinked, feeling ridiculous wearing nothing but high heels, hands braced against an appliance. Relieved he'd let his question go, she peeked over her shoulder as Cutter returned with a dishtowel, and her eyebrows drew together in question.

He paused behind her, his gaze intense. "Do you trust me?"

Unnerved, struggling for air, she hesitated...and realized the answer was yes. The irreverent rebel was too bold, too blunt and occasionally rude, but he wouldn't hurt her.

When she nodded, Cutter said, "If we break your need for safety and security, I might get an answer to my question." He covered her eyes with the makeshift blindfold, tying it behind her head.

Sweat pricked her temples. "Cutter..." The word ended with a nervous laugh. Unable to see, she heard the refrigerator open beside her, bottles being shuffled and then the door closed. What had she signed on for? "Cutter?" her nerves stretched with curiosity and apprehension, feeling exposed. "What are you doing?"

"Starting with my fantasy about you."

Thick liquid sloshed in a container, and Jessica's stomach flopped. "That better not be hot sauce."

A rusty chuckle came from behind. "Nope." Cutter swept her hair aside. "I've thought about this since I tasted your creamy vanilla shoulders at the Aquarium."

Jessica smelled chocolate before she felt a cool drizzle on a shoulder. His finger smoothed the slick circle, sensitizing her skin, which grew worse when his mouth sampled his creation.

"Definitely the right mix of flavors," he rumbled against her.

She swallowed hard. "I think chocolate syrup qualifies as a cliché."

"Yeah." He removed his mouth from her shoulder. "It's a good one, too."

Enclosed in the dark, she wondered what would come next. Her muscles tensed when a wet finger touched her back, tracing syrup between her shoulder blades, and his mouth followed to clean the mess, searing her skin. After a pause, a chocolaty dollop hit the opposing shoulder, lips nibbling next, and Jessica sucked in a breath. A brief lull…and a syrupy finger slicked down the curve of her waist, a tongue licked it clean and perspiration pricked Jessica's neck.

Desire spiraled higher as, between each of Cutter's choices, Jessica tensed, vulnerable and sightless—waiting for what would follow. The sweet smell of chocolate, the sound of her harsh breathing and the scrape of Cutter's teeth filled her heightened senses. As the pleasure curled tighter, her visionless world condensed to the feel of Cutter, her body's response and the cool refrigerator beneath her palms.

With each new spot, he moved lower, until her body was singing. When he knelt on the floor behind her, her head spun.

"What do you dream about?" Cutter drew a line of chocolate up one buttock, across the small of her back, and down the other cheek. And then he held her hips, feeding on her flesh with his lips, tongue and teeth. Driving her mad.

Engulfing her in flames.

By the end, Jessica's need was urgent. Stronger than any reservations. More powerful than her need to maintain a little control. Cutter stood and wrapped his arms around her, his hard body plastered behind hers. One hand on her breast, teasing the tip, the other stroked between her thighs, an agonizing pressure building as hot moisture made his fingers slick.

His tone was sinfully dark. "What qualifies as original to Jessica Wilson?"

Blindfolded, trembling and desperate, the last of her cool slipped, and she gave in to the desire, pressing back against his hard shaft. "This."

Cutter went still, obviously not following her vague answer. And then understanding filled his tone. "You mean this position."

A flush heated her face. Embarrassingly enough, it was just that simple. "Yes."

Without a word, Cutter released his zipper and kneed her thighs apart. Breath frozen, heart bashing her ribs, she tipped her hips back to meet him, and Cutter plunged inside her wet folds.

With a gasp of shocked pleasure, she arched her back, damp palms braced against the chilled stainless steel in front of her. Cutter wrapped his arms back around her, leaning over her, thrusting deep again and again, fingers stroking her between the legs. His free hand captured her jaw, turned her mouth to meet his. Hard, chocolaty lips devoured hers in a moist, open-mouthed kiss.

It was just as delicious as she'd imagined, as decadent as she'd dreamed, smashing her last thoughts of control. Defenseless, caught in his strong embrace, Jessica turned herself over to the wickedly primitive need as Cutter consumed her from behind.

"Tell me again why I'm here?" Cutter said into his cellular.

Jessica's chuckle was low in his ear. "The celebrity originally scheduled to appear for the Battle of the Sexes photo op had to cancel." Her voice sounded amused. "And *you* volunteered to come in his place."

"Oh, yeah." Cutter gripped his phone. "Remind me to be more careful when you're naked in my bed." Hoping to spot Jessica, he wove his way through the throng of locals filling the new gymnasium at the Boys and Girls Club, all funded by Jessica's ex. Bleachers lined two sides, with basketball hoops mounted at either end. On the polished maple floor of the court, round tables had been set up for the grand opening dinner.

"How did the photo op go?" she said.

"I sidestepped the reporter's questions and smiled for the camera."

"You smiled?"

Cutter bit back the grin and finally spied Jessica across the crowd. Cellphone pressed against her ear, she was dressed in a denim skirt that ended a tantalizing several inches above the knees and dainty flat sandals. Despite the casual attire, she managed to look as beautiful as she had in her formal wear.

The long expanse of bare legs was definitely a winner in his book.

"Could be *smile* is an exaggeration," he said. "But I definitely managed not to be disagreeable. Which is amazing considering the torture this event is turning out to be." He threaded his way through the people and leaned against the basketball pole, ten feet from Jessica and her gorgeous display of legs. "I wouldn't have volunteered if I'd known I still had to keep my hands to myself in public."

Jessica's eyes found his from across the crowd, and she sent him a sultry smile. Despite the distance, the effect was like a wrecking ball to the gut. "As far as the guests are concerned," she said. "I'm here with Steve." She turned to the wall plastered with the simplistic artwork of kids. Hand prints. Stick figures. And the swirls of abstract finger paints. "And *we* are just friends. So remember," she went on, her voice low and exquisitely sexy, "no touching."

In the past three days and two delicious nights, they'd done a lot of touching.

After the interlude at his refrigerator, the online flirting they'd finished with the contestants had been the most stimulating to date. But trying to keep his mind on their task—much less his comments PG-rated—was damn near impossible with her lounging naked in his bed.

He looked at the poster Jessica was pretending to examine. Even from a distance, it was obvious it was by a small child, the features on the face grossly out of proportion. "That one is definitely a Picasso in the making." The responding chuckle in his ear was low. Her gauzy, off-the-shoulder blouse exposed the creamy shoulders, and the memory of the taste of her skin set his body on fire. "It's killing me that I can't touch you."

"It'll be good for you." She targeted him with her wide, brown gaze, her face glowing with humor. "Encourage a little self-discipline."

A couple strolled between them, and he waited until his line of sight cleared before speaking. "Problem is," he said. "I have none around you. And that blouse isn't helping."

"Cutter," she said. "Stop looking at me like that."

"No one knows we're talking to each other." He turned to lean his back against the pole, eyes scanning the crowd, but unable to prevent them from returning to the beautiful woman. And even though it was impossible, he swore he smelled her delicate scent. Or maybe after the past three days it was simply seared into his memory. "I figured out your smell."

She turned her profile to him, examining another poster on the wall. "What are you talking about?"

"Sweet, with a hint of cinnamon," he said. "It reminds me of apple cider."

Christ, when had he started sounding so romantic?

"That's my shampoo," she said.

He looked at her again, the woman who, if he wasn't careful, would soon have him spouting compliments and smiling like a moron. He still couldn't figure out why making love to her was different. "Can't I at least meet you secretly behind the bleachers? Just a quick kiss and a grope to get me through until dinner?"

She wrinkled her nose in what looked like an amused grimace. "FYI, the word *grope* is never associated with anything appealing."

"Is *fondle* better?"

"Most women would prefer the term *caress*."

He gripped his cellular and looked back at the crowd milling about, trying to pretend the beautiful lady didn't have his total attention. "*Caress* isn't in my vocabulary. But I'll agree to the term if you'll agree to my offer of a secret meeting."

"Not going to happen, Mr. Wildcard," she said. "We'll sit at Steve's table for dinner. But that's it for the contact."

He pursed his lips and deliberately dropped his voice to a suggestive tone. "Not even if I promise to do something spectacularly original to you?"

There was a pause on the line, and Jessica turned to look at him. Even from ten feet away he could see her gaze was hot. Every cell in his body was blitzed with an energy that left him sizzling, as if he'd been shoved in a microwave set on high.

Her voice was husky. "In that case, I might be open to hearing about your plans."

A bonfire set up residence in his gut and spread lower, and Cutter could practically see the sparks arcing in the air between them.

"Jess," a masculine voice called.

Beating his libido into submission, Cutter hit the disconnect button on his cellular and watched Jessica's ex approach her as she slipped her phone into her purse. Dressed in a sharp navy suit, Steve Brice still looked relaxed enough to blend in with the casual crowd. The dark-haired man stopped and kissed Jessica on the cheek. When Steve's gaze caught Cutter's, he steered Jessica in Cutter's direction.

"Good to see you again," Steve said as he stuck out his hand.

"Nice gym." Cutter returned the handshake.

Steve gave a no-big-deal shrug. "It helps keep the kids out of trouble."

Cutter's lips twisted at the irony. "I'm sure the community appreciates your efforts. I would have been better off spending time at my local Boys and Girls Club as a boy." Would have made his mother happy, too. She'd made it clear she'd never wanted him, and had lived to get her moody teen out of the house, not caring where he was…as long as it was somewhere else. "'Course, by the time I had my driver's license, proving I had the fastest car in the neighborhood was my only goal."

Truthfully, getting away from home had been his initial goal. And then he'd hooked up with a crowd of racers, discovering the thrill of high speeds. Beating the competition. *Winning.* The only worries he'd had were his opponent and the possibility of dying. The first had driven him to go faster.

The second hadn't scared him at all.

Steve smiled. "The whole point of the club is to keep the kids *off* the streets."

"True," Cutter said. He let out a wry scoff. "But I never was much for conformity."

The man's grin grew bigger, and his sidelong glance at his ex was less than subtle. "And how's that working out for you now?"

Cutter did his best to keep the smile from his face. "So far so good."

"You haven't caved under the pressure?" Steve said.

Cutter's lips twisted in amusement. "Not yet." Though his thoughts about Jessica's scent did make his response questionable.

Jessica glanced suspiciously from Cutter and then back to Steve. "What exactly are we discussing here?"

"I'm not sure," Steve said with a grin.

She shot Cutter a this-better-not-be-about-me look as her ex went on.

"I've got to go get this dinner started with a speech." Steve jerked his head in the direction of a podium along the far wall, amusement dancing in his eyes. "I'll let you two get back to your phone conversation now."

Steve headed off, and Cutter turned to Jessica, trying to decide which he liked more...the old standby roll-of-her-eyes-heavenward or the I-was-so-right look currently inhabiting her face now.

But he had no regrets about the phone call. "Smug becomes you."

"I knew we were being too obvious."

"How about we play footsy under the dinner table instead?"

She shot him a faux menacing look. "Only if you promise to be discreet."

"Sunshine, Mr. Discretion is my other nickname."

She turned and headed for their table, shooting him an amused, doubtful expression over her shoulder. "Come on, Wildcard. Let's see if you can live up to that misnomer."

Cutter clearly was trying to make her pay for her teasing comment.

With Steve to her left, and Cutter to her right, Jessica tried to pay attention to the conversation at the table. But it was difficult to follow the discussion with Cutter's hand on her knee. He was debating the present-day status of racing with the man sitting beside him, and all the while his thumb was stroking her thigh beneath the curtain of the tablecloth.

It made focusing impossible; she was unable to get past the delicious circles he was drawing on the skin just above her knee.

The smell of rich, spicy tomato sauce seeped into her consciousness, and Jessica finally noticed the man delivering food to a nearby group of guests. But, on closer inspection, he wasn't a man. It was a pimply-faced adolescent. She managed to refocus on her surroundings and saw a dozen or so teens, all wearing black jeans and white shirts, carrying out trays laden with plates of lasagna, distributing them to the tables.

Cutter leaned in to address Steve, allowing his tormenting hand to conveniently inch a fraction higher up her leg. Jessica shot him a warning look, but, without even a glance in Jessica's direction, Cutter addressed her ex. "I was expecting pizza or hamburgers."

Clearly oblivious to Jessica's predicament, Steve said, "The local Italian restaurant donated the food, and the teens at the club volunteered to serve the dinner."

Cutter's fingers reached her inner thigh, blistering her skin, and her heart pumped harder, sweat dotting the nape of her neck as the conversation between the two men blurred.

This kind of behavior was exactly what she'd expected from a rebel bad boy. She *should* be disturbed by the illicit thrill shooting through her veins. But she hadn't counted on enjoying the clandestine caresses of one man while the table guests assumed she was here with another.

Lovely. Next she'd be changing her slogan from 'fostering honest dialogue in finding The One' to a women's-magazine version of 'how to kink up your sex life.'

And she was beginning to question her skepticism of

Calamity Jane, because Cutter put out her fire like no man ever had.

"Mr. Thompson?" a voice called, interrupting the conversation.

Jessica looked up to see a teen who looked vaguely familiar. Shaggy dark hair brushed his shoulders, and his oversize jeans hung low on his hips, the waistband of his orange boxers barely peeking above the denim. The brown eyes were still dark, but the belligerent look from the photo Jessica had shown Cutter was tempered with an emotion that surprised her.

Adoration.

The teen stuck out a paper napkin and a pen towards Cutter. "Can I have your autograph?"

Cutter's thumb ceased its disturbing caress, and his grip on her leg grew tight with tension. She shot him a curious look, and the expression on his face was a shock. She'd seen him on TV in the past, meeting and greeting kids, and he'd always been friendly.

But this time, he had a faint frown.

Cutter's head thumped with a familiar, gnawing pain, and he stared at the kid who looked barely old enough to shave. It took five seconds for full recognition to trigger his memory.

Emmanuel. The adolescent dropout. Big fan of the Wildcard. The belligerent teen who'd gone back to finish high school with the goal of following in Cutter Thompson's footsteps.

Damn. Why would the kid still want to be a screwup like him?

Years of experience had trained Cutter how to deal with fans, but he hated the goofy, almost fanatical expression the teen was wearing. Hadn't the kid heard the news? That Cutter had pulled a reckless stunt that cost him his career?

He beat back the urge to tell the boy to scram. Struggling

to take control of his suddenly sour mood, Cutter paused until he couldn't stand the hero worship on the adolescent's face any longer.

"Sure, kid," he said gruffly. He did his best not to snatch the napkin from the boy, to hurry the process along. But the need to get him to move on about his business was hard to suppress. After scribbling his signature, he stuck the paper out, hoping this would be the end of it.

But Emmanuel, wannabe Cutter Thompson, wasn't done yet.

"I watched you bump Chester Coon on TV," he said, taking the napkin back. Cutter's head thumped harder, the pain piercing, and a wave of nausea hit as the kid continued, his eyes glowing with excitement. "Dude, it was freakin' awesome!" he said, pumping the air with a fist that was like a head-on collision with Cutter's head. "The way you slid across the finish line on your roof. *Sweet!* And still pulled off second place, too."

Bile rose in Cutter's throat as memory engulfed him, and he was back in the stock car. He could smell burning rubber, feel the heart-pounding speed, his fingers gripping the wheel.

Oblivious, Emmanuel went on, his eyes shining with hero worship. "And you were the only one brave enough to take on that dirtbag Chester Coon."

Brave.

Sweat broke out on Cutter's lip, but the teen continued with his relentless, blow-by-blow account. His whole face lit with a smile, Emmanuel said, "And you so totally *owned* that track—"

The searing pain of his crash hit like a sledgehammer. "Hey," Cutter interjected, his voice low, body seized by ache and memory. "Don't you have other guests to serve?"

Through the haze of agony, Cutter watched the kid step

back, the excitement wiped from his face. "Sure." Emmanuel's face was nonchalant, his eyes flat. "Sure thing, man."

The teen turned and headed off, and Cutter fought the violent urge to vomit. Because the kid had called him *brave*. But Cutter knew better.

In truth, maybe he'd always known better.

Head pounding with the return of his memories of the crash, he watched Emmanuel walk away with his shoulders hunched, and the cauldron of dark emotion boiled higher in Cutter's gut, charring his insides. He recognized the blank look on the kid's face. Cutter had worn it a million times himself. And the adoration, too. But his father hadn't deserved his hero worship, and Cutter sure as hell didn't deserve Emmanuel's now.

He closed his eyes as his memories of the wreck, his *emotions,* came tumbling back. There had been no self-sacrifice on his part. Cutter had simply been incensed at Chester Coon's gall, threatened by the driver's hard racing as he'd challenged Cutter for the lead. Because…that track had been *Cutter's*.

He'd taken a risky move, had lost his career, all because of his anger and conceit.

The aroma of lasagna, which had smelled so mouthwatering before, almost finished him off. Battling the nausea that was growing hotter by the minute, Cutter slowly became aware of the rest of the table.

Jessica was staring at him, wide-eyed, with a look of pure disappointment on her face, and Cutter's stomach took on the festering essence of a primordial ooze. Poisoning him from the inside out.

Shit.

She finally spoke, her tone low and laced with disapproval. "What was that all about?"

He forced his expression to remain neutral. "What?"

Jessica turned in her seat to face him. "You just crushed that kid's heart."

Amidst all the roiling emotions, another stab of guilt slashed deep. He dropped his eyes to the table and reached for his glass of iced tea, his hand clammy. "I doubt that."

"Oh, *please.*"

Cutter cleared his throat, shifting in his seat, suppressing the need to bolt. To *run* from the bitter truth. But Jessica was waiting for a response, so he tried to give her one. "Even if I did, he'll get over it." He glanced at her from the corner of his eye, and her feelings were stamped clearly in her posture. Her back looked as if she had just traded her spine for an axle.

And although her words came out quietly, the low tone did nothing to detract from their impact. "That boy looks up to you."

Cutter gripped his tea glass, his fingertips blanching from the pressure, resisting the urge to crush the glass with his hand. Or at least hurl it against the wall. But he couldn't do that. Because here he sat, fool that he was, next to Jessica at this quaint little community party.

A brand-spanking-new gymnasium—funded by her honorable ex-husband—and full of nothing but do-gooders and one adoring, deluded juvenile fan.

And then there was him. Cutter Thompson.

Just who the hell was *he?*

He sucked in a breath and then quietly blew it out, loosening his grip on his drink, forcing himself to let it all go. He'd built a life out of not caring what people thought. It was how he'd survived. "Since when is some kid's misplaced idol worship *my* problem?"

Anger clouded her eyes. "But you at least have to try—"

"Sunshine," he said, cutting her off, aware of the stares of their table companions as the two of them argued. He couldn't take it anymore, hating the look of utter disenchantment in her face. But he hadn't asked for the teenager's hero-worship. He used to want it. But not anymore. He used to think he deserved it.

And it was a hell of a thing to look back on his career and realize he *didn't*.

"I don't owe anybody anything," he said. Her flush grew brighter as he continued. "And just because some starry-eyed kid—"

She held up her hand. "That starry-eyed kid needs as many positive male influences in his life as he can get," she said, staring at him. "He's growing up without a father." His conscience took another thrashing, and Jessica's tone was laced with accusation. "Which means you, of *all* people, should be extra kind."

Extra kind?

He raised an eyebrow. "Sunshine," he said softly. Her persistent optimism defied reason. "Do you think the rest of the world is gonna treat him with kid gloves because of his crappy childhood?" She frowned, a small furrow appearing between her brows, and he knew she knew the answer was no. "Exactly," he said.

Cutter had learned it over and over again. And just when he'd thought he couldn't take any more, the world had turned around and kicked him in the ass again. And as a teen he'd raced those cars, angry and getting into trouble, until he'd learned that no one cared. But he hadn't really learned anything. Because he'd let his anger control him again…and lost his racing career.

And there was no undoing that now.

With a defeated sigh, he passed a frustrated hand through his hair. "The kid might as well learn that when life sucks, you just have to deal with it."

Her face grew dark. "That's a horrible—"

"That's right," Cutter said as he stood, his chair scraping on the wood floor, the need to retreat overwhelming him. "It *is* horrible." He looked down on Miss Perpetual Pollyanna. "Life can *be* horrible." They stared at each other for a moment longer, until Cutter went on. "I'm not hungry," he said, tossing his napkin on his empty plate. "Enjoy your meal."

CHAPTER TEN

THE next afternoon Jessica made her way around the side of Cutter's house, sandals crunching on the sunlight-dappled gravel walk. His sports car was parked in the driveway, so she knew he was home. But he wasn't answering her knock at the front door. Which meant he was either in the backyard…

Or he was refusing to talk to her. With Cutter, you just never knew.

Gnawing on her lower lip, she rounded the corner of the house and spied him by the pool, hosing off the deck. Her stomach vaulted, flipped and then landed. Only now it was positioned lower in her abdomen. She stopped and let the sight of swaying palms, green grass and the sea-green waters of Biscayne Bay beyond soothe her nerves. Which would have worked if the handsome man had been dressed in more than a bathing suit, chest and legs exposed.

And if the memory of how they had ended last night wasn't embossed in her brain.

If ever there was a sign that Cutter Thompson was the kind of man she needed to stay away from, she now had proof. After he'd cut that poor boy off at his knees, and Cutter's face had closed down, it had taken Jessica about two seconds to realize that he had emotionally and mentally checked out.

Problems? Time to clam up. Bothered about something? Insult someone and retreat into your emotion-free hole. It didn't take a doctorate in psychology—or even regular viewing of the daytime TV talk shows—to realize that in every relationship, he would do the same thing.

Steve hadn't been fond of expressing himself either, and Jessica was one-hundred-percent sure that it had been the beginning of the end of their marriage. But even at his worst, Steve had never been this reticent. He'd even been willing to marry her.

And he would *never* treat someone as callously as Cutter had Emmanuel.

Last night Jessica had gone to bed livid, woken up disturbed and then spent the rest of the day trying to sort through her emotions. Which was a frustratingly difficult task. Because when it came to her feelings about the man standing on the teak deck, Jessica vacillated wildly. It was like riding a pendulum, swinging back and forth, trying to figure out when it would stop. She just wasn't clear if, when the pendulum finally came to a halt, she'd even *like* the real Cutter Thompson.

Lovely. Wasn't that a depressing thought?

Water jetted from the hose, hitting the wood with a forceful stream as Cutter herded the leaves from the pool area and under the tall hedge that provided a living privacy fence. Jessica smoothed her hand down her peasant blouse, steadying her nerves, and stepped up onto the deck.

Cutter shot her a glance and then returned his gaze to his task, his expression still shuttered.

Nice, this should go well.

"You here to read me the riot act again?" he asked.

Jessica curled her fingers against her shorts. "No," she said, crossing closer to him. "I came to discuss our plan for the last session." Among other things, but she wasn't sure how to broach the subject of Emmanuel. Easing into it seemed best. "I want to make sure we end the publicity stunt on the right note."

He lifted a brow, and Jessica was stumped. The facial cue could have meant anything. Was he questioning her topic, or waiting for her to explain what note she wanted to achieve? Or perhaps, considering the way things had ended between them last night, he was simply noting the irony of her statement.

She let out a quiet sigh and gave up on the impossible task of translating his expression. "Steve and I discussed you after you left the gym."

After a brief pause, he released the lever on the hose, shutting off the water, and turned to face her. Despite the guarded look in Cutter's eyes, he didn't ask what they had talked about. She suspected he was too proud to ask.

Or maybe he didn't care.

But she told him anyway. "Steve read *me* the riot act and said I should cut you some slack." She chewed on her lip before going on. "He also said I was wrong for calling you out in public like that."

Cutter gave a nonchalant shrug and depressed the handle again, eyes on the aim of his hose. "We didn't raise our voices. It wasn't a big scene."

It had felt *massive* to her, and his insistence on treating it with a casual air made the nervous tension worse instead of better. But the cool mist created by the spray of water felt good. She gave a halfhearted lift of her shoulder. "Better than getting caught making out behind the bleachers." Her stomach clenched.

She shouldn't have said that.

But at least she finally got an authentic response, the old Cutter reappearing with a dry twist of an amused mouth. "Sunshine, if anything, our fight just *confirmed* we're sleeping together."

This surprised her. "Do you always get into fights with the women you're involved with?"

"I've never been involved with someone quite so demanding before."

She hiked a brow dryly. "They must not have expected much."

"I guess I had other things to recommend me. It certainly wasn't my sparkling charm."

Despite her nerves, and the crackling tension, heat flared in her belly. Oh yeah, she'd been privy to a good bit of the things he did well. Had tossed every one of her plans aside when she'd signed on for more.

The tangle of emotions in her chest grew tighter, cinching into a knot.

"Have you *ever* been charming?" she said.

Cutter turned his hose on the next section of the deck, and the pause lengthened, filled only with the sound of water beating on wood. The moment stretched so long, Jessica thought he wasn't going to respond. But when she was about to ask again, Cutter finally spoke.

"I spent my preteen and teenage years angry at the world. Angry at my dad for leaving. I was even angry at my mom." He cut her a sideways glance. "It didn't leave much room for charm."

She studied him. The similarities between Cutter and the sullen teen from last night were impossible to ignore. And that seemed a nice segue into making that point to the stubborn man. "I'm sure Emmanuel feels the same way."

"He's just doing his time. He's *supposed* to be pissed off at the world."

"Fine. So he's dutifully being the sullen and disagreeable teen. But you are an *adult*." She swept a lock of hair from her damp cheek, the bright sun and her nerves heating her skin, and sent him a pointed look. "You should be better than that by now."

He stared at her for a long moment before answering. "Yeah," he said, his voice even. "Maybe I should."

His tone wasn't thoughtful in an I'm-contemplating-changing-my-ways fashion, it was more of a statement of fact. As if he knew how he was supposed to behave, yet still refused to comply. Cutter Thompson apparently didn't conform, no matter *what*.

She watched him return to his task of wielding the hose, driving the sprigs of greenery off the deck edge. Unsure where to go next, she said, "I watched the wreck again."

It had been disturbing to scrutinize, inch by pixilated inch, the stock car spin out, flip onto its back and slide across the track before busting into the wall, scattering parts across the pavement, all the while knowing Cutter had been inside. As a fan, it had been horrifying. Now that she knew him personally, it was terrifying. Because it made her realize she was beginning to *care* about him. The thought scared her senseless. And, ultimately, this conversation was about one thing.

She desperately needed to believe he was better than his actions last night.

"You're lucky to be alive," she said.

"You think I don't know that?"

She shook her head softly. "I honestly don't know what you think or feel." She was still trying to figure it out.

Still trying to figure *him* out. Because being with a guy who was the antithesis of everything she'd ever hoped for was wringing her emotions dry. She was now running around outside that comfort zone with those sharp scissors aimed at her heart.

When he didn't respond, Jessica stepped closer, staring at his profile. Because, bitter or not, the way Cutter had treated Emmanuel was wrong. Okay, so she should have discussed it with him in private, but that didn't excuse his behavior.

"Sometimes you have to take the higher road, Cutter," she said. His movements slowed, as if listening, but he kept his attention on his task. "Be the better person," she continued. "Yes, I realize it was painful hearing a tactless reminder about your crash. What you've lost." She hooked her hands on her hips, wanting him to recognize why she had been so disappointed in him. "But Emmanuel is just a seventeen-year-old kid. You can't expect him to comprehen—"

"It's not just about *what* I lost," Cutter said, cutting her and the hose off at the same time. "It's about *why*."

Confusion forced her brow downward. "I don't understand." As she stood there, studying his expression, it dawned on her what he meant. "You got your memory back."

"Yes." He tossed the hose onto the teak wood and it landed with a thunk. "I did," he said, and then he strode to the far end of the deck. He turned to face her, his expression hard. "In a fit of ego, I decided a rookie needed a lesson. Not to remind him of the rules so it's safer for everybody. And not just to win a single event." He jabbed his thumb at his chest. "I did it to show him that that track was *mine*." The arrogant words, the bluntly honest look on his face, sank her stomach lower in her belly, leaving her stunned as he went on. "He threatened my number-one status so I wanted to teach him a lesson. But what I got was an injury that guaranteed I'd never race again." He turned his face away from her, his profile lit by the bright sunlight, his expression harsh.

When she finally found her voice, it felt weak. "*That's* why you bumped Chester Coon?"

He passed a hand down his face, as if fatigued, but his words were no less candid. "Yes. It was all about *me*," he said. "Most people would say I got what I deserved. Ruining my own career." Cutter looked at her again, not bothering to hide the fiery emotion. "And it just so happens…I agree." She could hear the regret in his tone, see the stark expression on his face before it went bitter. "So I damn sure don't want any misplaced idolism from a kid searching for a father figure via a has-been sports star."

She blinked. "Maybe your memory is wrong. Maybe you—"

"No, Jessica," he said. "It's not."

It took a moment for the reality to fully sink in. And she shook her head, trying to wrap her head around the news. "It was just one split-second stupid mistake. It doesn't mean that you're unworthy of the kid's respect—"

"Christ, Jessica," Cutter said, frustration filling his face. "Don't start reading something into this that isn't there." The frown grew deeply skeptical. "This isn't about some pity-party, talk-show feeling of unworthiness." He stepped closer, exchanging cynicism for callous candor. "It is about my actions *being* unworthy."

She blew out a breath. After crossing her arms, she studied him carefully, trying to make sense of his words. To sort it all out. But it didn't compute. "You were the number-one driver for *six years*. You had to work like a dog to get to the top. And even harder to stay there. It took discipline and determination. One impulsive mistake does not erase everything that you've accomplished." She was feeling more confident in her words, but he was still looking at her as if about to refute her claim, so she continued. "Especially considering that, during all your years of hard work, while at the top of your game, you made sure your sponsors supported the causes that were important to you."

"That was just business."

"You chose to single out kids in need as your focus," she said. "I don't think that was a coincidence."

"Sunshine." He stared at her as if she were a new flavor of crazy. "The only humanitarian around here is you."

She was one-hundred-percent convinced his choice of charities was influenced by his childhood. He might not be able to see it, but *she* could. "I hate to break it to you, Mr. Thompson," she said. "You do have a few nice-guy qualities. Good-guy qualities."

He reached out and gripped her wrist, his voice low. "Cut it out."

Heart pounding in her chest, she stared up at him. He stepped closer, and the moment lengthened until Jessica thought it would squeal in protest from the stretch.

The hard look in Cutter's gaze didn't budge, but his voice turned deceptively quiet. "You were so mad at me after Emmanuel left I knew I'd never get to touch you again. Which would have been just as well."

They were the very words she'd been telling herself all day, yet the need that engulfed her now was stronger, and her whole world converged on the hand around her wrist. With one touch, he made her doubt her decisions. She should agree with him. Tell him he was right. But she couldn't do it. The muscles in her throat contracted, making her voice tight. "It wouldn't have been just as well."

He continued, his tone serious. And deliberate. "But I'm still the same person now as I was last night, Jessica." His fingers on her wrist were firm. "And I am *not* going to continue having sex with a woman who twists me into something I'm not, just so you can feel better about sleeping with me."

Denial surged. "What are you talking about? I don't do that."

"Sunshine—" he pulled her another half step closer, and her heart moved closer to her throat "—you just did."

Her breaths came shallow and fast, the intensity in his stare pinning her to the ground. "I never said—"

"You say I was an insensitive jerk to Emmanuel, and most people would agree," he said, his voice now dangerously low. "It wasn't my first mistake in your eyes, and it won't be the last. But you either want to be with me or you don't. And you can't divide people up into black and white, good or bad."

Her mouth dropped open. "That's not what I'm trying to do."

The frustration on his face was profound. "Then what *are* you trying to do?"

Her mind swimming, she blurted out the truth. "I'm trying to figure out who you are."

"You don't want to know."

But she did—because she'd fallen so completely under his spell. One touch and she chucked all her goals out the door. And she couldn't figure out *why*.

"Yes," she said firmly. "I want to know."

Cutter's face went rock-solid. "Fine. I told you that first day in my garage, but I'll spell it out for you again." He pulled her another half step closer. "I was a cocky, arrogant bastard. I enjoyed the public's attention. And I loved signing photographs." His words were blunt, his tone firm. "I chose the charities, yes, but the real kick for me was the interaction with the fans." He lifted an eyebrow for emphasis. "And that was ninety-eight percent about stroking my ego. Because I liked the way it made *me* feel." He paused, as if allowing time for the heavy words to sink further to the bottom of her heart. "The remaining two percent was to please the sponsors. For me, it's always been about the angle."

She pressed her eyes closed, trying to take it all in. But the truth was too awful to comprehend. "Is that it?" she said softly, lifting her lids and scanning his face. "Is that all there is to you?"

Something flashed in his eyes she couldn't interpret. "Even I haven't figured that out. But let me tell you what I *do* know," he said, pulling her until they were almost toe to toe. "I'm a shade of gray, Jessica. Darker on some days, lighter on others. But the real question is…" He lowered his head, his face only inches from hers. "Is that good enough for Jessica Wilson to sleep with or not?"

She stared into those sea-green eyes so turbulent with frustration. Resentment. And at the heart of it…desire. His fingers were warm on her wrist, but her skin burned. His musky scent, his presence, swamping her in a sensual fog. There was no redeeming feature about his past. He was all about Cutter. His actions had been selfish through and through.

But God help her, she still wanted him.

The sensual fog closed in around her, and she was powerless to stop it. "Yes."

He pulled her arm, and her body collided with his, his mouth crashing into hers. An instant battle for supremacy, with Cutter the clear winner. He took what he wanted, not looking for submission, simply demanding she keep up. Barely leaving her room to breathe.

He was giving her a full taste of what she'd been fantasizing about since she'd watched his crash again last night. She'd been horrified by the sight. Grateful he was alive. And she was still angry at him for letting her down. But she was also disappointed in herself for wanting him—whoever he was—and *this,* despite his actions.

The power, the pace of the kiss was exhilarating. A slice of the out-of-control passion he'd only hinted at in the past. The kind she'd never experienced before, had never really wanted in a man.

Until she met him.

She clung to his upper arms, trying to steady herself under the onslaught. Cutter had one hand behind her head, sealing her mouth to his, while his other yanked at their clothes. His biceps alternately bulged and lengthened beneath her hands as he pulled on buttons and zippers, impatiently sweeping the fabric aside. When she tried to help, desperate to make it happen, her hands kept getting in the way, and wound up hindering his efforts instead of helping.

"Don't," he said, his voice gruff, pushing her hand away.

Jessica abandoned the plan, and he pulled off her shirt. He clasped her face, pulling her lips back to his, and she met him now, taste for taste. Her passion was running at high speed, catching up with him. She ran her hands down his chest, his skin hot, yet damp. The chest hair crisp beneath her fingers.

Cutter pushed her shorts and his swimsuit down, and the fabric dropped to the teak at their feet.

And as he backed her towards the lounge chair behind her, both stepping out of their clothes, they stumbled back in a tangle of legs and lips. Cutter stuck out an arm, catching their drop onto the chaise, cushioning their fall. He landed on top of her, not missing a beat, continuing his full-speed-ahead clip. If anything, as if sensing she'd caught up, he shifted into higher gear.

It was maddeningly intense.

His hands and mouth were everywhere, her breasts, her stomach, between her thighs. Caressing, kissing, nipping and then moving on, leaving her in a breathless daze, trying to match his pace. Overwhelmed by the barrage of sensations. As her skin burned from his tongue, the rasp of his chin and from the hot sun blaring down on them, Cutter consumed her as if she was in danger of disappearing if he slowed down. All the rough, raw edges present since the day they'd first met highlighted in bold.

It was as if he was determined to show her the full force of the darker shade of Cutter Thompson.

Hands on her hips, he nipped his way up her belly, her breasts, and took her mouth as, in one swift movement, Cutter arched his hips, driving deep into her. Jessica cried out in relief.

He paused, capturing her head between his hands, and looked down on her, his face close. Her mind spinning, she gazed into his hard eyes, the steel muscles of his thighs pressed between the soft inner of her own.

Hands on her head, Cutter began to move between her legs. Swift. Sure. No holding back and no apologies. Taking what he wanted. A massive force of need.

But she hadn't counted on feeding his need being a catalyst for her own. His earlier frustration and his overwhelming desire stamped his every move. She arched beneath him, her hips meeting his, the sensual haze tightening her muscles in anticipation yet turning her body to gel. She clung to his arms, his muscles hard beneath her fingers, her body insisting she comply.

His gaze bored into hers as his movements swept her along in an undertow that sucked her down, skirting the edges between dark desire and danger, threatening to close over her head. She felt as if she'd stepped into the deep end of a pool of need, barely able to touch the bottom with her tiptoes, struggling to keep her face above water. To breathe.

She shut her eyes as the pool climbed higher, closing over her head, cutting off everything but her ability to feel the pleasure taking root in her body. Until she finally went under, vibrant bits of light bursting behind her eyelids as she came, the violent shocks gripping her body.

The sun bore down on Cutter's back as he gradually became aware of his surroundings. His chest heaved with every breath, his muscles were spent. His ribs ached and his left arm burned. Sweat trickled down his back, and his thighs felt slick between Jessica's. He opened his eyes to the sight of her face, lids closed, cheeks flushed. Her temples were damp, dark hair stuck to her skin.

She'd never looked more beautiful, and the terrible reality of what they'd shared clobbered his pounding head.

Bad enough that last night had been long and agonizing as he'd stared up at his bedroom ceiling, angry at her for calling him out, but mostly angry at himself for his behavior. But then she'd shown up at his house…

And he'd wanted her anyway.

So much so, his frightening need had caused him to come completely unhinged, and now he felt damaged. Ripped open, bleeding and exposed, and he grappled with the rising lump of terror.

Because he'd wanted her, but she'd come here only because she still clung to the hope he was some sort of friggin' closet humanitarian. Well, he'd cleared that notion up. He'd snatched off those sunshiny-colored glasses of hers and stomped on them within an inch of their life. And then he'd run them over, just to be sure.

His gut slowly cinched tighter, hating that he'd had to say all those words.

And he suddenly realized he *wasn't* the same person he'd been last night. He had finally figured out why making love to Jessica was different.

Because he cared what she thought of him.

The terrifying realization dwarfed him, looming over his consciousness. He'd spent a lifetime earning a reputation for not giving a rat's ass about people's opinions of him, and now, he finally did.

Damn, he'd vowed to never put himself through that kind of agony again.

He closed his eyes, remembering the naive seven-year-old who used to wait by the phone for his dad to call. After his father had driven away and left him behind, Cutter had desperately clung to the hope it wasn't over. So he'd left messages on his father's voice mail. His dad's return calls grew fewer and farther between, until Cutter's ninth birthday. After that, there was only silence. On the day of his tenth birthday, Cutter called to leave yet another message, and got a number-no-longer-in-service recording.

And Cutter had finally given up the last bit of optimism he'd had left.

He frowned, swimming in a sea of suck. But then Jessica Wilson, the consummate Pollyanna, had shown up and dragged him down the path of hope again, only to crush the tender, spring-like growth.

Body tense, he lifted his lids, scanning Jessica's lovely face again. Worried he was squashing her, he shifted slightly.

Her eyes flew open. "Wait," she said, her fingers increasing their grip on his forearm.

He hesitated, hating the intense uncertainty in her face. But as long as he lived he would never forget her big, you-just-shot-me, Bambi eyes when he'd finally come clean about Cutter Thompson.

The Wildcard…asshole extraordinaire.

With a curse, Cutter rolled off, instantly missing the feel of Jessica's skin. The sweat cooled his body, leaving him chilled. He tugged on his swimsuit as he stared down at her. He could never be the kind of guy she wanted.

He couldn't even come *close*.

"Jessica, I'm the man you'd pass over in your online list of potential dates." He raked a hand through his hair and then dropped it to his side in defeat. "Every single time."

Jessica blinked. The expression on her beautiful face did nothing to deny his claim.

His heart pumped like the pistons of an engine doing a thousand rpms, because a man couldn't spend his whole life being left behind by those he cared about. He remembered too well how it wreaked havoc on the psyche.

Of course, the devastating events by the pool had already laid waste to his last protective barrier. Cutter had feared nothing on the track, least of all death, but the terror inside him now forced him to go on.

"I won't survive the cut being compared to the guy to my left and my right," he said. "In a list of my pros and cons, the cons win by a mile." Unable to stop himself, his pounding chest painful, he swept a sweat-soaked strand of hair from her forehead, his eyes holding hers. "I think we both know this has to end."

Not trusting himself to wait for a response, he turned and headed into his house, quietly shutting the door behind him.

CHAPTER ELEVEN

"AND she was constantly complaining about my dog." The middle-aged, balding man blew his nose into a handkerchief and looked around the circle of divorce survivors sitting in the reception area of Perfect Pairs, clearly looking for support. "She *never* liked Darth," he went on, sniffing with a mix of anger and allergies. "And when she told me it was either her or the mutt, I told her at least Darth Vader never mocked my love for Civilization."

Bewildered, Jessica stared at him. "Civilization?"

The man blinked at her, eyes watering, either from hay fever or emotional pain. "The computer game."

"Oh, yes," Jessica said. She didn't know whether to be amused, disgusted or disheartened by the man's reasons for ending his marriage. And when the perfect reply escaped her, she simply cleared her throat and glanced at her watch, grateful the hour of horror was finally over. "Well…" she said, forcing a smile for the circle of faces, "if no one else has anything to share, why don't we call it an evening?"

There was a chorus of murmuring voices as the small band of people gathered their belongings. Jessica rose from her seat on the couch. With a combination of dread and relief, she saw the last of the support-group attendees out the door, locking it behind them.

One obstacle cleared. Now she had the worst one to go.

A knot of anxiety gnawed at her insides, and she turned and leaned her back against the door, closing her eyes. Cutter had left a message about their final session, the one she'd been too distracted by the events at the pool to discuss. And, too chicken to call him on the phone, she'd texted him back. Thank God he'd agreed to meet her here tonight to post his last question for the contest. She couldn't stomach the thought of returning to his home.

Memories of the blow-up by the pool three days ago washed through her. His anger. Her crushing disappointment.

And the combustible desire.

A burn began in her belly, her palms grew damp and she longed for a chilled glass of wine. Because, after all the eventful emotions, Cutter's text had seemed so normal, including a little sarcastic comment that had made her laugh.

When he'd told her it was over, intellectually she'd had to agree, but her body—and a big chunk of her heart—had screamed *no*.

Jessica threaded her fingers through her hair, trying to soothe the war being waged inside. It had been an ongoing battle since she'd first fallen under Cutter's spell, and she should be grateful he'd done what she'd been too weak to do to date. Last night she'd walked the hallway in her home, searching for an answer to the Cutter conundrum.

But there wasn't one. And in her rather extensive history of setting herself up for failure—in marriage, in dating—this one would be legendary.

Worth its own wing in the Romance Blunders Hall of Fame.

Unfortunately, her relationship with Cutter was doing more than just messing with her head, it was also mucking up the rest of her well-ordered life. She never used to feel irritated during the support groups before, impatient with the occasional silly reasons for the end of a marriage. And she hadn't had time to continue her search for the right guy because she was too busy wanting to be with the *wrong* one.

And when had her parents realized they were wrong for each other?

The thought snuck up on her, and once it had made itself known, she couldn't ignore it. What had caused her parents to wake up one morning, look at each other, and think—hey, this isn't working out? Had they started out good together and slowly grown apart? Or were they just a bad match to begin with?

Like her and Cutter.

The sadness that had been building for years threatened to breech the dam and come pouring out. Her parents' divorce. Her own. Now Cutter. And though she'd always strived for optimism, it was growing harder and harder to maintain.

She rubbed her forehead, smoothing away the frown lines, turning the questions over in her head. But leaning here against this door wasn't going to solve her problems. And no one liked a whiner either. She had to somehow prepare for Cutter's arrival.

With a sigh, she straightened her shoulders and headed down the hallway towards her office. As she crossed the threshold, she spotted Cutter at her desk. She stopped short, but her heart kept going, slamming into the front of her chest.

He was thumbing through one of her brochures, one hip perched on the edge of her desk, muscular legs bared beneath his shorts. When he looked up at her, her world reduced itself to the masculine cut of his face and his expression—as if he was just as clueless how to handle her as she was him.

She held her breath for the umpteenth time since she'd met the man. Much more training like this and she'd be ready for an underwater-swimming competition. All the way across the blue waters of the Atlantic and back. Or maybe green... like Cutter's eyes.

It was a moment before he spoke. "Are Sneezy and his merry band of pessimists finally gone?"

Her legs finally remembered their purpose in life, and she moved to the chair opposite the desk, slowly lowering herself into the seat. "How long have you been here?"

"Long enough to hear that the computer-gaming geek should get rid of his dog or make an appointment for allergy shots."

"But how did you get in?"

His lips twisted dryly. "Through the front door. No one noticed me go by. You all were too engrossed in the story about the cheating ex."

She shook her head lightly, trying to focus on the conversation. How could he act so normal? "There were two cheating stories tonight."

"The one whose wife was supposed to be a computer analyst for the CIA." He tossed the brochure onto her desk and shot her a skeptical look. "Must be shocking to discover that, in lieu of the Pentagon, your spouse was working the street corner in front of the local crappy motel."

They stared at each other, and Cutter looked as if he was waiting for her to respond. But she'd exhausted her ability for status quo conversation with Cutter after their explosion by the pool. As the seconds passed without a comment from her, the atmosphere grew strained. Until Cutter leaned forward, his eyes intent on hers.

"Why do you do it?" he asked, his face radiating curiosity. Her nerves stretched tighter, and when she didn't answer, he went on. "The support group." He seemed genuinely interested, no mocking tone. "Why is someone who is so bound and determined to look on the bright side of life actively seeking out other people's misery?"

There wasn't much of a bright side to see lately. She dropped her gaze to the armrest of her chair, tracing the pattern in the wood with her finger, her mind turning the question over. "I find it helpful to hear why other people failed."

When he didn't reply, she looked up, and Cutter's expression was doubtful. "How does listening to the million and one ways people botch their relationships benefit you?"

With a small frown, she combed her fingers through the tips of her hair. "I think I know why *my* marriage ended. But my parents' is a complete mystery." Cutter was watching her, clearly expecting more of an explanation. She wished she had one for him.

"What excuse did they give?" he said.

"They said they didn't want to be married anymore."

"Sounds honest enough to me."

The old guest that had been rattling around the empty hallways of her heart stopped and faced her head-on. Refused to let her pass. Her brows drew together, and her whole face felt tight. "Well, that's not good enough." Embarrassed by the words, Jessica closed her eyes, rubbing her forehead, trying to ease the tension. "For the first fourteen years of my life they seemed perfectly happy." She dropped her hand to her lap and looked at Cutter. "And then one night at dinner they simply announced it was over."

His eyebrows slowly crept higher, and then he leaned back, hands on the edge of the desk, as if trying to process the news. "Just like that?" He hesitated, as if waiting for more. But there *wasn't* anymore, and that was the hardest part to fathom. It felt so incomplete. Cutter tipped his head and said, "You had no idea something was wrong?"

Her chest grew tight, and she dropped her attention to her skirt, smoothing out nonexistent wrinkles and trying to ignore the ache in her heart. "None whatsoever. They never fought in front of me. They seemed happy." Still focused on her lap, she linked her fingers together. "The week my father moved out of the house, I sat in my bedroom, waiting for them to tell me it was all a mistake—all the while they were calmly discussing how to divvy up the furniture." After sixteen years of marriage their conversation had been reduced to who would get what. Her voice dropped an octave, the memory washing over her. The disbelief. The grief. And the *confusion*. "And all I wanted to do was scream."

The silence that followed was loud, and when she looked up, Cutter was studying her with an expression that she couldn't decipher. Jessica had a powerful urge to fill in the gap with something.

Anything.

"Most people say I should be grateful the end was amicable." She gave a little laugh that sounded pathetic. "My parents told me the same thing."

Stunned, Cutter stared at her, until a small scowl overtook his face. "To hell with what they say, Jessica," he said softly. And when he went on, each word was enunciated clearly, emphasizing his point. "You do not have to feel grateful."

Her lids stung from the threat of tears and her lips twitched at one corner, a mix of a forlorn smile and a grimace. "Cutter Thompson says I'm allowed to feel like shit about it?"

His eyes held hers. There was no cynicism, no suppressed humor, just the frank gaze that never failed to draw her in. "Cutter Thompson says you are allowed to feel like shit about it."

She stared up at him, moved by the emotion in his voice. After all these years, it was odd to have someone give her permission to still feel sad.

And how could someone so wrong for her feel so *right*?

Because currently Cutter was looking at her as if he wanted to hold her. To comfort her. Every cell in her body leaned in his direction, wanting—needing—him to do just that. But it was the set of his posture that told the complete story.

Much as he might want to, he was not going to take her in his arms.

The ache that had started when he'd called it off grew

deeper, and the ripple of confusion grew wider. He was one of the most truthful people she'd ever encountered. He might avoid discussing his feelings, but he was always honest when he did. Often brutally so. He'd told her from that first day in the garage that he was all about Cutter Thompson. The more she'd grown to enjoy the bad boy's company, the more she'd needed to believe his claim wasn't true. But that wasn't his fault. It was hers.

More importantly, she'd heard the remorse in his words, seen the doubt in his face when he'd told her the truth by the pool. Cutter had come face to face with his mistakes and it had been clear he was questioning the choices he'd made. And didn't that constitute a positive change?

Cutter cleared his throat and sat back, and the moment was gone. "So what's the last Battle question going to be?"

She had several burning questions she'd like to ask.

Had they just been exploring their mutual appreciation of each other's bodies? Had they become friends with oh-so-not-boring benefits?

Or had they been—*could* they be—more?

Heart pounding, she finally settled on the new plan that had eluded her last night, and offered up the idea that was so close to her heart that it hurt.

"How about..." her voice faltered a fraction, but she pressed on. "What's a deal-breaker in a relationship?"

He lifted a brow dryly. "Doesn't sound particularly optimistic."

"Maybe it is," she said as she leaned forward, her heart rate climbing higher. "We're two intelligent adults. Maybe we haven't reached our own deal-breaker yet." His lids flickered in surprise, but she refused to chicken out, and hope was taking hold of her. Driving her forward. Because she couldn't stand the thought of the two of them being done.

She clamped her hand in a fist. "Maybe if we're willing to try—"

"Try?" he said, cutting her off. "Sunshine," he said, the flash of emotion crossing his face not encouraging, "I'll agree you're an intelligent woman." He folded his arms, giving her that boldly frank appraisal that often ended with him saying something she didn't want to hear. "But right now you're not being smart."

They were the same words that had been whispering in her head since their fight over Emmanuel. But that seemed like a lifetime ago.

His eyes perused her face, and her apprehension grew as he went on, his voice low. "And you know what else I think?"

Her fingers gripped the wooden armrests, troubled by his tone. She didn't respond to his question, afraid to hear his thoughts.

He went on anyway. "I think you're stuck on an endless manhunt because the guy you're looking for doesn't exist," he said, the words knocking her even further off kilter.

How could he say that? "That's not true. I'm just looking for…" The words sputtered, struggling to gain traction as her mind scrambled to get the statement right. "I'm just looking for…"

"The Prince of Darkness?" he said dryly.

"No."

The sarcasm disappeared. "A shinier shiny object?"

"No."

The look he shot her held no mercy. "Perfection?"

"No."

His eyes scanned hers, as if trying to read the answer in her face. "Then why do you keep rejecting every man that comes your way? They couldn't all have been crying about their ex-wives and living in their parents' garage."

She refused to let his cynical views belittle her priorities. And his words reminded her of exactly how far Cutter Thompson had to go. "I want someone who will work with me." She lifted an eyebrow that was aimed squarely at him.

"I don't want to get involved with another man who emotionally retreats and refuses to discuss where the relationship is going wrong."

The pause was longer than she expected, and when it ended, Cutter's expression had shifted from not encouraging to actively *dis*couraging.

"Is that how it was with Steve?" Cutter's eyes narrowed. "You telling him where he was going wrong?" His tone implied the conversation encompassed more than just her ex. It was personal.

"No," she said, hating that she was growing defensive. And hating even more that she felt the need to explain. "I just suggested he see a marriage counselor with me, or at least *consider* looking at a few books that might help," she said, gesturing to her bookshelf in the corner to her left.

Cutter faced the direction she was pointing, his whole body radiating his reservation as he gave the floor-to-ceiling shelves the once-over. "What are those?"

"Books on relationships."

The doubt and disbelief were huge. "*All* of them?"

His questioning tone held more than its fair share of accusation, and she bit back a retort as he rose from his seat to survey her collection.

As Jessica fought to control her irritation, Cutter pulled down a book and began to flip through the well-worn pages—his movements growing slower and slower, until the frown gradually overtook his entire face. He pulled down a second one entitled *How to Strengthen Your Marriage* and gave it a quick skim. The margin markings on this one were even more pronounced.

"Christ, Jessica," he said, raising his head to stare at her, his expression giving way to one of complete shock. "And I thought I was screwed up."

A cold hand gripped her heart. She'd expected sarcasm

from him, not a frustrating mix of censure and pity. "What are you talking about?"

"Your insecurities are incapacitating."

Anger sent her bolting from her seat, infuriated by his audacious claim. "Well I don't need a man whose first instinct when threatened by an idea is to *insult* me and push me away."

His green eyes, simultaneously brutally hard and painfully honest, bored into hers. "Yes, I was rude to Emmanuel, but I am not insulting you. I am telling you like it is. But you're so busy clinging to those damn everything's-just-fine glasses that you want to ignore the truths that are too inconvenient for you."

She planted a hand on her hip. "And which truth would *that* be?"

"Like the fact that you *drove* your husband away."

With a frigid flash, her heart froze, sending icy crystals through her veins, the shards stinging as they went and draining the blood from her face. "That is not true," she ground out. Her heart hammered at a pace that seemed to shake her whole body.

"Yes, it is." Cutter stepped closer. He wasn't angry. The only thing radiating from his face was absolute conviction. "Not only do you *not* want the guy to the left or the right, you don't want the guy right in front of you. You want to change him. Turn him into your ideal man. You haul out your books, tell him where he went wrong and give him a list to follow." Still clutching the hardcover, he held it up higher, more in frustration than anger. "Who could live with that?"

"I do not have lists."

Cutter barked out a scoff and turned the book in his hand, displaying a page. "What do you call this?"

She stared at the text she had marked up, passages underlined, notes scribbled in the margins...and fluorescent highlights through the author's bullet points on how to argue effectively.

The ice crystals vaporized from the flaming heat that swept up her face. "I just wanted Steve—"

"No," he said, slapping the book closed and cutting her off. "That's the problem. You didn't want Steve. You wanted the idealized version of him."

Her whole body rejected his claim, her mind circling in a whirlpool of disbelief, desperately scrabbling for the safety of logic. "There is nothing wrong with trying to improve yourself."

Cutter's face went so hard it could have deflected a bullet at close range. "Let me be the one to tell you how demoralizing living with that would be." He tossed the book to her desk, and it landed with a loud thump that echoed in her small office. "I spent my entire childhood *not* being wanted by my parents. And until I was ten years old, I thought if I tried a little harder, was a better kid, a little *nicer,* more *agreeable*—" the sarcasm dripped from his voice "—one of them might change their mind." The awful words hung between them, and Jessica's eyes began to burn. "But my dad left and never came back, and my mother never stopped talking about how her life got worse after I was born." He raked his fingers through his hair, spiking his bangs in all directions, and his tone morphed from hard cynicism to biting bitterness. "So put me down as someone who refuses to try and *improve* myself anymore."

Years of adulation from his adoring fans could never undo the damage done by those who really mattered—rejecting him time and again. The tragic reality of his past added to her pain, boosting her sorrow exponentially, and her chest grew tight again, making it impossible to breathe. Everything about Cutter, the anger, the cynicism, and even the no-holds-barred honesty suddenly became clear. Unfortunately, the knowledge came too late. "You know what the problem with your theory is?" she said quietly.

"No," he said, his voice dangerously low. "But I bet you're about to spell it out for me."

She ignored the dig and pushed on, before she collapsed from the feeling of futility. "You've given up." She shook her head, sadness overwhelming her. "No, that's not true. You haven't just stopped trying, you go out of your *way* to tick people off. But it hasn't made you happy."

The hot color of anger tinted his cheeks. "And you're so blinded by everyone else's faults that you can't see your own."

She blinked back the burning threat of tears, realizing that she hadn't fully grasped the extent of their relationship. They weren't just wrong for each other...

They were *bad* for each other.

And the misery ended all hope for any kind of a future with Cutter Thompson. "I think you can handle the last debate alone."

Eyes dark, he said, "I think you're right."

And with that, Cutter pivoted on his heel and left.

Cutter parked the 'Cuda at the curb in front of the Boys and Girls Club, wondering what the hell he was doing here. After calling Steve to locate Emmanuel's whereabouts, and then learning the news about the kid's latest troubles, coming had seemed the right thing to do. Now he wasn't so sure. Of course, nothing felt right anymore.

And he doubted it ever would again.

Gut churning, he gripped the gearshift, remembering how *alive* he'd felt the night he was here with Jessica. It had been six days since he'd last seen her. Six horrendous, crappy days that had felt like infinity.

After their blowup, he'd stormed home and finished the competition alone. Annoyed with every response his contestants had sent, he'd bitten his tongue—or his texting fingers, in this case—and finished the job. Numb from his fight with

Jessica, he'd suffered through two hours of response after response, forcing himself to participate.

With the competition over, and the benefit dinner behind him, he'd buried himself in his work, finishing the 'Cuda and focusing on his new business. He'd ordered the equipment for the shop, and had even hired a third mechanic to start next month. All in all, Cutter's life was back on track.

But with Jessica gone, it felt as if every bad event in his life—his dad, his mom and his horrific career-ending wreck—had all been rolled into one and magnified by a hundred.

A fresh wave of agony bowled over him, and he dropped his head back against the seat and closed his eyes. Since he'd left Jessica's office, his mind had been spinning its wheels but never gaining traction. He'd been stuck in a never-ending neutral hell. Time and again he'd contemplated seeking her out, and to heck with how sorry he'd be in the end. Or how much it would cost his dignity to be with someone who didn't *really* want him, outside of the sexual sense of the word.

He would have shoved aside every semblance of self-respect and groveled like that seven-year-old boy who'd chased his father down the road. Or the ten-year-old who had sat by the phone, waiting for his dad to call him back.

But he couldn't get past the memory of Jessica's expression when he'd accused her of causing the destruction of her marriage. In honor of the cocky bastard he used to be, and apparently *still* could be, he'd dragged out her painful past and flogged it again, ensuring the wounds would be fresh forever.

These last six days, it was the image of her devastated expression by the bookshelf—juxtaposed with the you-just-shot-me, Bambi eyes by the pool—that had precipitated his perpetual orbit around the ninth circle of hell.

And while he'd finally concluded he could never fix things between the two of them, he could at least mend one fence he'd smashed. And maybe it would make up for a little of the pain he'd inflicted on Jessica, as if, in some minor way, he could become the man she'd hoped she'd seen in him all along.

He blew out a breath and stared at the Boys and Girls Club. Steve had said Emmanuel would probably be here. But if Cutter sat here any longer, the boy would leave and the opportunity would be gone.

With renewed determination, Cutter exited the 'Cuda and entered the building. When he asked about the kid, the gray-haired lady at the front desk directed him out back, and Cutter passed through the beautiful new gym where a dozen teens were playing basketball.

He eventually found Emmanuel outside, alone, shooting hoops on an old concrete court. Unlike the teens inside who wore athletic wear, Emmanuel was dressed in black cargo pants and a black T-shirt that swallowed his tall, lanky body. His hair was dyed an unnatural color that matched his clothes.

When the teen caught sight of Cutter, his face reflected the mood of his dark attire. "Why are you here?"

"To talk to you." Cutter waited a moment, feeling totally out of his element. Being on the receiving end of an adoring teen had been easy in comparison to the stone wall he now faced; Emmanuel had obviously changed his mind about the Wildcard.

Smart kid.

Cutter went on. "Heard you were caught racing a few days ago and got tossed in the clinker overnight."

"What's it to you? You're not my dad, so beat it."

Cutter regarded him for a moment. The animosity seeping from the kid was daunting. But, instead of leaving, Cutter crossed to a box of basketballs, pulled one out and sat on the ball. He stared at the teen, the wall of fury seemingly unscalable. "Don't have a clue how to go fatherly on a teen." He gave a small shrug. "My old man split when I was a kid."

Emmanuel cast him a scathing look. "Yeah?" He took the jump shot, missing by a mile. "So cry me a river."

Cutter's forehead wrinkled in brief amusement. It was interesting to be on the receiving end of his teenage self. "I also heard you got fired at the auto parts store as a result of your escapade."

This time Emmanuel didn't even acknowledge his presence, dribbling down the court and successfully planting a hook shot. When the ball bounced to the ground, the teen begin making shots from the foul line, his back facing Cutter.

Damn, disagreeable was hard to hold a conversation with.

But Cutter tried again. "I'm here to offer you a job."

"I don't want your charity."

"Gonna be hard to get hired anywhere with a record."

"So?" Like a cannon, Emmanuel shot the ball and it slapped against the backboard, the sound echoing on the small court.

A part of Cutter wanted to give up. He didn't need this. He had a fledgling business to get back to. Taking on an angry teen would hardly be the smart thing to do.

He swiped a hand through his hair and stared at the boy's back, remembering all the times Jessica had hunted him down. No matter how rude he'd been, or undeserving of her efforts, she still had come back.

At least until he'd accused her of destroying her marriage and killed all hope of her retaining any lingering affection.

The knifing pain in his chest didn't come from his now-healed rib injury. It was from the band encircling his heart, making each breath hurt. But he'd spent a lifetime feeling sorry for himself and he was tired of the emotion.

And it was time to just step up and take the higher road. At least put in the effort to *be* the better person, instead of going out of his way to piss everyone off.

Just like Emmanuel.

Cutter stood, picked up his ball and found a new location

on the sidelines, balancing on his makeshift seat. From this angle, he could see the profile of the teen's face, but the boy continued to mutely dribble his ball, clearly unhappy with Cutter's persistent presence.

With a sigh, Cutter said, "It's easy to blame yourself when a parent splits."

Emmanuel's hand fumbled briefly on the ball, but he recovered quickly. But the scowl that had settled on his face was *Psycho,* knife-through-the-shower-curtain worthy.

Cutter had definitely scored a hit with his comment.

"'Course, I was pretty little when my dad took off," Cutter said, feeling stupid, but staying anyway. "But for a long time I thought if I'd been a better kid, he wouldn't have left…"

His voice died as he remembered all those times his dad had dropped him off after a visit. Cutter would sit on the front porch, wondering why the man always left. After his father had moved, Cutter had manned the chair next to the phone, dreaming of the day his father would come back for good. Hoping his old man would come clean about why he'd left, and maybe even convince his mother it wasn't because of Cutter.

He blinked, pushing the memory aside. Dumb dreams. They'd never done him any good. But Jessica was right.

Adopting the screw-the-world attitude hadn't helped either.

Elbows on his knees, fingers linked, Cutter watched Emmanuel ignore him and said, "Take it from someone who's been there. The anger will eat you up if you let it." The kid continued to bounce the ball, and Cutter wasn't sure if the surly teen was listening or not. If he was anything like Cutter at that age, probably not. "I let it control me when I bumped Chester, and I blew my racing career." Funny how that didn't hurt near as much as losing Jessica. His breath escaped with a whoosh, and he swiped a frustrated hand through his hair. "Not the kind of thing a hero does."

The pause was filled with the sound of a dribbling ball as Emmanuel continued to refuse to acknowledge his presence. After several minutes passed with no response from the kid, Cutter pushed up to his feet. He'd said his piece. He'd made his offer.

It was up to the kid either to accept it or not.

"I'll leave my number inside in case you change your mind," Cutter said.

CHAPTER TWELVE

Trying to work, Jessica sat in her office, used tissues strewn across her desk, eyes puffy from lack of sleep. The frequent crying binges weren't helping their appearance either.

It had been exactly seven days since Cutter had walked out, and she'd spent most of it bawling her eyes out. A massive crying jag that had been thirteen years in the making. And once she had started, she couldn't seem to stop.

She'd indulged in a whine festival that would put most vineyards to shame.

Some of her tears were a little girl's grief over the end of what she had *thought* was a happy family, and some were a grown woman's hurt over Cutter's claim she had ruined her marriage.

But the biggest trigger by far was the unbearable pain of missing Cutter.

An ache the size of the Atlantic had taken up residence in her heart, and there was no ignoring this unwanted guest. Every time she closed her eyes, the horrid memory of Cutter's past, and his stunned expression at the bookshelf—one part censure and two parts pity—had hit her again. And yet, despite everything he'd said to her, she missed his cutting sarcasm, his cynical take on life, and that rare almost-smile that lit her world.

Toss in her body's intense longing for the fire in his touch, and she was a mess of gigantic proportions.

Between the huge hole Cutter had left in his wake and the nagging fear that she might have messed up worse than the majority of the ludicrous divorce stories she'd heard over the years, she wasn't getting much rest.

She was hoping her personal, in-depth exploration into the effects of sleep deprivation would end soon—but so far, no such luck. Especially on the night Cutter was supposedly sitting at the charity banquet with Calamity Jane.

By all accounts the dinner had been a huge hit. The Brice Foundation had made more money than ever before. And what had started as a potential publicity disaster had ended on a personal one of cataclysmic proportions.

For the millionth time since Cutter's awful claim, her gaze drifted to the wall sporting the shelves of self-help books. At first she'd been too angry for an objective look, convinced that Cutter had lashed out in his usual fashion, choosing to come out swinging when he felt pushed into a corner. But as time had passed, she remembered the open honesty in his eyes, the conviction in his voice, and—most damning by far—the lack of anger. Doubt had taken hold, and the shelf had loomed larger and larger, until now it was an ominous beast that seemed to sop up every oxygen molecule from the room.

It was draining her of any capacity for hope, much less optimism.

Miserable, Jessica slumped deeper into her chair, eyeing the tower of books warily. To be so thoroughly paralyzed by a stack of paper and ink was dispiriting. To be forced to live without Cutter was brutal.

Heart thumping painfully, her mind pushed away the implications of the thought. Her precarious—and entirely questionable—ability to function could shut down altogether if she began to explore why she missed Cutter.

Fear squeezed her chest at the idea. "God," she said, and snatched up her cell phone. Facing her past had to be easier than facing her feelings for Cutter. She dialed Steve's number, and when he answered, she didn't bother with a hello. "When did you first realize it wasn't going to work?"

She heard jazz music in the background. "Jess?" he said, his voice confused. "You haven't returned my calls. I've been worried—"

"I'm talking about us, Steve," she said. She took a breath and forced herself to slow down. It had been five years since their divorce. Giving him a minute to catch up would only be fair. "I want to know when you first thought we were a mistake."

"Jess," Steve groaned. There was no confusion now, only a man who didn't want to have this conversation. And she was very familiar with the reluctant tone. "It hardly matters any—"

"Don't," she said. More evasion on Steve's part. Or maybe it was simply a delay tactic. She remembered those, too. The jazz music in the background took on a lively tune, and her fingers clamped harder around her phone. "When was the first time you remember thinking you wanted out?" When the moment stretched to uncomfortable levels, Jessica said, "The truth, Steve." She hoped she wasn't hurting her cellular with her grip. "Please."

The sound of his sigh was loud. "I guess it would be when the CEO of the Wallace Corporation was flying down from New York for our meeting."

Stunned, Jessica sat up in her chair. The visit had taken place only four months into a marriage that had lasted for fifteen. Shock made her words sluggish. "You were positive he was going to hate your presentation."

Steve had never been a workaholic before, and his late hours and distracted mindset had started to wear her down.

She knew he'd been working hard, but a little part of her had been hurt.

And worried.

Okay, actually she'd been scared stiff. Especially after she flipped through a woman's magazine and landed on a survey that asked the readers how they first realized their relationship was in bad straits. The working-late excuse had been the number-one-reported sign.

Looking back, the fear seemed terribly ridiculous, but it had felt so *real.*

"Yes," Steve went on. "The morning of the presentation I was stressed and forgot to say goodbye when I left. After I got home, you asked if I was mad at you. But when I said no...you didn't believe me." His pause was longer this time, but there was a ton of meaning in the silence. Her heart grew heavy, and he went on. "It took me two hours to persuade you it wasn't a sign of a bigger issue."

She didn't bother to tell him that, deep down, she'd never really believed it wasn't. Four months later, after multiple similar episodes, and with Steve burying himself further in his work, she'd purchased her first book. She remembered the look on Steve's face when she brought it home. But that was nothing compared to his horrified expression when she purchased the second one three weeks later. At the time, she thought he was avoiding talking about their problems.

And it had certainly never occurred to her that *she* might be the biggest part of the problem.

Defeated, she slumped back in her chair. "Why didn't you tell me?" she said.

"I tried." Steve's sigh was huge. "But you weren't picking up on my hints."

Hints. She scrunched up her face, trying to recall any clues. But if he'd been tossing them out, she had missed every one. "Why didn't you just flat out *tell* me?"

Steve's voice went low. "Come on, Jess," he said softly.

Clearly he hadn't felt the direct route was an option. "You wouldn't have believed me. And all I would have accomplished was to hurt your feelings."

Jessica closed her eyes.

It's not you, it's me.

It's not your crippling insecure ways—it's my reluctance to tell you that you're driving me insane.

She stared blankly at the wall beyond her desk, the truth settling around her like an ugly, uncomfortable dress. She could have spent the rest of her life lining up the world's most perfect male, but it still wouldn't have worked. Because she'd always insisted on picking the *nice* guys—when all along what she'd needed was a brash, ex-race-car driver with a cutting mouth, a whole lot of attitude…

And a penchant for brutal honesty.

She needed Cutter Thompson because she was in love with him, and no one else would ever be more right.

Jessica blinked against the instant sting beneath her lids, knowing it was now an artesian well of tears that would never stop. Her nose grew stuffy, and she sniffed, reaching for another tissue in her severely dwindling supply.

"What's up with you and Cutter?" Steve said quietly, clearly oblivious to the momentous revelation she'd just endured, and that the answer to his question was so complicated it required its own internet support forum. There was concern in Steve's voice. "Do I need to send someone over to break his knees?"

"No." Jessica planted her elbow on her desk, wearily resting her forehead on her palm. "I'm the one who messed up."

The silence was long and heavy as Jessica waited for Steve to ask what else was new. Instead, he said, "So what's your plan?"

Jessica looked at the wall of books that had been read, reread, highlighted and underscored within an inch of their printed little lives. There was nothing on those shelves that could help her with Cutter. There was no analyzing her way out of the mess she'd created, and logic wouldn't solve her problems.

Ultimately, the only thing strong enough to overcome it all was her love for Cutter.

"No plan," she said, her heart tapping harder. "I'll just have to improvise."

Jessica followed her GPS to the upscale industrial park located in a high-end business district. It wasn't hard to identify which building was Cutter's. The 'Cuda parked in front was a dead giveaway.

It was strange to see the car in the parking lot lined with oak trees. Glossy black, the new coat of paint glistened in the sun. The brawny vehicle oozed raw power, as if poised to release its barely restrained speed at a moment's notice. Just the right touch, and all the pent-up energy would be unleashed. Much like its owner.

Memory welled higher, and Jessica's body went taut as she parked next to the 'Cuda. With a growing apprehension, she eyed the front of the building. The gargantuan garage door to the left was closed, the sound of muted music thumping from within. Not The Boss, but someone she didn't recognize. Harder. Angrier.

Which didn't bode well for Cutter's mood.

Her stomach slid lower in her belly, and she shifted her gaze to the smaller office door on the right, gnawing on her lip, gathering her courage. Improvising didn't seem like a good idea now that she was confronted with actually pulling it off. But loving Cutter and living without him was torment. Her heart lurched every time she thought of him. And that was so frequent it was like a streaming banner in her mind—similar to the news feeds that ran along the bottom of the CNN channel.

When the office door opened and Cutter appeared in the

doorway, the scrolling news feed in her mind went ultra-caps, a deafening screaming in her brain. Jessica could barely muddle through the process of breathing. Battered jeans clung to his body, and a smudged T-shirt stretched across his chest. Cutter looked beautiful.

But gawking like an idiot wasn't going to get her any closer to ending her agony. Heart pounding, she exited her car and closed the door, hand clinging to the handle, eyes on Cutter. He was leaning against the open doorway, thumbs hooked in his belt loops, his face guarded. And she instantly knew this wasn't going to be easy. *Nothing* with Cutter had been easy. But there was more than just wariness in his expression.

Was he trying to decide how to tell her to leave?

Fear joined the mix of emotions, and she didn't step closer. Without any idea of where to start, she said, "How was the benefit dinner with your online groupie?"

The only movement on his face was the lift of a single brow. *"Groupies,"* he corrected, and it took a moment to sink in. Jessica frowned in confusion until Cutter went on. "Calamity Jane was four retired bridge-club ladies ranging from seventy-eight to eighty-two years old."

She did her best not to gape at him, floored by the news, trying to picture their dinner.

"It was a hell of a date," he added dryly.

A ghost of a smile flickered across Cutter's face, but his fatalistic undertones brought a familiar wave of sorrow. She longed to throw herself on the ground and tell him she was sorry for letting her doubts rule her actions. She wanted to rewind the clock and—after shooting a chastising email to her silly, insecure self—try again. To quit *pushing* so hard.

A breeze blew, rustling the oak overhead. Light played across Cutter's face, and Jessica's eyes wandered over the tall form of this man she loved.

The lean muscle, dark energy and raw edges.

But he was definitely looking at her as if there was something he wanted to say that she wouldn't like, and a tight knot of panic formed. The pressure beneath her artesian well of tears increased, and she briefly pressed her eyelids together, forcing them back. Because honest dialogue had to begin with, well—honest *dialogue*.

"I spoke to Steve today," she said. Cutter didn't say anything, just regarded her with that coiled-spring edginess, until shame pushed her on. "You were right. I drove him away."

Cutter's eyebrows moved a fraction higher and, as if sensing she was about to shovel out a pile of misgivings, odoriferous stench and all, he crossed the pavement to lean his back against the door of the 'Cuda. Now four feet from her, he folded his beautiful arms across his chest.

And waited.

She cleared her throat, pushing past the fear. "I was always overly aware of the little things," she said. "Worried they were signs of a pending relationship apocalypse."

Cutter's face gave nothing away, and she longed for some sort of emotion, even anger. At least then she'd know he felt *something*. But…nothing was forthcoming.

His words were careful. "Understandable, given the way your parents split."

Which was so much more leeway than she'd ever afforded him, and his childhood had been light years ahead of hers in the misery department. Her piddly complaints were insignificant in comparison.

Guilt hit, and she lifted a shoulder listlessly. "I guess so," she said. "It's just…" She smoothed the knotted muscles on her neck, trying to ease the tension. To explain her desperate, foolish behavior. "All these years I believed my marriage failed because I chose the wrong guy." She gave a laugh that was more humiliation than humor and dropped her hand. "It's hard to face the mistakes I've made."

His gaze held hers, as honest as ever. "I'm sure your heart was in the right place."

A tidal wave of remorse threatened to swamp her. He was generously giving her the benefit of the doubt, and she didn't deserve it. She didn't deserve *him*. Not once when confronted with his questionable behavior had she ever afforded him the same latitude.

Instead, she'd been critical. Every moment he'd failed to live up to her expectations, she'd made it clear.

It was time to come clean. "My list was nonsense," she said. When his expression didn't budge, the tiny bud of terror expanded in her chest, and her grip on the car-door handle grew tight. "For fourteen years I was absolutely sure my parents loved each other. And then suddenly, they didn't. And I've never trusted myself to recognize love—or the lack of— since." It was a pathetic excuse, and she knew it. She fisted her free hand at her side. All the worry and second-guessing that had paralyzed her for years piled higher, making the words difficult. "So I pressed Steve too hard and drove him away." She'd made a plan, set an expectation and pushed. Just like she'd pushed Cutter. Blinking back the sting of tears, she went on. "I just needed—"

"A guarantee it would work out?"

"Yes."

Cutter stared at her warily. "Hence the rules and lists."

Heat seared her face. "They were my pitiful way of trying to ensure I found the right guy." But nothing on her bookshelf applied to the man who challenged her views on life, shooting holes in her theories, one biting remark after another. "And you were so different from what I thought I needed to make a relationship succeed, it scared me." Her throat ached from the pressure of tears, and her words came out weak. "But I wanted you so much…"

Something flashed in his eyes. An emotion she didn't recognize. Whatever it was, it didn't look encouraging.

Pushing forward grew more difficult. "So I kept trying to turn you into something I'd recognize." She rubbed her temple wearily and sent him a frown that held all the helplessness she'd felt to date. "But you weren't following the rules."

"I rarely do."

"Which was disastrous for my comfort levels."

His pause was brief. "Which would continue if we stayed together."

Was he still writing the two of them off?

Anxiety spiraled in her belly, drawing it tight. "But, Cutter," she finally let go of the car and stepped closer, halving the distance between them, "you are *The One*." She looked up at him, pushing aside every crippling ocean of fear, hoping the truth showed on her face because she felt it to the deepest depths of her being. "We are perfect together. You are perfect for *me*." She mustered up a wobbly smile. "Many shades of gray and all." When he didn't respond, didn't even look *moved,* she played her final card. Her pièce de résistance. Jessica drew in a shaky breath and spoke the most honest words of her twenty-seven years. "Cutter, I'm in love with you."

His stupefied expression did nothing to alleviate her adrenaline-induced state. Every muscle in her body tensed, and she slowed her breaths to help control the ungodly rate of her heart. Overhead, trees shifted in the breeze. Leaves rustled. And the world waited for Cutter's reaction. She wasn't sure how long the pause lasted, but it felt as if she lived, died and was resurrected a hundred times over.

Until a squeaking sound split the air as the garage door was rolled up by someone inside, and a male voice called out, "Mr. Thompson?"

Heart still throbbing, dying for Cutter's reply to her confession, Jessica turned to find Emmanuel standing in the doorway to the garage.

The teen's gaze shifted warily between Jessica and Cutter. "I'm ready to tighten the calipers on the brakes."

It took several seconds for Cutter to respond. "Use the torque wrench."

Emmanuel looked at him skeptically, a hint of defiance in his tone. "What happens if I don't?"

Cutter nodded at the two-foot wrench the teen was holding. "That monstrosity you have in your hand might break the bolt."

Instantly the defiance in the boy's face was gone. "Oh," Emmanuel said. And with that, the dark-haired teen turned and headed back into the shop.

Stunned by the exchange and the implications behind the teenager's presence, Jessica was still trying to recover from the boy's appearance when she aimed her gaze at Cutter. "How long has he been here?"

"Two hours."

"How long has he been working on the brakes?"

"Two hours."

Something in his tone alerted her to his frustration. "How long would it have taken you?"

"Thirty minutes."

Jessica glanced at Emmanuel, watching him wrestle clumsily with his tool at the wheelbase of Cutter's sports car in the garage, and then turned her attention back to Cutter. Her mind was frantically trying to keep up with the unexpected event. "So where is the angle for Cutter Thompson?"

He paused, staring at her. "There isn't one."

Her gaze roamed his handsome face, the sea-green eyes, and the glints of gold in his brown hair. He'd faced so much and come so far, and she hadn't made it easy for him.

"Why?" she asked softly.

A moment passed as he returned her stare, as if struggling with his answer. "I guess I'm going for a paler gray." But before hope could take root inside her, reservation infiltrated his face. "But I'll never be a light enough shade for you."

The tears welled higher, burning her lids. "I've done nice

and it didn't work." She'd spent their entire relationship telling Cutter how he wasn't measuring up. No wonder he was looking at her with such monstrous misgivings. "I *need* the bad boy. You are the right guy, just as you are." She gave a watery sniff and tried to smile, but her mouth twitched with guilt. "And I promise to quit nagging."

His brow crinkled in instant irony. "Sunshine, nobody makes an ass-kicking more fun than you." His tone went dry. "Something I clearly need on a regular basis. But Jessica…" The reservation returned, and he plowed a hand through his hair.

The frustration in his gesture and the flash of hesitation in his eyes gave her the courage to step closer. She wasn't sure if his doubts were about the two of them or about his continued resistance to her pleas. Praying it was the latter, she placed a hand on his chest. His thumping heart beneath her palm matched hers. Her first solid clue to his emotion.

She stared up into all that uncertainty in his face. "Tell me what you're feeling."

Eyes troubled, he blew out a breath, until his expression eased a bit, the candid words full of self-derision. "All I know is, since I left you, I've been to hell and haven't been able to find my way back." The honesty in his face was encouraging, but the continual apprehension in his eyes was heartbreaking. His words came out low. "But I don't want to turn out like my parents."

This was about more than just their relationship. It was his past, and hers.

"What *do* you want?" she said.

With a small frown he brushed her hair from her forehead. When his answer came, it was simple, but it was all she needed to hear.

"You," he said. "I just want you."

Eyes burning with unshed tears, she clutched his shirt. "I *am* yours." When his apprehension didn't ease, she went on, her fingers crushing the cotton. "Cutter, I had the marriage license and failed. The legal route didn't work for our parents either. And all I really want—" She pressed her lips together, intent on getting it right. "The only part of the marriage vow I need from you is a promise of till death do us part."

Eyes pained, expression stark, he said, "Jessica, I love you so much it hurts to live without you." He looked at her with that love—and a measure of surrender—in his eyes. "Forever is the only way to end my misery."

The relief was profound. She leaned against him, and he wrapped his arms around her. With his heart beating beneath her ear, slowly she allowed herself to feel the joy, to let herself believe it was real. That somehow, somewhere during her Battle of the Sexes with the Wildcard, he'd fallen in love with her as well. It was almost too good to be true.

But she would never doubt the two of them.

Smiling, she looked up at him, relishing the hard muscle. The wall of steel. He stroked the small of her back, sending decadent messages to her body. Cutter's eyes grew dark, and her smile grew bigger as he leaned in for a kiss.

"Mr. Thompson?" Emmanuel called from inside the shop, and Cutter froze, lips halfway to hers. The teen's voice was triumphant. "I'm finished."

Cutter briefly closed his eyes. "Great timing," he muttered, his expression one of barely maintained patience, lips hovering above her mouth. "Would it be rude if I tossed him out so I could make love to you?" The long-suffering expression on his face was adorable.

"Extremely rude."

"Damn." He pursed his lips, as if considering his options. "And taking off in the 'Cuda for a repeat backseat rendezvous? Rude?" Gaze smoldering, he pulled her flush against him. "Or acceptably wicked?"

In response to his hard body, delight spread through her. "Definitely acceptable."

A brow lifted suggestively. "You in?"

"Absolutely," she said with a grin. "You see, I've developed a thing for the wicked boy with a bad attitude."

* * * * *